Praise for the novels of
annie england noblin

pupcakes

"Noblin's tale of self-discovery, populated with a colorful cast of characters, is both lighthearted and life-affirming. Readers are in for a sweet treat."
—*USA Today*

just fine with caroline

"*Just Fine With Caroline* is all heart. Annie England Noblin knows how to make characters come to life. I was completely charmed on my trip to Cold River."
—*Stephanie Evanovich*

"Fans of Mary Kay Andrews and Mary Alice Monroe will enjoy Noblin's lighthearted second novel. For many readers, spending time immersed in Caroline's world might be just the ticket."
—*Library Journal*

sit! stay! speak!

"This author has much to recommend her to *Bark* readers, including her decade-long work in animal rescue and this charming debut novel . . . a touching and engaging book about friendships, family, and the power of dogs to inspire changes in our lives."
—*Bark Magazine*

"Full of southern charm and colloquialisms, Noblin's first novel explores the curious bond between man and beast. Noblin expertly blends the lingo of an insider and the angst of an outsider, giving readers the full experience of life in a tiny southern town. Addie's story is wrapped up neatly, full of romance, mystery, and a few new furry (and not-so-furry) friends to save the day. A warm, emotionally grounded story that will delight fans of Mary Kay Andrews and contemporary women's fiction."
—*Booklist*

By Annie England Noblin

THE SISTERS HEMINGWAY
PUPCAKES
JUST FINE WITH CAROLINE
SIT! STAY! SPEAK!

annie england noblin

pupcakes

A Christmas Novel

AVONBOOKS

An Imprint of HarperCollinsPublishers

Photo on pages v, 331, and puppy on page 379 © B.Stefanov/Shutterstock, Inc.
Photo on page 1 © fongleon356/Shutterstock, Inc.
Chapter opener photo © OxfordSquare/Shutterstock, Inc.
Photo on page 99 © Liliya Kulianionak/Shuttstock, Inc.
Older dog photo on page 379 © Erik Lam/Shutterstock, Inc.

First Avon Books mass market printing: November 2019
First William Morrow paperback printing: October 2017
First William Morrow hardcover printing: October 2017

Print Edition ISBN: 978-0-06-291796-6
Digital Edition ISBN: 978-0-06-256380-4

Cover design by Mumtaz Mustafa
Cover photograph © JanuarySkyePhotography/Getty Images

For Emilia,
the most perfect three pounds
I've ever held in my arms,
and for Nikki,
who is now holding her in heaven.

October

Chapter 1

THE DOG CAME WITH THE HOUSE. OR MAYBE the house came with the dog. Either way, no matter how the sentence was constructed, the house and the dog came together.

Brydie Benson looked down at the fat wad of fur on the floor in front of her. Its tongue hung out of its mouth, fixed in what seemed to be a permanent pant. Bits of drool dripped from the protruding tongue and pooled onto the hardwood floor between them.

Brydie took a step back. "Are you sure it can't go live with a relative or something?" she asked. "I'm not really a dog person." Although she wasn't really certain that what she was looking at *was* in fact a dog.

"There are no relatives," Elliott Jones, Brydie's best friend, said. She bent down and gave the drooling mess a pat on the head. "There is no one to take care of Teddy Roosevelt here."

"His name is Teddy Roosevelt?"

"It is."

Brydie stifled a giggle. Elliott couldn't be serious. "Are you kidding?"

"I'm not," Elliott replied, putting on her best Realtor voice. "Are you interested or not? I mean it's not that I don't *love* having you live with me and Leo and Mia, but it's been six months."

It was true. She did need a place to live, and although Elliott loved her, she was busy with her husband, Leo; her four-year-old daughter, Mia; and her ever-expanding belly, a boy, due in January. It had been fun at first, reliving their early days back in their hometown of Jonesboro, Arkansas, before Elliott moved down to Memphis to be with Leo, who was a successful personal injury lawyer in Tennessee.

But it was October, and Brydie knew she couldn't live in her friend's basement forever. She couldn't keep allowing Elliott to take care of her. It was time she lived on her own again.

Brydie said she'd take a place anywhere, as long as she could afford it, and she couldn't afford much. She glanced around the house. It was a beautiful and immaculately kept two-story brownstone in Memphis's well-to-do Germantown, and she'd been giddy when Elliott told her that she could live there rent-free if only she'd agree to a couple of "minor details." The elderly woman, she'd been told, was friends with Elliott's boss at the real estate company where Elliott worked. She hadn't wanted to sell the house when she moved to the home, so Elliott's boss told the woman that she would find a caretaker until it was time to sell.

"What kind of a dog is he?" Brydie asked.

Elliott shrugged. "I think he's a pug, and an old one, too. He's been boarded since his owner went to live in the nursing home two months ago. He seems glad to be home."

"How can you tell?" Brydie wasn't sure what kind of emotion her friend could see between the bug eyes and the wrinkles.

"I don't think he'll be much trouble," Elliott replied, resting her hands on her stomach. "But if you don't think it's going to work out, I need to know now. I had to beg for this. My boss wanted to let her deadbeat son into the place."

"Okay," Brydie said with a heaving sigh. "I'm in."

Elliott pulled a stack of papers out of a leather briefcase and said, "Read over the agreement. It's month to month, renewable after Mrs. Neumann's approval."

"Who is Mrs. Neumann?"

"The owner of the house."

Brydie knitted her eyebrows together. "But I thought the owner of the house was in a nursing home."

"She is," Elliott replied, circling a portion of the contract laid out in front of them. "You'll meet her when you take Teddy Roosevelt to see her in the nursing home every Sunday for a visit."

"Wait," Brydie said. "You mean not only do I have to look after that thing you're calling a dog, but I have to take it to visit an old lady in a nursing home, too?"

"You know what they say," Elliott said. "Beggars can't be choosers."

Brydie didn't consider herself a beggar, not really. Although at thirty-four, this was certainly not the position in which she'd ever imagined herself. She was in a tight spot, and she knew she ought to be grateful. She was trying to be grateful, but it was difficult to feel that way when everything in her life had gone so far to the other side of awful that she didn't even know where she was anymore. *I'm here,* she thought. *In this house, and I'm going to make the best of it.* She glanced back down at the dog. It had fallen asleep sitting up, eyes half-closed, tongue still lolling to the right side of its mouth.

Maybe it wouldn't be so bad. "Where do I sign?"

Elliott licked her finger and leafed through the pages. "Here," she said, "and initial here."

Brydie did as she was told. "Think I can get moved in today?"

"I'd planned on it," Elliott said. "That's why I picked the dog up from boarding."

"We can get my clothes and things from your place," Brydie replied. "Shouldn't take more than a couple of trips."

"I'm going to call Mrs. Neumann," Elliott said, and she disappeared out the door, leaving Brydie alone in the big house, with the exception of the sleeping pug.

She'd been surprised when she'd first entered the house to find that it was completely furnished, all the way down to the four-poster beds in each of the four bedrooms and the plush bathmats in each of the three bathrooms. Since she had nothing left to speak of, with the exception of her clothes and a few other things she could fit into Elliott's basement, it came as a relief to know that she wouldn't be sleeping on the lovely wooden floors.

Had it really been just six months ago that she'd had her own business, her own home, her own husband? How could it be gone? Just like that? These thoughts made Brydie's head hurt, and she wanted nothing more than to sink down onto the plush, peach couch in the living room and fall asleep. Instead, she looked around the house, absently twirling the house keys around her fingernails, bits of burgundy nail polish flaking off onto the metal.

Everything was pristine, a perfectly kept house. Brydie was sure that the old woman had housekeepers, a luxury she herself wouldn't be able to afford. She realized that she was now responsible for the upkeep of the whole house. She traced her steps back over to the hallway, stepping over the dog. She'd merely glanced at the house as Elliott showed it to her, her mind coiled like a snake around the life she no longer had.

She walked down the hallway, flipping the light switch. She expected to see pictures lining the walls, but there were none. The master bedroom was the same way, as were all of the other rooms. No pictures, no real decorations of any kind that might tell Brydie who the owner was or what she looked like. However, much to Brydie's relief, all of the kitchen supplies were there, and a little thrill ran through her when she realized she had the kitchen and all of its stainless-steel appliances to herself. In one of the pantries she found a bag of dog food as well as a food and water bowl. A leash and a harness hung next to them.

Brydie took down the bowls and filled one with water. The other she filled with the food from the pantry. She sat both bowls in front of Teddy Roosevelt. "Here," she said. "Eat up."

The dog opened up one eye, sniffing at the bowls. Then he sneezed into them before promptly going back to sleep.

"Suit yourself," Brydie replied with a shrug. She'd never owned a dog before, not even as a kid, and she didn't quite know what to expect. When she'd wanted a baby the year before she and her husband had divorced, he'd suggested a dog instead, to "break them in," he said, before having a child. She'd explained that having a dog wasn't at all the same thing as having a child. He'd said she'd never had a dog *or* a child and wouldn't know. They'd fought about it, the first of many fights about that particular subject. Wouldn't Allan be stunned to see her now, crouching in front of this odd-looking little dog. Brydie reached out and gave Teddy Roosevelt a hesitant pat. Maybe this wasn't how she'd imagined her life, but for now, at least, it *was* her life.

CHAPTER 2

IN BRYDIE'S PREVIOUS LIFE, SHE'D BEEN A BAKER. She and her husband had owned a bakery in Jonesboro, Arkansas, called Bake Me A Cake. The day they opened their doors had been the happiest day of Brydie's life. In truth, owning a bakery had been her husband Allan's dream, but Brydie couldn't have imagined anything better than the day they opened their doors.

She'd met Allan in culinary school. She'd been a nineteen-year-old student and he'd been her twenty-nine-year-old pastry instructor. Despite the reservations of her family and friends, as he was famed around town as something of a playboy bachelor, Brydie married Allan the next year. Five years later, they opened their bakery, and she thought the rest would be all creampuffs and buttercream frosting. Then, only eight years after they opened the doors of their shop, Brydie walked in one morning to find her husband *baking* with someone else.

That had been almost a year ago, and after

months of living with her mother while going through painful divorce proceedings, Brydie packed up everything she could fit into her Honda Civic and drove the forty-five minutes to Memphis and Elliott. She'd thought she could leave her pain behind and start fresh, but it had followed her, and although her best friend was trying to help her by finding her a new place to live, she couldn't help but feel a bit rejected as Elliott and Leo unloaded the boxes from their car and placed them in the living room. She couldn't help but feel a little jealous as Elliott drove away with her husband and child and pregnant belly—a painful reminder that Brydie didn't have any of those things, and she was beginning to feel like she probably never would.

She sat down among the boxes. When her phone began to ring from the kitchen table, she looked up at it, knowing she should answer. Her mother had already called three times that day, and she knew it would be her now. Brydie couldn't muster the energy to talk to her. Every time they spoke, her mother spent her time trying to convince Brydie that she needed to start dating again, or needed to find a new career, or needed a haircut. In Ruth Benson's eyes, there was very little a good haircut couldn't fix, and there were *many* things about Brydie that she thought needed to be fixed.

Brydie let out the breath she'd been holding when the phone stopped ringing. What she really wanted was to talk to her father. He wouldn't have tried to fix anything, but he would have listened. She would have felt better after talking to him, calmer and more confident somehow. But wishing she could talk to her father was even more useless than wishing she had a family like Elliott's. Gerald Benson had been dead nearly three years.

And so, since it was too late for a haircut, Brydie instead busied herself opening the first box in her new home.

CHAPTER 3

Teddy Roosevelt wouldn't poop. In fact, he wouldn't do anything. He wouldn't eat. He wouldn't drink. He wouldn't even move. Brydie didn't know much about dogs, but she knew enough to know that the pug should be doing . . . *something*. She'd left him on the kitchen floor the night before, and when she woke up the next morning, he was still there. Brydie couldn't even tell that he'd woken up.

Bending down, she slipped the harness over his head and around his middle, attaching it to the leash. "Come on," Brydie said. "Let's go outside."

The dog's ears perked up at the word *outside,* but he made no attempt to stand.

"Don't you want to go outside?"

Teddy ignored her.

"Fine," Brydie said, reaching down to pick him up. "I'll carry you."

He was heavier than he looked, and Brydie struggled to hold him and open the door to the backyard at the same time. She sat him down in the yard and, realizing that the yard was fenced, unhooked the leash from the harness. "Go on," she said to him. "Go potty."

Teddy lay down in the grass and began to snore.

Brydie threw up her hands. "Fine! Do whatever you want!" She stalked back up onto the porch and threw herself down on one of the wrought-iron chairs. "You're making me look like a crazy person, you know. Talking to a damn dog like it's a person."

She stared at him for a few seconds as if waiting for the dog to respond, before surveying the yard. It was neatly kept, like the house. Brydie found herself wishing for summertime so that she could plant a garden. But now it was October, not the best time to be doing much of anything except preparing for the holidays, which was Brydie's favorite time of year. A thrill went through her when she thought about decorating the house for Halloween, Thanksgiving, and Christmas. She thought about baking witch-and-ghost-shaped cookies and her special ingredient eggnog, which was so popular with her friends. *My old friends,* Brydie thought. *Allan's friends.*

Brydie loved the holidays. Despite being reserved much of the time, the holidays brought out the best, or worst, depending upon whom you talked to, in her. She especially loved Christmastime. She started counting down the days in October, recording all of her favorite Lifetime Christmas movies, and drinking eggnog way ahead of season when she could find it. Allan rolled his eyes at her excitement, since the only thing he really loved about the holidays was the money to be made at the bakery. But Brydie didn't care. She set up that countdown and reminded him every single day that it was one day closer to Christmas morning.

And that was when Brydie had an idea. She'd have a countdown to Christmas this year, just like she did every year—but that countdown would have a twist. Instead of simply counting down to Christmas morning, she'd use this countdown as a way to get over Allan. She'd get over the entire sordid affair, pun intended, by Christmastime, even if it absolutely killed her. Yes, she decided, by Christmas morning she'd be over Allan entirely, and what a Merry Christmas it would be.

She stood up, feeling the strength of her new resolve in her legs, and went back down the steps to retrieve Teddy, who of course hadn't moved. "Maybe I should start baking again," she said out loud, reaching down to pick him up. "Maybe I should start baking for you!"

Brydie sat Teddy down in the kitchen and headed toward the bathroom to get ready for the day. Elliott was coming over later to help her unpack, in between showing houses. There were many for sale on this street, and as Elliott explained it, that was because so many residents were like Mrs. Neumann—elderly. They were moving off to nursing homes or being buried in the Germantown cemetery.

It had been the same way in her Jonesboro neighborhood when she and Allan bought their first house. Her mother found it, and she'd gotten them a good deal, but it was the kitchen that sold them. It needed work—new cabinets and new flooring. The oven would need to be replaced, but the room was large and inviting, a complete change from the tiny apartment kitchen Brydie and Allan had been using for years.

After the divorce, they'd sold the house at a loss, and Brydie had to leave her gorgeous convection oven behind because she had nowhere to keep it. In fact, she'd sold or let Allan keep almost everything, an action for which her mother and Elliott chastised her. But she hadn't wanted anything. The life she'd lived with Allan was over, and all of those things represented that life. It was the same reason she'd wanted to sell the house, even after Allan offered to let her have it. She knew he'd moved in with his new girlfriend, and if she stayed in that house, she'd be stuck in her old life, *their old life,* while he moved on with someone else.

Now Brydie heard a commotion in her new kitchen. She hurried out of the bathroom and found herself staring down at a tipped-over trash can and trash strewn all over the kitchen and living room. "Did you do this?" Brydie demanded. She glared at Teddy Roosevelt.

The dog stared up at her for a moment before lifting his leg as a stream of urine shot out all over the trash can and the floor.

"*No!*" Brydie screamed. She ran over to him, her bare feet losing grip, and began sliding along the slick tile, before landing on her bottom in a puddle of urine.

"Gross!" Brydie scrambled up. "You are the worst dog, ever!"

She pulled off her jeans and kicked them over to the corner of the kitchen and began searching the cabinets for something to clean up the mess with. She was on her hands and knees, in her underwear, scrubbing the floor, her earlier resolve melting away underneath her, when Elliott walked in.

"What in the hell happened in here?"

Brydie pointed over at Teddy. "He happened."

Elliott glanced from the clothes wadded up on the floor to Brydie. After a moment of confusion, she burst out laughing. "Oh my God!"

"He's a menace."

"Well, I was wondering how things were going, but I guess now I know," Elliott said.

"I don't understand this dog," Brydie said. "I have to *carry* him outside. All he does is sleep . . . and snore . . . and fart."

Elliott wrinkled her nose. "Maybe he misses his Mrs. Neumann," she said. "I've met her a few times. She's a really sweet old lady."

"I can't imagine a sweet old lady owning a dog like this."

"I guess you'll find out in a couple of days when you meet her."

Brydie rolled her eyes. "Great."

"Why don't you take him to the dog park down the street?" Elliott offered. "I bet you could both use some fresh air."

"He won't go anywhere in that harness," Brydie replied. "We went outside earlier. He just lay in the grass."

Elliott bit at the corners of her lip to keep from laughing. She had a large, wide smile that hid two perfect rows of white teeth. People were all the time comparing her to a younger, tanner version of Julia Roberts. It was a feature of which Brydie was insanely jealous, as her own bow-shaped mouth made her look as if she were in a constant pout. "He won't have to wear his harness at the dog park. And it's a gorgeous day outside."

It *was* a pretty day. It was the beginning of October, and still quite warm, even for Memphis. "I guess it's worth a shot," Brydie said. She tucked a piece of brown hair behind her ear. The short haircut she'd had a year ago was still in that awkward stage and wouldn't quite go into a ponytail. She looked down at herself. Her five-foot-six frame had always been voluptuous, her "baker's body," as she called it. Now her clothes hung on her. Months of stress created an effect that she'd never been able to achieve when she was married. "But everything I own makes me look like a homeless person."

"Hush," Elliott replied. "You look great."

"I just don't want to go anywhere."

Elliott narrowed her eyes at her friend. "You can't trade one couch for another," she said. "You *have got* to get out. You've got to find a job."

"I will."

"Will you?" Elliott asked. "Because you've been saying that for the last six months. I love you, Brydie, but it's time to stop feeling sorry for yourself and do something with your life."

"I know, I know." Brydie waved her off, blinking back tears.

"The dog park would be a good start," Elliott said, her voice softening. "I know it's hard. But you can't ignore the rest of the world forever."

"Fine," Brydie said, putting her emotions in check and heading to the bedroom to find a new pair of pants. "But you're carrying Teddy Roosevelt to the car for me."

THE GERMANTOWN DOG PARK was just two blocks from Brydie's house. She'd never been to a dog park before, but Elliott told her that it was a place where people could let their dogs run around leash-free. This didn't sound like such a good idea to Brydie—all those dogs running around with nobody controlling them—but Elliott assured her it was perfectly fine. She parked and turned around to look at Teddy Roosevelt in the backseat. He was standing up on his back legs and panting hard, looking out the window. "Do you want to go outside?" she asked.

Teddy Roosevelt pawed at the window, making little whining noises in his throat.

"Let's go, then." Brydie opened the back passenger door and picked him up, carrying him to the gate of the park. There were about ten other people there, and none of them seemed to notice Brydie and Teddy Roosevelt. They continued playing fetch with their dogs, chatting with each other, or drinking coffee on one of the park benches. The sun was shining and the grass had been freshly cut, filling Brydie's nose with a sweet, soft scent. She loved it there.

She sat Teddy Roosevelt down on the ground and watched him lumber off, hiking his leg at the first tree he encountered. His change in demeanor surprised her. *Maybe this was a good idea,* she thought. Everyone else around her seemed to be having a good time. There was a woman to Brydie's right, a squat woman with blunt bangs and a cardigan, feeding treats to a huge harlequin Great Dane. When the Dane jumped up to grab the treat, he stood taller than his owner. After the dog gobbled up the treat, the woman said as if she were talking to an infant, "Good boy, Thor. You're such a good boy!" Then the dog licked her entire face with a tongue that was at least half the length of his body.

One man was throwing a ball while an elderly beagle chased it. Actually, the man and the beagle looked about the same age—ancient. Both were completely gray, and both had a slight limp in their gait.

Brydie was so entranced watching the Great Dane and the beagle that she didn't notice that Teddy Roosevelt had wandered off until she looked down and realized he was no longer near the tree. Feeling panic rising in her throat, she scanned the park. She didn't see him anywhere.

"Teddy!" she yelled, while other people in the park stared at her. "Teddy Roosevelt! Where are you?"

Then she saw him—at the other end of the park, sniffing at a dog, a huge, furry dog three times his size. There was a man leaning down and petting the heads of both dogs. Brydie trotted up to them, breathless.

"Is this your dog?" the man said, looking up at Brydie. He had a thick mass of curly black hair and eyes almost the same color. Stubble lined his jaws.

"I, uh . . ." Brydie couldn't think of what to say. Teddy Roosevelt wasn't really her dog. Not exactly.

The man straightened up, tucking an errant curl behind his ear. He looked at her expectantly.

"Yes," Brydie said quickly. "He's my dog."

"He seems to have taken a fancy to Sasha here."

"I'm sorry." Brydie reached down and pulled on Teddy Roosevelt's collar. "It's our first time here."

"Oh, it's fine," he replied. "She loves other dogs." He reached out his hand to Brydie. "I'm Nathan."

"Brydie."

"It's nice to meet you."

"It's nice to meet you, too." She smiled at him. He looked about her age—maybe a little younger—closer to thirty, and nice looking in a friendly sort of way. He was wearing dark wash jeans and an unbuttoned flannel shirt with a crisp, white T-shirt underneath. Brydie couldn't help but imagine that up close he probably smelled nice, too. "What kind of dog is Sasha? She's the size of a horse."

Nathan chuckled. "Maybe a pony, but you're right. She's a big dog. She's an Irish wolfhound, and still a bit of a puppy, and clumsy as hell."

Brydie giggled. "I don't think Teddy Roosevelt minds."

The two dogs were lying on the grass, Teddy giving Sasha's ears a good once-over.

"Your dog's name is Teddy Roosevelt?"

Brydie felt herself blush. "I didn't name him."

"Your husband, then?"

"No, no husband." Brydie's cheeks were burning. "It's just an, uh, old family name."

"I see."

The sun had begun to set and the wind had picked up. It was starting to feel chilly. Brydie hadn't been prepared for someone to ask her . . . well, anything about her life. *My life,* she thought. *Oh, you know, I'm a broke divorcée who's been forced into playing butler to a surly, trash-eating, old pug because my best friend can't stand to see me mope around her house anymore?*

She looked down at Teddy. He'd moved from investigating Sasha's ears to investigating Nathan's shoes. And then her borrowed dog began to make a hacking noise that sounded an awful lot like sneezing—backward sneezing. Before Brydie could do anything, and to her abject horror, Teddy Roosevelt opened his mouth and vomited.

He vomited all over the grass, all over himself, and worst of all—all over Nathan's shoes. Brydie couldn't do anything but watch, frozen, until the whole, disgusting performance was over.

"Oh my God," she said. "Oh. My. God. I'm so sorry!" She reached down to grab the dog. "He got into the garbage today. He must've . . . He must've eaten something . . ." she trailed off, unable to tear her eyes away from the man's shoes. Without another word, she turned and raced out of the park with Teddy Roosevelt tucked under her arm like a wiggly, barfing bowling ball, cursing Elliott the whole way home.

CHAPTER 4

I CAN'T BELIEVE YOU JUST TOOK OFF WITHOUT saying anything to him," Elliott said as she pushed a plastic cart through ShopCo, one of the largest superstores in Memphis. "I mean, you just picked up the pug and ran?"

Brydie nodded. "I panicked. I didn't know what to do."

"The least you could have done was offer to buy him a new pair of shoes."

"They looked pretty expensive."

Elliott laughed. "Maybe you can make it up to him the next time you see him at the dog park."

"Oh, I'm never going back there," Brydie replied.

"Somehow I knew you were going to say that."

Brydie picked up a bottle of Moscato from an endcap and inspected it. "I tried going out like you wanted me to. It was a disaster. So I'm going to buy enough food here to get me through the winter, and then I'm going to get under the covers and stay there until Easter."

"Why do you suppose they make bottles of wine this big?" Elliott asked, ignoring her friend. "Who could possibly drink this much?"

Brydie took the bottle back from her friend and put it into the cart. "Better get two of them just to be safe."

"You're going to drink this in front of me even though you know I can't have any?"

Brydie nodded, unable to stop the grin spreading across her face.

"Fine," Elliott said. "But I think we need cupcakes to go with the wine."

"I'm not baking for you, if that's what you're getting at," Brydie said.

"You haven't baked for me in ages."

"I haven't baked for anyone in ages," Brydie replied. "Surely we can find some cupcakes the size of these wine bottles somewhere."

ShopCo reminded Brydie of a store in Jonesboro. It was a big-box store like this one, although not quite so big. They'd given her little bakery a run for its money when it was first built, offering cheaper versions of what she and Allan created. As they passed through the deli and made their way into the bakery, Brydie saw a sign sitting atop two wax versions of cakes.

"Now Hiring!" the sign boasted. "Seasonal Employees!"

"Look, Brydie," Elliott said. "You can work *here*."

Brydie inspected the sign more closely. "It says they're hiring in the bakery and the deli."

"Oh, you can't be serious."

"Why not?"

"For one, this place is almost an hour with traffic

from where you live," Elliott replied. "For another, this place is a cesspool. We just came her for the cheap wine."

"What was it you said about beggars not being choosers?"

"I didn't mean you should work *here*."

Brydie shrugged. Sure, it wasn't her dream job, but her dream job had turned out to be more of a nightmare than anything else. "It's just for the holidays."

"I guess any job is better than no job," Elliott said. "And, hey, if they hired you in the bakery, at least you'd get to do what you love again."

"Maybe." Brydie wasn't so sure she loved baking anymore. She'd hardly baked a single thing since the night she caught Allan and one of their employees spread out on the bakery's kitchen floor like pieces of puff pastry. Allan hadn't even tried to stop her as she ran out of the shop in horror. Now baking reminded her too much of what she'd had—and lost.

"It says to apply on their website," Elliott said, pointing to the sign. "You can come over to my place and apply if you want. I know you don't have Internet at Mrs. Neumann's."

"You'll have to help me with a resume," Brydie replied. "I haven't had one since before the shop opened."

Elliott nodded. "Fine, but first things first—let's find some cupcakes to match our wine."

ELLIOTT AND BRYDIE stared down at Teddy Roosevelt from their perch on the couch. He hadn't moved since they sat down.

"What do you think he wants?" Brydie whispered.

Elliott stifled a giggle, leaned in closer to her friend, and said, "Your immortal soul!"

"Shut up!" Brydie pushed Elliott away from her. Her wine sloshed out of her glass and landed at the dog's feet. He leaned down to sniff the liquid and then resumed his gaze at the two women.

"Give him a cupcake," Elliott said. She scooped a glob of frosting onto one of her fingertips and held it out for Teddy Roosevelt to sniff.

Before Brydie could respond, the dog's tongue had uncurled from his mouth and practically swallowed Elliott's hand. "Don't give that to him!" Brydie yelped. "It's not good for him!"

"Frosting isn't going to hurt him." Elliott rolled her eyes and wiped her hand on her shirt. "It's vanilla, not chocolate."

"Still, he shouldn't be having it," Brydie chided. "I don't want to kill this dog before I've lived here a week."

"He eats the damn trash," Elliott muttered. "Or have you already forgotten your little incident at the dog park?"

Brydie felt herself flush. "No."

"He sort of seems amiss in this house, don't you think?" Elliott asked.

"Huh?" Brydie turned her attention to her friend. She'd been thinking about Nathan and his dark eyes and curly hair. "Who seems amiss?"

"The dog," Elliott replied. "He's sort of gross, you know? He's old and smells and eats the trash. And this house, well"—Elliott gestured to the grand living room—"is perfect."

Brydie nodded. Elliott was right. Teddy didn't fit with the house. A house like this should have come with a different sort of dog . . . maybe an Irish wolf-hound like Sasha—something regal, or at the very least taller. She looked down at the little dog. He wasn't the only one out of place. Hesitantly, she reached down and gave him a scratch under the chin. *Maybe,* she thought as she scratched him, *maybe I'm not quite alone.* Before she could take her hand away from his chin, Teddy Roosevelt sneezed.

"Yep," Elliott said, sticking her finger back into the frosting of her cupcake, "this dog is a real keeper."

CHAPTER 5

BRYDIE STARED UP AT THE GERMANTOWN
Retirement Village as it loomed in front of her.
It was a big, beautiful building—it didn't look like a
nursing home at all—with white pillars and carefully
laid brickwork. It didn't resemble the nursing home
her grandparents ended up at in Piggott, Arkansas.
This facility was trying hard to appear more like
a mansion than anything else and the courtyard
surrounding the building only added to that image.
All around, orderlies in crisp white uniforms laughed
and talked with elderly people as if they were at a
party.

To say this surprised Brydie was an understatement.
She'd assumed that the nursing home would be drab
and smell bad. However, as she and Teddy entered
the foyer, the entire place smelled of rich mahogany
and some kind of spice that Brydie couldn't place.
This is Germantown, she reminded herself, setting
the dog down on the tiled floor. *Rich people don't
live in holes.*

The woman behind the desk smiled up at Brydie. "Hello. How may I help you?"

"I'm here to see . . ." Brydie trailed off, nervous. "I'm here to see Mrs. Pauline Neumann."

The woman knitted her eyebrows together. "Are you family?"

"No," Brydie replied. "I'm living in her house, and I have her dog."

The woman's expression didn't change.

"I mean," Brydie continued hastily, "I'm house-sitting for her. I'm supposed to bring her dog by every week for a visit. This is a new arrangement."

"I'll just need to check the list for approval," the woman replied. "And I'll need an ID."

Brydie fumbled in her purse and handed over her driver's license. The woman eyed her and then turned and disappeared into an office behind the desk. Brydie gripped Teddy's leash. She wondered if the woman thought she was trying to pull one over on her—maybe she thought Brydie was lying about something. She couldn't understand why anyone would want to come to a nursing home if they didn't have to, but she figured this was probably the nicest nursing home she'd ever seen. Maybe people tried all the time to get in to visit people they didn't really know.

As Brydie continued to stare down at the dog, now sprawled out on the floor, she became keenly aware that she was being watched. It was probably the woman from the front counter, come to tell her that she wasn't welcome. She whisked around, ready to speak, then saw a familiar face and stopped cold.

It was Nathan.

The man from the dog park.

He was standing in front of her, a mix of confusion and amusement playing on his face. He folded his arms across his plaid button-up shirt. After what seemed like forever, he finally said, "Well, this is the last place I thought I'd see the two of you."

Brydie felt her cheeks burn. "I'm here for a visit," she said, because it was the only thing she could think to say. *I'm supposed to be here,* she reminded herself. There was no reason for her to be embarrassed. It was *he* who was out of place.

Nathan stared at her from over the top of a pair of wire-rimmed glasses. He looked dapper and professional, with the exception of his unruly, curly hair, which spilled down his forehead and threatened to cover his eyes. He looked confused for a moment, and then he brightened. "Oh, yes. I know who you're here to see." And then he said, more to himself, "I can't believe I didn't put it together before."

"Put what together?" Brydie asked. "Are you visiting someone here, too?"

By then the woman from the front desk had returned, and she stood watching them for a moment before interrupting. "Ms. Benson," she said, looking down at Brydie's license, "I'll go ahead and show you back to Mrs. Neumann's suite."

"Don't worry about it, Sylvia." Nathan waved her off. "I'll show her on my way to make the rounds."

The woman smiled a kind of thin, waxy smile at Brydie. She wasn't sure, but Brydie could have sworn she saw a look of jealousy come over Sylvia's face before she said, "Whatever you'd like, Dr. Reid."

Brydie could hardly believe her ears. Doctor? *Doctor?* He was a doctor? *Here?* Trying to keep her jaw from hitting the floor, she tugged at Teddy's leash, but he didn't move, and she groaned leaning down to pick him up. She didn't even know why she bothered with the damned leash and harness.

"Are you coming?" Dr. Reid turned around to look at Brydie. And then, with a smirk, he said, "Keep him away from my shoes, if you don't mind."

Brydie scurried after him, the dog tucked into the crook of her arm. "About that," she said, catching up with him. "I'm sorry. I shouldn't have run off like that. I was embarrassed. Let me pay for your shoes. I'm sure they're ruined."

"It's not the first time I've had vomit on my shoes, actually," the doctor replied. "Although I'm generally at work when that happens."

"So you work here? At the nursing home? You're a doctor?"

He nodded. "I'm usually at Baptist Memorial in the ER, but we doctors take turns at the home, here, as a bit of respite from the hectic schedule in Emergency. I'll be here until the new year."

"Oh," was all Brydie could think of to say.

"You're related to Mrs. Neumann somehow?" the doctor asked, stopping at last in front of a white door at the end of the hallway.

Brydie stared at the door in front of her. Behind it was a woman she'd never met, *a woman whose life,* she thought, *I've been living.*

Dr. Reid looked at her expectantly.

"Sort of," she said, not meeting his gaze. "Can I go in?"

"Of course," he replied. "When she said Teddy Roosevelt was coming to visit today, well, I didn't know what to think." He broke into a wide grin.

Brydie peered into the suite, but before she had

time to focus on anything, Teddy jumped out of her arms and bolted inside. He jumped right into the lap of the woman sitting at the window, causing her to drop the book she'd been reading.

Brydie rushed in after him, leaning down to pick up the book. "I'm so sorry," she said, handing the woman the book. "He got away from me."

The woman didn't answer; she was too busy greeting her dog as he showered her with kisses. After a few moments, she looked down at Brydie. She was no longer smiling. Positioning Teddy Roosevelt into her lap, she said, "Is this a habit of yours? Letting my dog *get away* from you?"

Brydie straightened herself. She thought about how Teddy Roosevelt had escaped from her at the dog park. Without realizing it, she turned her attention toward the doorway where Nathan had stood. He was already gone.

"Hello? Young lady?" The woman stuck a foot out and kicked Brydie in her shin. "I'm talking to you!"

"Ow," Brydie replied, stepping back. "No, um, I'm sorry. No, I'm certainly not in the habit of letting Teddy Roosevelt get away from me."

The woman narrowed her eyes at Brydie. "Sit down," she said. "I suppose you already know that I'm Pauline Neumann. I've heard quite a lot about you, but I can't for the life of me remember your name."

"Yes, ma'am. I'm Brydie Benson."

"This dog smells like garbage."

"He keeps getting into the trash," Brydie said. She bit at the corner of her bottom lip. "I sometimes forget to put the trash can up at night."

"How old are you?" Pauline asked. "They told me

a *young* woman would be taking care of my Teddy. You look at least thirty."

"I'm thirty-four."

"And you're not married?"

"No."

Pauline made a quiet harrumph under her breath before she said, "No children, either, I suppose?"

Brydie felt her chest tighten. How many times had she been forced to say the words "no, I don't have any children"?

"Children aren't for everyone," Pauline replied. Then a warm smile crossed her face, changing her angles, softening them. "Taking care of a dog is not entirely unlike taking care of a child sometimes."

Brydie took a moment to study the woman in front of her. She was dressed in a crisp linen dress and her legs were neatly crossed at the ankle. Her hair was completely white and had been braided and wound into a bun on the top of her head. Despite her deeply wrinkled face, her eyes were bright and blue, twinkling ever so slightly. The dog on her lap looked as out of place with her as he did at her house, but it was obvious she adored him, for reasons that Brydie had herself not yet figured out. "You don't have any children either?"

"I've had four husbands, my dear," Pauline replied. "They were children enough for me."

Brydie suppressed a smile.

"Teddy," the old woman continued, "was a present from my fourth husband. He passed on four years ago, and this dog is all I have left of him. When the stroke took my legs and I came to live here, I worried I might never see Teddy again."

"I'll make sure you see him often," Brydie said, her heart breaking for the elderly woman in front of her.

Pauline nodded. "I'm sure that you will, my dear."

"It's just . . ." Brydie hesitated. She didn't want to show the old woman how ignorant she was or make her think she actually wouldn't do a good job taking care of Teddy. "It's just I'm having a hard time getting him to eat. Or go outside on the leash. Or anything really," she finished.

"Oh, he likes to be carried," Pauline replied. She gave her dog a scratch between his ears. "It wasn't until recently, when I lost the ability to pick him up, that we tried the harness. The woman at the pet store said it was the best kind they made, but as you can see, he doesn't care for it much."

"And his food?"

Pauline shrugged. "Oh, I fed him table scraps, mostly. I bought him that dog food when I bought the harness. I'm sure it's old and stale by now."

"I'll buy him some more," Brydie replied.

"I know it's not good to give him table scraps. It gives him awful gas." Pauline wrinkled her nose. "But I can't seem to help it."

"I imagine table scraps taste better than dog food," Brydie said.

"I imagine you're right," Pauline replied. "And you know, the next time you visit, he ought not to smell like he lives in a junkyard."

"I'll work on that," Brydie replied. After a moment's hesitation, she blurted, "He's my first dog. I've never taken care of one before."

The old woman cocked her head from one side to the other, looking very much like Teddy in that moment. "No husband, no kids, and no dog?" Pauline asked. "How does a woman get so far along in life without any of those things?"

"I'm divorced," Brydie replied.

"Newly."

It wasn't a question. Brydie wondered how she could tell that her divorce was *new*. "It's been six months."

"New enough," Pauline replied with a shrug. "That's about how long my third marriage lasted."

"We were married for over a decade," Brydie replied, her hackles rising. She didn't know why, but she wanted to make sure the old woman knew that it hadn't been *that kind* of marriage.

"Takes some people longer than others to figure out they're not right for each other," Pauline said.

Brydie swallowed. She wanted to argue, but she couldn't. Clearly, since Allan met Cassandra and asked Brydie for a divorce, they hadn't been right for each other. Still, that wasn't a fact she was ready to admit to herself, let alone to anybody else. Rather, she hadn't been right for him. However, in the spirit of her new resolve to *move on,* Brydie said, "I suppose that's true."

"I'm sorry," Pauline said, breaking the silence. "I wish I could tell you that saying whatever pops into my head is a flaw that's come with age, but it isn't. I've always been this way."

"I've always wanted to be able to do that," Brydie replied. "Say whatever I'm thinking. Instead, I roll the words around in my head for just long enough to become worried that they're the wrong ones."

"Well, together we'll make a perfect team," Pauline. "You can help me think more, and maybe I can help you think less."

Brydie grinned at the woman sitting across from her. "It's a deal."

BRYDIE EXPECTED THAT after a long, hot bath in the master bedroom, she'd find Teddy in the trash, since she'd once again forgotten to put it up. But he was in the exact same spot as she'd left him. He usually delighted in ravaging the trash for goodies, and Mrs. Neumann had been right—her dog *did* smell like garbage.

Brydie retreated to the bedroom and threw on an oversize shirt—one of Allan's that she couldn't bear to part with—and began to run another bath. She felt a bit guilty for not having thought of it before. He would certainly smell better afterward, *and maybe,* she thought, *he'll feel better, too.*

She half-expected Teddy to protest, especially once she eased him down into the water, but he didn't. Instead he sat there while Brydie took a cup and poured warm water over him, his eyes half-closed. Brydie couldn't find any dog shampoo, but she did have her own strawberry-scented kind, and she figured that was better than nothing at all. She lathered him up, careful not to get the shampoo in his eyes or ears. When they were finished, she toweled him off, gently rubbing his fur in a circular motion, from his head all the way down to his paws. It amazed her how good he was being, but of course, she'd never had a dog before. The way he sat, so perfectly still and upright, reminded her of the way she used to sit after bath time as a child, when her father would help her out of the tub and make sure she was dry enough for her nightclothes.

Her mother had often worked late at night, leaving

Brydie's father at home alone to care for her. Ruth and Gerald Benson had both started out as real estate agents, and it was how they'd met as young adults. However, after Ruth became the more successful of the two, and after Brydie was born, Gerald stayed home to care for her until she went off to school. Brydie adored being with her father. He was warm and gentle, and told the best stories. They went to the park and to the swimming pool in the summertime and to the movies and museums in the wintertime, sometimes driving all the way to Memphis to find interesting things to do.

Her mother never went with them.

Even before she went to kindergarten, Brydie knew and understood that her mother worked, *needed* to work, in order to support the family. Brydie didn't mind it, and couldn't remember a time in her life when she felt resentful for the work her mother did and the late hours she kept. No, it wasn't resentment she felt when, after taking a bath and scrubbing herself clean and sitting on the couch fresh and pink in her pajamas, her mother would pass by her going to her office at the back of the house without so much as a look or a hug or a kiss. It wasn't resentment that she felt when after dinner her father sat down in front of the television with a rum and Coke and zoned out past Brydie's bedtime because it was her mother's night to put her to bed and they'd both forgotten.

No, it was something else that she felt, a feeling she'd had as long as she could remember, a feeling that lingered still, more than thirty years later. It was a feeling she'd been battling since her divorce from Allan. If Brydie had to put a finger on it, if she had to name this feeling, she guessed she would say it was loneliness.

Maybe Teddy Roosevelt was lonely.

Brydie shook her head. It was silly to place human feelings on a dog. But looking down into his wrinkled little face, she saw something she recognized. She gave his head a final rub with the towel and sat down beside him. At least if they were going to be alone, they could be alone together.

CHAPTER 6

THE NEXT MORNING, BRYDIE SAT IN HER FIAT and stared at the ShopCo building looming in front of her. Someone named Bernice had called her that morning for an interview. She'd been thick with sleep and when the phone call was over, she half-believed she'd dreamed it.

"Thanks for coming over on such short notice. I figured I'd get a couple of days' notice for an interview," she'd said to Elliott when she and Mia arrived to watch over Teddy. "I just don't want to leave him alone right now."

Elliott bent down to give Teddy Roosevelt a pat. "Changing your mind about him, are you?"

"He's hardly moved," Brydie replied. "He hasn't eaten hardly anything, either, even though I got him some new food."

"Poor guy."

"I don't know how to make him feel better."

"Give him some time," Elliott said. "I'm sure he'll come around."

"He's slobbery," Mia said, plopping down onto the floor next to Teddy. She took off her shoes and wiggled her toes.

"Be careful," Brydie said with mock seriousness. "Teddy might lick your feet!"

"Ewww!" the little girl squealed. "That would be funny."

Brydie smiled down at Mia. She had all of the best parts of Elliott and Leo. She had Elliott's wide mouth and laugh and Leo's dark hair and eyes. "Can you take care of Teddy while I'm gone?" she asked.

Mia nodded solemnly.

"We'll take great care of him," Elliott said. "Good luck at your interview!"

Brydie stepped out of the car and into the sunlight. She straightened her black knit pencil skirt. She wasn't sure where she was supposed to be going—the woman on the phone told her to find customer service, which was easier said than done in this colossal store. When she finally found the service counter, slightly sweaty and out of breath, she said, "I'm Brydie Benson. I'm here to see Bernice."

"You here for a position at the bakery?"

"Yes?" Brydie didn't mean for it to, but her response came out as more of a question.

He looked her up and down in that greasy sort of way some men are capable of doing. He said, "Looks like the bakery is movin' on up in the world."

Brydie followed him to the back of the store. ShopCo was huge—one of those big retail chains that sell in bulk. She'd never understood why someone would need a six-hundred-ounce jar of pickles, and she for sure never thought she'd be working at a store that sold them. What would it be like in the bakery?

The man led her back through heavy, plastic double doors and into what looked like a break room. There a woman sat, her back to them, wearing a purple hairnet that glistened in the fluorescent lighting. "Yo, Bernie, you got a lady here to see you."

Bernice turned around and gave the two of them a half smile. "Sit down," she said to Brydie. "I was just finishin' up my lunch."

Brydie sat down in front of the woman. She pulled her resume out from her bag and handed it over. "Hi, I'm Brydie Benson."

"Interesting name," Bernice grunted, licking Cheetos dust from her fingertips.

"It's Gaelic for Bridget."

"Well, Bridget, I'm Bernice. But everybody calls me Bernie," the woman said. "I looked over your resume. Impressive."

"Thank you."

"You owned your own bakery?"

"I did." Brydie shifted in her chair. "With my husband."

"And you did well? At this bakery of yours?"

"We did," Brydie replied. "For a little while."

Bernice made a scratch on the pad of paper in front of her with a dull pencil. "And how long did you own this bakery?"

"About five years," Brydie said. "Until . . ." She trailed off.

"Until what?"

"Until we got divorced."

Bernice's straight line of a mouth didn't change. She looked down at Brydie's resume. "Here's what I need, Bridget—I need someone to make sure the damn cakes get done. My overnight manager needs someone reliable."

"Overnight?"

Bernice nodded. "It's full-time. Benefits after three months, but right now you'll be seasonal. There is no guarantee of a full-time job after the holidays. The job is eight P.M. to five A.M. Four nights on, three nights off."

Brydie sat back in her chair. The ad she'd seen hadn't said anything about the position being overnight, and neither had the application. "It's overnight?"

"It's the only position we got left. Filled the other holiday jobs yesterday," Bernice replied. She licked the rest of the Cheetos dust off her fingers. "But I got about ten other people to get to today, so if you ain't interested, that's fine by me."

"No," Brydie said, taking her time with the word. "It's not that I'm not interested, but I just didn't know the job would be overnight."

"Well, now ya do."

"When does it start?"

"As soon as your background check goes through, and we can get ya through orientation."

"Okay," Brydie replied.

"Good." Bernice sat back. "Joe will give you a call in a couple of days. Get your schedule set up."

"Who's Joe?"

"The nighttime bakery manager."

Brydie knew she shouldn't be asking too many questions, especially since she'd only just been hired, but she couldn't help herself. "Why didn't Joe interview me?"

"Joe don't like to do the interview part," Bernice

said. "And he ain't up at this ungodly hour." She stood up, taking her clipboard and the remaining Cheetos dust with her. "He tends to scare people at first. He ain't much of a conversationalist, that one."

Brydie watched her go, not sure if she ought to be excited or terrified. She guessed she was a little bit of both. It felt like an eternity since she'd done any work, any baking, and she was woefully out of practice. She didn't need any reason to give Joe, the boss she'd never met, any reason to dislike her.

Maybe it was time she started practicing.

CHAPTER 7

LATER THAT AFTERNOON, BRYDIE LEANED THE back of her head against the locked door in the hallway, repeating the motion over and over again as the phone rang on the other end of the line. It soothed slightly the nervousness she felt about calling her mother.

"Benson Realty."

"Hey, Margie," Brydie said, releasing a breath she hadn't realize she'd been holding. "Is my mom busy?"

"Hey, honey," Margie said with her smooth Arkansas Delta twang. "Let me transfer you over. It sure is good to hear your voice!"

Brydie smiled into her phone. She'd always liked Margie. She'd been her mother's secretary at the agency since Brydie was in high school, and she was the complete opposite of Brydie's mother—cheerful and soft around the edges.

"Well, it's about time," her mother said, piercing Brydie's ear. "I thought that I was going to have to hear about everything through Elliott."

"I'm sorry," Brydie replied. She should have known her mother would call Elliott when she failed to get a hold of her. "I've just been really busy sorting things out."

"Too busy to call your mother?"

Brydie sighed. "Well, I'm mostly all settled," she said. "I start a new job in a few days."

"I heard you applied for a job at that ShopCo," was all her mother said. It was clear in her tone that Ruth Benson didn't approve.

"It'll be good to be working again," Brydie replied. "Even if it is at night."

"Elliott didn't tell me it was overnight," her mother said. "What kind of a bakery is open at night?"

"It's preparation for the daytime," Brydie said. "Allan and I used to be up at all hours of the night preparing cakes for customers."

"Yes," her mother agreed, "but that was at *your own* shop in Jonesboro, not at a bargain store in a sketchy part of Memphis."

Brydie rolled her eyes, and was glad her mother couldn't see her. "Maybe I'll have better luck with the bargain store."

"Why don't you just come home?"

It shouldn't have surprised Brydie, her mother's response. After her father died, her mother decided she hated being alone, and Ruth spent a good deal of her time making her only child feel guilty for not calling or coming to visit.

During her divorce, Brydie had been convinced by her mother to move in with her. It hadn't ended well, and Brydie sometimes wondered if her mother remembered that. "It'll be fun," her mother had said. "Just we gals, having a good time."

For Brydie, moving in with her mother had been anything but fun. What she'd needed, what she'd thought her mother would understand she'd needed, was quiet. Instead what she got was a cocktail party every night with her mother's middle-aged work colleagues. She missed her father more then, at that time, than she ever had before. If *he'd* been there, *he* would have known what to do to make her feel better. *He* never would have tried to set her up with a fifty-year-old real estate agent named Ralph. He'd have simply poured two drinks instead of one, sat down next to her on the couch, and not said a word.

Brydie forced herself to concentrate on the conversation she was having and said to her mother, "You know I can't."

"I don't know that," her mother replied. "I don't see any reason for you to be in Memphis playing nanny to an overweight dog."

Brydie looked over at Teddy Roosevelt, sleeping at the foot of the couch. "He's not overweight . . . not really. Anyway, this is a ridiculous argument to be having. You know why I don't want to come home, and you know why I left."

"I saw Allan last week," her mother said, hitting the nail right on the head.

Brydie felt a lump form in her throat. "Oh?"

"At the gas station by the office on Caraway."

"Did you talk to him?"

"No," her mother replied. "He was with *That Girl*."

The lump tightened. *That Girl* was the term she and her mother used to refer to Cassandra Burr, the woman with whom Allan had had an affair. Now, of course, it was no longer an affair, but a legitimate relationship, a thought that enraged Brydie. "I should probably get off the phone," she said, finally. "It's time for Teddy's walk."

"Headed to the dog park?"

"Maybe," Brydie said.

"Wouldn't kill you to be friendly with that doctor," her mother replied. "Sure be better than your last husband."

"I'll talk to you later, Mom."

She shoved the phone back in her pocket and turned around to face the door she'd been leaning against. She'd tried every key she could find, but none of them fit.

Frustrated, she kicked the door, and a string of expletives escaped her mouth as her bare toe met the wood. Teddy looked up at her and cocked his head to the side as if asking her why she'd gone and done such a stupid thing. "Why is this door locked?" she asked him.

Teddy cocked his head to the other side and then rested his chin on the floor once again.

I'm losing my mind, Brydie thought. *I'm talking to a dog.* She walked over to the hallway closet and retrieved Teddy's harness and leash. She needed to talk to an actual human being, and maybe, just maybe, the dog park wasn't such a bad idea.

CHAPTER 8

Try as she might, Brydie simply couldn't get used to how much *warmer* it was in Memphis. Even though Jonesboro was just seventy miles north of the city, hardly more than an hour and almost a straight shot up Interstate 55, the weather clearly hadn't gotten the memo.

Or maybe, Brydie mused, standing with Teddy in the all but abandoned dog park, maybe it was the people who were so different. It was fifty degrees outside, and *October,* for Christ's sake, but everywhere she went, people seemed to be bundled up and gloomy, complaining that winter was upon them. In Jonesboro, most people would have thrown on a sweatshirt and moved on with their lives.

City people, she thought.

Teddy didn't seem to notice the blustery weather and happily zipped away from her to explore the park. She'd been glad to see his energy back this morning, but worried that their Sunday visit with Pauline, just two days away, would bring him back down again.

He'd moved from sleeping in the kitchen to in the hallway just outside the spare bedroom door. Brydie thought it was progress. She slept in the spare room just across the hall from the master bedroom. Something seemed wrong about sleeping in Pauline Neumann's room, even if she wasn't around to use it. It wasn't Brydie's, and that certainty, that it wasn't hers and would never be hers, was unsettling. She was already pretending enough as it was, and she half-worried that if she slept in the master bedroom she'd wake up one morning to find Pauline's wrinkled face and cascade of white hair looking back at her.

"It ain't too cold out here for ya, missy?"

Brydie looked up, startled out of her thought, to see a familiar face smiling back at her. It was the old man in the overalls. His beagle waddled behind him, a stuffed duck hanging out either side of its mouth.

"It's barely sweatshirt weather," Brydie replied, grinning. "It's just October, after all."

"That's what me 'n' Arlow here think." The man jabbed a thumb down at his dog, who was now panting at his feet. "Name's Fred."

"I'm Brydie," she said, sticking out her hand. "And that weird little ball of hair over there is Teddy Roosevelt."

"No shit?" he replied, rubbing his chin. "I ain't seen him in ages. Not since he was just a pup an' Talbert Neumann used ta bring him round to play."

"I'm dog-sitting," Brydie confessed. "Well, house-sitting really. His owner went into a nursing home and needed someone to look after Teddy."

"I heard about her and was sorry fer it," Fred said. His face was kind and ruddy. He wiped his nose with a handkerchief and then placed it back in the front pocket of his overalls. "I'm mighty glad to meet ya. It's usually just me 'n' that doctor boy up the road on chilly days like this. It'll be good ta have some fresh blood around."

"Oh?" Brydie's heart skipped a beat. *Is he talking about Nathan? Were they friends?* She hoped the old man wouldn't tell him about why she was living in Pauline Neumann's house. Of course, it was always possible that Pauline had already told him, but she didn't want him to know. Not yet, at least.

"And speak of the devil!" Fred nodded his head toward something *or someone* behind Brydie. "If it ain't the good doctor in the flesh."

Sasha reached them first, racing past Brydie and planting her front paws squarely on Fred's chest, giving him a lick before they all heard Nathan say, "Get down, Sash!"

With a whimper, Sasha obliged and sat at Fred's feet, tongue hanging out.

"Sorry about that, Fred," Nathan said.

"Ain't no harm," Fred replied. "That's how Arlow gets me up every mornin'."

Nathan's back was to her as he continued to talk to Fred. For a moment Brydie thought that he wasn't going to acknowledge her. She felt her face redden at the thought, and searched around for Teddy. Maybe she should just walk away while she still could and save herself the embarrassment of having to admit to herself that she'd been hoping to see him.

Before Brydie could decide what to do, Nathan turned around and said, "Hey, Brydie."

His voice slid over her like warm butter, and her need to escape vanished. "Hey."

"I see you've met Fred and Arlow."

Brydie nodded. "I have."

"They're regulars at the park, just like Sasha and me," Nathan said. "She and I are here pretty much whenever we have time off."

"This is just our second time," Brydie replied. "Well, my second time. I think Teddy's been here lots of times."

"I moved into my grandparents' house about six months ago," Nathan said. "I thought I might sell it, but I like the quiet neighborhood."

Brydie looked over to see Sasha on her back with Arlow and Teddy taking turns licking her face. Fred watched in amusement. "I like it, too."

"Mrs. Neumann tells me you're watching her place for a while?"

"I am," Brydie said. "And Teddy, of course." She hoped he wasn't going to ask her anything else.

"I'd never met Mrs. Neumann before she came to live at the nursing home. I think our houses are a couple of blocks away," Nathan said, reaching down to pat Sasha's head when she came panting over. "She was very depressed after moving in. I think your visit with Teddy has really improved her mood."

"She and Teddy were thrilled to see each other," Brydie replied, relieved the conversation had moved off her and back to Mrs. Neumann.

"She's had very few visitors," Nathan said. "But the staff does a great job of keeping the residents busy and entertained. In fact, in a couple of weeks we're having a Halloween party."

"That sounds fun."

"It's just like a carnival—we have games and snacks, and we even have a costume contest. I dress Sasha up every year."

Brydie couldn't help but giggle. "You dress your dog in a costume?"

Nathan grinned. "Sounds weird, right?"

"Maybe a little."

"I'm training her to be a therapy dog for the elderly, and I tell people that dressing her up is part of her training," he said, leaning in closer to Brydie. "But the truth is, picking out her Halloween costume is my favorite thing to do."

Brydie grinned. "How does one go about finding a Halloween costume for their dog?"

"You can find them just about anywhere," Nathan replied. He reached down to pat Sasha's head as she settled herself in between him and Brydie. "But Sasha is so big, I have to order her costume online or have someone make it especially for her."

"I should dress Teddy up as a gremlin," Brydie said.

"You should come to the party," Nathan replied. "I'm sure Mrs. Neumann would love to see Teddy dressed up."

"Oh, I don't know," Brydie said. "I'm getting ready to start a new job. I'm not sure if I'll have time."

"Congratulations," Nathan said. "What is it that you do?"

"I'm a baker," Brydie replied. It was an automatic reply, one that she was so used to giving, she hadn't even thought about it.

"Really?" Nathan asked. "Where will you be working? Maybe I know the place. There used to be a great little bakery downtown, but it closed last year."

Brydie was starting to feel nervous. She was standing there talking to a *hunky doctor,* who had a *therapy dog,* and who enjoyed his grandparents' *quiet neighborhood.* Meanwhile she was just trying to keep her head above water in her *borrowed house* and keep her *borrowed dog* from eating the trash. "I doubt you'd know it," she said, finally. "It's about forty-five minutes from here."

Nathan was about to respond when a buzzing in his pocket distracted him. He pulled out his phone and looked down at the screen. "I've got to head out," he said, clipping Sasha's leash to her collar. "There's an all-hands-on-deck type of emergency at the hospital."

"That sounds serious."

"At least think about the Halloween party, okay?"

"Okay."

Brydie watched him go, both he and Sasha moving quickly, purposely toward the other end of the park. She was relieved that she hadn't had to tell him where she worked or anything else about herself, but she couldn't help but smile when she thought about Nathan's invite to the Halloween party. It did sound like fun. Maybe she and Teddy would go.

"That boy is like a mirage," Fred said, ambling back up to her, Arlow panting in tow.

"What do you mean?"

"He's here, and then he's gone. Never quite know if I'm seein' the real thing or not."

"He is a doctor," Brydie reminded him.

"Them ER doctors got a hankerin' for drama," Fred said. "They like all that rushin' about, never quite knowin' which way's up. Probably why he ain't found himself a wife."

"Maybe he just likes saving lives," Brydie replied. She'd have been annoyed if his drawl weren't so endearing. "Besides, he does work at the nursing home."

"True 'nuff," Fred conceded. "But you be careful with 'im all the same. Married to his work, that one."

Brydie knew all about what it meant to be a workaholic. Her mother was a workaholic, and she'd been one, too, once upon a time. Before the affair, before the divorce, Brydie's devotion to her work was the thing she and Allan fought about the most. He'd thought she worked too much, and he'd told her on several occasions that the reason he'd been an instructor at the culinary school was that he liked the regular and shorter hours. Allan wanted to work nine to five. He wanted to be able to go out with friends on the weekends. He didn't want to take his work home with him.

Brydie, however, didn't know any other way. She wasn't sure if it was genetic or maybe because as a child she saw her mother come home with a stack of paperwork every night, but she couldn't imagine closing up the bakery and not thinking about it again until it opened the next morning. She knew now that when Allan started working late with Cassandra, it should have been a clue that something was up, but instead she'd been thrilled that Allan was showing such initiative.

Now, as she began to feel a slight chill in her bones for the first time since moving to Memphis, Brydie knew that initiative wasn't what anyone would have called it.

CHAPTER 9

SHOPCO AT NIGHT LIT UP AN ENTIRE BLOCK, OR so it seemed to Brydie, who practically had to shield her eyes as she made her way inside. She was nervous and, she had to admit, exhausted. The orientation the day before was simply a two-hour video she and the new hires had to watch. She hadn't met her boss at the bakery or anybody else she was going to work with. She'd tried to sleep earlier during the day, but her brain just wouldn't shut *off*, worrying about things like baking professionally for the first time in nearly a year and how she was going to manage to stay up all night tonight and still make it for her Sunday meeting with Mrs. Neumann.

Teddy seemed confused as Brydie left for the night, but Elliott and little Mia had been kind enough to come and spend the night with him just for this first time so that Brydie wouldn't have to worry. She was sure he'd get used to it eventually. They both would, she guessed.

It surprised Brydie that there were so many people

out shopping at midnight. Her shift ran from 10 P.M. until 6 A.M., and she assumed the place would be empty, but that couldn't have been further from the truth. Doing her best to ignore the throng of people, she made her way up to the bakery counter and stood uncertainly in front of it, where a man had his back to her, scrawling something in icing on a cake.

"Excuse me?" Brydie said, standing on her tiptoes to see over the counter. "Excuse me, are you Joe?"

The man didn't turn around.

Brydie continued to stare at the man's back. She wasn't sure what to do. Bernice had told her to go straight to the bakery and find Joe. But if the man with his back to her was Joe, well, he wasn't paying any attention to her. She called out to him a few more times before giving up and walking around to one side of the counter, where she pushed her way through the yellow double doors and into the bakery.

The little room hidden behind the outside wall and racks of packaged bread smelled like dough and fresh icing, and Brydie inhaled deeply, closing her eyes. It had been a long time, *such a long time* since she'd smelled this smell, and she couldn't help but smile as the memories of her own bakery flooded back to her. It had been the only place she'd felt at home, the only place where she felt she could be herself. *For a little while, at least,* she thought. *Until that day.*

She shook her head to clear her thoughts and made her way back behind the counter where the man still stood. Brydie realized that he was wearing earbuds. She could hear the music blaring through them from where she was standing.

"Excuse me?" she said to him, getting as close as she could without actually touching him.

He didn't notice her.

"Excuse me?"

Still nothing.

This time Brydie reached out to touch him. "Excuse me?"

The man jumped back, dragging a line of purple icing across a white sheet cake. "Shit!"

"Oh, I'm sorry!"

"What the hell are you doing sneaking up on me like that?" The man pawed at his face, pulling the hairnet away from his beard, which unfurled into a long braid. "What are you doing back here? Customers stay behind the counter."

"I'm . . . I'm not a customer," Brydie replied, unable to keep herself from staring at his beard. "I'm Brydie Benson. I'm new."

"Bernie didn't mention you."

"But I'm the new hire."

The man frowned at her, and then his eyes lit up. "Oh, you're Bridget!"

"Brydie."

"Well, Bernie had your name tag made up. I'm Joe. You can call me Joe, not Joseph and not Joey." He pushed past her and lumbered into the back. When he emerged, he handed her the tag. "You'll have to wear this until we can get a new one made up."

"I told her my name was Gaelic for Bridget, not that my actual *name* was Bridget," Brydie replied, grudgingly placing the name tag on her shirt.

"Well, you ruined my cake, whatever your name is."

Brydie looked down at the cake. "I can fix it."

"I ain't even trained you yet."

"I know how to fix a cake," Brydie replied. "It's pretty basic."

"Fine," Joe replied. "Go wash up. I'll get you a hairnet." He disappeared into the back once again.

Brydie scrubbed her hands, dried them, and then walked back over to the cake. Without thinking, she picked up the frosting and began to create a flower over where the accidental line had been made. By the time she finished, Brydie found herself quite pleased and rather breathless. It was the first time she'd been this close to a cake without eating it in months.

"Nice job," Joe said. He was suddenly hovering over her, his beard braid covered once again.

"Thanks," Brydie replied. She smiled up at him. Maybe she was going to like this overnight thing after all.

Joe handed her a hairnet. "But if you ever go to work on anything without a hairnet ever again, I'll fire your ass."

"Don't listen to him," came a voice from the other side of the counter. "He's all bark."

"Watch it, Rosa," Joe replied, without turning around. His voice was gruff, but he was smiling, something Brydie could tell he didn't do often—it made his face look awkward and stretched. "You'll be next."

Brydie watched as two little women walked around the front counter, through the double doors, and finally to where she and Joe were standing. At first she thought they were sisters. Then she realized one of them, the one who spoke and the shorter of the two, was leading the other, holding her hand as if she were a child.

"I've been working for you for five years," the first woman said. "How often do you threaten to fire me?"

"Every day."

"And he never does," the woman said, grinning at Brydie. "I'm Rosa. This here is my daughter, Lillian."

"Hi," Brydie replied, relieved that she and Joe were no longer alone together. "It's nice to meet you both. I'm Brydie."

Rosa let go of her daughter's hand and reached out to Brydie. "Your name tag says Bridget."

"Bernie made a mistake," Joe said. "Big surprise there."

Rosa laughed. "Don't worry about it," she said. "We asked her to put 'Lillie' on Lillian's name tag, and when we showed up for our first night of work, she'd put 'Billie' instead."

"Took them six months to fix it," Joe chimed in.

"My Lillie doesn't always respond well in general," Rosa said. "You can imagine how well it went over with people calling her Billie."

Brydie looked at the woman behind Rosa. She hung back, her head covered by a St. Louis Cardinals baseball cap. She looked a lot like Rosa—they were both short and petite, with smooth caramel-colored skin and a smattering of sprinkles across the bridge of their nose. But there was something different about Lillian that Brydie couldn't put her finger on. She made no attempt to talk to any of them and was instead staring intently at the cake on the table.

"But she's the best cake decorator in the South," Rosa finished, her voice barely above a whisper. "Been here five years, and ain't had a complaint yet."

"Well, it's nice to meet you both," Brydie said.

"That's enough chitchat," Joe said, clapping his hands together. "We've got five orders to fill and a new employee to train."

"See?" Rosa whispered to Brydie. "All talk."

Brydie grinned. It was true that working at ShopCo wasn't going to be anything like owning her own bakery. She was no longer the boss, and she was going to have to learn to follow someone else's lead. But for now, her big, gruff new boss didn't bother her. For now, she was just happy to be doing what she loved.

CHAPTER 10

Brydie knew that she should go straight to bed once she got home, but she simply couldn't. She found herself feeling more awake, more alive than she had in a long time. She felt awake, but at the same time exhausted, a delicious mix she wasn't used to. It made her feel drunk. Although her first night at work had gotten off to a rocky start, the rest of it had been more exciting than she'd expected. Joe and Rosa showed her how to take orders and fill them, and how to stock the bakery so that everything looked lovely and fresh. Then she'd spent at least two hours watching Lillie decorate a cake with the most intricate design she'd ever seen, without messing up or stopping once. Joe practically had to pull her away to clock out at the end of her shift.

All she wanted to do once she got home was bake, and although Teddy was more than a little disgruntled by the time she returned that morning, he sat in the kitchen and watched her curiously as she went to work, cocking his head from side to side as Brydie whisked the cookie dough batter together, dropping in miniature chocolate chips as she went.

She'd done a bit of shopping after work—just enough to get supplies to bake with. On a whim, she'd also purchased some dog treats for Teddy. "Here you go," she said to him. "Try one."

Teddy gave the treat a sniff, took a step back, and promptly sneezed.

"You don't want it?" Brydie held the treat up to her own nose. "Ew," she said, nodding in agreement. "It does smell pretty gross."

As she turned away from the dog and continued on with her baking, she wondered if she would ever find anything that suited Teddy. He all but refused to eat his food, and he clearly didn't want the treats, the fairly expensive ones, she'd bought for him at work. She looked down into her batter and decided she would make him a couple of cookies without the chocolate chips. The rest of the ingredients wouldn't hurt him, and maybe she could win him over with her cookies—she'd never met *anyone* she couldn't win over with her cookies.

In fact, that was how Brydie and Allan had gotten the idea for their bakery. She'd made four dozen cookies for a fundraiser at her mother's realty company, and she'd sold out within fifteen minutes of being there. After the umpteenth person told her she should have her own bakery, Allan had said to her, "You know, it's not a bad idea. Why should we work for someone else, when we can work for ourselves?"

It was an idea that had never occurred to Brydie. In fact, she'd been thinking about trying to get a job at the culinary school. She liked the idea of teaching others to bake, but she also liked the idea of working alongside Allan. She couldn't help but feel that their chemistry in the kitchen was unrivaled. By the end of the next week, Allan had turned in his resignation and they were well on their way to starting their own business.

They started Bake Me A Cake from their apartment kitchen, baking birthday cakes, cookies, anything really. It caught on, and after two years, the business was too big for them to continue in the cramped conditions, so they began searching for a storefront.

Everything was so expensive, and there were problems no matter where they turned. Allan's credit and finances were less than desirable, and Brydie was just twenty-one and had hardly any credit of her own. If the bakery was going to become reality, Brydie would need to quit her retail job—which she'd kept to make ends meet—to bake full-time, and they'd have to use what little money they'd managed to save over the last two years. The way it looked to them, nearly all they had saved would go into the start-up, leaving little room to survive.

"I have a solution," Brydie's mother said to them one afternoon over lunch. "I own a couple of stores in that strip mall on Caraway—you know, over by the Elephant Carwash? One of the tenants skipped out of the rent last month and it's sitting empty, which looks bad for the other businesses there, *and*," her mother emphasized, "*it looks bad for me.*"

Brydie told her mother they'd have to think about it, and she and Allan went home to discuss the possibility of renting from her mother.

"Absolutely not," Brydie had said. "She'll never leave us alone. She'll pester us all the time. She'll tell us how to do *everything*."

"Your mother's never baked a cake in her life!" Allan replied.

"Exactly," Brydie said. "That's what will make it so awful."

Allan, of course, couldn't understand why she thought it was such a bad idea. He'd never understood why Brydie was so hesitant to take anything from her mother, and truthfully, Brydie didn't know, either. It wasn't like her mother was an ogre. It was nice of her to offer her help. But Brydie always worried that there would be strings attached, that her mother would storm in and take control just like she did at home with Brydie's father and every other aspect of Ruth Benson's life.

In the end, they rented the storefront from her mother. She gave them a good deal, much less than they would have paid anywhere else, even though it was located on a prime street. Brydie was thankful, she had to admit, for her mother's smart business sense.

It ended up being Gerald Benson who spent most of his time at the bakery, not his wife. He'd show up in the mornings with a copy of the *Jonesboro Sun* tucked under one arm. He'd sit at the smallest table by the window and wait for his coffee and cranberry scone, tippling whiskey into his coffee and chatting idly with Brydie as she prepared for the morning rush of people grabbing breakfast on their way to work.

Gerald hadn't gone to work since not long after Brydie was born. He stayed home with her while her mother went to work. Once she started school, her father went back to the real estate business part-time and had just hedged into full-time when the accident happened. It had been a small accident, really, almost comedic—Brydie's father falling off a ladder while hanging Christmas lights the year Brydie was sixteen. He'd joked he was Clark Griswold, as he told the story from his recliner, over and over again into the new year.

The reality was something grimmer, crushed disks in his back leading to degenerative disk disease and constant pain. The next year he could scarcely get out of bed at Christmas, let alone attempt to hang Christmas lights. The jokes stopped. Everything stopped but rye whiskey, doctor's visits, and fights with Brydie's mother.

By the time Brydie and Allan opened the shop almost a decade later, Gerald Benson had been subjected to more than a dozen surgeries and was on a daily cocktail of medication and monthly epidural injections in his back. It hurt to walk. It hurt to sit down. It hurt to sleep. Basically, everything hurt. But Brydie's father tried not to complain, at least not in public, and it seemed to Brydie that getting out of the house and coming to her bakery in the mornings was better medicine than most of what he was already choking down with his coffee.

It was around this time that he began asking Brydie and Allan when they were going to make him a grandfather.

"You know I love children," Brydie's father would say. "I wanted your mother and I to have more, but work just got in the way."

"I'm glad you didn't have any more," Brydie said, pouring him more coffee. "I don't like to share much."

"That's the truth," Allan grumbled from behind the counter. "She thinks this whole place belongs to her!"

It wasn't as if Brydie hadn't thought about having children. She had. She and Allan always said they'd have children *someday*. They wanted to wait until they got their business off the ground and had more money. They wanted to wait until they had a bigger house. They decided to wait until they had more time. There was always a reason that the timing wasn't right.

"There is no perfect time to have children," Brydie's father said. "If you wait too much longer, you'll run out of time."

As much as Brydie loved her father, she chafed against his insistence. She couldn't have known that in the end, he wouldn't live to argue much longer. She couldn't have known that her father would die before she had a baby or that the weight of that guilt would follow her all the way across state lines and into the iridescent lights of Memphis.

BRYDIE FELT ALMOST human again after a shower, but it was difficult to appear awake as she entered the nursing home, even after what amounted to an entire pot of coffee. The effects of the night before, coupled with her frenzied baking afterward, hadn't given her much time to sleep or wind down.

Teddy, however, was full of spit and vinegar. This time when they entered the building, Teddy wiggled to free himself from Brydie and pranced right up to the receptionist's desk.

"Hello," the receptionist said. She was the same woman from last time. "Ms. Pauline has been expecting you."

"I'm sorry we're a bit late," Brydie replied.

"Oh it's fine," she said. "Y'all can go on back if

you'd like. Just sign here for me." She pointed to the same book Brydie signed on her first visit.

"Okay, thank you." Brydie tugged on Teddy's leash, and he trotted happily in front of her. She smiled to herself, despite her exhaustion. Teddy seemed to know where he was going, as if he remembered their last visit. Maybe he knew they were going to see his real owner.

When they got to Mrs. Neumann's suite, she was sitting in the same place she'd been last time. This time a woolen blanket covered her, and instead of reading a book, she was staring out of the window.

Brydie knocked on the door as Teddy struggled to free himself from the leash she held. "Mrs. Neumann? Is it okay if we come inside?"

"Of course," she said, turning around to greet them. She patted her lap, and Teddy scurried over and jumped up. "I've been waiting for your visit all week."

"I'm sorry we're late," Brydie said as she sat down. "It took me longer than I thought it would to get ready this morning."

The old woman studied Brydie, narrowing her clear, blue eyes at her. "You look tired, my dear."

"I am," Brydie confessed.

"You're quite a lot younger than me," Pauline replied. "But you're not so young that you don't need your beauty sleep."

"I started my new job," Brydie said. "And it's overnights. It's going to take some getting used to."

"You haven't slept all night?"

"No." Brydie saw the worry in the old woman's eyes and was quick to continue, "But I promise Teddy won't be neglected. We'll both feel better once we're adjusted to the schedule. And I won't always work on the Saturday before we come to visit. It's just through training."

"My first husband was a delivery driver for a dairy in Stuttgart, Arkansas," Pauline said. "He had to get up at three o'clock in the morning to make his deliveries. I used to get up at two o'clock to make his breakfast and pack his lunch for the day. Sometimes he would come home from work to find me asleep on the couch with a magazine in my lap, dinner burning in the oven."

"I don't blame you," Brydie said. "I thought that I was going to fall asleep on top of the counter at about four A.M."

"Six months of that and I was done," Pauline replied. "I left him to make his own breakfast and moved to Jackson, Mississippi, with husband number two."

Brydie remembered Mrs. Neumann telling her on her first visit that she'd been married four times, and she wondered what happened with numbers two and three. The person sitting in front of her looked like any other little old lady, but it was clear Pauline Neumann had lived quite an interesting life, and Brydie found herself wondering what she'd been like as a young woman.

"Anyway," Pauline continued, "you've got to make sure you get your beauty sleep."

"I will," Brydie replied, a smile playing at her lips.

Just then Teddy let out a woof and jumped down from Pauline's lap. Brydie turned around to see Dr. Nathan Reid standing in the doorway. He bent down to give Teddy a pat on the head.

"I was just making the rounds," he said. "I saw you

and Teddy in here and thought I'd stop to say hello and apologize for rushing off the other day."

"Oh, that's okay," Brydie replied, trying to ignore the nervous flutter in her stomach. "I hope that whatever it was wasn't too awful."

"An entire wedding party showed up to the ER with food poisoning after the reception," Nathan said. "Nobody died, but it sure wasn't a lot of fun for anybody."

"I can't imagine anyone not having fun with you, Doctor Sexy," Pauline said, winking at Nathan.

Brydie looked quizzically at Pauline and then at Nathan. "Doctor. . . . Sexy?" she asked.

"It's just a nickname," Nathan said. His cheeks were pink. "A nickname I've asked Mrs. Neumann several times not to use."

"It's because he's such a dish," Pauline replied, ignoring the doctor. "We all call him that." She leaned in closer to Brydie. "Even the nurses."

Brydie tried to stifle a giggle, but couldn't.

"Don't you think he's a dish?" Pauline asked, giving one of Brydie's arms a pinch.

Brydie stopped giggling and cleared her throat. Now the fluttering in her stomach felt like a swarm of butterflies doing somersaults. Without looking at Nathan, she said, "Yes."

"See?" Pauline said, lifting her chin up into the air. "It's unanimous."

"Okay." Nathan lifted his hands into the air. "You win, Mrs. Neumann."

Pauline smiled, and Teddy jumped back into her lap. "Oh, my darling boy," she said. "How I miss you."

"I've invited Brydie to bring Teddy to the Halloween party," Nathan said, stepping farther into the suite.

Pauline clapped her hands together around Teddy. "Oh! That would be lovely."

"I'm not sure what my work schedule will be," Brydie said. It was a lie, and Brydie didn't even know why she was telling it. She wanted to go, and it would be a nice thing to do for Mrs. Neumann. Still, it had been so long since she'd gone out and done anything that the thought of the effort made her nervous. "But I'll try to make it."

"Please do," Pauline replied. "It would make me very happy."

"I promise I'll do my very best to be here."

"I should probably get going," Nathan said. "I hope you two enjoy the rest of your visit."

Once he was gone, Pauline turned her attention back to Brydie. "Dr. Sexy says he sees you at the dog park."

"The first time, Teddy threw up on his shoes," Brydie confessed. "I didn't think I'd see him again, but then he was here when Teddy and I came to see you."

"That's Germantown for you," Pauline replied. "Memphis is a big city, but Germantown can feel very, very small."

"I'm from Jonesboro," Brydie said. "It's not a small town, but I know what you mean. Sometimes it seems like everybody knows everybody."

"So we're both Arkansas girls," Pauline said. "Well, from one Arkansas girl to another, I think the doctor is sweet on you."

This time it was Brydie's turn to blush. "He's just very nice."

"Honey, I've had four husbands. I know what it looks like when a man is sweet on a woman."

Brydie was beginning to wonder how often Mrs. Neumann was going to mention her four husbands. "Well, I've just had one husband, and he was sweet on me for over a decade until one day he wasn't."

"And that's why he's not your husband anymore."

"Now he's sweet on someone else."

The old woman nodded. "We don't always get it right on the first try."

"Or the second or the third," Brydie replied with a wry smile.

"Right you are, kiddo. Right you are." Pauline laughed. "Although I am sorry. Husband number three was a bit like that. We never should have gotten married in the first place."

"Why did you?" Brydie asked, unable to help herself.

"I was on the run," Pauline said, raising one of her penciled-in eyebrows ever so slightly. "I wasn't even divorced from husband number two when we met, but that chemistry!" She raised her hands up in the air in mock praise. "It was too much to resist."

"You were on the run from your second husband?"

"Oh, he wasn't abusive, if that's what you're thinking," Pauline said, adjusting the blanket on her lap after Teddy jumped down to inspect breakfast crumbs under the bed. "I was on the run from Stuttgart. From his family. From mine. From tiny minds in a tiny town."

Brydie nodded. She knew what Pauline meant. Jonesboro wasn't a small town, not really, but that didn't mean that after Allan and Cassandra got together people didn't talk, because they did—

especially her own mother. "I can understand that," she said.

"I was never meant for small town life," Pauline continued. "I wanted to experience things. I wanted to see things. I wanted to *live*."

"I grew up in Jonesboro," Brydie said. "I always lived in Jonesboro until I moved here."

"It's a might better than Stuttgart," Pauline replied. "But you mean to say you've never lived anywhere else?"

"Not until now."

"And this ex-husband of yours . . ."

"Allan."

"This, *Allan*, was he your first boyfriend?"

Brydie thought about that. She'd dated in high school before she met Allan, but it had never been anything serious. "I was nineteen when I met him," she said, finally. "He was older than me, and I guess you could say he was my first serious boyfriend."

"And was he . . . your first everything?"

It took Brydie a moment to figure out what Pauline was asking her. When she did, her face turned bright red. "I, uh, I . . ."

"Oh for goodness' sakes!" Pauline exclaimed, so loud it startled Teddy, who knocked his head against the underside of the bed. "It's just sex. No need to be embarrassed."

Brydie let out a laugh that sounded more like a cough and said, "My grandmother never would have asked anyone about sex, let alone said the word."

"Bless your heart," Pauline replied. "I'm nobody's grandmother."

"Well," Brydie said, recovering slightly. "Yes. I guess you could say he was my first everything. I just . . ." Brydie trailed off, shrugging. "I thought he was perfect, you know?"

"Nobody, especially no man, is perfect."

"I know," Brydie said.

"Do you?" Pauline replied. "You don't sound so sure."

Brydie let out a breath. She knew Pauline was right. Obviously Allan wasn't perfect. But she sometimes felt like it was her fault, everything that happened, and that if she'd just been *more* in some way, none of this would have happened. "I do," she said at last, trying to sound more confident. "Of course I know that."

Pauline's blue eyes narrowed into slits and with a wave of her hand she said, "Well, at least now you're in Memphis." Her eyes were sparkling. "The city that never sleeps."

"I thought that was New York City," Brydie said. "And I'm pretty sure there is a curfew in Germantown."

"Nonsense," Pauline said. "This is the perfect city to find yourself inside when you feel like you may never recover." The old woman took Brydie's hand and squeezed it. "Trust me, I know."

Brydie thought about Mrs. Neumann's words on the way back from the nursing home. She hadn't ever given much thought to the fact that Allan had been her first for so many things. She'd been just nineteen when they met, and was inexperienced. Elliott had been the same way when she met Leo, but many of their other friends were sexually active from the time they were in high school. Brydie, quiet and self-conscious, wasn't the kind of girl in whom most boys were interested. It was one of the reasons she'd fallen so hard for Allan. He was an experienced *man*, and he was interested in her. In her! He'd taken his time with her. He'd never pushed her to do anything she didn't want to do, and in turn, Brydie worshipped him.

She'd always thought Allan would be her husband forever, right up until the moment she'd signed the divorce papers. She hadn't thought of her marriage as right or wrong, but rather that her marriage had been good and then bad. Now she was beginning to think that maybe it had been wrong the whole time. And if that was true, maybe she was going to get a second chance to find out for herself what was right.

CHAPTER 11

THE REST OF THE WORKWEEK PASSED SURPRIS-ingly fast for Brydie, and before she knew it, it was her last night at ShopCo before her three days off.

"If I never see another ghost-shaped cookie, it'll be too soon," Joe grumbled, squeezing the last of the white icing out of his icing gun.

"You say that every year," Rosa replied, refilling his gun. "You'll feel the same way about turkeys next month."

"I love Halloween," Brydie said. "Actually, I love just about every holiday. It's an excuse to bake."

"You don't need an excuse to bake," Joe said. "You work in a bakery."

"But I don't get to bake ghosts in July."

"No, in July it's fucking American flags."

"Language!" Rosa said. She wagged her finger at Joe. "You know what you have to do now."

"I'm not putting money into that fucking swear jar."

"That's two dollars!" Rosa reached underneath the

counter and pulled out a mason jar with "Swear Jar" painted on the side.

"No."

"Joe."

"Rosa."

Rosa shook the jar at Joe's face. "You promised."

"Fine," Joe said, letting out a deep sigh. He pulled off the plastic gloves he was wearing, reached into the pocket of his pants, and pulled out his wallet. "Here."

"We started a swear jar a few months ago," Rosa explained to Brydie as she put the two crisp one-dollar bills into the jar. "Joe swears like a sailor, and Lillian has a tendency to repeat things. She called the priest a rat bastard as we accepted communion last month."

Brydie burst out laughing. She looked over at Joe, who was smiling down into the ghost cookies. "I understand why you started a swear jar, but it doesn't sound like it's helped much."

"It hasn't," Rosa agreed. "My favorite holiday is Christmas," she said. "It always has been."

"Mine, too!" Brydie said. "I love picking out a tree and caroling and baking gingerbread cookies." She paused, and then continued with a laugh, "Basically, I love anything clichéd about Christmas."

"My parents emigrated here from Venezuela before I was born," Rosa said. "They were devout Catholics. We had the most beautiful nativity that my mother brought over, carefully packed in one of the two suitcases she came with. She told me once that she had to leave half of her clothing behind just to make it fit. Now I have it, and it's the very first thing

Lillie and I do when we decorate. It goes up the first week of November, and we don't take it down until after the New Year."

"Wow," Brydie murmured. "My nativity is from Dollar General."

"And my absolute favorite part of Christmas is the food," Rosa continued. "December twenty-first is El Día de los Reyes Magos, and that's the day we prepare *hallacas*, my favorite dish."

"What is that?"

"Oh, Brydie, I'll have to make some for you sometime," Rosa replied. "It's usually a mixture of beef, pork, chicken, capers, raisins, and olives. We wrap it in maize and plantation leaves and tie it up and boil it. It's like nothing you've ever tasted."

"I would love that," Brydie said in earnest. "My mother never cooked much, and since my father died, and even more so after my divorce, I don't get a home-cooked meal by anyone other than myself."

"Oh, sweetheart," Rosa said. She reached out and stroked Brydie's cheek. "I'm so sorry about your father."

"It's okay," Brydie replied, her face warming to Rosa's touch. "It was a few years ago."

"And now you live alone," Rosa said, turning her gaze to Lillian. "Everybody ought to have somebody."

Brydie followed Rosa's eyes to Lillian, whose back was to them. She'd been standing there for almost two hours, working on cake after cake. It amazed Brydie that all Rosa had to do was read the cake order to Lillian, and she could create exactly what the client asked for. Each cake was more gorgeous than the last. Brydie had to admit that she was more than a little jealous of Lillian's artistic abilities.

She walked over and stood next to Lillian. "That looks gorgeous," Brydie said.

Lillian didn't look up. She was instead swaying back and forth, from one foot to the other, whispering, "Four tulips. Red, yellow, pink, purple. Happy Birthday, Jessica. Four tulips. Red, yellow, pink, purple. Happy Birthday, Jessica. Four tulips. Red, yellow, pink, purple. Happy Birthday, Jessica," over and over and over.

"Did you take those witch's hats out of the oven?" Joe asked Brydie, turning away from his ghost cookies. "It smells like something is burning."

"Shit!" Brydie ran to the back and pulled open the oven. "Oh no. No, no, no, no, no."

"Well, at least they're the right color," Rosa said, nodding toward the now-charred hats.

"Great," Joe said, throwing the door open to the back. "Just great. That's a hundred cookies we have to redo."

"I'm sorry," Brydie replied. "I set the timer, but I guess I didn't hear it go off."

"None of us heard it," Rosa said, patting Brydie on the arm.

"Now we're gonna be here an extra *two hours* fixing your mistake," Joe continued. "Two hours we won't get paid for."

"I can stay," Brydie said. "I'll stay and make sure they get done."

"I don't know if you can be trusted to fix it," Joe said.

Brydie felt on the verge of tears. She couldn't believe she'd made such a dumb mistake—a rookie mistake. She was supposed to be a professional. "I'm sorry," she said again.

Joe opened his mouth to speak, but Rosa cut him off. "It's okay," she said. "Lillian and I will stay to help. It's just a batch of cookies. It's really not the end of the world."

Joe let out a snort, but didn't say anything else. Instead he turned around and trudged out of the room.

Once he was gone, Brydie let out a breath she hadn't known she'd been holding. "Thank you," she said to Rosa. "I thought Joe was going to fire me."

"Ignore him," Rosa replied. "Well, don't ignore him. He's our boss. But you just have to know when to take what he says to heart and when to ignore it."

"He seemed pretty angry."

"He'll get over it," Rosa said. "He burns cookies all the time. He's hard on everybody at first."

"You really don't have to stay and help me," Brydie said. "This wasn't your mistake."

"Lillian and I don't mind. Besides, you won't get any help from that morning crew, that's for sure."

"Thank you." Brydie felt the tears welling up again. "I've just been kind of distracted tonight."

"You got family troubles?" Rosa asked. "Man troubles?"

Brydie grinned, despite her embarrassment. "That would take longer to explain than those cookies will," she said.

"Kid, we've got all night."

"I got invited to a Halloween party," Brydie said. "By this guy I kind of know."

Rosa clapped her hands together. "Oh, it *is* a man!"

"It's not like that," Brydie replied. "It's at a nursing home."

"Your man lives in a nursing home?" Rosa asked.

She wrinkled her nose. "You got a thing for older men? I thought you said you had an ex-husband, not a dead husband."

"No!" Brydie said. "The guy is a doctor at the nursing home. I'm dog-sitting for a woman who lives there. Last week the doctor invited me to the Halloween party at the nursing home."

"Oh." Rosa was visibly relieved. "Do you like this doctor?"

Brydie shrugged. "I think so."

"You think so?"

"It's been so long since I've done this," Brydie said. "I can't tell if he's interested in me or if he's just being nice."

"Honey, a man doesn't invite a woman to a party if he isn't interested," Rosa said.

"Even a party at a nursing home?"

Rosa chuckled, covering her mouth with her hands in an effort to stop. "Even at a nursing home."

Brydie was encouraged. "Well, if I go, I'm going to need to find a Halloween costume for me and Teddy."

"Who's Teddy?" Rosa asked. "The doctor?"

"He's the dog," Brydie said. "But I don't even know where to *get* a Halloween costume for a dog."

"You can get one of those here," Rosa said. "There's a whole aisle dedicated to pet costumes at the back of the store with the rest of the Halloween stuff."

"Really?"

"Sure," Rosa replied. "I'll show you after we finish with the cookies."

"You two are wasting my time!" Joe bellowed from the front. "Chat later!"

"I'd better not waste any more of Joe's time tonight," Brydie said, rolling her eyes slightly. "Thanks for being so nice to me, Rosa."

Rosa smiled. "Don't thank me just yet," she said. "You still owe a dollar to the swear jar."

CHAPTER 12

For the most part, Teddy seemed to adjust to the new schedule, but Brydie thought it was more because Teddy slept twenty-three hours a day than from anything she was doing to keep him happy. They'd continued their routine of baking after work, and Teddy was usually satisfied enough after his snack not to root around in the trash.

"So you're liking your job?" Elliott asked on Saturday morning, easing down onto the couch and resting her hands on her belly. "I told Leo we'd order Mia's birthday cake from you."

"Mia's birthday isn't for another six months," Brydie replied. She squinted at the recipe for peanut butter dog treats she'd printed out. For the last week, she'd been experimenting with a couple of different recipes to take to the party. So far, this recipe had been Teddy's favorite, Brydie thought because of the combinations of peanut butter and mashed banana. "And yes, I like it. It's nice to be baking again, but it's not been easy getting used to staying up all night."

"Have a kid," Elliott joked. "You'll learn how to be up twenty-four/seven." Then, as she realized what she'd said, her cheeks turned pink. "I'm sorry. I didn't mean it like that."

"I know. It's okay."

"Oh, I could just kick Allan in the balls," Elliott said. "I could just kick him for what he did to you."

"It's not his fault I never got pregnant," Brydie replied, but she knew what her friend meant. She wished she could kick Allan, too.

"I guess it ended up being for the best, anyway."

Brydie winced. That's what everybody said when they found out that she and Allan had gotten divorced. She'd be a rich woman if she had a dollar for every time someone mentioned "how lucky" it was that she and Allan hadn't had any children. They said it made the split easier. They said it was a clean break. But nothing about the divorce felt easy or clean. She'd lost her husband. Her husband. She'd lost not only the life she was living, but her future life as well. Maybe she hadn't had children with Allan, but now she never would. Brydie mourned that life, too—the life that would never be. "Yeah, I guess."

"He's a jerk, Brydie," Elliott continued. "I'd call him worse, but I don't want the baby to hear me swearing."

Brydie leaned down to Elliott's belly and whispered, "Shit."

"Brydie!"

Brydie giggled. "I'm sorry. I couldn't help it."

"You'll be a great mother someday," Elliott said. "Don't let this thing with Allan spoil it for you."

"Thanks," Brydie replied. "I don't know, though.

I'm thirty-four. Maybe it's time to have more realistic dreams."

"That's not old," Elliott protested. "I mean, you're older than you were a decade ago, obviously, but women older than you have babies all the time. Don't give up."

Brydie squinted down at the recipe in an effort to keep from looking over at her friend. Having a baby was a dream she'd shared with Allan. It felt too burdensome to carry all on her own. "I'll try not to," she said.

"It's not easy," Elliott said, "to want a child and not be able to have one. I understand."

Brydie nodded, feeling a lump in her throat begin to rise. Elliott did know what that was like. She'd had a miscarriage in between Mia and the baby she was now carrying, and it had been awful. They'd already announced the pregnancy to everyone. They'd posted a cute ultrasound picture on social media with Mia holding a sign about becoming a big sister. A couple of weeks later, Brydie had gotten a phone call from Elliott's mother about something "going wrong" with the pregnancy. She'd dropped everything at the bakery and driven as fast as she could to Memphis, but by the time she got there, it was already over. *The procedure,* as Elliott referred to it, was over. Her baby was gone. No, not gone, dead. Her baby was dead, and she'd told Brydie that she didn't think she and Leo could handle something like that happening again. She didn't know if they'd have more children. It was just too hard.

But two years later Elliott was pregnant again with a healthy baby boy, a Rainbow Baby, Elliott called him. Brydie had to look it up online to find out exactly what she meant. She'd learned that a Rainbow Baby is a baby that is born following a miscarriage, still-birth, or another kind of loss of an infant. The website she'd visited compared the baby to a beautiful and bright rainbow that follows a storm and gives hope of things getting better, that the rainbow is more appreciated when one has just experienced the storm in comparison.

"So are you excited about the Halloween party tonight?" Elliott asked, slicing through the thoughtful silence that had settled between them.

"I am," Brydie replied, thankful for the subject change. "I found the cutest lion costume for Teddy. It's hilarious."

True to her word, Rosa had shown Brydie the Halloween costumes after their shift. There were so many that Brydie felt overwhelmed. She smiled to herself thinking about Teddy being a chubby lobster or bumblebee or hot dog. But when she saw the lion costume, she knew that it was the one for her dog. *My dog,* she thought. She'd never thought of Teddy that way before. She guessed, for now, he was her dog.

"So what are you going to be?" Elliott asked.

"I thought I'd be a lion tamer," Brydie said. "But I'm having trouble coming up with the costume."

"What do you need?" Elliott asked. "Surely we can put it together before you have to leave."

Brydie slid the pan of dog treats into the oven and motioned for her friend to follow her to the master bedroom. "Let me show you what I've got so far."

"They didn't have a costume at ShopCo?"

"No," Brydie said. "I thought I might find one that I could alter, but they were all so *skimpy*."

"I know!" Elliott exclaimed. "It's like every costume

for women is a sexy nurse or a sexy firefighter or a sexy skunk. I mean, how can *anybody* be a *sexy* skunk?"

Brydie giggled. "I wouldn't mind being sexy, but I'm not going to wrap myself up in a piece of plastic the size of a Band-Aid to do it."

Elliott surveyed the items Brydie had laid out on the bed. "Okay, so you've got a black tube dress, fishnets, and black boots."

"The tube dress is pretty short," Brydie said. "That's why I bought the fishnets. But I'm missing the jacket and a whip."

"Oh, I've got a whip at the house," Elliott replied.

"You do?"

"Yes." Elliott's cheeks were pink. "It's not like *that,* if that's what you're thinking. Leo got it at the Indiana Jones ride at Disney World last year. I'm sure he won't mind if you borrow it."

"What about a jacket?" Brydie asked. "Without the jacket, I'm just going to look like a dominatrix."

"You wouldn't want to give the old people a heart attack," Elliott agreed. "But at least you'd have a sexy doctor there to save some lives."

"I doubt he would like it if I showed up looking like a hooker at his place of employment," Brydie replied.

"Trust me, *all* men like that."

"Allan wouldn't have liked it."

"Dr. Reid isn't Allan," Elliott reminded her. "Besides, Allan wouldn't have wanted you to dress provocatively because he'd be afraid everybody else would see how gorgeous you are."

Brydie rolled her eyes, but secretly she was touched. "Well, thanks. But I'd still like to find a jacket."

"Have you searched through Mrs. Neumann's closets?"

"No," Brydie replied. "I was hoping you might have something."

Elliott was already opening the closet doors. "Surely she's got something."

"I don't feel right about going through her things," Brydie protested.

"There's not a lot in here," Elliott said, her voice muffled through the closet doors. "She must have taken most of it with her."

"Maybe I've got something that will work," Brydie said, even though she knew she didn't. "Just get out of her closet."

Elliott ignored her. "Come over here and help me," she said. "You're taller than me, and I can't reach the top shelf."

"She'll notice if I wear something of hers," Brydie replied. She went over to the closet and stepped inside.

"She's like ninety years old," Elliott said. "She's lucky to know her own name."

"Elliott!"

"What?"

Brydie stood on her tiptoes and reached for the clothing that was folded neatly on the top shelf. As she felt along the shelf, her fingers grazed something cold and hard. Curious, Brydie pulled it from the shelf to get a better look. It was a key. Her heart skipped a beat. *Could this be the key for the door in the hallway?* she asked herself.

"I found something!" Elliott hollered from one end of the closet. "I must have missed it the first time."

Brydie shoved the key into the pocket of her jeans. "Let me see."

Triumphant, Elliott held up a red knit jacket. "It's perfect!"

"I don't know." Brydie eyed the jacket skeptically. "It looks kind of small."

"Try it on."

Brydie took the jacket from Elliott and pulled it on over her T-shirt. "It's too small," she said. "It won't button over my boobs."

"So?" Elliott asked. "You don't need to button it over your boobs."

"It won't work."

"Of course it will!" Elliott stood in front of Brydie. "The buttons are even gold! I have a couple of gold tassels from Mia's dance recital that we can sew on. I'll grab them when I go get the whip."

"I don't know."

Elliott crossed her arms over her chest and said, "Do you want to go to this party?"

Brydie nodded.

"Then stop looking for excuses," Elliott said, "and let me fix this jacket for you."

"Fine."

"Good," Elliott said, helping Brydie out of the jacket. "You stay here and get Teddy ready. I'll be back in a jiff."

A FEW HOURS LATER, Brydie sat in the parking lot at the Germantown Retirement Center, readying herself to go inside. Although Elliott had basically kicked her out the door, telling her that she looked perfect, Brydie felt ridiculous. She hadn't dressed up for Halloween in years, unless she counted wearing a witch's hat to hand out candy to kids in her neighborhood in Jonesboro.

Teddy Roosevelt, however, looked fantastic. When Elliott saw him, she'd laughed until she cried, and surprisingly, Teddy seemed to love being dressed up, minus the lion mane. He'd tried chewing it off several times as they drove to the party.

All around them, people streamed in. There were whole families dressed up, people with dogs, and so many doctors and nurses that Brydie couldn't tell which were the real nurses and doctors and which ones were dressed up for Halloween. There were many "sexy nurses," and Brydie wished Elliott were with her to see it. Actually, she wished Elliott were with her so that she wouldn't have to go inside alone.

In the seat next to her, Teddy chewed on his mane. Brydie guessed she wasn't entirely alone. "Okay, pup," she said, grabbing the plastic tub full of dog treats she'd made. "Let's do this."

Inside, the nursing home was decorated for Halloween, complete with cobwebs at the entryway that got stuck in Brydie's hair. She set Teddy down on the tiled floor and wrapped his leash around her hand. She looked around for Mrs. Neumann or Nathan, but she didn't see anybody she knew. Thinking that maybe the older woman was back in her room, she maneuvered Teddy through the throng of people and into the hallway.

Mrs. Neumann wasn't in her room. Brydie turned around and led Teddy back out. Now the hallway was beginning to fill up with orderlies and family members helping the nursing home residents out into the large cafeteria, where she heard someone say most everybody had gathered. Brydie picked Teddy up and followed them.

"Oh my goodness!" one woman said to Brydie as they walked. "Your costume is just the *cutest*. And look at your dog!"

"Thanks," Brydie replied, starting to relax for the first time since she'd arrived.

"Is he a pug? I had a pug when I was a little girl. He was the best dog."

"Yes," Brydie replied. "His name is Teddy."

The woman reached out and gave Teddy's mane-covered head a pat. "He's so sweet!"

Brydie felt a swell of pride that she hadn't anticipated. "He's a good boy," she said.

As they entered the cafeteria and the crowd thinned out, Brydie saw Mrs. Neumann sitting in a wheelchair at a table surrounded by other people Brydie guessed lived there as well. When Teddy saw her, he began to whine, and Brydie set him down on the floor so he could go to her.

"Brydie!" Pauline said, clapping her hands together. "You came!"

"I thought you might like to see Teddy," Brydie replied.

"I'm happy to see you both," Pauline said. "Everyone, this is Brydie. She's looking after Teddy."

"It's nice to meet you, honey," said a bespectacled woman with a shock of short white hair.

"Is that the dog you're always going on about?" said a man sitting next to Pauline. His eyebrows, Brydie noticed, looked like two fuzzy caterpillars stuck together at his forehead. "He's got to be the ugliest dog I've ever seen."

"Oh, hush up, George," the woman with the white hair said, rapping his arm with her cane. "Don't talk to us about ugly until you've looked in the mirror."

Brydie stifled a giggle.

"Has Dr. Sexy found you yet?" Pauline asked Brydie. "He was looking for you earlier."

"No," Brydie said. She felt those familiar flutters in her stomach. "I haven't seen him."

"Hey," said the man with the eyebrows. "You're young and on your first legs. How about you go get us some punch?" He pointed to the table filled with food on the other side of the cafeteria.

"George!" the white haired lady gasped. "Where are your manners tonight?"

"It's okay," Brydie said. She handed Pauline Teddy's leash and set the plastic tub full of cookies on the table. "Would anybody else like some?"

"I would," Pauline replied. "And if there are any oatmeal raisin cookies, I'll take one of those, too."

Brydie nodded and headed off toward the refreshments. All around her people were laughing and having a good time. There was an area where people were playing bingo, a fortune-teller in one corner, games for children to play, and tables of food and drinks spanning almost the length of the entire cafeteria. Brydie wasn't sure what kind of punch George and Pauline wanted, but she grabbed the handle of the first ladle she came to and filled two cups.

"Are you having a good time?" said a voice behind her.

Brydie turned around to see Dr. Nathan Reid standing there, a white mask covering half of his face. "I don't know," she said with a grin. "It depends on who's asking me."

Nathan took off his mask. "Can I help you with those?"

"Sure," Brydie replied. She handed him the cups full of punch and led him back over to the table where the older people were sitting.

"Who ordered punch?" Nathan asked once they were at the table.

"I did," Pauline said. "Thank you, Doctor."

"Look there, ladies," George said, motioning to Brydie and Nathan. "Looks like y'all have some competition when it comes to the young doctor," he paused, clearing his throat, "*Sexy.*"

"I'm guessing this second cup is yours, George," Nathan replied.

"You guessed right," George said, grabbing the cup from Nathan and sloshing half of the contents onto the table.

"Watch it, George!" one of the women sitting beside him said. "For heaven's sake!"

George ignored the woman. "Aren't you supposed to be working, Dr. Reid? Not gallivanting around with scantily clad young women?"

Brydie looked down at herself. She wasn't scantily clad. Almost every inch of her was covered.

"Nobody is working tonight, George," Nathan replied. "We're having a party."

"What if I have a heart attack?" George countered. "What if I have a heart attack right here at this table?"

"We'd all be eternally grateful," the woman beside him muttered.

"I'm serious!"

"George, if you have a heart attack, I'll not let the party distract me from saving your life," Nathan said. "You have my word."

George made a quiet harrumph under his breath but didn't say anything else.

"Oh, Mrs. Neumann," Brydie said suddenly, "I forgot your oatmeal raisin cookie. Let me go get it for you."

"It's fine, my dear," Pauline replied. "I'll just eat one of the cookies you brought. George says they're quite good. He ate one while you were getting us punch."

Brydie clapped a hand over her mouth. After a few seconds, she mustered up the courage to say, "Those aren't cookies for people."

"What's that supposed to mean?" George asked, his bushy eyebrows drawing even closer together. "Who else eats cookies?"

"They're dog cookies," Brydie replied, her voice barely above a whisper. "I . . . I made them for Sasha."

"Who's Sasha?"

"Dr. Reid's dog."

There was a collective gasp by everyone at the table, followed by laughter. Pauline was laughing so hard she had tears streaming down her face. George stood up, his face more than one shade of green, and hobbled off without saying another word.

"I feel so bad," Brydie said after the laughter had subsided. "I should have told you all that those were dog cookies."

"Don't feel bad," said the woman with the short white hair. "He's a crotchety old man. He deserved it."

"Well, Teddy sure does seem to love these cookies," Pauline said. She had both Teddy and the plastic bin full of the treats on her lap. "He's eaten at least six."

"It's the banana," Brydie said, her voice tinged

with pride. "I tried a few different recipes, but this was the one he liked the best."

"Sasha likes banana, too," Nathan said.

"Where is she?" Brydie asked, realizing she hadn't seen Sasha all night. "I thought she was going to be here."

"She sprained a paw at agility class," Nathan replied. "She's been ordered to stay off it for a couple of weeks, which means she has to stay in her crate most of the time. I was afraid bringing her here tonight would be too exciting and might make the injury worse."

"I'm so sorry."

"But you made her cookies?" Nathan asked. "Now I really feel bad for not letting her come tonight."

"Well, for her and any other dogs that came tonight," Brydie replied. She could feel everyone at the table looking at them, at her, and her cheeks burned. "But it looks like Teddy may eat them all before they get a chance."

"Oh, look," Pauline said, pointing to a line already forming at the other end of the cafeteria. "They're starting the costume contest."

"You and Teddy better get over there," Nathan said.

"What about you?" Brydie asked.

"Employees can't participate," Nathan replied. "But I'll walk you over."

Pauline handed Teddy over to Brydie. "You two are already the best dressed, in my opinion," she said.

Brydie resisted the urge to lean down and hug the old woman. Pauline had been so kind to her, and for a moment she found herself wishing that Mrs. Neumann were her own grandmother. It was a shame, Brydie thought, that she didn't have any children.

Brydie sat Teddy down on the ground and said, "Come on, buddy."

Teddy stared up at her and yawned. He wasn't going anywhere. Brydie reached down into her jacket pocket. She'd prepared for this. "Here," she said, handing him a treat.

Teddy gobbled it up, and this time he followed her.

"Nice trick," Nathan said.

"Well, he's no agility master," Brydie replied. "But he will walk for treats."

"When I got Sasha, she was almost a year old," Nathan said. "One of the doctors bought her from a breeder without knowing anything about Irish wolfhounds. He actually thought she'd be a good apartment dog."

"Really?" Brydie asked, incredulous. "She's huge!"

"Some bigger dogs do okay in apartments," Nathan replied. "But not wolfhounds. He was getting ready to have her euthanized because she ate his expensive leather couch."

"That seems extreme."

"I agree."

"So you offered to take her instead?"

"I did," Nathan said. "And when I got her, she was a mess. She wasn't house-trained, and once I came home and she'd chewed out of her kennel and was sitting on my kitchen table eating what was left of an entire roasted chicken."

Brydie looked down at Teddy, suddenly feeling very lucky. "I guess getting into the trash is pretty minor compared to that."

"The agility classes helped with her destructive

behavior," Nathan continued. "I read up on wolf-hounds, and realized she needed more stimulation than she was getting. It's why we go to the park so much."

"She's probably not too thrilled about having to stay off her feet for a while," Brydie said.

"No, not at all," Nathan replied. "But she should be healed up by next week."

"That's good."

"So I was wondering," Nathan said, pausing as they walked. "I was wondering if next week you and Teddy might like to come over for dinner with me and Sasha."

There were those flutters again, and Brydie struggled to concentrate. "Are you sure Teddy won't hurt her by accident?" was all she could think of to say.

Nathan laughed, gesturing down to Teddy, who'd promptly taken advantage of the pause in their journey and fallen asleep. "I don't think that's going to be a problem."

"Well . . ." Brydie said, drawing out her response as long as she could. She didn't know why she was looking for an excuse to say no, when all she wanted at that moment was to say yes. She wanted to kick herself with one of the heavy combat boots she was wearing. "Okay, that sounds like fun."

"How's Saturday for you?"

"Perfect."

"Great," Nathan said. He took her elbow and guided her and the sleepy pug to where those in costume were lined up. "I'd better make myself scarce. I wouldn't want anyone to think I've given you an unfair advantage."

He replaced his Phantom of the Opera mask and

was gone, vanishing back into the crush of people. Brydie took her place in line, last, behind two women dressed up as a cat and a nurse, respectively. Brydie couldn't be sure, but she'd wager that each of their costumes had the word *sexy* somewhere in the title.

"Did you see Dr. Reid just a minute ago?" the cat asked the nurse.

The nurse nodded. "He's the hottest phantom of any opera I've ever seen, that's for sure."

The cat turned away from Brydie, so she had to strain to hear what she said next. "Do you think he's with that . . . woman . . . behind us?"

"Her?" the nurse whispered. She peered around the cat to catch a better look at Brydie. "I doubt it. She looks older than him."

"I don't know what I'd do if I found out he had a girlfriend," the cat continued. "I mean Dr. Reid is the only reason I come to visit my aunt."

"I know what you mean," the nurse replied. "And in a few weeks he'll be off the rotation, and we'll be stuck with that horrid old woman . . . what's her name?"

"Dr. Sower," the cat said with a giggle.

"Oh, that's right! What a name!"

The two women burst into a fit of laughter, until the nurse jabbed the cat in the ribs and said, "Shut up, the judges are headed this way."

Brydie was relieved by the distraction as three judges came into view and began to view her costume. She tugged on Teddy's leash just enough to get his attention and then handed him a treat. Teddy snapped it up and she now had his full attention.

"What an adorable dog," one of the judges said. "Oh, and he's a *lion*! How cute!"

"And you're the lion tamer, I suppose?" said another judge, looking Brydie up and down. "Well, show us what tricks your lion can do!"

Brydie hadn't prepared for there to be a performance aspect of the costume competition. She doubted very much that any of the judges would be impressed with Teddy's trash-eating or snoring capabilities, and she was keenly aware of the two women in front of her watching her every move, their eyes narrowed so that they were nothing more than slits on their faces.

Brydie fished the last treat out of her pocket and held it up in the air for Teddy to see. He stared at her for a second, confused. Brydie began to panic. She looked like an idiot standing there holding a treat out to a dog with a coif of polyester hair surrounding his head. She considered placing the treat back into her pocket, picking Teddy up, and darting out of the cafeteria before she could be embarrassed further, but instead she lowered the treat just a bit and said, "Up, up, up!"

To her surprise, and the surprise of everyone watching, she was sure, Teddy stood up on his hind legs and began to beg, his tongue lolling out of the side of his mouth and catching on his lion's mane.

"How positively adorable!" the first judge said. "I'm giving you the best in show for the dog costume portion." She handed Brydie an envelope, and the judges moved on.

Brydie leaned down and gave Teddy the treat. "I'm going to bake you the biggest batch of peanut butter banana cookies you've ever seen," she whispered to him.

When she stood back up, the cat and the nurse were

still staring at her. Maybe it was the thrill of winning or maybe it was because Dr. Nathan Reid wanted to have dinner with her next Saturday; Brydie didn't know, but as she passed the two women, one dressed as a cat and one dressed as a nurse, she couldn't help but say just loud enough for them to hear, "I guess you really can teach an old dog new tricks."

November

CHAPTER 13

IT HAD BEEN A LONG TIME SINCE BRYDIE BENSON
had been on a date. Her marriage to Allan lasted
almost thirteen years, and she figured that going on a
date, especially the first date, had probably changed
since Allan took her to the movies on their first date
more than a decade ago.

After Brydie's father died, her mother jumped back
into dating with both feet. She even started a sin-
gles group for middle-aged women called Fabulous
at Fifty, and they met every week at Ruth Benson's
house to drink cocktails and talk about the men they
were dating. When her mother brought a man she
was dating into the bakery one day just a month after her father died, Brydie felt as though she'd been
slapped.

"I can't believe you're dating already," Brydie said
to her mother on the phone that evening. "Dad has
barely been gone a month."

"We all grieve in different ways, Brydie," her
mother had replied.

Brydie rolled her eyes into the receiver. "And your way of coping is to bring a sixty-year-old investment banker named Collin into my bakery before noon?"

"Collin is a great catch," her mother said. "If you'd just give him a chance."

"Don't bring him back into my bakery."

"Oh, you mean the bakery in the *building I own*?"

"We'll move."

Her mother sighed audibly. "Let's not fight right now. You couldn't possibly understand what I'm going through."

Brydie had wanted to throw her phone into a batch of triple-fudge brownies. She'd just lost her father. *Her father.* The person she was closest to in the whole world. The last thing she wanted was for her mother to be looking for a new one.

But Brydie soon realized that her mother wasn't looking to replace her father. She was looking for a distraction, and when Brydie moved back home after she and Allan got divorced, her mother thought Brydie needed one as well.

"I've found you the perfect man," her mother said a few days after Brydie moved in. "His name is Steve Landon, and he's a senior partner at my realty company."

"No," Brydie replied. "Absolutely not."

"You'll love him," her mother went on, ignoring her. "He's good looking, owns his own home, and he has all of his own teeth and hair. What more could you ask for?"

"The ink isn't even dry on the divorce papers yet, Mom," Brydie said. "Could you at least wait a couple of weeks before setting me up for my next one?"

Her mother agreed, somewhat stiffly, and Brydie

tried to relax for the first time in months. A couple of months later, her mother threw a party, and Brydie came home to a house full of real estate agents, drinking and eating the croissants she'd made to have for breakfast the next morning. She gathered up the rest of the croissants to hide in her bedroom and was close to making her escape when her mother cornered her in the hallway.

"Brydie, honey, there you are! I've got someone I want you to meet," her mother said. "This is Steve, the guy I told you about!"

Brydie had a croissant in her mouth but managed to choke out a "hello" before she tried to get past them both and to the safety of her room.

"Don't be rude," her mother hissed, grabbing her by the arm. "He came here just to meet *you*."

"Well, I didn't ask him to do that," Brydie hissed right back. "All I want to do is go to my room and go to sleep."

"You can sleep when you're dead."

For some reason, her mother's words cut right through her, and it caught Brydie off guard. "Fine," she said, relenting. "I'll go talk to him."

"Good girl," her mother said. She took the croissants out of Brydie's hands. "Finish eating that first."

Brydie followed her mother and Steve out into the living room. He'd been older than she'd expected, his hair a distinguished salt-and-pepper mix. He was older than she, but younger than her mother, an indeterminable spot between thirty-five and forty-five. "So, my mom says you're a partner at her company?" she asked.

"The newest partner," Steve replied.

"Congratulations."

"So, how come I've never seen you," he paused, tapping her arm lightly with his beer bottle, "come in to the business to see your mom?"

"I own a bakery," Brydie replied.

"Oh really?" Steve asked. "Your mom never mentioned that."

"What a surprise."

"Where is this bakery?"

Brydie shifted from one foot to the other. She'd responded so automatically, she'd forgotten she in fact *did not* own a bakery. Not anymore. "It used to be on Caraway," she said. "But we closed a few months ago."

"Oh?"

"We weren't bankrupt or anything," Brydie said quickly. For some reason, it was easier for her to admit that it was her marriage that had failed and not her business. "My husband and I got divorced, and we decided it was best to go ahead and close. Neither one of us was willing to give it up to the other one."

"Sort of like when King Solomon threatened to cut the baby in half," Steve replied. "Better for no one to have it than let one person have it all."

Brydie nodded. She had never thought about it that way, but it was probably a pretty accurate analogy. "Yeah," she said, smiling despite her resolution to remain annoyed. "Something like that."

"I've been divorced for almost five years," Steve said. "It gets easier."

"Thank you."

Steve sat his empty beer bottle down on the coffee table. "You know, this isn't really my scene. Want to get out of here for a while?"

Brydie thought about it. She didn't even know this guy. For all she knew, he could be the next Buffalo Bill, interested in her size 12 skin suit. But the truth was that she wanted to be anywhere but here, even if that meant taking a risk on a potential serial killer. "Sure," she said. "Why not?"

The next morning Brydie woke up in Steve's house, in Steve's bed, on the other side of Jonesboro. When she had tried to leave, he'd woken up and told her how beautiful she was and how much fun he'd had, and it was all Brydie could do not to burst into tears in front of him. She let him think it was because she was so happy and so flattered by what he'd said to her, but really it was because she felt like she was dying inside. Worse than that, she felt like she'd just cheated on her husband.

Her mother wanted to know all about it. "Tell me everything," she'd said to Brydie. "Will you see him again?"

"No," Brydie replied. "I don't think I'll see him again."

"But why not? He is such a nice guy!"

"He is nice," Brydie agreed. "But I'm not ready."

"With that attitude, you'll never be ready," her mother replied. "I know it's hard . . ."

"It is hard," Brydie said, cutting her mother off. "It *is* hard. How can you go from Dad to someone like Collin?"

"I loved your father," her mother said, her tone softening. "But I like Collin. We have fun together. And it's not like your father was perfect. He had his faults."

Brydie didn't think so. "Everybody has faults," she said. "But he was a good dad. The best dad."

"He was a good dad," her mother conceded. "But he was a terrible husband."

Brydie rolled her eyes up to the ceiling in her bedroom and tried to think of a way out of the conversation. "Mom," she said finally, "I don't want to talk about this."

"Your father was an alcoholic," her mother continued, ignoring her.

"Mom," Brydie said. "Stop."

"No," her mother said. "You need to hear this. Maybe you'll stop putting your father up on a pedestal. He wasn't the man you think he was."

"Mom," Brydie pleaded. "Stop, please."

"He fell off that ladder when you were sixteen because he was drunk, Brydie. He was drunk before noon during the week. He was trying to hang Christmas lights in October."

Brydie knew her father drank. Sometimes he did drink too much. But it wasn't as bad as her mother was making it out to be. *It wasn't.* "I have to go," she said, standing up.

"Brydie." Her mother took her hand and pulled her back down onto the bed. "Your father was a nice person, a *good* person. He was just bad at being a husband. Allan is the same way. He's not a good husband. He's not the right husband for you."

Brydie shook her hand free and fled, locking herself in the bathroom until she heard her mother retreat from the bedroom and leave the house. That was the day Brydie packed her bags and left for Memphis. That conversation was the reason the relationship with her mother had been strained since she left. It was the reason she avoided her mother's phone calls and the reason she didn't go home.

Now Brydie was less than a week away from her first real date since the divorce, with someone she actually liked, and she hoped those same feelings wouldn't return. The Sunday after the Halloween party, Nathan found her while she was visiting Mrs. Neumann. They'd exchanged phone numbers, and they'd agreed Brydie and Teddy would be at Nathan's house about 7 P.M. for dinner and a playdate for Teddy and Sasha.

She hadn't told anyone about the date—not Elliott and certainly not her mother. She didn't want to answer questions. She just wanted to keep it to herself—a reason to smile when there was a lull in her day and she had a few moments to think about it.

At work, there were no lulls. They'd transitioned from Halloween to Thanksgiving on the first of November. All of the ghosts, and witches, and mummies were replaced with pilgrims and turkeys and filling the regular orders for weddings, baby showers, and other events.

"Who gets married in November?" Rosa asked as she filled a tube of red icing to hand to Lillian, who was busy making red roses on the top tier of a wedding cake. "Summertime is for weddings. I have never understood getting married in the cold. It starts a marriage off cold, if you believe that sort of thing."

Brydie shrugged. "I got married in July. But my best friend got married in February. There was an ice storm the day of her wedding. Half of us had to spend the night in the church."

"And your friend is still married?"

"She is."

"Good for her," Rosa said.

"Are you married?" Brydie asked. It wasn't normally a question she'd ask someone she hardly knew, but she figured it couldn't hurt since they were on the subject.

Rosa shook her head. "No, I've never been married." She turned around to look at Lillian and then said, her voice scarcely above a whisper, "Lillian's father is my younger brother. He and his girlfriend had Lillie when they were still just kids themselves. They couldn't care for her, and our parents are dead. So I took her. I was just twenty."

"Wow," Brydie replied.

"It wasn't even something I thought about. She's family, and I already knew I'd never be able to have children of my own," Rosa continued. "I adopted her, and then when she was three I found out she was on the autism spectrum."

Brydie stared at Rosa and then stole a glance at Lillian, who hadn't moved from in front of the cake she was decorating. "Do her parents ever . . . do they ever see her?"

"No," Rosa replied. "They moved to Florida, and they don't visit. But they did get married, and we keep in touch through phone calls and emails. They have three children now. It would just be too confusing for Lillie to try to explain it to her."

"I understand," Brydie said, even though she really didn't. She couldn't imagine having a baby and not wanting her. She felt a twinge of jealousy knowing that Rosa's brother and his wife had three more children—three more chances—to be parents. She must have been staring hard at Lillian, because after a few seconds of being lost in her thoughts, she felt Rosa's hand on her shoulder, warm and reassuring.

"Don't feel bad for us," Rosa said. "The two of

us, Lillie and me, well, we were meant for each other. We have everything we could ever want or need."

"Oh, I don't," Brydie said, quick to reply. "I'm glad. For both of you."

Rosa smiled a smile that went all the way up to her eyes. She was about to reply when they both saw Joe heading toward them, a scowl on his face. Trailing behind him was someone that Brydie had never met, but he looked important.

"Look busy," Rosa whispered.

Brydie picked up the icing she'd been using to ice pilgrims' hats and began outlining the white of the hats with black. She followed Rosa's lead and kept her head down, even when she knew Joe and the other man were standing right in front of them.

"And I'm telling you," Joe said, stopping just in front of the counter, "I need at least two part-timers. I'm down to half the number of employees I normally have during the holidays."

"And I'm telling you that you'll just have to do with what you've got," the man said. "We don't have the budget to hire anyone else."

"I find that very hard to believe," Joe said, laying his palm flat against the countertop. "Our orders are up fifteen percent from this time last year. You can't expect us to keep up with half the help."

"Can't be helped," the other man said.

"So move around a couple people from over-nights," Joe replied. "I know you can do that. You've done it before."

"We need everybody where they are." The other man leaned over the counter until Brydie looked up at him. "How long have you been here?" he asked her.

"She's new," Joe snapped. "We're still training her."

"What about that one," the man said, his eyes roving lazily over Lillian's form. "She hasn't moved since I got here two hours ago. No wonder you're falling so far behind."

Brydie saw the color rising in Rosa's cheeks, and she opened her mouth to say something, but Joe shot her a look and said, "Kent, she's the whole reason we have as many orders as we do. Hell, you ordered your wedding cake from us. Tell me you would have done that if you'd known anyone other than her was decorating it."

Kent shrugged. "You'll just have to make do. We aren't hiring anyone else."

"That's bullshit, Kent, and you know it."

"Watch it," Kent replied. "You'll do well to know who you're talking to. One more write-up and you're out of here."

"Fine," Joe said through clenched teeth. "We'll make due."

"Good man," Kent said, clapping Joe on the back before turning to walk away.

Brydie looked up in time to see Joe standing there, rigid from Kent's touch. His head was as red as a cherry tomato, and for a second it looked as if Joe's head might very well pop right off his neck. Instead he took a deep breath and walked around the counter and through the double doors. He didn't look at Brydie or Rosa and walked over to where Lillian was pasting lovely red roses around the side of the cake.

Brydie winced, thinking about the way he'd chastised her for burning the ghost cookies. Was he going to say something to Lillian about working so slowly? She knew Kent was right—a couple of part-time workers, one even, could work faster than Lillian. But Joe was right, too. Brydie had never seen a talent for decorating like Lillian had.

"You're doing a good job," Joe said. "The roses are perfect." He rested his hand on Lillian's shoulder. Lillian let it rest there for a moment before stepping away from Joe's grasp.

Rosa smiled at Joe, but her eyes were worried. "I'm sorry we are behind," she said. "Maybe it would be better if—"

"No," Joe said, cutting her off. "Ignore Kent. You know he hates me. He's always hated me. I won't let him take it out on you or anybody else."

"We're still behind a couple of orders a night," Rosa continued. "You heard Kent say that if you get written up one more time, he'll fire you."

"He's not going to do that," Joe replied. "Just do your best to be busy if you see him roaming around here, okay?"

Rosa nodded. "Okay."

Brydie turned back around and began tending to the pilgrim hats once more. She thought about the way Joe had tended to Lillian, and she warmed to him, despite the way he'd been so angry with her about burning a batch of cookies. At her own bakery, she'd very rarely gotten upset, even when they ran behind a bit. They always managed to deliver on time. Allan, however, liked to bark orders. They'd actually gone through a few part-time employees before they'd found Cassandra, recommended to them by one of their old contacts at the culinary school.

At first Brydie was pleased that Cassandra worked out so well. Allan rarely got angry with her, even though she often needed Brydie's help at the last minute to finish a cake. Now, of course, she knew why that was.

Brydie shook her head in a physical attempt to rid herself of these thoughts. This wasn't her bakery. She wasn't in Jonesboro. Cassandra and Allan would never step foot into this place, because it didn't belong to them. It belonged to her.

For the first time in a long time, Brydie felt like she belonged.

CHAPTER 14

THE NEXT EVENING, BRYDIE STOOD OUTSIDE Dr. Nathan Reid's door, poised to knock. She'd managed to get Teddy to walk the entire two blocks with only minimal bribing with treats. She wished now that she'd chosen to drive. The rain was coming down in a slow, cold drizzle and everything outside was starting to look like it had been thrown into the Mississippi River, especially her and Teddy.

She thought about turning around and going back home to change her clothes, but she was already late enough. As nervous as she was, Brydie knew that if she went home to change, she'd probably end up canceling altogether. So, despite the fact that her hair was matted to her forehead and Teddy was really starting to smell of wet dog, she rang the doorbell.

Nathan opened the door. "I was hoping you'd decide to stay," he said.

Brydie's cheeks immediately began to burn. "Were you watching me from inside?"

"Well, when you say it like that," Nathan replied, "it sounds kind of creepy."

"I hadn't anticipated the rain," Brydie said. She bent down to unhook Teddy's leash. Before she could say anything else, Sasha was in front of her, jumping up so that her paws were on Brydie's shoulders.

"Sasha!" Nathan scolded. "Get down!"

"It's okay," Brydie replied from somewhere buried in Sasha's fur.

Nathan pulled Sasha back and she went loping off with Teddy. "Sorry," he said.

"I guess she's all healed."

"She is," Nathan replied. "But she's still on tramadol for pain, and instead of making her calm, it gives her the energy of a jackrabbit."

There was an awkward silence as the two of them stared at each other. Brydie felt her cheeks warm, and so she looked down at her cardigan, pulling off long, wheat-colored strands of Sasha's hair. It occurred to Brydie just then how very little they knew about each other.

"Your hair is dripping," Nathan said finally, ending the intermission. "Hang on, I'll go grab you a towel."

He left Brydie standing alone in the hallway. On the outside, the house looked a lot like Mrs. Neumann's. All of the houses in the neighborhood did. But Nathan's house had been newly remodeled. In fact, the inside even smelled new. The tile in the hallway led to what Brydie assumed, from the fantastic smells emitting from it, was the kitchen. She was sure in the summertime the tile was nice and cool, and it made the house seem light and airy. But with November setting in, it just made Brydie shiver.

She walked the length of the hallway and stopped in front of a mirror with a gold, filigreed frame. Nathan was right—her hair was dripping down onto her cardigan, hanging in limp strands around her face. Her gold ballet flats were sopping and squishy when she walked, and the bottoms of her jeans were just as wet. However, she was pleased to see that her makeup, at least, had remained intact.

"Here you go," Nathan said, appearing from behind her. He handed her a fluffy white towel.

"Thanks," Brydie replied, taking the towel and putting it to the ends of her hair. "Whatever it is you're cooking smells delicious."

"Oh shit, the chicken!"

Brydie followed Nathan into the kitchen, where he was frantically opening the oven. She watched as he pulled out a steaming dish and set it down on the counter. "It doesn't look burned or anything," she said.

"It's not," Nathan replied, relief written all over his face. "But I have a tendency to forget and let food burn. It's not one of my better qualities, I'm afraid."

Brydie grinned. "Do you cook a lot?" she asked. *Do you cook for other women a lot?* was what she really wanted to ask. Visions of the two women at the Halloween party flashed in her mind.

"I try to cook for myself a few times a week," Nathan replied, "even if I'm exhausted after a shift. For some reason, it's completely—"

"Relaxing?" Brydie finished for him.

"Exactly!"

Nathan motioned for her to sit down on one of the bar stools at the island in the middle of the kitchen, but Brydie couldn't sit. She was too busy admiring his oven and everything else about the kitchen. "This is an amazing space," she said. "And you have a KitchenAid oven!" She ran one of her hands over the handle of the oven. "I always wanted one of these in my house, but by the time we furnished the bakery, we just couldn't afford it."

"Bakery?" Nathan asked. His eyebrows were knitted together. "We?"

Brydie looked up from the oven with the realization of what she'd just said. She hadn't been thinking. "Before I became nursemaid to a pug, I owned a bakery," she said. "With my hus—" Brydie stopped, and correcting herself, continued. "With my *ex*-husband."

Nathan pulled two wineglasses down from a shelf and set one in front of her, filling it up. "That explains your reaction to my oven."

"I do love a good oven," Brydie said. She took a drink of the wine. It tasted wonderful.

"I can't take credit for the kitchen," Nathan replied. "It was all my fiancée. Well, ex-fiancée now."

Brydie peered at him from over the top of her wineglass. She hadn't expected that. "She had good taste."

"She did," Nathan agreed. "But she hated it here. She missed the East Coast. She tried, but the mud of the Mississippi River isn't for everyone."

"And you wouldn't move back to be with her?"

Nathan busied himself with setting plates and placed a salad between the two of them. "My life is here now," he said. "Even if my grandparents hadn't died and left everything to me, I still would've found my way back to Memphis."

"I'm from Jonesboro," Brydie said. "That's where my bakery and my husband were."

"My grandfather used to take me there in the summertime when I came to visit as a kid," Nathan replied. "Well, we always stopped for lunch on our way down to Hardy for a weekend of fishing."

"Jonesboro is a nice town," Brydie said. "It was just too small for me, my ex-husband, his girlfriend, and our failed business."

Nathan sat down across from Brydie at the island. "Now I'm nervous that you'll think I'm a terrible cook. I should have waited until after dinner for the deep conversation about our failed relationships."

"I might judge your ability to ice a wedding cake," Brydie said, "but I promise not to judge any other of your culinary skills."

"This is fajita rollup chicken," Nathan said. "There's southwestern corn, too, if you'd like some."

"Thanks," Brydie said, popping a piece of chicken into her mouth. "The chicken tastes as good as it smells."

"So," Nathan said after a few minutes of quiet chewing, "how did you find Teddy and Mrs. Neumann?"

Brydie looked down at her plate, searching for the right words to say to keep her from looking like the near-destitute charity case she really was. "My best friend moved here five years ago after she got married," she said. "She's a Realtor, and her husband is an attorney. After my divorce, I just thought it would be a nice change. My friend's boss at the realty company knows Mrs. Neumann. She set everything up for me."

"Seems like a good friend."

"She is," Brydie said. "She's the best. I lived with her for almost six months. But she's about to have another baby in January, and they really needed the space."

"Did you and your ex-husband . . . ?"

Brydie shook her head. "No, we never had any children." She almost laughed at how easily she knew what he was going to ask. It was the next logical question. Besides, better to get that out of the way now, in the beginning.

"Do you want children?"

"I did," Brydie replied. "I mean, I do. But I'm thirty-four."

"Age isn't always a determining factor," Nathan replied, sounding very much like a doctor. "Women much older than you get pregnant all the time."

"I know," Brydie replied. She wasn't sure how to respond. She took a slow drink of wine. "But my ex-husband didn't want to have children. We put it off for a long time, and by the time we decided to start trying, our marriage wasn't in a good place. So, here I am," she took another drink, "thirty-four and starting all over again."

"It happens that way sometimes," Nathan said. "Starting over, I mean."

"I guess it was stupid of me to think that it was something I'd never have to do," Brydie said.

"My parents have started over more times than I ever thought possible," Nathan replied. He stabbed at the last of his chicken with his fork. "When I was a kid my dad had a habit of starting businesses he couldn't afford or maintain. My grandparents used to bail him out a lot, just like they'd always done for my mother. When I went away to college, my grandparents stopped helping them. I don't think my mother ever got over it."

"Did that hurt your mom's relationship with them?" Brydie asked. She thought about her own mother. She'd offered to help Brydie after the divorce. She'd offered to lend her money and even offered to buy her a house, both of which Brydie rejected. She couldn't let her mother help her. Her mother had been angry, but for Brydie, her mother's anger was better than allowing her mother to hand her money with strings attached.

"It did more than hurt it," Nathan replied. "My mother stopped talking to my grandparents altogether."

"I'm sorry," Brydie said.

"She feels a lot of guilt now that they're gone," Nathan continued. "She takes that guilt out on me."

"You and your mother don't get along?"

Nathan shrugged. "Now that I live in Memphis, there's less occasion for arguments, but seldom does she call and we don't disagree on something."

"My mother and I are the same way," Brydie said. "It's always been that way, though. Ever since I can remember."

"Family can be frustrating sometimes," Nathan said. "I guess that's why I have a dog instead of a wife and kids."

Brydie wondered if that was his way of saying that he didn't ever want to have a family. She couldn't imagine how difficult it must be to balance a demanding job like being a doctor with having a family. She knew only how difficult it had been for her and for Allan to find time for each other while running a business. But she didn't want to think about any of that. She especially didn't want to think about Allan. She wanted to be where she was, *right here*, drinking wine and contented with her life in the present.

AFTER DINNER, NATHAN refilled their wineglasses and led her into the living room. Sasha and Teddy had settled there as well, and when Nathan built a fire in the fireplace, Teddy dropped right in front of it and started to snore. Sasha wasn't far behind him.

"The living room at Mrs. Neumann's house has a fireplace, too," Brydie said. "I thought about lighting it the other night, but it hasn't been lit in ages."

"I'm sure she wouldn't appreciate it if you burned her house down trying to light the fireplace," Nathan replied.

"No, I can't imagine that would make her too happy."

"Listen," Nathan said, scooting closer to her on the couch. "I'm sorry if I asked too many intrusive questions earlier. I'm hopeless at small talk, and when I get nervous, I tend to fall back into doctor mode. I swear I didn't mean to interrogate you over chicken."

"That's okay," Brydie replied. "It was actually kind of nice to talk about it with someone who doesn't know anything about my life before I moved here."

"How do you like Memphis so far?"

"It's getting better," Brydie said with a sly grin. Between the wine and the fire, she felt deliciously warm.

"I'm glad to hear it."

Brydie watched him watching her. She liked the way his curly black hair fell in his eyes when he was concentrating. She liked the way his T-shirt fit, not too loose or too tight. She liked the way he asked her questions—soft, curious, but not intrusive. It made her want to tell him everything, anything, just to keep him looking at her. *Paying attention to her.*

But more than that, she realized, there was something familiar about him, comfortable. She couldn't put her finger on what it was, but despite the constant butterflies in her stomach, he made her feel calmer somehow. She could understand why people would be drawn to him as a doctor. She could even understand why a woman might visit her elderly aunt in order to be near him.

Nathan moved a hand up to Brydie's face, tucking a wandering strand of damp hair behind her ear. It sent a bolt of electricity through her, and when he moved his hand away, Brydie felt herself grabbing a fistful of his T-shirt and pulling him closer to her until her mouth was on his, and she could taste the wine on his lips.

Brydie fell back into the couch and pulled Nathan down on top of her. She could feel his hands exploring her body underneath her T-shirt, and she burned with a need she hadn't known existed until that very moment.

"Do you want—" Nathan began in between frenzied kisses, but before he could finish, the ringing of his phone in his pocket cut him off.

"Ignore it," Brydie murmured.

"I can't," Nathan said, pulling himself away from her with a groan. "I'm on call at the nursing home tonight."

Brydie propped herself up on one elbow as Nathan answered the call. He walked back toward the kitchen as he talked, and Brydie hoped that he wouldn't have to leave for an emergency. It occurred to her that if there was indeed an emergency, it could be Mrs. Neumann. She got up to follow Nathan, straining to hear his conversation. As she stood, her own phone buzzed in her pocket.

Again.

And again.

Annoyed by the interruption to her eavesdropping, she pulled her phone out and looked at it. There were three text messages from her mother. The first one asked Brydie to call her, and so did the second. The third was a screenshot from the *Jonesboro Sun*. Brydie squinted down at the screen on her phone. It took her a second to recognize the people in the picture—Allan and Cassandra. Brydie read the first line: "Susan and Ira Burr of Jonesboro are pleased to announce the engagement of their daughter . . ."

Brydie couldn't read the rest. She shoved her phone back into her pocket, the butterflies she'd had earlier turned to stone and were now hammering at her stomach with a sickening precision.

At the end of the hallway, she could hear Nathan end his conversation. He walked back into the living room. "I have to go in to the hospital," he said.

Brydie tried to put the image she'd just seen out of her head. "Does this happen a lot?"

"What?"

"Getting called in to the hospital?"

Nathan shrugged. "I'm pretty much always on call, even when it's my shift at the nursing home."

"Seems unfair for you to *always* be on call."

"I don't mind," Nathan replied. And then, thinking better of it, he said, "I mean, obviously I mind right *now*, but I don't generally mind."

She thought about what Fred had said to her about Nathan being a workaholic. She wondered if it was true. She thought about Allan and Cassandra, and all of Allan's late nights at work, and despite herself, she couldn't help but wonder if there were any women like Cassandra whom Nathan worked with. She wondered if Nathan was like Allan. She'd already been fooled once. "I think I would mind," Brydie said at last.

"What, there aren't baking emergencies? An all-hands-on-deck situation to finish that wedding cake?" Nathan asked, a grin forming on his face.

Brydie didn't know why, but his comment made her stiffen. Was he making fun of her? She couldn't tell. "Well, if I wanted to be a workaholic, I guess I would have become a doctor."

"Brydie," Nathan said, "I don't have a job where I can just choose not to come in. It's not about wanting to go in or not wanting to go in. It's about saving lives. Surely you understand that."

"I understand," Brydie said, standing up and grabbing Teddy's collar. "Nobody's ever saved a life by *baking a cake*."

"That's not what I meant," Nathan said. "Look, I think there's been a misunderstanding or something."

"No misunderstanding," Brydie replied. She reached down in her pocket and felt for her keys, her fingers grazing against her phone, still warm from the text message she'd gotten. She felt sick. "I'll get out of here."

"Hey." Nathan reached out to touch her, but Brydie pulled away from his grasp.

"I don't want to hold you up," Brydie replied. "See you around."

"Don't leave like this," Nathan said. "Honestly, I don't understand what just happened."

"It's fine," Brydie said. "I should get going. See you around."

Without another word, Nathan stepped back, allowing Brydie to run out of the house and into the frigid November night.

CHAPTER 15

WHEN BRYDIE AND TEDDY GOT HOME THAT night, Brydie baked him some treats and then settled herself into a steaming bubble bath. Already she was feeling guilty for her overreaction at dinner, and she was more than a little aware that her behavior probably meant she wouldn't be seeing any more of Dr. Reid.

She decided she was genuinely terrible with men, and that it was probably a good thing she wouldn't be seeing him anymore. Maybe she'd saved herself a lot of heartache in the end. Maybe if she had been paying more attention, maybe if she'd spoken up with her ex-husband the way she spoke up with Nathan, she would have noticed that her husband was cheating on her. At least, that's what her mother said when Brydie came to see her at her office. It was eight o'clock at night, but Brydie knew that her mother would still be there, working.

"I could have told you five months ago that he was

cheating," Ruth Benson said, not looking up from her computer screen.

"Why didn't you?" Brydie asked between sobs.

"Well, I didn't have any proof," her mother replied. "But all the signs were there."

"What signs?"

Brydie's mother sighed, finally looking up at her daughter. "Coming home late, breaking plans, taking phone calls in the other room."

"*You* do all of those things," Brydie said. "Those things don't always mean someone is cheating."

"But they do in this case."

Brydie slumped back into her chair. She couldn't get the image of Allan, *her husband,* grinding on top of Cassandra, *their new and very pretty employee,* out of her head. Every time she closed her eyes, she saw them. "I just don't understand," she said. "We were trying . . . we were trying to have a *baby.*"

"No," her mother replied. "*You* were trying to have a baby."

"I can't get pregnant by myself."

"Allan didn't want to have a baby, and you know it."

Brydie stood up on wobbly legs. "I don't know why I came here," she said. "I should have known you weren't going to make me feel any better."

"It's not my job to make you feel better," her mother said. "It's my job to be honest with you."

"I wish Dad were here."

Hurt swept across her mother's face, and Brydie instantly regretted her words. But it was true, and they were both being truthful, weren't they? Still, she wished she hadn't said it. She left her mother's office and got back in her car. The only thing left to do was to go home and confront her husband.

By the time Brydie got home, Allan was waiting for her. He was sitting outside in one of the rocking chairs, as was their habit at night during the summer months. She contemplated turning around and going to her mother's house. At least there she wouldn't have to talk to him. Her mother might not be good at comfort, but she would make sure Allan didn't come within talking distance.

"I was going to tell you," Allan said when Brydie reached the first step on the porch.

"That's comforting," Brydie replied, trying not to look at him.

"I didn't want to hurt you," he continued, following her inside. "I swear I didn't."

"Is that why you've been fucking some girl in our bakery?" Brydie demanded. "Because you didn't want to hurt me?"

"You weren't supposed to be there."

"It's my bakery!"

"It's our bakery," Allan reminded her. "But that's not an excuse for what I did."

"There isn't an excuse for what you did," Brydie replied. She put a hand up to her throbbing temple. "I can't talk about this right now. I thought I could, but I can't."

"I understand."

"No you don't," Brydie said. "But you do know you have to end it, right? It has to end with her."

"Brydie," Allan said. "Brydie, wait."

Brydie turned around at the foot of the stairs. "What?"

"I'm not going to end it," he said.

"What do you mean?"

"Brydie, I love her."

Brydie felt like she'd been punched in the stomach. She'd expected to come home and have Allan apologize, cry with her, and tell her it would never happen again. She'd expected him to say that it just happened once. She'd expected him to tell her it meant nothing. "How long has it been going on?"

"A few months."

So her mother had been right. "Why?" she asked.

Allan shrugged. "I don't know. It just happened."

"That's not a reason," Brydie replied. She kept thinking that if she could just keep him there, if they could just talk about it, then maybe somehow it wouldn't be so bad. Maybe they could work it out. Maybe her marriage wasn't over.

"It's not that I don't love you," Allan replied. "I do. I'll always love you. But things have been different these last couple of years since your dad died. You're different. You're not the person I married."

"Oh, so this is my fault?" Brydie asked. "It's my fault you can't keep it in your goddamn pants, Allan?"

"That's not what I'm saying."

"So what *are* you saying?"

Allan held up his hands in defeat. "I'm going to go ahead and stay somewhere else for the night. We can talk tomorrow."

Brydie looked down at the bag in Allan's hand. He must have been holding on to it all along, but she'd been too distracted to notice. "Are you going to stay with her? With Cassandra?"

"We'll talk tomorrow," was all he said.

Brydie thought about that night all the time. She often wondered if she could have said or done something that would have made Allan want to stay. She wondered if it really was her fault, as he often said in the months to follow, that she'd changed, that she wasn't the woman he'd married. She wondered, too, what her life would be like if she hadn't walked in on Allan and Cassandra. Would they still be married? Would they have a child? Could she have been happy in her ignorance for the rest of her life?

She didn't know.

All she knew for sure right now was that Allan and Cassandra were getting married. During her weakest moments, alone in bed and wearing Allan's shirt, she'd hoped against hope that maybe he'd realize he made a mistake. Maybe he'd call her and say that *any* version of her was better than no version at all. He'd say he loved her. He'd say there was no one else. He'd say he wanted her to come home.

Home? There wasn't any home to go back to. The bakery was closed. The house was sold. She had proof right there on her phone that Allan was never going to say any of those things. He was going to be someone else's husband, and he was going to live a life that she knew nothing about.

Brydie toweled off and climbed into bed. She'd shut her phone off so that she wouldn't be tempted to look at the photo again. She was sure that by now her mother had called, and maybe even Nathan had called. She was too humiliated to call and apologize. All she wanted to do right now was sink down into the pillow and go to sleep until Christmas.

As she closed her eyes, she felt something wet and rough graze the top of her hand hanging off the side of the bed. She sat up and turned the lamp on to see Teddy sitting there, looking up at her expectantly.

"You want up here?" Brydie asked.

Teddy put his two front paws on the side of the mattress.

"Okay," Brydie said, getting out of bed and hoisting Teddy up. "But if you drool on me in the middle of the night, you're going right back down again."

Teddy pawed at the comforter and turned around a few times before nestling right up to her. In true Teddy fashion, he promptly began to snore.

Brydie looked at him in amazement. She reached out her hand and stroked him along his back until her eyes became heavy and her hand began to burn. Then she turned off the lamp and tried to get some sleep.

CHAPTER 16

Nот long after Brydie drifted to sleep, she bolted upright in bed when she heard a deafening crash coming from beneath her. Teddy was suddenly pressed up next to her, his breathing rough and ragged. She patted his side, trying to wake herself up enough to figure out what was going on.

"It's okay, buddy. It's okay."

She shifted over on her side to look at the clock on the nightstand, but it was off. When she went to turn on her phone, it wouldn't come on, the low-battery signal mocking her in the middle of the darkened screen.

Brydie lay down, wondering where the crash could have come from. It sounded as if it was below them. In the basement, maybe? She knew she should get up and see to it, but she didn't want to. It was probably nothing. She doubted there was anything at all in the basement. The crash had been in her head. She just wanted to sleep, but after a few minutes the fog in her brain lifted and she sat up yet again.

The basement?

That's when Brydie remembered that she had the key that might work on the basement door. She'd forgotten all about it since Halloween. *There's been a crash down there,* Brydie thought. *I should get up and check it out. I need to get up and check it out.*

She pushed aside her covers and switched on the light. She'd hidden the skeleton key in one of the porcelain jewelry boxes Mrs. Neumann kept on her dresser. It was the kind with serrated edges that opened locks of all kinds. Brydie had seen only one before, at her grandparents' house when she'd been helping her mother move them into the nursing home. But when she'd asked about it, her mother told her to put it away, and reminded her not to take anything that didn't belong to her. *As if I would have taken anything from my own grandparents,* Brydie thought, annoyed even now, years later, feeling her cheeks burn.

She turned the key over in her hands. This *had* to be the key to the basement. It just had to be. Brydie's heart skipped a beat when she put the key into the lock and it turned with ease. She opened the door and tried to switch on the light, but nothing happened. "Shit," she said. There was no way she was going to be able to see anything down there in the middle of the night in the dark. Then she remembered that she'd seen a flashlight in the bedroom closet.

She stood up on her tiptoes and felt along the shelf for the flashlight. When she felt it, she grabbed on to the handle but did not get a good grip, causing it to fall from the shelf down onto the top of her head and onto the floor. Ignoring the mess, the key in one hand and the flashlight in the other, she made her way triumphantly back to the now-open basement door. This time Teddy was by her side, his gaze shifting from the open doorway in front of them and back to her.

"This is how horror movies begin," she whispered to him. She was barefoot, and the dust from each step stirred and became lodged in between her toes. After a few halting seconds, Teddy was at her heels, his hot breath beating against her skin.

Once they got to the bottom of the stairs, the musty smell of the basement invaded Brydie's nostrils and she coughed to clear her lungs. She wasn't sure what she'd expected once she got down there, but as she shone the flashlight around the room, she found that the basement looked like, well, a basement. It reminded her of her grandparents' basement. There were boxes on shelves that were neatly labeled "Christmas supplies" or "tablecloths." There were canned goods and a hodgepodge of other items that people relegate to basements when they no longer have a place upstairs. Further inspection revealed an old couch and a broken-down table and chairs.

But the site of the crash was obvious—in one corner, an entire shelving unit had imploded, taking years of food-filled mason jars with them. The smell as Brydie got closer to the mess was overwhelming, and she had to cover her nose. There was no way she was going to be able to clean it up tonight—not in the dark and not barefoot. She crept closer, shining the light around the rest of that side of the basement to make sure no other rotting shelves had decided to commit suicide and spill their contents on the dirty concrete floor.

Behind her, Teddy jumped up on the couch and

nestled down onto one end where the stuffing was coming loose. She turned her attention back to the mess, and as she did, her light caught something in the corner opposite to the shelves. It looked like a trunk, and as she moved closer, she became even more curious. Surely an old trunk in a basement wasn't a rarity, but this trunk didn't match the rest of the ratty furniture and rotting food that filled the rest of the space. It was ornate, with metalwork scrolling up and down the wooden flanks. And there was something else, something even more curious—just in front of the trunk was a folding chair, and on top of the seat of the chair was a book lying open. If not for the dust and the cobwebs, Brydie would have guessed that she'd just missed the mysterious person who'd been sitting there, as if they'd just popped out for a moment and would be right back.

Brydie set the flashlight onto the concrete floor so that it shone upward, and gingerly picked up the book. It was damp and stank of mold, and when she held it closer to her face, she realized it was a photo album. The pages inside were yellowed, and so were the photos.

She retrieved the flashlight to get a better look and sat down gingerly in the chair. The first few pages were of people she'd never seen—members of Mrs. Neumann's family, she assumed, at a wedding. Then there was Mrs. Neumann, a much younger version of her, standing in a wedding dress next to a fair-haired, good-looking man in a suit. Brydie could tell by the cap-sleeved, A-line dress that it must have been sometime in the 1960s. The dress was short, just below the knee, and she was wearing a small white hat that fit close to her bobbed head of hair.

What struck Brydie most was that even with the poor lighting in the basement and the fading quality of the photograph, she could tell that Mrs. Neumann had been beautiful. She practically radiated warmth as she smiled up at the man next to her. Brydie wondered why the photo album was downstairs sitting on top of a folding chair.

When she turned to the next page, she found that it was blank. There had once been pictures inside the sleeve; she could tell because the spots where they had once been were not as yellowed as the rest of the page, leaving lighter boxes where the pictures had once been. There were at least ten pages where the pictures had been removed, and then suddenly the pages were filled once again. Mrs. Neumann and the man she'd been with in the earlier pictures were back, staring at the camera. Some of them were holidays, and some of them were random moments, the kind people caught on film before cell phones had been invented—imperfect moments printed for all to see. But what struck Brydie was that Mrs. Neumann and the man were no longer smiling . . . in any of the pictures. Gone was the radiant glow, replaced with, what? She didn't know exactly, but there was something in her face that Brydie recognized. Something she'd seen in herself more than once when she looked into the mirror.

Grief.

It was grief.

She thought about how there were no pictures anywhere upstairs. It had seemed odd the first time Brydie noticed it, but she'd grown accustomed to the naked walls. Now, with the photo album lying dusty in her lap, she thought it odd once more.

She was so busy contemplating the photo album that Brydie hadn't noticed that Teddy had jumped down from the couch and was standing motionless in front of one of the walls at the far end of the basement. There was a low growl coming from his throat. "What are you doing?" Brydie asked. "Stop being weird."

She shone the light over to where he was standing, but she didn't see anything but the wall. Teddy didn't move, and instead began to bark. It was a funny, little bark, and if Brydie hadn't been so busy replaying every scary movie she'd ever seen in her head, she might have laughed.

With her heart in her throat, she crept over to where Teddy was standing. She shone the flashlight just above his head, and that's when she saw them . . . all of them. They were crawling along the wall, one after another in an eight-legged pilgrimage to the floor, five granddaddy longlegs.

Brydie jumped, edging back toward the couch, not itching to let them crawl all over her. "Come on, Killer," she said to Teddy. "Let's go back upstairs."

Teddy looked from the spiders over to Brydie and back again, and before Brydie could stop him, Teddy unfurled his tongue and licked the wall, picking up each spider one by one. He was still chewing on them when he turned and scampered up the stairs.

Brydie stood there for a moment, not sure whether she should laugh or throw up. Instead she started up the stairs after him. Then, thinking better of it, she hurried back to the chair, picked up the photo album, and carried it up the stairs and into the wash of the early morning daylight.

CHAPTER 17

THE NEXT MORNING, BRYDIE STOOD OUTSIDE the nursing home with Teddy on his leash next to her. After a frantic call to Elliott and a Google search, she learned that the now deceased and digested granddaddy longlegs wouldn't hurt Teddy. Still, she figured she'd probably keep their late-night shenanigans out of the conversation with Mrs. Neumann. She knew that if the old woman had wanted the person staying in her house to have the key to the basement, she probably would have given it to her. She'd been so kind to Brydie so far, and Brydie couldn't shake the feeling that looking at Mrs. Neumann's photographs was a breach of her trust somehow. Besides, she still had to clean the mess up once she got home. She'd tell the old woman the next week—once she'd seen the basement in the daylight and the trash men had hauled off the rotting shelves and broken glass.

It was a steely day, and the sky hung heavy above her. With her gray cardigan and blue jeans, she almost faded into the background, and after the way she'd behaved at Nathan's house the day before, she wished she could indeed do just that.

However, she had an agreement with Mrs. Neumann, and besides, she was excited to show her the tricks she'd been able to teach Teddy with the new treats she'd baked for him—carrot-oat-applesauce treats—and the dog would do just about anything for them.

She waved at the receptionist as she walked by, and Pauline was waiting for them in the chair where she always sat, a blanket covering her legs. "Brydie and Teddy!" She clapped her hands together.

Brydie unhooked Teddy's leash so that he could run to her and jump on her lap. "He's learned some new tricks," she said. "And we're both excited to share them with you."

"How wonderful!" Pauline replied.

"How are you feeling today?" Brydie asked. "It's awful ugly outside."

"Oh, I like this kind of weather," Pauline replied. "It's good for the soul."

"I don't know about that," Brydie replied. "It depresses me."

"Don't you like to sit back and just reflect a bit?" Pauline asked. "Or cuddle up by the fire with a cup of hot chocolate," she looked around the room before whispering, "or bourbon, and read a good book?"

"The book and the bourbon I like," Brydie said. "The reflecting, not so much."

"You'll get there," she said. "When you're as old as me, you'll have more to reflect upon than you have time left on this earth."

"I can't imagine having that much to think about."

"Ah, that's yet another joy of getting old," Pauline replied. "Selective memory." She grinned and pointed to her head. "For example, I choose to think only about the parts of my marriages that I enjoyed."

"You've been married four times, right?"

Pauline nodded. "I have."

Brydie shifted from one foot to the other and then sat down in the chair opposite the old woman. "Well, I've just been married once, and I can't seem to move past it."

"The divorce wasn't your idea?"

"No."

"Ah," Pauline said, giving Teddy's back a stroke. "That was marriage number two for me."

"What happened?" Brydie asked. She wondered if the man in the pictures with Mrs. Neumann was the second husband. She wanted to ask, but held back.

"He was my childhood best friend," she replied. "When I came home to live with my parents after my second divorce, I was so depressed. My mother and father were embarrassed to have a child with a failed marriage. They hardly let me out in public."

"That must have been awful."

"The only person they let me see was Bill. He'd been widowed the year before. He had a good job as a car salesman. And oh, we loved spending time together," Pauline said. She was looking out the window, just like she'd been doing when Brydie arrived. "I think my parents thought that he could sand away my rough edges, you know, make me a proper southern woman. I think I thought that he could do those things, too."

"And he couldn't?"

"Nobody could ever do that for me," Pauline

replied. "I loved him more than I'd loved any of my other husbands combined. I'd loved him all along, you see. Since we were kids."

"He didn't love you as much as you loved him?" Brydie asked. That was something she could understand. That was something she knew too much about already.

"Oh, he loved me as much as I loved him," Pauline said. She smiled, her gaze catching something far away, a lost memory.

"Then I don't understand."

"You're so young," Pauline replied. "So young."

"I'm not so young," Brydie said, prickling. "I'm thirty-four."

"Just a baby," Pauline said.

"So what happened?" Brydie pressed, eager to hear the ending to the story.

"I had to move on," was all Pauline said. "And so do you."

"I don't know if I can."

"Then you're foolish," Pauline said, her eyes snapping back to Brydie, back to the present.

"I *want* to move on," Brydie said, feeling herself straighten. "I just don't know if I can."

"You are allowed to grieve over your marriage," Pauline said. "It's important to grieve. I grieved for every single one of my marriages. However, it's also important to move on. It may not seem like it now, but it will get better, easier."

"When?"

Pauline shrugged. "I can't tell you that."

Brydie stood up and pulled her phone out of one of her pockets. "Last night, my mother sent me this," she said. She handed the phone to Pauline with the picture of Allan and Cassandra on the screen. "That's my ex-husband and the woman he cheated on me with. They're getting married."

"Oh my."

"I was feeling better," Brydie continued. "I really was. I was feeling like maybe for the first time in months that I was ready to move on, to have something else." She sat back down. "Now I don't know what I feel."

"He had an affair then?" Pauline asked, still looking down at the picture.

"He did," Brydie replied. "And then he told me he didn't love me anymore because he was in love with her."

Pauline's eyes flicked up to Brydie. "Honey, that's terrible. I'm sorry."

The old woman's voice dripped with sympathy, and Brydie took a deep breath and let it back out again. She hadn't told anyone that before. She assumed everyone knew, since Allan left her for Cassandra, but saying it out loud made her feel better somehow, lighter even. "I guess this picture just proves what I've known for a long time."

"I'm glad we didn't have technology like this when I was your age," Pauline said, handing the phone back to Brydie. "When I was a young woman, if you wanted to take pictures, you had to buy a Kodak Cresta and send off your pictures and wait for them to be developed."

"I sometimes wish it was still that way," Brydie replied. She thought about the pictures she'd found in the basement, and she thought about asking the old woman about them. But she knew that she'd have a hard time explaining how she even *got* into the locked basement to begin with.

"Anyway," Pauline continued with a wave of her hand, "that was a different time—a much different time. And right now, it's time for you to look forward. Especially when there's a handsome young doctor after you."

"I don't think he's after me," Brydie said. "And if he was, after the way I behaved the last time I saw him, he's for sure not after me now."

As if on cue, there was a knock at the door. Brydie and Pauline looked up to see a short, squat woman with Harry Potter–esque glasses standing there with a clipboard.

"May I come in, Mrs. Neumann?" the woman said.

"Dr. Sower," Pauline said and shot a glance at Brydie, then added, "Where's Dr. Reid?"

Dr. Sower smiled. "He's gone on back to the hospital a couple of weeks early," she said. "He gave me a break, and I appreciate it." She looked from Pauline to Teddy to Brydie. "And who do we have here?"

"This handsome fellow is Teddy Roosevelt," Pauline said. "And this is his caretaker, Brydie Benson."

Brydie stuck out her hand. "It's nice to meet you." She wondered if Nathan had asked Dr. Sower to come in early because he didn't want to see her. If that was the case, she didn't blame him.

"It's nice to meet you, too."

"Brydie and Teddy were just about to show me a new trick," Pauline said. "Come in and sit down."

"Oh, I don't want to interrupt."

"Too late for that now," Pauline replied with a

good-natured wink. "Teddy always has liked an audience."

Brydie reached down into her purse and pulled out the bag of treats. Teddy jumped down and sat down in front of her as soon as he saw the bag. "Okay," Brydie said. "I hope you two aren't disappointed. We haven't been practicing anything fancy."

"I'm just impressed he's awake," Pauline replied.

"Okay, Teddy," Brydie said. She held out a treat to him. "Beg."

Teddy stood up on his hind legs, his tongue uncurling from his mouth.

"Good boy!" Brydie gave him a treat. "Now, roll over."

Teddy cocked his head to the side.

"You can do it."

Teddy lay down on the floor and rolled from one side to the other.

"Good boy!" Brydie gave him a treat. "Now play dead."

Teddy lay down on the floor once again, but this time he began to snore. And drool.

"Well, that's close enough," Brydie said.

"What kind of treats are those?" Dr. Sower asked. "They smell delicious."

"They're carrot, oats, and applesauce," Brydie replied. "Teddy loves them."

"Where did you get them?"

"I made them," Brydie said. "They're actually pretty easy."

"I bet my boys would love them," Dr. Sower said. "I have two Afghan hounds, Rufus and Oliver."

"Here." Brydie handed the doctor what was left of the treats. "Take the rest of these home."

"Really?"

"Oh sure. I have more at home."

"Thank you," Dr. Sower said. "I'd be happy to pay for them."

"It's really okay," Brydie replied, unable to hide her pleasure. She'd almost forgotten what it was like to bake just for fun. It was a feeling she'd missed.

"Be careful," Pauline said once Dr. Sower had gone. "Before you know it, you'll be baking for the whole darn place!"

CHAPTER 18

THE SMELL WAS EVEN WORSE LATER THAT AFTER-
noon when Brydie went down to the basement to
clean the mess. She tried breathing through her mouth
instead of her nose, but that only made it worse. It
was like she could actually *taste* the liquefied food and
mold and rotting wood. She armed herself with
rubber gloves, a bucket full of bleach, a mop, trash
bags, a box, and a broom with a dustpan.

Teddy sat at the top of the stairs and whined.

"I don't know what you're complaining about,"
she said to him. "You're not the one down here cleaning up this cesspool."

Brydie knelt down next to the broken shelves and
began to pick up glass and deposit it into the box
she'd brought down with her. She propped what was
left of the shelf up on its side, and stacked any stray
boards up along the wall.

Despite the smell and the occasional shard of glass
tearing through her gloves to prick one of her fingers,
Brydie found that she was enjoying clearing the base-

ment of the debris. It kept her from thinking about Cassandra and Allan and that horrid engagement announcement. She'd wasted too much time on it already, and if she was going to be over the whole thing by Christmas, she couldn't invest another second in it.

Really, what was her mother thinking by sending it to her?

Of course, Brydie already knew the answer to that—her mother hoped that it would help her move on. She hoped that it would break free the invisible tether holding Brydie to Allan and that she'd find herself a nice, preferably rich and older man with whom she could settle.

The thought made Brydie roll her eyes.

She'd known since she was four that she and her mother were different—that they went about things differently. It was a truth that both of them forgot, and often. When her mother was angry with her, it was Brydie's inclination to cry, which in turn made her mother even angrier. It was Ruth Benson's nature to be blunt, to always tell the harsh truth, and it was a trait that Brydie, most of the time, envied. She just wished her mother wouldn't be quite so blunt with her.

Brydie was more like her father, and her mother knew it. Brydie knew it, too, and that was one of the reasons she didn't drink much—she'd known before her mother told her that her father was an alcoholic. Of course she'd known. She just hadn't wanted to *ever* admit it or *ever* talk about it. She knew it just like she'd known that she and Allan were having problems in their marriage, long before Cassandra came into the picture. She just thought that maybe if she didn't admit it, didn't engage those thoughts, it would go away and work itself out.

It hadn't, and now she wondered if she would ever meet someone who could help her heal, both from her divorce and her father's death.

But she had met someone, hadn't she? She'd met Dr. Reid, and despite knowing she'd blown it with him, she held on to a small kernel of hope. She liked him, still, and she wanted, despite herself, to keep that hope alive. It wasn't just that Dr. Reid was kind and handsome and very probably doing well for himself; there was something more about him that made Brydie want to be near him, want to talk to him, want to know him. Maybe it was his unruly mop of thick, curly hair, or maybe it was his dark eyes. She didn't know, but she felt the pull nonetheless, deep down inside of her in a way she'd never experienced before—not even with Allan.

She wondered if that was what Pauline had felt with her second husband, Bill. If they had loved each other as much as she said they did, then how could their marriage have ended? Brydie wasn't naïve enough to still believe that love conquered all; she wasn't a child, and even when she had been, she'd never been one for fairy tales. But she'd always harbored a suspicion that no relationship truly ended with two people in love with each other equally. At least one of the responsible parties had to be in love with the other just a *little bit less*. It was possible to love someone without that love being enough to save the relationship, wasn't it? To love without actually *being* in love?

That's what Allan had told her more than once during their divorce. He loved her, but he wasn't *in love* with her. At the time, she'd scoffed at his assertion.

How could he love me at all, even a little, and be doing this to me? she'd thought.

She'd accused him of trying to placate her, trying to keep her from making his life and Cassandra's life miserable. She'd accused him of a lot of things in those early days, and some of them she wished she could take back.

Brydie's gaze fell to the trunk in the corner. She wondered idly if the pictures missing from the photo album were inside. Placing the mop down inside the bucket full of bleach, she walked over to the trunk and stood in front of it.

Just a peek inside of it wouldn't hurt.

Gingerly, she curled her fingers under the front of the lid and lifted up. A thick layer of dust puffed up and into Brydie's face, causing her to cough and sneeze, but the lid didn't budge. She gave it another, more forceful tug.

Still nothing.

Brydie stood back and blew a stray piece of hair out of her eyes. Pauline Neumann clearly didn't want anyone riffling through her life. Not that Brydie blamed her—everybody had secrets. But she found herself frustrated that the trunk was locked, and she considered for a moment trying to force it open.

Scolding herself for having such a thought, she was interrupted by Teddy's whining at the top of the stairs. "Hold on," she said to him in mock aggravation. "I know it's lunchtime."

Giving the trunk one last longing look, she gathered up her cleaning supplies and headed back up the stairs. The mystery, at least for today, would simply have to wait.

CHAPTER 19

B Y THE END OF HER WORKWEEK, BRYDIE WAS glad it was payday at ShopCo. Brydie wasn't used to regularly scheduled paydays, and she had to admit it was kind of nice. Since she worked Monday nights through Thursday nights, she got to pick up her paycheck on Friday morning before she left for her days off.

"I like it that way," Rosa said, opening one of the ovens to insert a cake. "I can pick up my and Lillie's checks, cash them at the service desk, and do our shopping before we go home. Then we have a few days off with a little money in our pockets."

"I was too tired on the first payday to do much of anything," Brydie replied. "But the second time around, I think I'll be able to stay conscious long enough to do the same thing."

"You've been here a month!" Rosa exclaimed, clapping Brydie on the back.

"It ain't somethin' to brag about," Joe said,

boxing a dozen cupcakes. "I've got milk in my fridge at home older than that."

"Yeah," Rosa replied, "but you probably shouldn't."

Brydie stifled a laugh. "I just hope I can make it through Christmas."

"Joe scared three girls off last year," Rosa said, giving Joe a sideways glance. "Two of them never even came back for their last check."

"They were hacks," Joe replied. "None of them had your eye, Bridget."

Brydie was so surprised by the compliment that she didn't even think to correct Joe on her name. "Thank you."

Joe nodded. "Now get back to work. You've still got two hours before those checks are ready."

BRYDIE PUSHED HER cart languidly down the aisles. She'd thought that she would be able to stay up to do grocery shopping, but now she just felt like crawling inside the cart and going to sleep. The only thing keeping her awake was her excitement about buying the ingredients for a few new recipes for dog treats as she browsed the Internet. In fact, she'd come up with one recipe all on her own—a doggie cupcake.

As she walked toward the front of the store, she saw that the little hair salon inside ShopCo had begun to open for the day. She'd never been there late enough in the morning to see it open. She thought it was a tad strange for a hair salon to be inside a grocery store, but Rosa told her that she and Lillian both got their hair done there. Of course, she'd always seen their hair inside a hairnet, or just out of a hairnet. Nobody's hair looked good after wearing a hairnet for a full eight hours. Maybe that's why Joe was bald.

Brydie was so preoccupied with thinking about hairnets and Joe's big, bald head that she didn't notice one of the women in the shop beckoning to her.

"Hey!" the woman said. "Hey, ma'am!"

"What?" Brydie looked around. "Me?"

"Yeah," the woman replied. "You need a cut and color."

"Oh, no," Brydie said. "I'm all right."

The woman held up her finger to Brydie and began fishing around in one of the drawers at her station. She pulled out a mirror and trotted toward her. "I wasn't asking a question," she said, holding up the mirror so Brydie could see her face.

Brydie had to force herself not to look away. Being up all night showed everywhere, especially around her eyes. And her hair. Oh, her hair. True, the hairnet hadn't done her any favors, but her hair was a mess even before. "Is it that bad?" she asked.

"It's not great," the woman said. "I don't have any appointments this morning. Why don't you come in and let me give you a nice cut and color."

"I don't know."

"I'm Mandy," the woman said. She pointed to Brydie's name tag, still hanging from her shirt. "Employees get a fifteen percent discount."

Brydie thought about it. She couldn't remember the last time she'd gotten her hair cut, and it had been years since she'd had it colored. Allan liked her hair long, and so she'd kept it long, a fact that drove her mother crazy—that Brydie would keep her hair a certain way *for a man*. But really, it was because

Brydie never really cared much about her hair. Now, looking in the mirror, she thought maybe she might consider giving caring about her hair a try. *One step at a time,* she told herself.

"Okay," Brydie said to Mandy, pushing her basket to the side of the salon. "Let's do it."

CHAPTER 20

B RYDIE LOOKED INTO THE MIRROR, MOVING HER head from side to side. She just couldn't believe how different she looked.

"Do you like it?" Mandy asked, standing behind the chair where Brydie sat. "I told you an all-over chocolate with caramel highlights would do the trick."

"You make my head sound like a cake," Brydie replied.

"Sorry," Mandy said. "I guess I've worked up an appetite."

"That's all right," Brydie said. "I like cake."

Mandy pulled out her straightening iron and smoothed a few unruly strands in the back. "What do you think of the cut?"

"I love it." Brydie touched the back of her hair. It felt soft and sleek. "I especially like the way it's swingy."

Mandy laughed. "It's a classic bob with a twist. It's just a little shorter in the back than in the front.

It does mean you'll need to have a trim every few weeks."

"Well, it'll be hard to forget about with the salon in the same building where I work," Brydie said. "Thank you so much. I had no idea that this was exactly what I needed today."

"You look like a whole new woman!"

"I do," Brydie replied. "And I think I like her."

BRYDIE DROVE HOME, checking the clock every couple of minutes. She was two hours later than normal, and she was worried about Teddy. Their routine of breakfast and a nap had been disturbed, and as silly as she knew it sounded, she was worried he would be upset. At least once she got to the house all she'd have to do was put groceries away, fix breakfast, and take Teddy out for a short walk. Then the two of them could snooze the day away.

She blinked her eyes, hard, trying to keep them focused, when from out of nowhere a flash of feet and fur darted out in front of her and across the street. Brydie slammed on her brakes, sending her car careening to the side of the street and up onto the grassy median.

Brydie sat there for a second, stunned, trying to collect herself. After a few seconds, she looked down to see that she was still gripping the steering wheel as if her life depended upon it. Unfurling her fingers, she got out of the car to inspect the damage. She walked around her Fiat and breathed a sigh of relief that there didn't seem to be a scratch or a dent or a popped tire or anything else. She was glad, too, that she hadn't hit whatever it was that ran out in front of her.

But what had it been? She looked around the empty street and houses nearby. She didn't see anything. Just as she was about to get back into her car and chalk the whole thing up to some kind of exhaustion-induced hallucination, she saw something large peeking out from behind one of the bushes in the yard of the house across the street. Brydie squinted and edged closer. Something about whatever it was looked oddly familiar. It took her just another second to realize she'd seen the thing before.

It was a dog.

And not just any dog—it was Nathan's huge Irish wolfhound, Sasha.

Panic began to fill Brydie's throat. She couldn't imagine Nathan ever letting Sasha outside to run around on her own. She must have escaped. Brydie abandoned her car and jogged across the street.

"Sasha!" she called. "Sasha! Come *here*!"

Sasha peeked out again from behind the bush and, realizing that it was Brydie, came lumbering toward her, full throttle.

"Wait!" Brydie shrieked. "Wait, wait! Sasha! *No!*"

But it was too late. Sasha was on top of Brydie, licking her face with her enormous, wet tongue. Brydie managed to push Sasha off her and grab hold of her collar. "Oh, you're in so much trouble," she said. "How did you get out?"

Sasha just panted and followed along, seemingly unbothered by Brydie dragging her back across the street and to Brydie's car. Sasha was roughly half the size of her Fiat, Brydie surmised, and that was without all the groceries filling her backseat. "Get in," she demanded, opening the front door.

Brydie hurried around to the driver's side and got

in. Sasha was hunched over in the seat next to her as Brydie eased off the median and back onto the road. It didn't take long for Sasha's nose to begin to twitch, taking in the scent of the groceries. "Don't even think about it," Brydie said.

By the time Brydie pulled into Nathan's driveway, Sasha had wiggled herself halfway into the backseat, happily sniffing her way through each bag. In the front yard was a woman, talking on her cell phone and waving her free arm about. When she saw Brydie get out of the car, she ran up to her.

"Oh my God," she said, out of breath and wheezing slightly. "You found her! Oh my *God,* thank you!" She threw her arms around Brydie as Brydie tried to open the passenger's-side door and pull Sasha out of whichever ShopCo bag she'd ravaged.

"Get her leash," Brydie said.

"Oh yeah, her leash!" The woman ran inside and emerged a few seconds later, triumphant. "I found it!"

Brydie took it from her and clipped it to Sasha's collar. "Come on," she said to the dog, who had half a head of lettuce still in her mouth.

"Where did you find her?" the woman asked. "I've been looking all over."

"She ran out in front of my car," Brydie replied.

"I couldn't catch her," the woman said. "She got through the door before I got her leash on, and she ran off."

Brydie studied the woman in front of her. She was young, maybe twenty-two, with long blond hair and a nice tan, despite it being November. She looked like she belonged on a college campus in Florida somewhere. "Well, she's okay now," Brydie said.

Just then, a black Range Rover pulled into the

driveway, and out hopped Nathan. He looked confusedly between Brydie and the woman, his eyes finally settling on Sasha, who'd lain down between the women, casually licking the lettuce. "What happened, Myriah?"

"She's back!" Myriah said. "I'm sorry I called you in such a panic, but this lady here found her."

Brydie tried to smile, but it came out as more of a grimace. All she wanted to do was get into her car and disappear back down the street, but they were both staring at her like they expected her to speak. "Well," she said. "It was no big deal. I'm glad she's all right. I'd better get home."

"Hey, wait," Nathan said. Then turning to Myriah said, "Take Sasha back inside. I'll be there in a second."

"I really need to get home," Brydie said.

"Thanks for finding Sasha," Nathan replied.

"She kind of found me," Brydie replied. "She ran out in front of my car. I almost hit her."

"She thinks it's a game when she gets loose," Nathan explained. "Myriah underestimates her, I think."

"Yeah, well," Brydie said with a shrug. "I'd better let you get back to them." She turned around and pulled open the door to her car.

"Did I do something to upset you?" Nathan pressed.

"No."

"Then why are you in such a big hurry to get away from me?"

"I'm not in a hurry," Brydie said. "I've been at work all night, and I should have been home by now. Instead, I just wasted an hour corralling your dog and then watching her eat an *entire head of lettuce*."

"I'll pay you for the lettuce."

Brydie rolled her eyes. "Don't worry about it," she said. "But you might want to tell your girlfriend to make sure she has Sasha's leash on before opening the door to go outside."

"Myriah?" Nathan glanced back at his house. "She's not my girlfriend."

"It doesn't matter," Brydie replied.

"It matters to me," Nathan said. "I thought we were having a good time the other night, you know, until we suddenly weren't."

"We were," Brydie said. "I mean we did. Look, I'm sorry about all of that. It wasn't your fault. I didn't mean to be so rude."

"I didn't like having to end our evening early," Nathan replied. "What we were doing before that phone call, well, I thought it was pretty great."

"It was," Brydie said, biting the bottom of her lip. "It's just been such a long time since I've, you know, dated anyone. I guess I got a little freaked out."

This response seemed to placate him. "I haven't dated anyone since I moved here," he said. "I'm a little rusty myself."

"You were doing a pretty good job."

"You've got a leaf in your hair," Nathan replied, reaching around to pluck the leaf from its resting spot.

"That must have happened when your gigantic dog wrestled me to the ground."

"Sasha only tackles people she really, really likes."

"Is that so?" Brydie asked, trying not to grin.

"I like your hair, by the way. I almost didn't recognize you."

"Thanks," Brydie replied.

"So," Nathan said, letting the leaf in his hand fall to the ground. "Do you want to try it again?"

Brydie hesitated. She did want to try again. That was all she wanted, but she was afraid she would mess it up again. "I don't know."

"Let's just start off slow," Nathan replied. "Let's meet up for coffee in the dog park tomorrow afternoon. I'll buy."

"I'll buy," Brydie said. "I owe you one."

Nathan grinned. "Okay, how about four o'clock?"

"Teddy and I will be there."

Nathan waved to her as he went back into his house, and Brydie got into her car, finally releasing the smile she'd been holding. She looked into the rearview mirror at herself, at her new hair. Maybe it was silly, but for the first time in a long time, she thought maybe she really could see the beginnings of a whole new person.

CHAPTER 21

S O YOU'RE TELLING ME THAT YOU BASICALLY
started a fight and then ran out of his house in
the middle of a make-out session, and he still wants
to see you again?" Elliott asked the next morning,
resting her water bottle on her protruding stomach.
"Look! No hands!"

"That's what I'm telling you." Brydie licked chocolate off the tip of her thumb and placed two chocolate
bars in the center of the dough in front of her. "I
can't believe he even wanted to talk to me, let alone
see me again."

"He's a keeper," Elliott replied. She eyed the pastry Brydie was perfecting. "Please tell me you're making enough of whatever that is to give some to me."

"It's a chocolate croissant braid," Brydie said. "I
thought it would go well with the coffee I'm taking
to the dog park."

"I'm so glad you're baking again," Elliott said.
"Everyone in my house is glad you're baking again."

Brydie looked over at Mia, who was sitting in

front of the television next to Teddy. "I'll send one home with you."

"She talks about Teddy all the time," Elliott said, nodding her head toward Mia. She wants a dog of her own."

"So get her one," Brydie replied.

"Do you have a fever?" Elliott asked. "Aren't you the same person who called that pug over there an 'it' for the first two weeks you lived here?"

Brydie shrugged. "Things change."

"Obviously."

"I don't know," Brydie said. "He just makes me feel less alone."

"I read a study once that said having a pet can reduce depression," Elliott replied. "Do you think that's true?"

Brydie thought about it. A doctor she'd seen just after the divorce suggested she get Prozac and a cat. At the time, it brought images to her mind of the crazy cat lady who lived down the street from her as a child. Brydie's mother had hated the house. She said the whole neighborhood smelled like cats because of the woman who lived there, an aging German woman named Uta. When Uta died, the Humane Society had to come in and take the cats. Brydie begged her mother for one, but Ruth Benson said she would rather take Uta's place in the grave than clean a litter box.

Uta had been old, yes, and maybe her house did smell a little bit like kitty litter. However, she always had the best candy at Halloween, and Uta had always been kind to Brydie. She thought maybe if her mother let her adopt a cat, everybody in her house might be a bit happier.

"I think that it's probably true," Brydie said finally. "Nathan said he's training Sasha to be a therapy dog at the nursing home. I'm sure part of that therapy is to help with feelings of depression while living there."

"You mean the huge dog that escaped from him and tackled you?" Elliott asked, a smirk appearing on her face. "Seems legit."

"She didn't escape from him," Brydie corrected her. "She escaped from her dog sitter or something."

"Or something?"

"I don't know who the woman was."

"Woman?"

Brydie sighed. She loved her friend, but she didn't know when to stop asking questions. "I assume she was the dog sitter," she said. "I made some crack about how Nathan could go back inside to his girlfriend, and he said she wasn't his girlfriend."

"But he didn't explain it any further?"

"I didn't ask him to."

"And he didn't offer?"

Brydie turned around to face her friend. "I thought you said he was a keeper?"

"I'm sure he is," Elliott replied. "I'm just looking out for you. You're fragile right now."

"I'm fragile?" Brydie set the timer on the oven. "I'm not the one two months away from giving birth."

Elliott looked down at her stomach. "I'm a force to be reckoned with right now," she said. "Nobody wants to piss a pregnant lady off."

Brydie laughed. "That's probably true."

"Well, as long as he's not an ax murderer with a closet full of ex-wives, I'm sure I'll like him very much," Elliott said.

"Speaking of ex-wives," Brydie said, shutting the oven, "I have something I want to show you."

"Ooh, what is it?"

"Remember when I told you I found a photo album down in the basement?"

"Was that before or after Teddy ate an entire family of granddaddy longlegs?" Elliott asked.

"Before." Brydie led Elliott to the basement door. "Remember I told you that the album is missing a bunch of pictures?"

"Yeah," Elliott replied. "But that's not so strange, is it? People take pictures out of albums all the time. Remember how in seventh grade I got pissed at Samantha Siebert for stealing my boyfriend? I cut her face out of every single picture I had of her."

Brydie grinned. "I remember."

"What was his name?" Elliott mused. "Mason? Mark?"

"Maxwell!" they said in unison before dissolving into a fit of giggles.

"Oh, Maxwell," Elliott said once she'd recovered. "I still haven't forgiven Samantha."

"You were thirteen," Brydie reminded her friend. "The pictures in Mrs. Neumann's album are just *gone*. It's like something happened in the middle of the album, and it changed everything. She looks so happy in the pictures at the beginning, at her wedding. Then there's these blank spaces where pictures ought to be, and when the pictures begin again, she looks miserable. She's not smiling in a single picture."

"I still think you're making more out of it than you need to."

Brydie unlocked the basement door and a gust of

stale air hit them both in the face. "I found something else down there, too."

"I'm not going down there," Elliott said, bumping her belly on the door frame. "No way."

"Why not?" Brydie asked. "We can shut the door so Mia doesn't come down."

"She knows how to open a door, genius," Elliott replied. "But it's not that. She's so absorbed in *Bubble Guppies,* she won't even notice. I'm not going down there because it looks less like *Bubble Guppies* and more like *American Horror Story* down there."

Brydie rolled her eyes. "Come on, you'll be fine."

"Fine, but if my baby ends up possessed by an angry spirit, I'm sending it after you."

When they got to the bottom of the steps, Brydie led Elliott over to the trunk in the corner. "See that chair by the trunk?" she asked. "It was sitting there just like that with the photo album lying open on top of it."

"Creepy."

"It's like Mrs. Neumann would just come down here and sit," Brydie said. "Sit down in the chair and look at the pictures."

"And stare at the trunk," Elliott said.

"And stare at the trunk," Brydie agreed.

"What's in the trunk?" Elliott asked.

Brydie shrugged. "I don't know. It's locked."

"You brought me down here to stare at a locked trunk?"

"Did you get any other keys when you got the keys to this house?" Brydie asked.

Elliott screwed up her nose as she thought, and then said, "I don't think so. It would make more sense that the keys are in the house somewhere."

"I can't find them anywhere."

"Well, maybe she doesn't want you to find them," Elliott replied pointedly. "We shouldn't even be down here. This isn't your house."

Brydie knew that Elliott was right, but the words still stung. She forgot sometimes that nothing about her life at the moment was permanent. She really had no idea how long she would be here in Germantown. She didn't know how much longer she would be caring for Teddy, and that thought gave her an unexpected lump in her throat. "Let's go back upstairs," she said, turning away from the trunk. "I need to check on the croissant braid."

"What's wrong?"

"Nothing."

"Are you sure?"

Brydie nodded. "Yeah, I just don't want to burn the croissant."

"Okay. Well, I've been meaning to ask you, have you thought about your plans for Thanksgiving yet?" Elliott asked, following her. "Are you going home?"

"I doubt it," Brydie replied, relieved that Elliott wasn't asking any more questions about Mrs. Neumann. "I'll have to work that night."

"My mom and dad are going to Florida to see my brother and his wife," Elliott said. "We'd go, but I don't want to travel that far so close to my due date. I was thinking maybe we could get together and have dinner. Me, you, Leo, and Mia . . . and maybe that doctor of yours."

"Let's not get ahead of ourselves," Brydie said. "Five minutes ago you were grilling me about his possible girlfriend."

"Well, just you then."

"Is this your way of asking me if I'll make you a pumpkin pie?"

Elliott rolled her eyes. "It's not always about your pie."

"It's not?"

"Okay," Elliott said. "It's about your pie. But I'll bake the turkey!"

BRYDIE STOOD AT the entrance to the dog park, one hand wrapped around Teddy's leash and one hand holding a thermos of coffee and a ShopCo bag filled with an old tablecloth she'd found in the hallway closet and the pastry she'd baked.

Nathan waved her over to where he was standing with Sasha. "This looks like a little more than coffee," he said, bending down and unhooking Teddy's leash. "What's in the bag?"

Brydie set the thermos down on the ground and handed Nathan the pastry. "You can't have coffee without something to eat."

"Oh, really?" Nathan asked, a small smile appearing on his face.

"Everything goes better with something to eat."

"I guess you're probably right."

Brydie spread the blanket down on the ground. "I love to eat almost as much as I love to bake."

"I don't think I've ever dated a girl who felt that way," Nathan replied, sitting down.

"Are we dating?" Brydie teased. "I thought this was just coffee."

"But you brought food."

"I guess I can't argue with that," she replied.

Brydie had been nervous when she first got there, afraid that maybe their conversation would be awkward after what happened the last time. But Nathan's smile was so easy, and his eyes were so kind. She felt her heart skip a beat when she looked at him, and she had to admit that it made her feel a bit foolish.

"So, did you always know you wanted to be a cook?" Nathan asked. "Or, what is it that you said? A pastry chef?"

"I think I figured it out when I was in high school," Brydie replied. "I like cooking in general, but desserts have always been my favorite."

"My mom is a great cook," Nathan said. "I have two older sisters, and they're also fantastic cooks. My dad cooks, too, but I don't think I'd ever even boiled water until I went to college."

"My mom is a Realtor, and she works a lot," Brydie continued. "My dad mostly stayed home when I was little, and even though he went back to work part-time, he cooked all the meals. Then, when I was sixteen, he suffered a back injury and for a while, he couldn't cook or do much of anything. My mom didn't have time, so that left me. Instead of feeling like it was a burden, I ended up really enjoying it."

"I'm sorry about your dad," Nathan said. "Back injuries can be one of the worst kinds of injuries for a person to bear."

"It was hard on him," Brydie agreed. "He tried surgery and therapy, but nothing really ever worked."

"We're coming up with new treatments all the time," Nathan replied. "There's always hope. I can refer him to some specialists up here if you think he might be receptive to that."

Brydie looked away from Nathan and down into her lap. "Thanks," she said. "But he died three years ago."

"I'm so sorry."

"It was a brain aneurism," she said. "He was fine when my mom left for work, but by the time she got home that night, he was already gone."

Nathan reached over and took Brydie's hand in his. He held it for a minute, not saying a word. It was a surprising act of intimacy that Brydie hadn't expected, but it was one that she was grateful for. She didn't know why she felt compelled to tell him these things. It was like the night they'd had dinner, all over again. She could have told him about her love for cooking without mentioning that her father had been hurt. She could have merely said *thank you* when he offered to help, without telling him that her father was dead. But for some reason, a reason she'd yet to figure out, she couldn't keep quiet around him. She couldn't *not* tell him what she was thinking, and it was an altogether new experience for her. All she knew was that he made her feel better about . . . everything.

After a few minutes, Brydie saw Fred and Arlow scampering over to them, followed by the woman and Great Dane she'd seen her first day in the park.

"How're you young'uns today?" Fred asked. "Looks like yer havin' quite a picnic."

"We were just about to have some chocolate croissant," Brydie replied. "Would you like some?"

"Oh, no, thank ya," Fred said. "I've got the diabetes. Can't be havin' none of that. But Dr. Reid here gave me some of those treats you made for Sasha. My Arlow loved 'em, and so did MaryAnn's Thor over there."

Brydie looked past Fred to the woman and dog standing behind him. "I'm so glad to hear that," she said.

"We'd both like to place an order fer more, if yer willin' to make us some."

"Really?"

MaryAnn stepped out from behind Fred and said, "You made those treats? Thor loved them. Ate them right up."

"I did," Brydie replied, nodding.

"And the ingredients are all natural?"

"They are."

MaryAnn shifted Thor's leash from one hand to another. "Could you make a treat that's grain-free? I like to try to keep Thor on a grain-free diet. It's best for his skin."

"I'm sure that I could," Brydie replied. "In fact, I think I have a recipe for a grain-free treat that I've been meaning to try."

"Great," MaryAnn replied. Drool from Thor's massive tongue dripped down and splashed onto her shoes. "I'll take five dozen."

"Oh, um, okay," Brydie replied. "When would you need them?"

"Could you have them ready by Sunday?" Mary-Ann asked. "I'd like to have them for Thor's third birthday party. If they're a hit, I'm sure some of my Dane friends will want to order some as well. Do you have a card?"

Brydie stood up and dusted herself off. "I don't have a card," she said. "But let me give you my number."

"Just give me a couple dozen of them peanut butter banana treats," Fred said. "Ain't no rush on 'em."

Teddy wandered up to Brydie and nudged her leg. She reached down to pet him, while she used her other hand to log the numbers of Fred and MaryAnn into her phone. "I'll get started on these ASAP and give you both a call once they're ready to go."

Brydie watched MaryAnn and Thor walk off, followed by Fred, who mumbled something about being sorry to have interrupted them. Sasha and Teddy ambled off after the other two dogs, Teddy jumping up every so often to try to sniff Thor's back end, the big dog merely swatting his tail at the pug.

"I hope it was okay that I gave some of those treats to Fred," Nathan said once everyone had gone. "Sasha loved them so much, and then so did Arlow. Now I guess Thor does, too."

"Are you kidding?" Brydie asked. "It's fantastic!" She sat back down, feeling a little dazed. She couldn't believe that she'd just gotten two orders for *dog treats*. "But a dog birthday party? Do people really have those?"

Nathan laughed. "MaryAnn does. Sasha and I were invited last year. It was an interesting experience.

"Have you thought about trying to sell your treats at pet stores?" Nathan asked. "It seems like there's a market."

"I've never thought about selling my treats anywhere," Brydie replied. "But I don't think I need to worry about it just yet. I've just gotten my first two orders."

"Thanks to me," Nathan said, giving her a mischievous grin.

"Thanks to you."

Nathan took apart a piece of croissant and popped it into his mouth. After a moment of thoughtful chewing, he said, "So, I have this friend whose husband owns a restaurant. It's in downtown Memphis, close to Beale Street. The chef is absolutely amazing."

"Oh yeah?"

"Yeah, and I think you'd really like the food."

Brydie tried to hide a grin by eating a piece of the croissant. "Are you asking me out on an actual date?"

"I'd like to take you there, if you want to go," Nathan replied. "Next Friday night?"

"I think I have that night open."

"Great," Nathan said. "Do you want to bring Teddy over that night? My dog sitter can watch him and Sasha together."

"Is that the same woman who lost Sasha the other day?"

"I promise she won't lose Teddy."

Brydie wasn't so sure that was true, but she was too excited to think much about it right then. It had been the perfect day, and now she had actual orders for something she'd created. It had been so long since she'd had that feeling. She enjoyed making cakes and everything else at ShopCo, but the customers didn't come because *she* was baking them. It was the first time in a long time that she felt excited to bake, and it was a feeling she was going to hold on to for as long as she possibly could.

CHAPTER 22

B Y THE DAY OF THOR'S PARTY, IT LOOKED LIKE the Pillsbury Doughboy had exploded all over Brydie's kitchen. Actually, it looked a little like she'd slaughtered him and his whole family. Every single utensil was dirty, and remnants of Brydie's test runs of treats were strewn about the table and the countertops. She'd been through five different grain-free recipes before she found something Teddy would even sniff, let alone eat. In the end, it was the pumpkin treats that won out.

She'd found a cookie cutter in the shape of a paw at ShopCo the night before, and after baking the regular batch for Fred, all she had left to do was package them up in the red cellophane bags she'd found. Brydie looked around the kitchen, feeling exhausted, but satisfied. It would take her at least an hour to get herself cleaned up and package the cookies, which didn't leave her much time to get ready for work and deliver them, if she didn't get lost on the way to Fred's and to MaryAnn's. Cleaning the kitchen, she realized, would have to wait.

Teddy looked up at her and licked his lips.

"Is this what you want?" she asked him, holding out the can of pureed pumpkin that was left over from the treats. "Well, come on."

Brydie bent down over Teddy's bowl. Up until she began living with Teddy, she hadn't known that dogs could eat anything other than regular dog food. She hadn't known what human foods were good and which were bad, and she certainly hadn't known that there was a community of dog lovers big enough to bake treats for. Now she was spooning pumpkin out into a dog dish.

She put the empty can into the trash and headed back into the bedroom to get dressed. She pulled her khaki pants and blue ShopCo shirt out of the closet, her gaze moving across the box of photo albums up on the shelf. Brydie knew she should probably take the box back to the basement, but she hadn't been able to bring herself to do it, especially after not even being able to see the older woman once she and Teddy got to the nursing home. It had taken more treats than Brydie was willing to admit in order to get Teddy back up to his old self. Well, that and letting him sleep right next to her on her pillow.

Brydie laid her clothes out on the bed and then turned on the shower in the bathroom. As she let the water rush over her and she began to relax, it occurred to her that when she'd packed up and left the house she and Allan had shared; she hadn't taken much of anything—no pictures or keepsakes. Why would she? Their marriage had been over.

She wondered what Allan had done with everything. Had he thrown everything away? Had he left everything in the house after it sold? Surely he wouldn't have taken it with him. Brydie couldn't imagine Cassandra, *his soon-to-be wife*, wanting any reminders of the woman who'd come before her—the woman he'd been married to for more than a decade. Maybe there were people in her old house right now wondering what to do with the memories she and Allan had collected. Things like the wedding topper from their cake, and photo albums with pictures not unlike the ones she'd found in Mrs. Neumann's basement. She couldn't think of a single picture where she and Allan weren't smiling, happy. All of the vacations and holidays and monumental moments in their lives had been photographed and saved for posterity; for a day, she'd always thought, that she'd be able to show their children and grandchildren.

Now she didn't even know where those pictures were.

But those pictures, she knew, told only half of the story. There were other memories, not so happy memories, which were not in any kind of album. Brydie knew that the same thing was true for the younger version of Mrs. Neumann and the man she was with. There was a reason nobody took pictures of *those* memories.

Brydie turned off the shower and reached for her towel, only to realize that it was no longer hanging on the towel rack. She looked down to see Teddy nestled into it, snoring away. "I need my towel," she whispered to him.

ALTHOUGH IT HAD been easy to find Fred's house, just a few doors down from hers, Brydie had a harder time with MaryAnn's. It was clear on the other side of Germantown, the newer side, and Brydie got lost so many times she thought she was going to have to call Elliott to rescue her.

"Brydie!" MaryAnn said, opening the huge, oak door to her house. "I was afraid I might miss you. It's almost time for my meeting."

"I'm sorry," Brydie replied, struggling with the box containing all of the wrapped treats. "I guess I don't know the area as well as I thought I did."

"It's a new development," MaryAnn replied, waving her hands in a wide circle. "Nobody knows where I live.

"Come on in," MaryAnn added. She led Brydie down a long, marble hallway.

Everything in the house smelled new, and Brydie had to hold her breath to keep from gagging on the new-paint smell. At the end of the hallway was a huge room with a fireplace, and above the fireplace was an even larger portrait of MaryAnn and Thor. It took up half of the wall space, and everything from the floor to the ceiling was decorated with balloons and banners and streamers. The custom-made "Happy Birthday, Thor" banner was hanging across the painting.

"Fantastic, isn't it?" MaryAnn asked, nodding toward the painting. "Just got it hung up last week. It cost a fortune, but Thor looks perfect."

"It's impressive," Brydie replied. "Where would you like me to set these?"

"Oh, over here," MaryAnn said. "Right here on the coffee table."

"I put each dozen in a cellophane bag," Brydie said. "If you place another order, I can do boxes next time if you'd rather."

"Mind if I take a peek?"

"Of course."

MaryAnn plucked one of the bags out of the box and opened it up. She took one of the cookies out, sniffed it, and then, to Brydie's astonishment, popped the entire thing into her mouth, chewing thoughtfully for a moment before shrieking, "Thor! Where are you, my babykins?"

Thor came crashing into the room, his tail thwacking against everything he passed by, knocking two framed pictures of himself off shelves in the process.

MaryAnn leaned down and gave Thor one of the treats. His tongue covered the length of her hand, and she made no effort to wipe the slobber off it after Thor had taken the treat. After feeding him a few more treats, MaryAnn grabbed the wallet that was also sitting on the coffee table and said to Brydie, "Mother tested, Thor approved. How much do I owe you?"

Brydie handed her the bill. It was a habit she'd gotten into when she delivered cakes for weddings and other events. People liked to see a broken-down list with a total at the bottom. It helped them understand what exactly they were paying for before they got the bright idea that it was *just some flour and eggs* and they could do it themselves. "Here you go," she said.

"Lovely," MaryAnn replied. "You know," she said, "why don't you and Teddy come to the party today?"

"Oh, we'd love to," Brydie replied. "But today is the day we visit Mrs. Neumann."

"Bring her!" MaryAnn exclaimed, ripping a check out of her bedazzled checkbook. "She came last year and the year before that. I can't believe I didn't think to invite you earlier. I'm so sorry, my dear."

"Oh, it's okay," Brydie replied. "I'll ask when we get to the retirement village. What time does it start?"

"One o'clock," MaryAnn said. "Presents are optional, but of course appreciated."

THERE WAS A nurse in Pauline's room when Brydie got there. They were chitchatting about the nurse's son who was graduating from high school in the spring and had been accepted to Stanford University. Brydie stood in the doorway holding Teddy for a few minutes and listened to them.

"He must be a very smart young man," Pauline was saying, "to be accepted to such a prestigious school."

"He's very smart," the nurse replied. "But now his father and I are going to have to figure out how we're going to pay the bill. I told my son he'd better get some scholarships!"

"My second husband was accepted to Yale," Pauline replied. "In the end, he couldn't go. It was too far away, and he needed to stay home and help his family."

"That's so sad," the nurse said. "I guess back then, it happened quite a lot."

"It still happens quite a lot," Pauline said. "Bill always said that if we had a child, he would want them to go away to college . . . have the experience he didn't."

The nurse removed the blood pressure cuff from

Pauline's arm and said, "Do you ever think about where—"

"No." Pauline cut the nurse off before she could finish. "It does no good to dwell on those things."

"I'm sorry," the nurse replied. "Sometimes I don't think before I speak."

Pauline patted her hand. "It's okay, sugar. Don't think a thing of it."

Brydie crept closer, hoping to hear more of the conversation. But when she did, Teddy wiggled free from her grasp and hit the floor with a thunk.

"What on earth?" The nurse looked up just as Teddy came flying into the room, full of snorts and wiggles.

"Teddy!" Pauline said, delighted. "Brydie, how long have you two been standing there?"

"We just got here," Brydie replied, relieved that Teddy seemed to be fine after plummeting to the tiled floor. "How are you today?"

"I feel good today," Pauline replied. "My blood pressure is good?"

"As always," the nurse said, giving the older woman a smile.

"You're early today," Pauline said, nodding her head over at Brydie. "Aren't you?"

"A bit," Brydie replied. "I had to take some treats over to MaryAnn's house for Thor's birthday party. She invited me . . . well, us . . . to his party this afternoon."

"Oh, those parties are a hoot," Pauline said. "Last year Thor and another dog ate MaryAnn's brand-new chaise longue. She threw a huge fit and told the other dog's owner that he owed her three thousand dollars—until she found a big strip of fabric in Thor's mouth!"

"I figure Teddy will sleep through most of it," Brydie replied.

"He usually does."

"So," Brydie said. "Do you want to, I mean, *can you* go?"

"Oh, I don't think that's a good idea," the nurse said, cutting in. "We usually like for day trips to be approved at least a week in advance, and we really like for a doctor to sign off."

Brydie felt a pang of disappointment. "Oh, okay."

"But it is a beautiful day," the nurse continued. "Why don't we get a wheelchair and you can take Mrs. Neumann outside?"

"Okay," Brydie replied, smiling at Pauline. "How does that sound?"

"Oh, fine," Pauline said. "Will I need a coat?"

"Maybe a light jacket," the nurse said. "Why doesn't your friend get your jacket, and I'll send for the chair?"

Brydie did as she was told and opened Pauline's closet. "Which jacket would you like?"

"The gold one," Pauline replied. "With little red mulberries on it. It's festive, don't you think?"

"Very."

Pauline stood shakily, bracing herself against the railing of her bed. "Oh, I'm so stiff."

Brydie took the wheelchair from the nurse and rolled it over to Pauline. "I didn't know you could walk."

"I can get up and down," Pauline replied. "I can shuffle enough to get from my bed to the chair by the window or to the bathroom. But my legs just won't do much more than that."

"My grandmother had legs that worked perfectly," Brydie said. "But there was something wrong with her brain. It wouldn't tell her legs to move."

"I talk to my legs all the time," Pauline said, easing herself down into the wheelchair. "But they never listen."

Brydie pushed the wheelchair out of the room and down the hallway. "It really is a pretty day," she said. "I think you'll enjoy being outside."

"I wish we could have gone to the party," Pauline replied. "It seems like it's been an age since I've seen anyone I know."

"I wish you could, too," Brydie said.

"Sometimes I feel like a prisoner here," Pauline said. "It's a lovely place, but I don't enjoy being told when to eat and when to go to the bathroom and when to sleep. It's hard getting old, Brydie."

Brydie was glad she couldn't see Pauline's face. She sounded like she might cry, and it seemed like such a small thing—leaving for a couple of hours to travel two or three miles for a party.

When they reached the front desk, the receptionist looked up at them and smiled. "Headed out to the courtyard, are we?"

Brydie began to nod her head and say yes when she changed her mind. "No," she said. "Uh, I'm actually taking Mrs. Neumann out for the afternoon."

"You are?"

"Yes, to a friend's house for a birthday party. We won't be gone more than a couple of hours."

The receptionist, a slight woman with frizzy red hair whom Brydie had never seen, pushed around a stack of papers in front of her. "I don't have that approved request anywhere in my paperwork."

"Well, it should be there," Brydie said, feeling a twinge of guilt. It was an outright lie. And she could get caught. She glanced down at Pauline, who gave her a sly wink, and Brydie was emboldened. "We're running a bit late, actually, if you don't mind."

"I, uh . . ." the receptionist said, still going through her papers. "I really better check with someone."

"She's not allowed to leave the grounds without the paperwork?" Brydie asked.

The receptionist looked up. "It's just that they like to have the request," she said. "It's procedure more than anything else."

"We're just going a few blocks away," Brydie pressed. "We aren't even leaving Germantown."

"It's just that I can't find the paperwork."

"You cannot keep me here," Pauline said, indignant. "I can check out anytime I'd like. I read the agreement."

"It's just they like to have the paperwork," the receptionist replied, her cheeks turning pink. "I'm sure it's in here somewhere."

"Well, if you're so sure, then we'll be on our way," Pauline said.

The receptionist looked helplessly from Brydie to Pauline, and then gave them a thin, tight-lipped smile. "I'll find it. You go on ahead."

CHAPTER 23

BRYDIE WAS SURPRISED AT THE NUMBER OF CARS already in front of MaryAnn's house when she and Pauline arrived. She was still feeling guilty about lying to the receptionist, but Pauline's excitement over the party was contagious, and she pushed those pesky thoughts out of her head.

"Last year there was a canine hypnotist," Pauline said as Brydie helped her into her wheelchair. "I let her try it out on Teddy, but I think it just made his gas worse!"

"There are hypnotists for dogs?" Brydie wondered aloud. "That seems . . ."

"Weird?"

"A little."

"MaryAnn wrote the book on weird."

"Would you like me to put Teddy in your lap?" Brydie asked.

"Yes, please," Pauline replied. "He likes to ride on my lap, I think."

As Brydie pushed Pauline and Teddy up the walkway, she thought about how the three of them must look—an old woman and an old pug in a wheelchair being pushed by someone who looked wildly out of place in this upscale Germantown neighborhood, with her sneakers and worn-out cardigan. They were a ragtag group for sure, and Brydie figured that they probably had at least one chapter in that book Mary-Ann must have written.

"Pauline!" MaryAnn exclaimed when she opened the door. She was wearing a sweater with Thor's face stitched onto it. "I can't believe you actually made it!"

"I wouldn't miss it for the world," Pauline replied. "Your sweater is very festive."

"Isn't it?" MaryAnn looked down at herself. "I had a designer friend in Italy make it especially for today. It cost a fortune."

Brydie silently wondered just how many items of MaryAnn's *cost a fortune.* What she said out loud was, "Thank you so much for inviting us."

"Nonsense," MaryAnn said. "I can't wait to introduce you to everyone. The dogs are loving the treats you made!"

"I'm thrilled," Brydie replied, allowing MaryAnn to take over pushing Pauline.

MaryAnn led them into the living room, where at least a dozen people and dogs were milling about, including Fred and Arlow. Some of the people Brydie recognized from the dog park as well. Some of them, like a short, bald man in a butter-colored leather jacket, she'd never seen before. He had an empty martini glass in one hand and a tiny Yorkie in the other.

"Brydie and Pauline, I want you to meet Lloyd Jefferson," MaryAnn said, motioning to the man.

"He plays trumpet for the Memphis Symphony Orchestra, and this is his dog, Alice."

"It's nice to meet you," Brydie said, extending her hand.

Lloyd looked at her as if she'd presented him with a Venus flytrap. "Hello."

"Lloyd, Brydie is the one who made those treats your little Alice has been scarfing down for the last half an hour," MaryAnn said, winking at Brydie. "Remember, you said you wanted to meet her?"

"Oh, yes," Lloyd said, his eyes brightening. "Alice is very picky, you know. I've never been able to get her to eat a regular dog treat."

"So is Teddy," Pauline spoke up, patting the top of Teddy's head. "But he likes Brydie's treats."

"Do you have a shop somewhere?" Lloyd asked.

"No," Brydie said. "I don't."

"A card or a website, maybe?"

"No," Brydie said. Lloyd was looking at her disapprovingly again, and so she continued, "This is a new venture for me. I've been a baker for the last fifteen years, but I've only started baking dog treats in the last few weeks."

Lloyd handed her his empty martini glass and pulled out a gold money clip from his pocket. "Here's my card," he said. "Alice has a birthday in March. Let's talk."

"Thank you," Brydie said.

In Pauline's lap, Teddy began to whine and wiggle, and he jumped down just in time for Sasha to tear into the living room and jump on top of him, bathing him with her tongue.

"Oh my God," Lloyd said, taking a step back from the two dogs. As he moved, Alice wiggled out of his grasp and leapt to the ground, joining in on the chaos that ensued. "Alice! No!" He looked helplessly at Brydie, Pauline, and MaryAnn. "She has soft bones!"

Brydie resisted the urge to laugh, instead bending down to pick up Teddy. "Grab her now," she said. "While you still have a chance."

Lloyd bent down to do as he was told, but Alice gave chase, and he stumbled off after her, calling her name and lamenting about her bones.

"He's a bit high-strung," MaryAnn said. "But he's an amazing trumpeter."

Brydie looked all around the room for Nathan. Surely if Sasha were here, Nathan would be, too. "Have you seen Dr. Reid?" she asked Pauline. "Sasha can't be here alone."

"I sent him and that darling dog sitter, Myriah, of his outside to set up the games for the dogs," MaryAnn cut in. "They got here just before you did. I guess Sasha was ready to come back inside."

"Myriah?" Pauline asked. "Dog sitter?"

"She is an absolute doll. Just a doll," MaryAnn continued. "I've told Nathan a hundred times that he needs to make her more than just his dog sitter. I don't see the big deal with the age difference."

Pauline's eyes snapped up to Brydie. For some reason, she couldn't bring herself to look down at her. It wasn't as if she was going to explain her relationship with Nathan to Pauline in front of MaryAnn. Besides, she reminded herself, it wasn't like they were in a relationship. They were just . . . well, she didn't know quite what they were doing, but if MaryAnn wanted to talk about how wonderful and perfect Myriah was, then that was *fine. It was just fine.*

"Ah, there they are," MaryAnn said. "Did you get it all set up?"

"We did," Myriah replied. "Although I don't think that the dogs are going to be able to play pin the tail on the golden retriever."

"Mrs. Neumann?" Nathan was looking down at Pauline, his brow furrowed. "What are you doing here?"

"I was invited," Pauline replied. "Same as you, Dr. Reid."

Nathan looked to Brydie. "Did you bring her here with you?"

"I did," Brydie replied, suddenly realizing that Nathan being at the party could be a problem. "We just got here."

"I didn't know they'd released you to come."

"Well, how could you know?" Pauline replied, slight annoyance in her voice. "You've been gone, and now Dr. Sower is in charge."

"And she signed off on the paperwork for you to come here today?"

"They seem to have misplaced it."

Nathan turned his attention to Brydie. "Could we maybe talk for a minute?" he asked.

"Okay."

He led her away from the crowd, while Pauline continued to chat with Myriah and MaryAnn. "Did you really get permission for Mrs. Neumann to be here today?" he asked when they were out of earshot of everyone. "I can't imagine that anyone there, especially Dr. Sower, would give her a release."

"Why not?" Brydie asked.

"She has congestive heart failure," Nathan replied. "She had a stroke mere months ago, and she doesn't have full motor control, in case you haven't noticed."

"She's done pretty well today."

"Today," Nathan said, "is a good day. Yesterday, she was on oxygen for most of the day. She had chest pains." He took a step closer to her. "She's not well, Brydie, and it was incredibly irresponsible of you to bring her out here today."

"I didn't know that," Brydie said, feeling her chest tighten. "I just wanted to give her a good day. She was so upset when I mentioned it and the nurse said it wasn't a great idea, and I just thought . . . I just thought she might enjoy herself for a little while."

"Of course you didn't know," he replied. "She doesn't want you to know. She doesn't want anybody to know, and I can't say that I blame her."

"I can take her back right now," Brydie replied.

"No," Nathan said, his tone softening. "Let her stay. She seems to be having a good time."

"I think she is."

"I'll call Dr. Sower myself when I get home," Nathan said. "I'll tell her that it's my fault about the paperwork, because I know just as well as you do that it was never filed."

"Thank you."

"But don't do it again," he continued. "They could take away your visiting privileges, and that would devastate Mrs. Neumann."

"It really did seem like a good idea at the time," Brydie said.

"As a doctor, I have to say it was a terrible idea," Nathan replied. "As a person who hopes to have dinner with you on Friday, I have to admit that I think it was a rather kind thing you did."

Brydie grinned and looked back over at Pauline. MaryAnn had settled her onto the couch, and she was busy talking to a woman around her age with two miniature dachshunds on her lap. They were wearing matching sweaters. "I think she's really enjoying herself."

"I'm sure she misses it," Nathan said. "Living at home and being able to see her friends and go out. It's one of the hardest parts of assisted living, especially when they live like she does, without a lot of visitors."

"Are you coming back to the party anytime soon?" Myriah asked Nathan, cutting into their conversation. She curled her fingers around one of his biceps.

Brydie narrowed her eyes at the other woman. Myriah wasn't Cassandra and Nathan wasn't Allan, but it didn't matter. Memories back to that time in her not-so-distant past were still right there, waiting to be used against people she barely knew. She wondered if Nathan was interested in Myriah just a little more than he let on. Why wouldn't he like her? She was sleek and put together. She, at least, looked like she belonged here, with her French-manicured nails and shiny hair, and the yoga pants Brydie was sure were from Lululemon and not from the bargain bin at Target.

"So we're still on for Friday?" Brydie asked, unable to keep from saying it in front of Myriah.

Nathan nodded. "Yep. Myriah has already agreed to dog-sit while we're out."

Brydie smiled at Myriah, trying to be as genuine as possible. "Sounds great."

Myriah unfurled her fingers from Nathan's arm

and smiled back. "Of course. I have a test to study for anyway. I always study better at Nathan's."

Before Brydie could respond, MaryAnn stood up and announced, "It's such a gorgeous day outside! Let's go out and let the dog games commence! The winner of each game will receive a framed eighty-by-ten of Thor as a prize!"

"We'd better get outside," Nathan said, grinning at both women. "I wouldn't want to miss out on that framed picture."

THREE HOURS LATER, Pauline and Brydie were headed back to the Germantown Retirement Village with not one but two framed pictures of Thor. Brydie had no idea what she was going to do with them, but MaryAnn had kindly suggested she hang them in the living room.

"The party was so much fun," Pauline said. "Even if we did have to take home pictures of Thor."

Brydie grinned. "I'm glad we got to go."

"Me too," Pauline replied. "I do miss going home sometimes. I miss sitting on my couch. I miss watching television without nurses coming in to check my blood pressure. I miss having Teddy there with me all the time."

Brydie wasn't sure what to say. She wished all of those things for Pauline, too, and she wanted to do more to help her. "Is there anything I could bring to you from your house to make it better?"

Pauline was quiet for a moment, thinking it over. After a while, she said, "There are a couple of quilts in the closet in my bedroom. Maybe you could bring them next time?"

"Of course," Brydie replied. "Is there anything else?"

"No," Pauline said. "Not anything you can get to."

"What do you mean?"

"Nothing," Pauline replied, turning her head and looking out the window. "The blankets will do just fine."

"Pauline," Brydie said, reaching over with one hand to touch the old woman. "Why don't you have any pictures up in your house?"

"What?"

"Pictures," Brydie repeated. "There aren't any on the walls. There aren't any sitting around."

"I don't like clutter," Pauline said.

Brydie knew this wasn't true. Pauline's house, while immaculate, wasn't immune to clutter. She had knickknacks everywhere. She took a deep breath and said, "A shelf collapsed in your basement the other night. It woke me up from a dead sleep."

"How do you know it was a shelf?"

"The door to the basement was locked," Brydie said. "But I found the key. I wouldn't have gone down there except for the crash."

"The basement was locked for a reason," Pauline replied. "I don't want anyone down there."

"But there was a mess."

"It could have waited."

"For what?"

Pauline turned and looked at Brydie. Her eyes were wet around the rims, but her mouth was set in a firm, ugly line. "I don't want anybody snooping in my basement," she said. "You had no business going down there."

"I wasn't snooping," Brydie protested. She turned

into the parking lot of the nursing home. "I was try-ing to clean up a mess. It would have stunk up your whole house if I hadn't cleaned it up."

"You had no business going down there," Pauline repeated. "No business."

Brydie sighed. This was getting her nowhere, and now Pauline was upset with her. "I didn't know you didn't want me down there," she said. "I'm sorry."

"Don't go down there again."

Brydie didn't want to promise that she wouldn't go back down there, especially since she had an entire album of photos that she'd brought upstairs—photos that she now knew for sure that Pauline didn't want her to see.

"Did you hear me?" Now Pauline was turned fully in her seat. The lipstick she'd applied on the drive over was now settling in the fine lines around her mouth. "Don't go back down there."

"I won't," Brydie said, despite herself. "I won't, I promise."

CHAPTER 24

I T WAS MONDAY NIGHT, AND BRYDIE WAS RUN-
ning late. She'd gotten caught in traffic and was
already fifteen minutes behind schedule by the time
she pulled into the parking lot at ShopCo.

"I'm so sorry I'm late!" Brydie said, hurrying to
the bakery, her eyes scanning the scene for Joe. "I
ran into traffic."

"Joe just went to the back to look for you," Rosa
replied, her voice sympathetic.

Brydie sighed. "I guess I better go back there and
find him. I need to clock in anyway."

"Good luck!" Rosa called after her. "He's on a
roll tonight!"

Brydie could have kicked herself for thinking she
could sleep an extra fifteen minutes that evening.
Time management had never been her forte, and
now, by the time she got to the back to find Joe, she
was going to be *twenty-five* minutes late.

Joe was standing by the time clock, his big arms

crossed over one another. "Where have you been?" he demanded when he saw her.

"I'm sorry," Brydie huffed. She was out of breath from traipsing all the way from the bakery. "I hit traffic at Midtown."

Joe pulled at the fabric of her T-shirt, moving her over to the side and closer to him. "Listen," he whispered, bending down so that he was eye level with her. "I'm going to yell at you, and I need you to act like you're upset. Got it?"

"What?"

"Do. You. Understand."

Brydie nodded.

"I thought I told you when I hired you that it was unacceptable for you to be late!" he bellowed. "And what, now you've worked here a month and a half and think that you can just show up whenever you fucking feel like it?"

"I'm . . . I'm sorry," Brydie stuttered. She felt her face grow hot as two employees scurried past them. "I hit traffic. It wasn't my fault."

"I don't want to hear your excuses," he said. "You're an adult."

Brydie had to bite back the urge to argue with him. If this was his fake anger, she sure didn't want to be on the other side of any actual anger. Being scolded for burning cookies her first week had been enough for her to last a lifetime. "I'm sorry," she said.

"One more time, and I'll fire your ass. You got me?"

"I got you."

"Good," Joe replied. "Now clock in, and make it quick."

"Okay," Brydie said. She pulled out her time

card from her purse as Joe stalked out of the back room.

Joe was waiting for Brydie when she emerged. He was still scowling, but he no longer appeared angry, real or otherwise. "I'm sorry," he said to her under his breath as they walked. "I just got my ass reamed for not taking my job seriously enough. I needed to do something to show I'm still an asshole."

"You're the most serious person I know," Brydie said. She meant it. She didn't know anybody who took his job as seriously as Joe.

"Thanks," he said. "I normally wouldn't give you such a hard time for being late."

"I really am sorry."

"Don't let it become a habit," Joe replied.

"I won't."

"I like you," he continued. "You work well with Rosa and Lillie. I'll try my best to keep you after the holidays are over."

"You really look after them, don't you?" Brydie asked.

"They're not blood," Joe said. "But they're family all the same."

A FEW HOURS LATER, Brydie watched Lillian working. Her concentration on the cake in front of her was amazing. She never looked up, never got distracted, and never made a mistake. Brydie wasn't sure if she ever saw her take a bathroom break or eat or even sit down. She admired the way Rosa took care of Lillian, not overbearing, but never too far away, ready to refill the icing or move a finished cake to its plastic container.

"How do you know when Lillian is done with a

cake?" Brydie asked Rosa. "She never says anything to you, does she?"

Rosa shook her head. "No, she doesn't have to say anything," she said. "I know when she's done, because when she works, she hums a bit. It's very quiet, and I'm sure you haven't noticed it. But I know that when she stops humming, she's done."

"Does she talk to you at home?" Brydie asked. She didn't want to pry, but she couldn't help herself.

"Sometimes," Rosa replied. "She's certainly more open. She has a personality that most people don't see. She's just . . . my Lillian."

Joe walked past them and over to Lillian, bending over slightly to see her work. "That's the best damn turkey on a cake I've ever seen," he said.

"Language," Rosa scolded, but she was smiling.

Brydie felt like an interloper watching an intimate conversation, and she thought about what Joe said to her about Rosa and Lillian being family. It really did seem like they took care of each other. Brydie felt an unfamiliar pang of longing for something similar.

"Go back and check on those cupcakes," Joe said to Brydie, turning around to face her. "We need to get at least four more dozen finished before the end of the night."

Brydie went into the back to check on the cupcakes. She pulled them out and started on the next batch. She wanted to feel like she belonged here, with the people that she worked with at ShopCo. She wanted to do something nice for them, especially for Joe.

"Hey," she said when she emerged from the back room. "What are you three doing for Thanksgiving?"

"Sleeping," Joe grunted. "ShopCo is closed that day. I'm going to sleep all day long. It's tradition."

"But I'm going to be cooking Thanksgiving dinner at my house. My best friend and her family are coming. I thought maybe you all would like to come, too," Brydie said. "Maybe you could make a new tradition?"

"Lillie and I usually just go to Denny's," Rosa replied. "It's too much trouble to cook a huge dinner for just the two of us."

"You won't have to bring anything," Brydie said. "Just yourselves."

"We'd love to come," Rosa said. "*And* bring something."

"I'm sleeping," Joe repeated. "All day."

"Joe, you cannot be serious," Rosa replied. "It's Thanksgiving."

"And I'm thankful to be asleep. Alone. In my apartment. Not talking to anyone."

"I'd really like it if you'd come," Brydie said.

Joe looked at Rosa and Brydie, the permanent scowl on his face fading ever so slightly. "Fine," he said, throwing his hands up in the air. "But I don't want any of you dragging ass once we open back up because you're too full of turkey to work."

"Language!" Brydie and Rosa said in unison.

CHAPTER 25

B Y MIDWEEK, BRYDIE FELT AS IF SHE'D TRIED EV-
ery single dog treat recipe available on Pinterest.
She spent her mornings and her money perusing
ShopCo for ingredients before coming home to spend
a few hours baking. Some of her ideas she got from
work, trying out dog-friendly versions of the cookies they baked, but most of her ideas came from the
Internet, and she was beginning to understand what
Elliott meant when she talked about a Pinterest fail.
Who had time to create organic virgin coconut oil
dog paws with every single essential daily vitamin
that a dog needed? She hadn't even *known* dogs
needed vitamins until two days ago, and Teddy
was less than thrilled with the glucosamine supple-
ments she'd bought. He'd spit them right back out at
her the first morning, five times, until she wrapped
them in a piece of cheese. Didn't wrapping them in
cheese defeat the whole purpose?

Brydie looked around the kitchen. She'd gotten a
surprise call from the guy named Lloyd she'd met at

Thor's party, who'd gotten her number from Mary-Ann. He wanted a trial run of a few treats before booking her to bake for Alice's party, and Brydie had been forced to reassure him that Sasha and Teddy would be nowhere within licking distance of Alice when she delivered the treats. So far, she'd baked cinnamon apple treats, sweet potato treats, and a zucchini vegetarian treat that was supposed to be hypoallergenic, whatever that meant, since Lloyd had reminded her that Alice had a very delicate digestive system. She'd also created a strawberry and banana smoothie dog bone that had to be kept frozen.

She was proud of herself, she had to admit. Sure, the kale and apple treats hadn't turned out the way she'd planned, and neither had the chicken meatball treats, but the trial and error was fun.

CHAPTER 26

IT WAS FRIDAY NIGHT, AND BRYDIE WAS NERVOUS. She didn't know what to wear, she didn't know where they were going, and right that second, she didn't know if she wanted to get dressed or crawl back into bed for the next fifteen years.

She wanted to call Elliott and ask her to come over, but Elliott was at a dinner with some of Leo's clients.

Brydie was on her own.

Staring at her closet, she had no idea what to wear. Hanging out at Nathan's house or at the dog park was one thing. Going out for an actual dinner at a restaurant was another. Picking out clothes had never been her strong point. She'd wear jeans and a baggy T-shirt every day if she thought she could get away with it. She'd tried to be a fashionista like her mother or Elliott, but creating outfits just wasn't something that clicked with her brain. She was much more like her father in that way, in every way, really, and she found herself missing him.

He couldn't have given her fashion advice, but he would have said something hilarious and insightful to put her at ease. That was what she missed the most—just talking to him.

Brydie thought about the tender way Nathan had held her hand at the park, and she felt her heart skip a beat. Talking to him had become something she looked forward to almost as much as seeing him. Tonight, however, she didn't want to spend all of her time regaling him with stories about her past. Tonight, she wanted everything to be about the present.

She pulled out a red strappy dress from the closet. It was something her mother had bought her just after her divorce, when Ruth Benson was still enticing her daughter to move on from Allan and enjoy her life. Brydie had shoved it to the back of her closet and forgotten about it.

It was a little too chilly to wear it alone, but with a pair of boots and a jacket, she thought, maybe it could look cute. She wiggled into the dress and pulled from the closet a pair of black boots that came up just past her knees and a gauzy black cardigan. When she went to the bathroom and looked in the mirror, Brydie was surprised at how good she looked. Her hair was glossy and fell perfectly around her face. Her skin, which sometimes felt greasy and uneven after spending so much time in a kitchen, seemed to glow. She looked like she was ready for a night out in a big city with a sexy doctor.

Teddy, however, looked like he was ready for a night of sleeping at the foot of Brydie's bed. "Sorry, buddy," she said, slipping the harness over him. "But you're going to have to snore and fart in someone else's house tonight."

AN HOUR LATER, Brydie found herself sitting on Nathan's couch with Myriah, the dog sitter, waiting for him to come home.

"He said he wouldn't be more than twenty minutes late," Myriah said, giving Brydie a sympathetic smile. "You look really pretty."

"Thanks," Brydie replied. She watched Sasha chew on Teddy's ear as he slept. "And it's okay. I don't mind waiting for a little while. I know his work isn't really something he can walk away from."

"He's worked almost twenty-four hours straight," Myriah replied. "I can't even stay up past midnight to study for a bio exam."

"You're in college?" Brydie asked. She wondered if Myriah had been at Nathan's house the entire time. Did she sleep there sometimes?

Myriah nodded. "Premed. My dad is a cardiologist at Baptist."

"Oh."

"What do you do?"

"I'm a baker," Brydie replied. It was an automatic response, and not one that usually made her feel nervous. But right now, sitting in a doctor's house with a beautiful and young premed student, she wished she had something more impressive to say.

"That's awesome," Myriah said. "Do you have a shop or something?"

"No."

"Oh."

The two women sat there in silence for a minute, and Brydie felt bad for not explaining to Myriah where she worked. Maybe she could have worked it into the conversation that she had owned her own shop, but at the moment, explaining any of it made her feel silly. She doubted Myriah cared, and she was starting to think maybe she should just go ahead and call it a night.

"Hey, wait!" Myriah said, standing up and jogging toward the kitchen, motioning for Brydie to follow her. "Did you make these treats that I give Sasha? She *loves* them."

"I did," Brydie said, grinning as Myriah pulled the bag from the cabinet. "How did you know?"

"I just now remembered that Nathan mentioned it. He said to remind him to ask you for more. Sasha is about out," Myriah replied. "He told me that like a week ago. I can be kind of a ditz sometimes."

Brydie grinned. "That much we have in common," she said.

"My dad says I shouldn't use that word if I'm going to be a doctor," Myriah continued. "He says it'll make patients lose faith." She laughed nervously. "But I can't think of a more perfect word to describe me!"

Brydie was about to respond when she heard the front door open and Sasha's loud, joyful bark echoing down the hallway.

"I'm sorry I'm late," Nathan said, rounding the corner and into the kitchen. He stopped short when he saw Brydie. "Wow, you look fantastic." His eyes roamed playfully over her body. "Now I feel even worse for keeping you waiting."

"Thanks," Brydie replied, feeling herself blush. She hoped her cheeks weren't as red as her dress.

Myriah looked from Nathan to Brydie and back again, a small smile forming at the corners of her mouth. "Let me just get Sasha out of here," she said, shaking the bag of treats at the dog. "Come on, you canine tornado. You want a treat?"

Brydie watched Nathan set his coat down on the countertop, his shoulder slouching slightly. There were dark circles under his eyes and at least two days of stubble jutting across his jawline. "You look exhausted," she said, finally. "Are you sure you want to go out tonight? We can reschedule if you're too tired."

"Do I look that bad?"

"No!" Brydie said. "But Myriah said that you've been at work for hours and hours. I just don't want you to feel obligated, that's all."

"Well, I won't lie, I'd prefer to go on up to the bedroom and take you with me," Nathan said. He reached out and put one hand on her waist. "But I've already switched our reservation around, and Neil will kill me if I take up a table on the busiest night of the week and don't use it."

Brydie cleared her throat. The bedroom option sounded better to her as well. "Okay," she said.

"Give me fifteen minutes."

MEMPHIS AT NIGHT was glorious. In the eight months that Brydie had lived in Memphis, she'd never been downtown at night. Even in the fall, Beale Street was vibrant and buzzing with locals wandering around and popping into restaurants to eat dinner.

Fish, the restaurant where Nathan had taken her, was no different. They breezed past the maître d', who merely nodded at them and said, "He's in the back, Dr. Reid."

Nathan led Brydie to the back part of the restaurant, all the way to a round booth where four people sat, cloaked in warm, yellow lighting. One of the men, slim and balding, stood up when he saw them coming.

"Nate!" he howled, extending his arms to bring Nathan into a hug. "I thought you'd stood me up!"

"Oh, come on. You know me better than that," Nathan replied. "I couldn't come straight from the hospital. I figured the whole restaurant would appreciate it if I showered."

"As much as I'd like to hear about that shower," the man said, turning his attention to Brydie, "I'm going to need you to tell me who this dish is first."

"Neil, this is Brydie, my neighbor from down the street . . . Brydie, this is Neil. He owns this restaurant."

"It's nice to meet you," Brydie said, extending her hand, trying not to be bothered by Nathan introducing her as his neighbor. She guessed it was true, at least.

"Oh, honey," Neil replied. "I'm a hugger. Get in here!"

Brydie's face was suddenly planted firmly into Neil's starched, white collar. "Frumpumph," she said.

Neil took her by the hand and led her closer to the booth. "Everyone, this is Brydie. Nathan's *date*."

"Hi," Brydie said to the two men and one woman sitting at the booth.

"Brydie, this is Warren, my husband." Neil nodded toward one of the men. "He's a lawyer, but don't hold that against him. And beside him is Jasper Floyd and his wife, Adelaide."

"Call me Addie," the blond woman said. "It's nice to meet you."

The man beside Addie named Jasper smiled at Brydie. "Hello," he said. "Dr. Reid, did you save any lives today?"

"Probably not as many as you ruined," Nathan replied.

"I'm not in the habit of setting criminals free anymore," Jasper replied. "I mostly just argue with cattle now."

"Jasper used to be a lawyer here in Memphis," Neil explained to Brydie. "But then he left us all for the life of a farmer. Have you ever heard anything more quaint?"

"I'm from Jonesboro," Brydie said. "Lots of quaint farms up that way."

"I know it well," Jasper replied. "I have a buddy who went to Arkansas State."

"It's where both of my parents went."

"I like to go to Hardy for the antiques," Addie cut in. "I've found some spectacular deals up that way. It's just a little past Jonesboro, isn't it?"

Brydie nodded. "Just about an hour."

"Addie has her own shop in Eunice," Neil said. "It's full of repurposed furniture and some of the sweetest little knickknacks."

"I've never been to Eunice," Brydie admitted.

"Come on down anytime," Jasper said. "Make that doctor of yours take a break once in a while."

"What this doctor needs," Nathan said, rubbing his stomach, "is something to eat. I can't remember the last time I had an actual meal."

"Let me get you all a table," Neil said. "I saved you one with a view."

"It was nice to meet you," Addie called over her shoulder as Brydie was ushered off.

Neil led them to a table near the front, next to a window with a view of the street. "I'll get a server right over," he said. "Come and find me if you need anything."

"Thanks," Nathan said, sitting down with a grateful sigh. "Appreciate it, man."

"Thanks," Brydie echoed.

Once Neil had gone and they were comfortable with their menus in front of them, Brydie stole a glance at Nathan. He still looked worn out, but less so than when he'd gotten home earlier. She couldn't help but feel a little insecure at how quickly he'd changed the subject when Jasper invited them to Eunice and called Nathan *her* doctor.

She tried not to let it bother her. It was silly, she knew, but that didn't make her feel any better. "Is everything here good?" she asked.

Nathan looked over his menu at her. "Everything I've tried has been good, but catfish is their specialty."

Brydie wrinkled her nose. She wasn't a fan of catfish. "I was thinking about the chicken Parmesan and a nice glass of wine."

"That sounds perfect," Nathan replied. He closed his menu and handed it to a waiter who seemed to appear out of thin air. "I think I'll have the same thing, and could we get a bottle of the Viognier?"

"Your friends were nice," Brydie said once the waiter had gone.

"They're a good group of people," Nathan agreed. "I didn't know Jasper and Addie were in town. You'd really like them both if you got to know them. Jasper and Warren helped my family settle my grandparents' estate, and Jasper and Addie have about five dogs. I swear their farm doubles as an animal sanctuary."

"I should have mentioned my dog treats to them," Brydie replied.

"You should have." Nathan grinned at her for the first time since they got to the restaurant. "Speaking of which, I need to order some more. We're almost out."

"Myriah told me," Brydie replied. "I made some extra when I baked for MaryAnn and Fred. I will bring some over."

"I'll pay you," Nathan said.

"Of course you won't," Brydie scoffed. "Consider it compensation for setting me up with MaryAnn and Fred.

"I've never owned a pet before," Brydie said. "I have to admit that I didn't realize so many people treated their dogs like their children."

"MaryAnn has three kids. I'm pretty sure she loves Thor more than all of them put together."

"I'm sure she's made her kids well aware of that fact."

"In a way, I understand it," Nathan replied. "We had dogs when I was growing up, but I didn't really know what it meant to take care of another living being until I got Sasha. I've never thrown her a birthday party, but I have to admit that she has her own side of the bed."

"I wasn't thrilled about dog-sitting when I first met Teddy," Brydie said. "I thought he was kind of ugly and smelled bad. But I have to admit that I've grown pretty attached to him."

"Mrs. Neumann loves him, too," Nathan replied. "I know she worried about what was going to happen to him when she moved to the nursing home. You've been a savior for her."

Brydie felt a twinge of guilt at what Nathan said. She knew she hadn't taken the responsibility of caring for him very seriously at first, and she certainly hadn't accepted the responsibility to help Pauline. She'd accepted because she was broke and semi-homeless. "I hope I can take care of him even half as well as she did."

"I think you're doing a great job," Nathan said, giving her the smile that made her heart skip a beat. "At the end of the day, I really think all dogs want from us is for us to love them. Well, that and for us to come home after work. I've been feeling pretty guilty about leaving Sasha with Myriah so much. But they love each other, so I guess it works out."

"She was pretty excited to see you tonight," Brydie replied.

"She's always excited," Nathan said with a laugh. "But after a long day, especially a day like I had to-day, it's nice to come home to pure joy on the face of my dog."

"I know what you mean," Brydie replied. "Teddy is a little too old and too fat to get very excited, but he always greets me at the door. And he follows me everywhere for the first couple of hours I'm home after work."

"Sasha does, too," Nathan said. "And she always seems to know when I've had a bad day."

"Was today one of those days?"

Nathan looked down at the table. He didn't look up for a few seconds, until the waiter whisked in with the wine and poured them each a glass, obviously grateful for the interruption to their conversation. "Today was one of those days," he said finally, giving her a half smile. "Being an ER doctor can be difficult sometimes."

"I'm sure being a doctor at any time is difficult,"

Brydie replied. "I can't imagine having people's lives in my hands every day."

"Sometimes I think I'll get out and start my own practice," Nathan said. "But I don't know how to function anymore without the stress of the ER."

Brydie didn't really know how to relate to the stress of the job that Nathan had. There were rarely life-threatening moments in baking. Sure, sometimes mothers got angry when a birthday cake for a little kid was a minute late to the party. And sometimes brides and grooms broke up before the wedding, leaving you with tiers upon tiers of wedding cake. But those were hardly relatable to trying and failing to save a person's life. She did, however, know about owning her own business. "Working for myself was stressful, but probably not as stressful as it is now, where I have to worry about several bosses *and* the customer," she said.

"Do you miss it?"

Brydie shrugged. "Some days. I miss having creative control, but I've met some really great people at ShopCo."

"It helps when you like the people you work with," Nathan said.

"I invited them to Thanksgiving dinner," Brydie replied. "My boss is kind of prickly, but I think he was secretly pleased to have been invited somewhere."

"I usually spend the day at the ER," Nathan said.

"Are you working this year?"

Nathan shook his head. "I'm on call, but I don't have to go there. This year, I'm not the new guy anymore."

Brydie bit at the corner of her lip. Should she invite

him to come over? Would he think that was weird? Would he feel obligated but not really want to come? "You know," she said carefully, "I've invited the three people I work with and my best friend Elliott and her family to Thanksgiving dinner. Would you like to come?"

"You wouldn't think I'm a party crasher?" Nathan asked.

"Of course not," Brydie replied. "You can't crash a party you're invited to."

"I'd love to come," he said. "What should I bring?"

"Just yourself," Brydie said. "And Sasha if you want."

Nathan picked up his fork when the chicken parm was put down in front of him and grinned at Brydie over the steam. "I have to tell you," he said. "I was so tired when I got home tonight. I thought I might cancel once I got there, and then I saw you in that dress, and I knew I couldn't. After the day I've had, all I wanted to do was go to sleep, but I'm so glad we came out tonight. You've made this day so much better than I can tell you."

"I would have been happy to reschedule," Brydie replied. "But I'm glad we came out, too."

Nathan took a swig of his wine—a larger drink than usual—and said, "I didn't want to come out tonight because before I came home, I had to tell a twelve-year-old girl that both of her parents were dead."

Brydie's eyes snapped up from her plate. "You had to do what?"

"There was a car accident on the Memphis-Arkansas Memorial Bridge. Her parents' car was rear-ended while they were at a dead stop, and the impact was so great, it slid their car underneath an eighteen-wheeler," Nathan said. "They were on their way to pick her up from her aunt's house in South-aven."

"How awful."

"It was worse than awful," Nathan said, looking down at his empty plate. "It was pure carnage, and there was nothing I could do to save either of them by the time they got to the hospital."

"That's not your fault," Brydie said. She reached out across the table to take his hand as it drummed nervously on the tablecloth.

"No," Nathan replied. "But it had been such a long shift already. All I wanted to do was go home, and I didn't have it in me to tell this little girl that her entire world had vanished, but I had to."

"I'm sure that you did the best you could."

"I didn't, though," Nathan said. "That's the thing. That's what I feel so shitty about. I hadn't had any sleep. I was . . . I am exhausted. I wasn't delicate with her like I should have been. I didn't sit down and hold her hand. I just . . . told her and then I walked away. I left with her crying on her aunt's shoulder."

"I'm sorry."

"She's going to live with this night for the rest of her life," Nathan replied. "She's going to remember my face and what I said forever, and I failed her."

"Don't be so hard on yourself," Brydie said. "You can't always say the perfect words. That little girl will remember that you tried to save her parents. That counts, too, you know."

Nathan squeezed her hand before he pulled away from her. "This is why I'm glad I didn't go to sleep as soon as I got home," he said. "Thank you."

"You're welcome."

It wasn't a sentiment that Brydie could explain, at least not yet, but it had been such a long time since she felt like she'd made anybody happy. In fact, lately she'd felt like a burden more than anything else. She'd been a burden on her mother, on Elliott, and sometimes, she even felt, on everyone. But tonight, in her red dress, sitting across from this handsome, curly-headed doctor, she felt like maybe she wasn't a burden after all. Maybe, just maybe, she had more to give than all she'd already lost.

CHAPTER 27

THANKSGIVING WAS LESS THAN A WEEK AWAY, and the weather in Memphis was starting to look like it. There were gray clouds low in the sky, and the wind stung. For most people, it would have been a good incentive to stay inside, but Brydie loved it. Teddy, however, wasn't excited at all about the weather. She had to carry him from the car into the nursing home.

Brydie felt as anxious to see Pauline as Teddy did. She wasn't sure what to expect after their last interaction. Pauline had hardly spoken to Brydie in the car after she told her to stay out of the basement, and the mood had been just as tense back inside the nursing home. Although the receptionist had long gone home, Dr. Sower made it a point to let Brydie know she wasn't buying Nathan's story at all. She made Brydie promise not to take Pauline anywhere from now on.

She planned to honor both of those promises, although the promise about staying out of the basement was proving to be the more difficult of the two.

Brydie and Teddy stood at the receptionist's desk at the nursing home while the receptionist was talking on the phone. She'd been on the phone since Brydie announced that she was there to see Pauline.

"Dr. Sower is coming up," the receptionist said, finally hanging up the phone. "You can have a seat if you want."

Brydie knitted her brows together. "Why? What's wrong? Is Mrs. Neumann sick?"

"Dr. Sower will be right out," was all she said.

Brydie led Teddy away from the desk and sat down on one of the couches facing the courtyard. It was a lovely day, and not too chilly out. The yard was littered with orderlies and the elderly, some of them walking around and many more sitting in chairs and drinking up the sunshine. She strained her eyes to see if maybe Pauline was among those outside, but Brydie couldn't find her anywhere. She hardly noticed when Dr. Sower came and sat down next to her.

"Brydie?"

Brydie jumped a little, accidentally jerking on Teddy's leash. He made an annoyed gurgling sound. She reached down to pet him and said, "I'm sorry, Doctor. I guess I didn't hear you sit down."

"Oh, it's all right," Dr. Sower replied, enticing Teddy to come over to her for head pats. "I'm sorry that nobody called you."

"What's wrong?" Brydie asked, feeling panic rise in her throat. "Is Mrs. Neumann okay? I was looking for her outside, but I don't see her anywhere."

"She had an episode last night."

"An episode?"

Dr. Sower nodded. "She had some trouble breathing. We had to give her oxygen. She was very scared and had to be sedated. She's still resting, and we've not yet been able to take her off the oxygen. I'm afraid it may be something she will need long term."

"Can I see her?" Brydie asked. The thought of Mrs. Neumann in her room, scared and alone, was enough to make her want to cry.

"Not today," the doctor replied. "She needs her rest."

"But Teddy makes her so happy," Brydie protested. "She looks forward to these visits."

"I know she does," Dr. Sower said. She cast an empathetic gaze at Brydie. "But even if she were awake, and she's not, she would be very groggy. I doubt she could enjoy much of anything right now."

"*Why didn't* anybody call me?"

Dr. Sower sat back, placing her hands across her middle, lacing her fingers through each other. "Mrs. Neumann has given us permission to share limited medical information with you," she said. "But we are not obligated to call you every time an issue arises. You aren't family."

Brydie didn't respond. She knew she wasn't family. She was hardly even Pauline Neumann's friend. She was the woman's dog sitter. She was her house sitter. She was just the person staying in her house and taking care of her dog until . . . until what? Until the old woman died? The thought gave Brydie pause. "I'm sorry," she said at last. "I wasn't trying to be rude. I know you aren't obligated to call me. I just wish you had, that's all."

Dr. Sower patted Brydie's arm. "I'll make you a deal—I'll call you if there is a problem that I think requires you to be here, if you'll trust us to make that decision."

"Okay," Brydie replied. "And you think she's going to be okay?"

"I do," the doctor said, and then added, "with a little more rest."

Brydie nodded and stood up. "Oh wait," she said, tugging at the purse on her shoulder. She pulled out a bag of treats. "I made these for you. Well, for your dog."

Dr. Sower's eyes lit up. "Oh thank you! Rufus and Oliver will be so pleased!"

"I'll bring more next week if Mrs. Neumann is up to visitors."

"I'm sure she will be."

Brydie gripped Teddy's leash and tugged gently. "Come on, buddy."

Teddy stood up and started down toward the hallway, where Mrs. Neumann's room was located.

"No," Brydie said.

A whimper escaped Teddy's throat, his body rigid. He didn't move.

"He knows we're here to see her," Brydie said, feeling helpless. She bent down in front of him and put her forehead to his. "Please could we see her? Just for a few minutes? I have these blankets she wanted from the house. I'd really like to give them to her personally."

Dr. Sower sighed. "Okay, but just for a few minutes. I'm serious."

"I promise we'll be quick."

Brydie's excitement faded when she saw the woman lying in bed in front of them. She was wrapped in several blankets with one of her feet sticking out. Brydie could see the pale blue of the veins in her leg just above her sock. Pauline was pale, so pale, and there were tubes going up each one of her nostrils, attached to an oxygen machine just to the side of her.

When Brydie reached down to undo Teddy's leash, the nurse in the room put her hand out and said, "He can be in here, but don't let him jump up on her, okay?"

"Okay," Brydie said. "Can he sit next to her on the bed?"

"Of course," Pauline said before the nurse had a chance to respond. "Lift him up here."

Brydie picked him up, ignoring the nurse's pursed lips. "Be sweet now," she said to him.

Teddy gave Pauline's hand a lick and then settled down next to her on the bed, seemingly aware that his master was out of sorts. Pauline patted him on the head and then turned her attention to Brydie. "You two are a sight for sore eyes, let me tell you."

"I brought you the blankets you asked for." Brydie tried to smile, forcing the corners of her mouth to turn up. Pauline's eyes did look sore. Everything about her looked sore. "How are you feeling?"

Pauline put her fist to her chest and rapped a few times. "The old ticker is still going, so I suppose I'll live.

"I woke up yesterday feeling right as rain," Pauline continued. "And then, for some reason, I just couldn't breathe. Been hooked up to one of these tank thingamajigs ever since." She jabbed her thumb in the direction of the oxygen.

"I'm so sorry."

"Don't be," Pauline replied. "It's just one of the many perks of getting old."

Brydie appreciated Pauline's lighthearted tone. She knew she was putting on a brave face for her and

Teddy, but the woman's watery, blue eyes told another story. She was tired, and Brydie thought maybe just a little scared. "Thanksgiving is on Thursday," she said. "I thought I might be able to bring you over some Thanksgiving dinner and you could have a visit with Teddy."

"I sure wouldn't say no to that," Pauline replied. "We'll have dinner here, but I can't imagine it could be better than anything you could whip up." Her hand went down to Teddy's head. "And you know I'm always happy to see my Teddy."

"Good," Brydie replied, clapping her hands together. "Then it's settled."

"Oh, and bring some of those treats you brought for Dr. Sower last week. She's been raving about them ever since."

Brydie grinned. "I will!"

"Dr. Sower is wonderful," Pauline continued. "But I think we all miss Dr. Reid when he's away." She paused to give Brydie a not-so-subtle wink. "Have you seen him lately?"

Brydie cleared her throat and stole a glance over at the nurse who was still inside Pauline's room. She didn't want to say anything in front of her. The last thing Brydie wanted was for a rumor about her and Nathan to get around the nursing home, around the hospital, and, most likely, around to Nathan. "I've seen him around the neighborhood," she said as casually as possible.

"On purpose?"

"We had coffee at the dog park once."

Now the nurse was paying attention. She'd turned so that her whole body was facing them, as she pretended to study the oxygen tank.

"Well, that's promising!" Pauline replied, clapping her hands together. "You should invite him for Thanksgiving dinner."

"I'll think about that," Brydie replied, still feeling the nurse's eyes on her.

"I've had some wonderful Thanksgivings," Pauline said. "Many of them right there in that house you're living in."

Brydie realized that she'd invited a whole bunch of people over for Thanksgiving dinner without even thinking about or asking permission from the house's actual owner. She winced at the thought. "Would you mind if I cooked a Thanksgiving dinner there . . . at your house?"

"Child, where else would you cook it?"

"I'm sorry I didn't ask earlier."

"As long as you don't burn the kitchen down," Pauline replied, "I certainly don't mind."

"I've set a stove on fire," Brydie admitted. "But I've never burned a kitchen down."

"Well, that makes one of us."

"You burned down a kitchen?"

"Honey," Pauline said, the twinkle returning to her eyes, "I burned down a *house*."

By now, the nurse had pulled up a chair and was sitting right next to Brydie, no longer able to pretend like she wasn't listening to their conversation. "You burned down a house?" she squeaked.

Pauline nodded. "It was 1963, and it was my first Thanksgiving with Bill," she said.

"Who's Bill?" the nurse asked.

"Her third husband," Brydie replied before Pauline had a chance to answer.

"Yes, my third husband," Pauline echoed. "We'd

just moved into this adorable little house across the street from his parents. His mother, Fredna, wanted to have Thanksgiving dinner at her house, but I insisted we have it at ours. I wanted to prove to her that I could cook a meal and feed my husband and his family."

"But instead you burned down the kitchen?" Brydie asked.

"Shhh . . . let her finish," the nurse said, putting her finger to her lips.

"I wanted to prove that I was a good wife," Pauline continued. "I'd had two failed marriages before this, mind you, and Mrs. Fredna Campbell was not at all thrilled that her only son had gone off and married a tainted woman." Pauline gave the women a mischievous half smile. "But the truth was that I couldn't boil water, and God love Bill, he knew it. All that week he was trying to convince me not to be in charge of Thanksgiving dinner, but I was bound and determined. I've always been a little headstrong, you know?"

"Oh, I know, Mrs. Neumann," the nurse said. "I've never had anyone fight me on that oxygen like you did last week."

"Imagine that my mother-in-law was just that much more stubborn," Pauline replied. "She came over that day ready to be disappointed, but I'd cooked a beautiful dinner, and for the first time since I'd known this woman, and I'd known her my whole life, she was paying me compliments. My head got so big that I forgot about the pot of green beans on the stove. I didn't realize it until the whole house started to smell and the kitchen was going up in flames. It didn't take long before the whole house was ablaze. That little house was a tinderbox."

"Good Lord," the nurse gasped.

"We lost everything," Pauline said. "Bill and I lost everything we owned in that fire, and all Fredna could holler about was how she left her brand-new mink coat. It was an anniversary gift from Bob, her husband. It was pastel, the fashion of the time, and quite costly. She told me right there on the spot that I'd be buying her a new fur."

"Did you?" Brydie asked.

"Of course not," Pauline replied. "I hated that thing, and she'd worn it over to my house only to taunt me. Even back then I knew that wearing the skin of other animals was ghastly, and I told her so every chance I got."

"So what happened?" the nurse asked. "After the fire?"

"We moved in with my parents for a while," Pauline replied. "And then we lived with Bill's parents. That next summer we started building our own house outside of town, and then before we knew it, I was . . ." Pauline trailed off.

"You were what?" Brydie asked.

Pauline looked away from the women sitting beside her. In a voice so low that it was barely a whisper, she said, "I'm tired." She closed her eyes.

As if on cue, the nurse stood up and dragged the chair she'd been sitting in back to the other side of the room. "Mrs. Neumann needs to rest now," she said. "I think it's probably best if you and the dog leave."

"Is she okay?" Brydie asked. "Did we say something that upset her?"

The nurse picked Teddy up from the bed and set him down on the floor, busying herself with

Mrs. Neumann's blankets. "She just gets worn out easily," the nurse replied. "She talked more to us today than she's talked in over a week—well, probably since the last time you visited."

"Okay," Brydie said. She clipped Teddy's leash to his harness. She didn't want to leave. Selfishly, she wanted to push the older woman for more information, to *make* her tell her about what happened with her marriage. Was the man in the pictures she found Bill? What was in the trunk? What happened with Bill? Did he cheat on her with another woman the way Allan had done? Did he just come home one day and tell her that he didn't love her anymore? Brydie desperately wanted to know the answers.

Brydie peeked over at Pauline. Her eyes were still closed, and if she was still awake, Brydie couldn't tell. She watched the ragged rise and fall of the woman's chest for a few seconds until, realizing she was no longer welcome, she set down the blankets, picked up Teddy Roosevelt and left the nursing home.

CHAPTER 28

B RYDIE HAD NEVER SEEN SHOPCO SO BUSY, ESPE-
cially at night. It was late Wednesday night, almost Thanksgiving Day, and people were rushing
around the store, grabbing and snatching at things
as if it were the zombie apocalypse and only frozen
turkeys and boxed stuffing could save them from the
advancing horde. She hoped that there would still be
something left for her to buy once her shift ended.

On Monday, Brydie had bought the turkey and the
ingredients for her favorite homemade stuffing recipe.
But she'd waited on the fresh fruits and vegetables.
Now she was wondering if that was a mistake.

"Don't worry," Rosa said to her, snapping the
plastic lid shut over a dozen cupcakes with turkeys
on them. "There will be enough for everyone. They
always keep a little in the back for the employees."

"That makes me feel better," Brydie replied. "So
far, there are seven people coming to dinner, not
including myself. I haven't cooked a meal for that
many people in a long time."

"Do you need some help?"

"Really?" Brydie asked.

"Of course," Rosa replied. "Lillian and I would love to help with the dinner."

"That would be wonderful," Brydie replied, feeling a flood of relief wash over her.

"Lillian and I made a cherry pie and a fruit-and-yogurt parfait this afternoon before work. We'll bring that over with us, and then you can put us to work doing whatever it is that you'd like us to do."

Without even thinking about it, Brydie reached out and hugged Rosa. "Thank you so much."

"Oh honey, it's our pleasure," Rosa said. She stroked Brydie's head. "Now, we better get back to work before Joe comes in and sees us showing affection for one another. He really hates hugging."

Brydie giggled. "That really doesn't surprise me."

"It's one of the reasons he and Lillian get along," Rosa replied. "Don't get me wrong, Lillian is affectionate in her own way, but it's a way that she and Joe seem to understand about one another." She grinned at Brydie. "I'm a hugger. I'm glad to have another one in the mix."

Brydie felt her phone buzz in her pocket. It was the third time that night, and every time she pulled it out to see who it was, it was the same person— her mother. She'd been avoiding talking to her since she'd found out about Allan and Cassandra, afraid her mother would offer up more information that would send her into a tailspin. She'd kept their conversations short, and she'd relegated their content to talk of the real estate business or baking sweet treats for the dogs of the neighborhood. Now she was starting to worry that something was wrong.

Her mother knew she'd be at work at this time of night.

"Do you care if I go ahead and take a break a little early?" Brydie asked Rosa. "My mom keeps calling me, and I'm worried that maybe there's been an accident or something."

"Sure thing," Rosa replied. "Take your time."

Brydie pulled her phone out of her pocket and dialed her mother's number as she walked back to the break room. When her mother answered, she said, "Mom? Is everything okay? You've called me three times, and I'm worried."

"What?" her mother asked. "No, everything is fine!"

Brydie pulled her phone down from her ear and stared at it, willing herself not to just hang up. "So there's no emergency? Why did you call me three times in a row when you know I'm at work?"

"Well, there's no reason to be crabby about it," her mother replied. "I just wanted to see what time you'd be here for Thanksgiving dinner tomorrow."

"When did we talk about me coming home for Thanksgiving?"

"We didn't. I just assumed you would."

"Why would you assume that?"

"Because you're my daughter, and you've spent the last thirty-three Thanksgivings at my house."

Brydie sighed. This conversation wasn't getting them anywhere. "I'm not coming home, Mom. I work until tomorrow morning, and then I'm cooking dinner up here for some friends."

"For that doctor?" Ruth Benson asked.

"He'll be there, yes."

"Perfect!" her mother said, practically cackling

with delight. "What time should Roger and I be there?"

"Who's Roger?" Brydie asked. "And what do you mean what time should you be here?"

"Since you can't come to me, I'll come to you, of course."

Brydie didn't know what to say. Her mother hadn't even mentioned Thanksgiving until now. She knew why, of course—so that Brydie didn't have time to think of an excuse, a reason why mother and daughter shouldn't be reunited for the holiday.

"We'll eat around six."

"Lovely!" her mother exclaimed. "Roger will be so happy to be invited."

Except, Brydie thought, *he hasn't been invited. Neither of you has been invited.* Instead, what she said was, "Okay, well, I'll see you then."

"Call me with directions tomorrow when you're off work?"

"Okay."

Brydie hung up the phone and shoved it back into her pocket. She knew she shouldn't be surprised about her mother's behavior, but for some reason, she was. Maybe it was because it had been nearly a year since she'd lived with her mother. Maybe it was because she'd simply been too busy to think about it. Now, however, Brydie was thinking about it. She was thinking about how she was going to have to introduce her mother to Nathan. The thought made her grimace. Now she had less than twenty-four hours to prepare and still not a damn clue who Roger was.

ROSA HAD BEEN RIGHT—just after the doors closed at 6 A.M., ShopCo brought out more of everything that could possibly be needed for Thanksgiving dinner *and* gave each of the employees a ham. Brydie rushed home to start on everything and feed Teddy so that she could at least get a couple of hours' sleep before the day got hectic.

Teddy looked at her curiously as she buzzed around the kitchen. He cocked his head from one side to another as pots and pans clanged around on the stove and Brydie talked to herself under her breath.

"Do I look like a crazy person?" she asked him, her hands coated in stuffing. "Because I feel like a crazy person."

Teddy rushed to her feet when he saw a bit of stuffing drop from her hands onto the tile. He snorted as he scarfed up the food, and Brydie couldn't help but laugh just a little at the symphony the combined noises made. She was just about to wrap up in the kitchen when her doorbell rang. It was just eleven o'clock and Brydie was surprised to see Elliott standing there on her doorstep holding Mia.

"Sorry for barging in," Elliott said, huffing into the hallway. "Leo and I had a horrible fight. He wasn't supposed to work today, but he scheduled two meetings with clients. *Two!* It's fucking Thanksgiving, and he's scheduling meetings with clients."

"Mommy!" Mia gasped. "Mommy, that's a bad word."

"I know," Elliott replied, setting Mia down and rubbing at her temples. "Mommy's sorry. Go play with Teddy, okay?"

"Okay!"

"Are you okay?" Brydie asked, beckoning Elliott into the living room. "Sit down. You look like you haven't slept in days."

"I'm having lots of Braxton Hicks contractions," Elliott replied. "I never had them with Mia. It's awful."

"I'm so sorry."

Elliott waved her off. "It's just, the only time I really have to sleep is during the day when I feel okay, but with Leo at work all the time and Mia out of preschool this week for Thanksgiving, well, I just haven't gotten a lot of rest."

Brydie looked longingly in the direction of her bedroom. If Elliott hadn't showed up, she'd be getting a few hours of sleep before people arrived for dinner. But she also knew that she had the next few days off from work, and Elliott really looked like she needed to sleep. "Why don't you go into the bedroom and take a nap?" Brydie offered. "I can watch Mia. I have a ton to do in the kitchen, anyway."

"I can't ask you to do that," Elliott replied, but she was already pushing herself up off the couch and heading toward the bedroom.

"Don't worry about it."

"Well, only if you're sure . . ." Elliott trailed off as she rounded the corner into the bedroom. "Wake me up in an hour or two, and I'll help you in the kitchen."

Brydie had no intention of waking her. She turned on the television and called out to Mia and Teddy, "What do you want to watch, Mia?"

Mia shrugged. "Do you have *Doc McStuffins*?"

"I don't even know what that is."

"It's a cartoon, silly!" Mia plopped herself down in front of the television. "About a doctor for toys!"

"Do you know what channel that is?" Brydie flipped to the program guide. "I don't know where the cartoon channels start."

Mia sighed. "It's Disney Junior!"

After a few minutes of searching and much complaining by Mia, Brydie was finally able to find the right channel. "Are you hungry?" Brydie asked, once she'd gotten the child settled.

"Mmmhmmm."

"What sounds good to you?"

Mia looked up at Brydie, a devilish grin on her face. "My mommy is asleep, right?"

"Yes."

"Can I have some candy?"

Brydie tried her best not to laugh and replied, "I don't think I have any candy. But I do have some chocolate chip cookies. Would you like two?"

"And milk?"

"Of course." Brydie padded off into the kitchen. Mia was like a miniature version of Elliott, all the way down to the way she spoke. She'd witnessed the two of them negotiating with each other, and it was usually pretty hard to tell which one came out on top.

Brydie opened up one of the cabinets and took down a cup and a plate. She'd often wondered if, when she was married, her children with Allan would be more like her or like him. She'd hoped that they would be outgoing like him, not afraid to try new things or speak their minds. Her own adventures were usually limited to the kitchen, despite Allan's best efforts to get her to spread her wings.

"Let's go skydiving," he'd say. "Let's buy an old stock car and fix it up to race! Maybe some weekend we could go rafting on the Buffalo National River!"

She and Allan had some pretty ugly fights about her "never wanting to do anything." But it wasn't that Brydie hadn't wanted to do anything. It was that Brydie hadn't wanted to do *those* things. When she'd suggested going away for the weekend to a vineyard for wine tasting, Allan told her they could drink wine together at home. When she'd said she wanted to visit the Gulf Coast for a week in the summertime, Allan told her the creeks and rivers in Arkansas were just as good as the ocean, a sight she'd still never seen.

Brydie wondered, as she set the plate of cookies and glass of milk in front of Mia on the floor, if Cassandra was willing to go white-water rafting and stock-car racing with Allan. Maybe the two of them would have lovely, outgoing children together. The thought should have made Brydie cringe, but for some reason, it didn't.

She'd always thought that if she and Allan had had children together, they never would have gotten divorced. She realized now that that probably wasn't the truth. It was just something she told herself when she was feeling her lowest, a way to blame herself for what happened between them, and even if they *had* stayed married, what then? What if she'd had a child just like Allan, and for the rest of her life she was subjected to skydiving and bungee jumping and hikes in the Grand freaking Canyon?

That thought *did* make her cringe.

"Bwydee?" Mia looked up at Brydie, who was still crouched down next to her. "Do you like this show, too?"

Brydie blinked, bringing herself back to reality. "What? Oh, yes. Yes. It's really good."

"I want to be a doctor someday," Mia replied. "But not for toys. For real people."

"Oh yeah?"

"Yeah. I want to cut people open!"

Brydie bit at the corner of her lip to keep from laughing. This kid was something else. "Well, I have a friend coming to dinner tonight who's a doctor. Maybe you can talk to him about it."

"Really?" Mia clambered to her feet, knocking the milk over onto the carpet in the process. "Oh no! I'm sorry!"

"It's okay," Brydie replied. "The carpet is white anyway. Nobody will ever know."

Mia looked up at Brydie through her eyelashes and said, "I stepped on a cookie, too."

BY THE TIME five o'clock rolled around, the entire house smelled like Thanksgiving, and despite Brydie's exhaustion, she was eager to have a house full of people to feed. Rosa and Lillian showed up at two o'clock on the nose to help prepare, their arms full of *hallaca*s.

"I know I said we would bring a pie, but I thought you might like to try the *hallaca*s," Rosa said, gesturing to the large tray Lillian was carrying.

"That's fantastic!" Brydie exclaimed, taking the tray from Lillian. "Thank you so much. I'm excited!"

The three of them and Mia were hard at work when Elliott wandered out from the bedroom, yawning.

"How long have I been asleep?"

"All *day*, Mommy," Mia replied, rolling her eyes at her mother.

Elliott glanced up at the clock above the stove. "You let me sleep all afternoon? I told you to wake me up!"

"I had plenty of help," Brydie said. She gestured

to Rosa and Lillian. "Elliott, this is Rosa and this is her daughter, Lillian. We work together at ShopCo. Rosa, Lillian, this is my best friend, Elliott."

"Hello," Rosa said, taking inventory of Elliott's round belly. "You're having a boy, yes?"

Elliott glanced from Rosa over to Brydie. "Um, yes. How did you know?"

Rosa reached out and put both of her palms flat on Elliott's stomach. "You're carrying low. And you're due soon? Next month?"

"January," Elliott replied. "Not until the middle."

"I wouldn't be surprised if that baby comes earlier," Rosa replied, turning back to her work. "He's going to be a big boy."

Elliott raised her eyebrow at Brydie.

Brydie only grinned and continued working. When the doorbell rang, Mia jumped down off the chair she was standing on and hollered, "Let me answer it!"

"Not without me!" Elliott trailed off behind her, and when the pair returned, Ruth Benson followed them with a man who, Brydie had to assume, was Roger.

"It's just an old man and an old lady," Mia said, clearly disappointed.

"Mia!" Elliott exclaimed, her cheeks turning pink. "What did we discuss about thinking before speaking?"

Mia shrugged and reached out for Rosa to hoist her back onto her chair.

Brydie gave Mia a sly wink and dried her hands off on a hand towel before approaching her mother. "Hi, Mom," she said, allowing herself to be drawn in for a hug. "I'm glad you made it."

"The traffic was awful," her mother replied. "I don't know how you drive in this every day."

"It's not so bad by the time I leave for work," Brydie replied. She turned her attention to the man beside her mother. "Hi. I'm Brydie."

"I'm Roger," the man said, holding out his hand to her. "Thanks for having me."

"Oh, it's my pleasure. Dinner won't be ready for another hour or so, but there's beer in the fridge, and you're welcome to find something on TV to watch."

"Actually," Roger replied, holding up a basket with his other hand, "I made green bean casserole, and I was wondering if I might be able to warm it up before dinner."

"Roger's quite the cook," Brydie's mother said, beaming. "He cooks for me almost every night!"

"Really?" Brydie asked. "Are you a real estate agent, too?"

Roger shook his head. "Nope. In fact, I met your mother when I went to list my house. I'm a contractor by trade."

"He came in to sell his house, but I guess I sold a little more than that," Ruth replied, giving Roger's arm a squeeze.

Brydie fought the urge to roll her eyes and said, "Well, come on into the kitchen."

"Where should I put our coats?" Ruth asked Brydie. "Do you have a place for them?"

"You can just put them in the living room."

"I don't want to leave them just lying around."

"Fine," Brydie replied. "You can take them back to the bedroom. I'll show you."

"This house is lovely," her mother said. "It could

use a few updates, but I'm impressed with how well it's been kept."

"You can just put them on the bed," Brydie said, motioning to her bed.

"You didn't bother to make your bed before company?" her mother asked, making a tsk-tsk noise under her breath.

"It was made," Brydie replied. "But Elliott took a nap earlier. I guess she forgot to make it back up. It's really not a big deal."

"Isn't that Mia of hers just a doll?"

"She is."

"And she's pregnant with a boy now?"

"Yep."

"Have they decided on a name?"

Brydie shrugged. "I don't think so just yet."

"I wish you'd had one. I'd love to be a grand-mother."

Brydie gritted her teeth. "Maybe Elliott and Leo will let you be the godmother," she said. *Then you can show up on their doorstep uninvited for Thanks-giving,* she thought.

"Where *is* Leo? I didn't see him."

"I think he had a meeting or something."

"On Thanksgiving?" Ruth looked down when Teddy shuffled into the room, snorting his displea-sure at all the people to Brydie.

"Had enough already?" Brydie asked him.

"Is that the," Ruth paused, taking inventory of the little pug beneath her feet, "the dog you've been charged to care for?"

Brydie nodded and reached down to scratch Teddy between the ears. "This is Teddy Roosevelt."

"I can't decide if he's cute or ugly."

"I felt the same way at first," Brydie said. "But he's really quite lovable."

"I sold a house for a couple who had four or five of this kind of dog," Ruth continued. "It took us hours to get that house ready to show. Dog hair was everywhere."

"He sheds some," Brydie admitted. "But I hardly notice. It's nothing a lint roller can't fix, anyway."

Brydie felt a shiver of relief run through her when she heard the doorbell ring. She wished her mother would just relax and have a good time instead of asking so many questions and lightly insulting Teddy, but she tried to remind herself that she didn't mean anything by it—that was just her mother, and it had been months since the two of them had been in the same room. "I'd better go see who that is," she said.

By the time Brydie got to the door, Mia had already answered it. Standing in the hallway were Nathan and Sasha, and behind them were Joe and Myriah. Brydie knitted her eyebrows together. She hadn't remembered Nathan telling her he was bringing Myriah.

Joe squeezed past Nathan and held up a covered dish. "Here," he said, his voice gruff as ever. "I thought you might need a pie, but I can see now that you didn't."

"No, it's great," Brydie replied, anxious to make Joe comfortable. "What is it?"

Joe grinned. "It's my specialty—shepherd's pie."

"I love shepherd's pie," Nathan cut in, releasing Sasha to find Teddy so that the two could begin their playful round of introductions. "I haven't had it in ages."

Joe beamed. "You've never had shepherd's pie like

my shepherd's pie," he replied. "Not even them Brits over there can make it like me."

"I'm looking forward to it," Nathan said.

"Come on inside," Brydie said, motioning for them to follow her. "There's no need to hang out in the hallway."

"I hope it's okay that I tagged along today," Myriah said. "It's just me and my dad, you know, and he had to work."

"Of course," Brydie replied. "The more the merrier." She felt a wave of guilt wash over her for being suspicious of Myriah. She really was a nice girl, even if she *did* tend to always be in the same spot as Nathan.

"Something tells me you don't really mean that," Nathan whispered to her when everyone had disseminated from the hallway and they were alone. "You look a little stressed."

"Yesterday there were six people coming to dinner. Now there are nine, and one of them is my *mother,*" Brydie whispered back. "*Stressed* doesn't even begin to cover it."

"Your mother?" Nathan raised his eyebrow at her. "Where?"

"Right here," came a voice from behind them. Ruth Benson swanned over to Nathan, her hand stuck out to him as if she expected him to kiss it. "I'm Ruth Benson."

"I'm Nathan Reid," Nathan replied. "It's nice to meet you."

"Are you that doctor?"

"I am."

"Well, aren't you just gorgeous!"

Brydie shot her mother a look before saying, "Mom,

why don't you let me introduce you to the people I work with."

"We can do that in a minute," her mother replied, not taking her eyes off Nathan.

"Let's do it now." Brydie grabbed her mother's arm and pulled her toward the kitchen. "Besides, I need to check on the pumpkin pie."

"He's very attractive," her mother said, waving goodbye to Nathan over her shoulder. "Much more good-looking than Allan ever was."

"Mom."

"What? I'm just saying."

"Well, don't."

"Fine."

The kitchen looked an awful lot like the bakery at ShopCo with Rosa, Lillian, and Joe all hovered around the stove, staring down at Brydie's pumpkin pie. "Is something wrong?" Brydie asked. "Did it not bake okay?"

"It looks amazing," Rosa said, holding the pie out for her to view. "We were just talking about how perfect it is."

"Oh good," Brydie replied, feeling at least part of her stress dissolve. "Everyone, this is my mother, Ruth. Mom, this is Rosa, her daughter Lillian, and Joe. We work together."

"Hello," Ruth said.

"Hello," Joe said, reaching out his hand to her. "Your daughter is a very talented baker. We're uh, we're real lucky to have her."

"Well, I'm happy to hear it," Ruth replied. "She does make the best pumpkin pie of anyone this side of the Mason-Dixon."

"Did she get her skill from you?"

Brydie's mother hesitated. "No . . . her late father, actually. He was always a much better cook than I."

"I'm so sorry," Joe said, looking helplessly from Brydie to her mother. "I didn't know."

"It's just fine," Ruth replied. "I'm sure you didn't know her mother was *still alive* until today."

"I don't know much of anything today," Joe admitted. "I'm usually sound asleep right about now."

"Why don't you all go on into the living room?" Brydie said, sensing that there were one too many cooks in the kitchen. "Let Rosa and I get everything out and onto the table."

Brydie took a deep breath once she was alone with Rosa and Lillian. It had been a long time since she'd cooked for so many people—since she'd hosted so many, and she was suddenly painfully aware of how little she'd missed it. There was something about the quiet of her life now that she'd not known she loved until this very second.

"Relax," Rosa said, resting her hand on Brydie's shoulder. "It will be fine. Everything will be fine."

"I know," Brydie replied, bending down to lift the massive turkey out of the oven. The smell filled her nose and lungs, and she began to feel herself relax. "Thanks, Rosa."

Rosa nodded and shooed Lillian out of the kitchen, following close behind her.

Brydie scanned the room. Everything else had been put out onto the table except for the turkey, which she'd bring out once the guests had been seated. She walked out from the kitchen, almost tripping over Teddy and then Sasha, who wasn't far behind him. "You two look guilty," she said to them, bypassing them and making her way into the living room.

She stood at the threshold for a few moments, taking in the sight in front of her. Brydie had a house full of people, and not just people—friends. She felt her heart swell, and she wished that Pauline could be there to see it. Something told her that she would enjoy this motley crew. Nathan and Joe were having a lively conversation about recipes for shepherd's pie. Her mother and Roger were playing with Mia, and Elliott was submitting to Rosa rubbing her belly, and telling her, Brydie could only guess, the exact due date of the baby.

"Is it time to eat?" Mia asked, looking up from the disappearing-quarter trick Roger was showing her.

Brydie grinned. "It is, kiddo."

"Can I have pumpkin pie first?"

"Absolutely not," Elliott interjected before Brydie had a chance to respond. "You've got to eat a real dinner first."

Mia stuck out her lip in a pout, and Brydie held out her hand to the little girl. "Come on, Amelia Bedelia," she said, winking at her.

"No pie!" Elliott called after them. "I mean it!"

Brydie and Mia rounded the corner and into the kitchen just in time to see what was left of the turkey sliding from the countertop to the floor. It was like slow motion—Sasha jumped up, her front paws on the counter, and sank her teeth into the side of the turkey, dragging it down with her. Together she and Teddy dug in, completely unaware that they'd been caught.

Brydie watched in horror for a few seconds before she found her voice. "Teddy! Sasha! *No!*"

Sasha completely ignored Brydie, but Teddy looked up at her for a brief second, a piece of turkey hanging out of his mouth, before plowing right back in. The temptation was just too great. Brydie let go of Mia's hand and charged over to them, desperate to save what was left of the battered carcass. She realized too late that she'd stepped right into a puddle of turkey juices, and felt herself falling backward, unable to catch herself before she landed with a thud right in front of the dogs. She could feel the liquid seeping into her jeans.

In a fit of giggles, Mia plopped down next to her. "Look, Brydie! It's a mud puddle!"

Brydie closed her eyes in a feeble attempt to collect herself, and when she opened them again, Nathan was there, pulling Sasha back by her collar and cursing at her under his breath. "I'm so sorry," he said, pulling her out of the kitchen.

"They ate the turkey," was all Brydie could say.

Nathan returned a few seconds later without Sasha and picked up the turkey, setting it out of Teddy's reach and back onto the counter. "They sure did," he replied. "I should have told you that you can't leave anything within Sasha's reach. Especially not something like an entire baked turkey. This is my fault."

Brydie reached out her hand to meet Nathan's and allowed him to pull her up. She looked down at Mia, still playing in her mud puddle made of turkey guts. "It's my fault," she replied. "I should have known better, and now the whole dinner is ruined."

"No, it's not," Nathan replied. "We still have plenty of food."

"But the turkey is the most important!" Brydie wailed, on the verge of tears. She didn't know why the turkey was so important. It just was. It was like the icing on top of a cake. You can't have a cake without icing, and you can't have Thanksgiving dinner without a turkey.

"We've got so much food that it won't even matter," Nathan said. "Nobody is going to be mad."

She knew he was probably right. Save for her mother, everyone would be kind about the destroyed turkey. But it galled her. Couldn't anything just *go right* for once? She wanted to stamp her foot and throw a fit as if she were Mia's age instead of a grown woman in her thirties. Instead Brydie reached down and picked up a couple of stray pieces of turkey, tossing them dejectedly at the sink. But they bounced off Nathan's arm and back onto the floor.

"Oh, so you're hitting me with food now?" Nathan asked, arching an eyebrow.

"No!" Brydie exclaimed. "I'm sorry! I didn't mean to . . ." She stopped abruptly when she felt a piece of turkey slap her cheek, and then her forehead.

Nathan was grinning over at her, fingers wrapped around the disconnected leg of the turkey.

"Don't you dare!" Brydie said, lunging toward him.

Nathan caught her by the wrist with his free hand and pulled her closer to him until there was no space between their bodies. Despite her despair over the ruined turkey, Brydie could feel her heart pounding in her chest as he drew her gaze up to his, refusing to release her with his eyes. "Not so bad, is it?" he said cozily, a smirk appearing on his lips—lips that Brydie had to fight furiously not to press against her own.

"I need to get this mess cleaned up," she said instead, but she made no effort to pull away from him.

"What on earth happened in here?" Ruth Benson demanded, suddenly there in the kitchen as if she were an apparition. She eyed the kitchen scene first—

the discombobulated turkey and Mia playing on the floor. Then her eyes snapped up to Brydie and Nathan, who by now had moved away from each other and were staring guiltily down at their feet. "What are *you two* doing?"

"Nothing," Brydie muttered, bending down to pick up Mia. "Come on," she said to the little girl. "Let's get you cleaned up."

"I'll take the dogs and get them hosed off," Nathan said. "You've got a hose out back, right?"

Brydie nodded. She walked into the living room. When Elliott saw them, she made an effort to stand up. "It's fine," she said to her friend. "We just had a little mishap in the kitchen. Is there an extra set of clothes in your bag?"

Elliott nodded. "Did Mia . . ."

"No," Brydie replied, choking back a laugh. "No, Mia didn't do anything. But it's going to be a few minutes before dinner is ready," she said. "The turkey . . . well, it looks worse than we do."

"Good thing we got more food than we can probably eat," Joe said, giving her a good-natured grin. "Nobody here is in a hurry."

Brydie mouthed a thank-you to him before saying to Elliott, "Just stay where you are. I'll get the both of us changed."

Ruth followed Brydie back to the bedroom. "What happened?" her mother asked.

"Sasha and Teddy happened," Brydie replied grimly.

"*The dogs?*"

"Yes, the dogs." Brydie hunched over the bag Elliott had discarded on her bed earlier that day. "Go on back into the living room with Roger."

"It looks like she went swimming in turkey gravy!" her mother said, ignoring Brydie's request. "Weren't you paying attention to anything at all except that doctor's hands on your rear end?"

Brydie felt herself flush hot with anger. "It was an accident," she hissed.

"His hands on your rear end were an accident?"

Brydie rolled her eyes and pulled Mia into the bathroom, where she discarded the little girl's stained clothes. Wetting a washcloth, she began to rub at the blotches of brown all over Mia's skin. "Is that too hot?" she asked her.

"No, it feels good," Mia replied, closing her eyes.

"Maybe after dinner," Brydie offered. She wiped at Mia's face. "This gunk is stuck on here good."

"Let me see that." Ruth snatched the washcloth out of Brydie's hands and began to rub Mia's forehead.

"Ow!" Mia screeched.

"Mom, that's too rough," Brydie replied, making an attempt to reclaim the washcloth. "Stop!"

"You have an entire room full of people waiting to eat," her mother said, continuing to scrub. "At the pace you were going, it would have taken all night long to get this child's face clean."

"Ow!"

"Mom!" Brydie said, her voice raising an octave. "You're hurting her!"

"She's fine!"

Brydie reached down and grabbed the washcloth out of her mother's hand, tossing it into the bathtub. "Mom, this isn't your house. Mia isn't your child. You aren't in charge here." She felt the words slide out of her mouth before she had the time to take them back. She bit her lip instead, turning back to Mia, who was now crying softly in the corner. "Shhhh," she said. "It's okay."

"*This*," her mother said acidly, expanding her arms and waving them about the room, "isn't your house. *She* isn't your child, either."

Brydie kept her back turned to her mother. "It's my house for now," she said. "And while you're in it, you'd do well to remember that you're a guest."

Her mother let out a noise that sounded like a cross between a snort and a sneeze. "I don't know why I thought coming here today was a good idea. It's obvious you don't want me here."

"That's not true," Brydie replied, feeling a slight pang of guilt knowing that she wasn't, in fact, telling the truth. She picked up Mia and carried her past her mother and to the bed. "But this is at least for now the place where I'm living. The people out there are my friends. You can't just come in and take over."

"That's not what I'm doing."

"That's what you always do."

Brydie's mother followed her out of the bathroom. "I don't understand why you're acting like this. I was just trying to help."

"I know," Brydie replied. She felt tired. She really didn't want to argue with her mother, but the woman just wouldn't listen.

"I really thought coming here today would be a nice reunion," her mother continued. "I thought you'd like Roger."

"I don't know Roger."

"He's a nice man," her mother said. "He's so much like your father."

"But he's not my father," Brydie said, cutting her off.

"If you'd just get to know him," her mother replied.

"He still won't be my father."

Brydie's mother sighed. It was a sigh she reserved for the times when her daughter was being her most insolent. "Your father would want me to be happy," she said.

Brydie closed her eyes and took a deep breath. "I want you to be happy, too, Mom," she said. "Does Roger make you happy?"

Her mother paused. "Yes," she said. "He does."

"I'm glad."

"Are you?"

"I said I was."

Her mother sat down on the bed, kneading her hands into her navy dress slacks. "Brydie, I want to apologize to you."

"It's okay, Mom," Brydie said. "Mia will be fine."

"Not about that," her mother replied. "Come here. Sit down."

"What is it?" Brydie asked, doing as she was told. "Mom, are you okay?"

Her mother nodded. "It's just that I feel terrible for the way we left things, you know, when you were staying with me. Before you left for this place."

"I know you were just trying to help," Brydie said. "I just wasn't ready to date anyone."

"No, I don't feel bad about that," her mother said, giving her daughter a sideways smile.

"Then what do you feel bad about?"

Her mother stopped kneading her pants. "I feel bad about what I said about your father. About his drinking. About him being a bad husband."

"Mom . . ."

"Let me finish," her mother said. "I shouldn't have said those things. Your father wasn't a *bad* husband any more than I was a *good* wife. We just . . ." She trailed off. "We just weren't good together."

"You were good together," Brydie protested. "Not always, but most of the time."

"We were good together at first," her mother continued. "We loved each other. But we got lost somewhere in the middle. I took it out on you that night, and I shouldn't have."

Brydie reached out to take her mother's shaking hand. "It's okay."

"It's not," her mother said, her voice cracking. "I'm sorry. Those things I said about Allan, those were the things I felt about your father. The things I never said."

"You weren't wrong."

"Maybe not," Ruth Benson replied. "Maybe not, but it wasn't my job to tell you. It was my job to be there for you and let you figure it out for yourself."

Brydie wasn't sure what to say. She'd never heard her mother apologize for anything—at work *or* at home. The concept was so foreign that the only thing she could think of to say was "I love you, Mom."

"Well," her mother replied, "I love you, too." She stood up and smoothed out the nonexistent wrinkles in her silk blouse. "I'd better go and find Roger."

Brydie watched her mother leave and heard her beckon to Roger, calling out to him about not letting his green bean casserole burn. She looked down at Mia, slightly red-faced and sniffling, and she was reminded of all the times she'd overheard her parents arguing. At least this time, there'd been a happy ending.

"Hey," Brydie said to her, touching her gently on the cheek. "How about we get you dressed and we'll go out there and have a piece of pumpkin pie right this very second?"

"Really?" Mia asked, hopeful.

"Really."

"Okay." Mia held out her arms to Brydie, and Brydie picked her up, carrying her as gently as she could into the living room full of waiting people.

CHAPTER 29

DESPITE THE TURKEY FIASCO, THANKSGIVING dinner went off without another hitch. Nobody seemed to mind not having the main course, and Brydie's anxiety over having ruined everything diminished completely when Leo appeared nearly half an hour after they'd all sat down to eat and claimed quite gallantly that he, for one, abhorred turkey. Not a single person mentioned anything other than the amazing pumpkin pie, shepherd's pie, and *hallaca*s.

Even Joe loosened up and talked with everyone, and Brydie could have sworn that she saw more than one smile out of him, although she would never mention it. For Joe, that would have been akin to an insult. As the evening wore down and she'd said goodbye to everyone but Nathan and Myriah, she began to clear the plates and pack a dinner for Pauline. She'd have just enough time to get it there before eight o'clock—the close of visiting hours at the nursing home.

"What are you doing?" Nathan asked, carrying in a stack full of plates from the table. "Are you still planning to go over to the nursing home tonight? It's getting late."

"I know," Brydie replied. "But I promised her I'd be there. I don't want her to wait up for me only to have me be a no-show."

"You could just call and tell her you'll bring it by tomorrow."

Brydie shook her head. "I want to take it to her tonight."

"Okay," Nathan said. He sat the dishes down with a plunk into the soapy water in the sink. "Do you think maybe afterwards you'd want to stop by?" He was looking at her like he'd looked at her earlier. They'd been standing in almost exactly the same spot.

"What about Myriah?" Brydie asked. She didn't know why she asked it, but she couldn't stop herself. That seemed to be a theme in her life at the moment. "Won't she be there?"

"No." Nathan looked at her, cocking his head to the side. "She drove herself here."

"Oh." Brydie peered around him and into the living room. "Where is she, anyway?"

"Outside with the dogs," he said. "So? How about it?"

"I probably shouldn't."

"Why not?" Nathan asked.

"I guess I don't have a very good reason."

"Good," Nathan said, brushing his lips up against hers. "You go and see Mrs. Neumann, and I'll see you in a couple of hours."

BRYDIE ARRIVED AT the nursing home with twenty minutes left to spare. She'd called just to let them know she was coming, afraid that holiday traffic might cause a delay. Teddy snored in the backseat. He'd been decidedly grumpy about being pulled out of the bed at so late an hour and had whined and snorted his displeasure until falling asleep.

She pulled on the dog's leash. "Come on," she said. "Let's go."

Teddy blinked up at her in the darkness, and smelling the food she carried, jumped down out of the car, happy to follow her. Once inside, the night receptionist smiled up at her, a hint of panic in her eyes at seeing a visitor so late.

"Hi," Brydie said. "I'm Brydie Benson. I called earlier."

"Oh, yes," the woman said. "I just about forgot you were coming."

"Is Mrs. Neumann already asleep?"

The woman, whose name tag read Rita, shook her head. "She was awake just a few minutes ago when the orderlies made their rounds. You can go on back."

"Thanks."

"That's a cute dog you've got there," Rita said. She bent over the desk and grinned down at Teddy. "He's a pug, right?"

"He is," Brydie replied.

"My aunt and uncle have two," she said. "I just love their little bug eyes. Can I pet him?"

"Sure."

Rita came around the desk and squatted down in front of Teddy, allowing him to smell her first and then scratching him under his chin. "I better let you get to it," she said, giving Teddy one final scratch. "You've just got about ten minutes before the doors lock."

Brydie pulled Teddy away from his adoring fan, much to his displeasure, and continued down the hallway to Pauline's room. Engrossed in an episode of *Diagnosis Murder,* she didn't notice them when they walked in.

"Hello?" Brydie asked, knocking quietly on the door frame. "Can we come inside?"

Pauline grabbed at the remote, but it slid from her hands and broke open onto the tile floor, spilling its batteries. "Well, fiddlesticks," she mumbled, making an unsuccessful attempt to sit up from the bed.

"I'll get it," Brydie offered, letting go of Teddy's leash and reaching down underneath the bed to retrieve the remote.

When she reappeared seconds later, Pauline was staring at her, glassy-eyed. It occurred to Brydie after a few awful moments of silence that the look on the older woman's face was one of confusion. She was trying to place Brydie . . . as if . . . as if she didn't know who she was.

Pauline was afraid.

Just as Brydie was about to speak, about to offer to get a nurse, Pauline's eyes cleared and she smiled. "Brydie, dear. I'd quite forgotten you were coming tonight."

Brydie felt a wave of relief wash over her. "I'm sorry I'm so late," she said. "Dinner ran longer than I thought it would."

"It always does," Pauline said. "What have you got there?"

Brydie held out the Tupperware dishes she'd brought with her. "You've got pumpkin pie, green bean casserole, mashed potatoes, cranberry sauce, and a good-sized helping of shepherd's pie."

"Sounds delightful." Pauline patted the bed for Brydie to lift Teddy up next to her. She stroked his ear.

"I'm sorry there's no turkey," Brydie said. "There was a mishap."

"Are you the mishap?" Pauline asked, glancing down at the dog nestled in her lap. "You smell like you might be."

"It wasn't *really* his fault," Brydie said. "Sasha knocked it down off the counter."

"Sasha?"

"Nathan, um, Dr. Reid's dog."

"Dr. Reid was there?"

Brydie nodded. "He was."

"Well, now," Pauline said. "That's certainly more interesting than the turkey."

Brydie tried to smile. She didn't have the heart to tell Pauline that she'd gone and messed it up. She'd messed it up every time, it seemed, and now he was done being patient. He was done waiting for her to make her move, to figure it out. "When his dog and Teddy get together, disaster usually ensues."

"I'm sorry I missed it."

"Me, too."

From behind them, an orderly tapped on the door. "It's really past time for visitors, Mrs. Neumann."

Pauline waved him away. "She's just leaving, Thomas."

Thomas made no move to leave. He just continued standing at the door, looking at Brydie as if she were keeping him from making the rest of his rounds.

"You'd better go on," Pauline whispered to her. "Thomas is a stickler for the rules. That's why he works nights here. Nobody else could keep Bob and

Phyllis from sneaking to the therapy pool after mid-night."

Brydie stifled a giggle. "Well, I wouldn't want to keep him from his duties," she said.

"His duty is to be a killjoy," Pauline replied, just loud enough for Thomas to hear.

Still, Thomas didn't move. He reminded Brydie of one of the guards people saw at Buckingham Palace—expressionless and yet at the same time very serious indeed. She couldn't imagine that the night-time antics of the elderly would get so crazy that they'd need such an enforcer, but perhaps Bob and Phyllis weren't the only offenders.

Brydie moved Teddy from Pauline's bed and down to the floor. "Where should I put this food?" she asked.

Pauline pointed to a mini fridge at the back of the room that Brydie had never noticed before. "Throw it in there. I'll have it for lunch tomorrow instead of having them bring me something from the cafeteria."

"Don't you go down there to eat anymore?"

"Heavens no," Pauline said. "I haven't been down there since the Halloween party." She pointed to her small frame, covered in thick blankets. "Nothing about me works well enough to get out of this bed anymore, it seems."

"They're bringing your food to your room?" Brydie asked, her brow furrowed.

"They are."

"How about on Sunday, I bring you lunch. From anywhere you want. Where would you like me to go?"

"Oh," Pauline said, clapping her hands together. "How delightful. Anywhere?"

"Anywhere!"

"Gus's," Pauline replied. "But you'll have to make sure you get enough for Teddy. It's his favorite, too."

"I've never heard of it," Brydie replied. "But if that's what you want, that's what I'll get."

Pauline opened her mouth to respond, but closed it when there was a not-so-subtle cough from Thomas in the doorway, and she rolled her eyes instead. "Listen, before you go, there is one more thing I want to talk to you about," she said, waving away Thomas's exasperated sigh.

"Sure," Brydie said. "What is it?"

"I want to apologize for the way I acted after Thor's birthday party," she said. "I know I was unkind to you, and I shouldn't have been."

"No, I should be the one apologizing," Brydie said. "I should have called first instead of just going downstairs."

"You did the right thing," Pauline continued. "You were charged with taking care of my house, and that's exactly what you did."

"I got everything cleaned up," Brydie said. "There wasn't any major damage."

"I haven't been down in that basement in a long time," Pauline replied. "It got too hard for me to go up and down the stairs."

"Did you go down there often?" Brydie desperately wanted to ask her about the photos and the trunk, but she was afraid of upsetting her. If Pauline had gotten so angry simply knowing Brydie was down there, she didn't want to know what she might say about the photo album.

"I used to," Pauline said. "I kept many memories down there. Memories I couldn't bear to look at every day, but memories I was afraid I might forget."

"I have some memories I really wish I could forget," Brydie mumbled.

Pauline reached out and took Brydie's hand. "Don't say that," she said. "Don't ever wish to forget *anything.*"

"Sometimes I think that if I forgot about certain things, I'd be a better person . . . an easier person to get along with," Brydie confessed.

Pauline shook her head, adamant, and said, "The minute you begin to forget what you've experienced is the minute you cease to become the person you were and begin to become someone else. Someone unrecognizable in the mirror in the morning."

"Would that be bad?"

"It wouldn't be you."

"And those memories in your basement . . ." Brydie said carefully, slowly. "You don't wish to forget them? Even though you can't bear to have them upstairs where you live your life?"

Pauline let out a sigh. A sigh so loud that Thomas hurried over to where they were and said to Brydie, "I think it's time for you to go now."

"I'm fine, Thomas," Pauline objected. "I'm fine."

"You need to *rest,*" he said, glaring over at Brydie. "I've been telling you that for half an hour."

"It's okay," Brydie said, freeing herself from Pauline's grasp. "Thomas is right. It's getting late."

As Brydie made her way with Teddy toward the thick double doors for exiting to the parking lot, she caught a glimpse of herself in the mirrored windows reflecting off the streetlights. The woman staring back at her looked worn down. She looked pinched and pained. She looked, she realized, just exactly as her mother had looked in the bedroom earlier that evening. It was no wonder Pauline scarcely recognized her, although she knew with a sinking realization that Pauline's health was failing right before her very eyes. It seemed odd that the vibrant old woman she'd met that first day could be the sickly creature she'd seen the past couple of weeks.

She wondered what it was that Nathan saw in her, what he saw that made him like her, made him want to be with her. It had been so long since she'd seen herself as desirable. If, in fact, she ever had. Sometimes Allan would tell her she was beautiful, but that had been long ago, when they were first married. Brydie sometimes felt like he said it out of obligation—because he thought it was something a husband *should* say. He'd never looked at her the way he'd been looking at Cassandra in the photograph her mother texted her.

But Nathan looks at me that way.

When Brydie thought about it, really thought about it, she couldn't imagine being Pauline's age and married to Allan. She couldn't imagine languishing in a nursing home, alone, only to realize that she'd spent her entire life with a man who didn't really love her. And even worse, that *she* hadn't really loved herself. Maybe that's what her mother had meant when she said she'd taken her anger out on Brydie. She'd been unhappy in her marriage and unhappy with herself. Brydie wished she and her mother had talked about it before now—about all of it, even the parts Brydie didn't want to admit to, like her father's drinking. Maybe if they'd had a better relationship, they both would have been happier.

Brydie stared back at her reflection, hard. At her feet, Teddy nudged her to keep moving. Instead she bent down and picked him up, awkwardly clutching him to her, breathing in his musty scent. She brought his face to eye level with hers, and when she did, Teddy unfurled his tongue and licked her.

"Come on," she said, putting him back down on the sidewalk. "Let's get out of here. We've got one more stop to make tonight."

CHAPTER 30

ALL OF THE LIGHTS WERE OFF AT NATHAN'S house by the time Brydie pulled into his driveway. She sat there for a few minutes, debating whether to knock on the door. She knew he probably had to be at work early the next day, and maybe he'd changed his mind about her coming over.

Brydie shook her head. No. He'd asked her over. She got out of the car and carried a snoring Teddy to the door and rang the bell.

Nathan answered, wearing a white shirt and fleece pajama bottoms with moose all over them.

"Nice pants," she said, grinning at him. She placed Teddy down on the floor and he melted into it, as if he hadn't even noticed he'd been moved from the back of the car.

"I thought you'd decided against coming over," he said. His voice was thick, husky from something. What was it? Sleep?

"Did I wake you up?"

"It's okay."

"I can go," Brydie said. She went to turn around, but Nathan took her hand.

"I want you to stay," he said. "Please."

He led her toward the stairs, not saying another word. The top floor in his house was almost completely dark, with the exception of a warm, yellow light coming from a room at the opposite end of the stairwell. Once inside the room, it became apparent to Brydie that this was Nathan's bedroom, and she felt herself blush at the intimacy of simply being there.

In the middle of the room was one of the largest beds that Brydie had ever seen. A thick white comforter and plush pillows covered it. There was a dark wooden desk in one corner, and a pair of discarded scrubs were slung over the chair in front of the desk. Magazines and books covered the top of the desk completely. The floor was almost as dark as the desk, but a gray rug covered much of it. It was a room that was meant to be comfortable. Lived in. Slept in.

"I spend a lot of my time in sterile places," Nathan said, as if reading her thoughts. "I never wanted my home to reflect that. Especially not the place where I close my eyes at night and open them in the morning."

"I'm sorry that I woke you up," Brydie said because she didn't know what else to say.

Nathan kissed her, and it was harder this time, with more force than he'd had when he was in the kitchen with her earlier that evening. "I couldn't sleep now if I tried."

Brydie pulled at him, an urgency that she hadn't known existed until now surging through her, and Nathan put his hand onto the small of her back to stay her, leading her over to the big bed.

She sat down, staring up at him as he took off his shirt. He lowered himself down on top of her and began to kiss her again, and this time she had trouble catching her breath in between the meeting of their lips. She allowed him to pull off her own shirt and then her jeans, her hands finding their way to the mass of curls on his head.

As Nathan's mouth made its way down from her lips to her collarbone to her breasts, Brydie felt herself opening up, blooming right there in his bedroom underneath him. It was a confidence she'd never known existed. A small, satisfied smile escaped her lips, and she closed her eyes.

When she opened them again, Nathan was watching her. Their eyes locked, and she managed to whisper, "Please."

Without breaking her gaze, he slid himself inside of her. Now Brydie sucked in her breath, air filling her lungs. Thoughts of everything else fled from her mind. She didn't think about Allan or Cassandra or the last year of her life spent in turbulence and virtual homelessness. She didn't think about the loss of her bakery or the fight she'd had with her mother or the withering old woman at the nursing home. There was nothing else but this moment, the here and now with Nathan Reid, and the exquisite moment that the two of them became one.

BRYDIE AWOKE THE next morning to the smell of coffee and bacon frying. She sat up, rubbing her eyes, for a moment forgetting where she was. As she stretched out, one of her feet hit a hard lump at the foot of the bed, and she realized that both Teddy and Sasha were there, fast asleep. She reached down and gave both dogs' ears a scratch before swinging her legs over the side of the bed and groping around the dimly lit room for her pants.

It was raining outside, a fine mist that seemed to coat everything, even inside the house, and Brydie shivered slightly when her bare feet left the carpet and hit the wooden floor in Nathan's bedroom. Downstairs the light was much better, and she followed the scent of coffee into the kitchen.

She watched him from the entryway for a second, her nervousness about seeing him in the daylight getting the better of her. She hadn't meant to spend the night, not really, although Brydie had to admit it was a happy accident. They'd stayed up for a while afterward, talking. She didn't remember falling asleep, but once during the night she'd woken up to find the bathroom and considered leaving. She hadn't wanted to make the morning awkward.

But she'd returned to the bed and watched him sleeping, the way his lips parted slightly as he breathed. The rhythmic motion of his chest moving up and down, up and down, up and down. She thought she might just slide into bed for a few more minutes to be next to him, and when she had, he'd reached over and grabbed her hand, whispering, "Don't go."

Before she could protest, she was fast asleep next to him. She hadn't woken up again until just a few minutes ago, slightly dazed and alone in the big bed.

"Oh, good morning," Nathan said when he saw her, making her jump. "I was wondering when you might wake up."

"What time is it?" Brydie asked, shaking her head to clear her thoughts. She still felt fuzzy from everything that happened the day . . . and night . . . before.

"Almost nine A.M."

Brydie accepted the cup of coffee he offered her and said, "But I thought you had to be at the hospital hours ago."

"I called in," he replied.

"You did?"

"First time, ever."

Brydie cocked her head to one side. "Oh?"

"I thought we might spend the day together," Nathan said. "I mean, if you didn't have any other plans."

Brydie was taken aback by this. She hadn't really expected to be asked to stay, especially after he'd told her he had to be at work before dawn. Truthfully, she'd expected a note and a promise for a phone call. "I don't," she said.

"You don't have to work tonight?"

Brydie shook her head. "I don't have to be back at work until Monday night."

"Great," Nathan replied, rubbing his hands together. "I have somewhere I want to take you."

"Where?"

"Nope." Nathan moved back over to the stove, flipping the bacon. "It's a surprise."

"Can I go home and shower after I eat? Change?" Brydie asked, feeling giddy. "I don't want to go anywhere in the same clothes I wore all day yesterday. I smell like turkey."

Nathan grinned. "Pick you up in an hour?"

"Sure," Brydie said. "But what'll I do with Teddy? He's still upstairs asleep with Sasha."

"Leave him here." Nathan waved her off. "Sasha got up early with me this morning, and we went for a jog. She got back up into bed with the two of you an hour ago, and neither you nor Teddy even rolled over. I'm sure he'll still be up there asleep when you get back."

"Okay," Brydie replied. "If he does get up, he'll want eggs for breakfast."

Nathan raised an eyebrow.

"Don't judge me," Brydie replied. "It's our routine."

"Will his highness want coffee or tea to drink?"

"Water will be just fine," Brydie said. "But if you have it, he'd probably prefer Earl Grey."

BY THE TIME Brydie was dressed and ready to go, the rain had begun to pour. She wondered for a moment if they should cancel their plans. It was silly, she knew, but driving in the rain made her nervous and Memphis drivers could be . . . well, eccentric. It wasn't particularly cold outside, in the mid-forties, but she'd heard that there was snow and ice in northern Arkansas and Missouri.

Since she didn't yet know where they were going, Brydie had opted out of her usual uniform of jeans and a T-shirt, instead choosing something just as comfortable if not altogether different. She'd pulled out the heavy combat boots she'd worn over Halloween and paired them with a long gray skirt with a slit up the side and a black three-quarter-sleeved cashmere sweater that sat right at her midriff. It left her navel *almost* in plain sight if she raised her arms up just right.

It was a very 1990s ensemble that left her yearning for the days of the dELiA*s catalog and YM magazine. It was also, she thought with relish, an outfit her mother hated. She'd worn it once or twice back in Jonesboro after her divorce, and her mother told her in no uncertain terms that she was neither young enough *nor* thin enough to be wearing it.

And maybe, she thought, she actually wasn't young enough or thin enough to be wearing it; she didn't care. It made her feel good, and today she was going to feel good. She'd woken up feeling good, and she was going to go to bed that night feeling good. Maybe even at Nathan's house.

When her phone began to ring, she looked down at it expectantly. Nathan should be here any minute. Instead it was her mother calling. She'd started calling while Brydie was in the shower, and she hadn't stopped since. Brydie knew she should answer it, but she didn't want to. She didn't want to fight with Ruth Benson. She didn't want to talk about the things either one of them had said. She didn't want to, and she wasn't *going to* think about it.

When Brydie heard a car pull into the driveway, she ran out to meet Nathan, making a vain attempt to shield herself from the rain.

"Don't you have an umbrella?"

"There are about twelve in the house," Brydie replied. "But I can never remember to grab one."

"I left Teddy at the house," Nathan said, shifting the Range Rover into reverse. "I don't think I could have gotten him outside in this mess if I'd wanted to anyway."

"He's getting pretty comfortable there," Brydie said. "You may never get rid of him."

"I'm hoping his owner will feel the same way soon."

Brydie grinned, feeling herself warm from the inside out. "So where are we going?"

"I told you it's a surprise."

"All right," she sighed with mock irritation. "Fine."

"It figures that the first day I've ever taken off from the hospital would be a rainy day," Nathan continued. "Maybe we should have just stayed at my place."

"It's all right," Brydie said. "I spend almost all of my time at home, at the nursing home, or at work. It's nice to get out somewhere different."

When they neared downtown Memphis and they turned onto Union Avenue, Brydie knew where they were. She hadn't been close to downtown since the night Nathan took her out to dinner, and she smiled to herself remembering it. A year ago she couldn't have imagined herself where she was now. She knew that not everything had changed—there were many parts of her life that weren't settled. She didn't know how long she'd be living in Mrs. Neumann's house, and she didn't know if her job would keep her past the holidays. In a few months, Brydie realized, everything could be much different than it was now. It occurred to her for the first time that if she had to move away from the house in Germantown, she might have to move away from Teddy as well. The thought made her feel a panic in her chest that she hadn't expected. She didn't want to leave Teddy. She didn't ever want to leave Teddy.

"We're here," Nathan said, drawing Brydie out of her thoughts. "The grandest hotel in the South—the Peabody Memphis."

Brydie blinked. She hadn't been paying attention, and now they were parked in a space in a large parking garage. She knew where they were, of course, because she'd been here before. "I love this place," she whispered.

"What?" Nathan asked. "Have you been here?"

Brydie glanced over at him. The look of disappointment on his face was palpable. It was obvious that he'd meant to take her somewhere she'd never been—the surprise he'd been so excited about. "No," she said, unable to tell him the truth and spoil it for him. "But I've heard about it."

"It's one of my favorite places."

"Well, then," Brydie said. "We'd better go inside."

"My grandparents brought me here every time I visited," Nathan said, slamming his door shut and leading her toward the big double doors at one end of the parking garage. "This way. We can walk down the covered overpass and stay out of the rain."

Brydie followed him, breathing in the smell of the rain on the asphalt. "Wow," Brydie said when they got inside. It had been so many years since she'd seen the place, at least eleven. Not too long after that, she'd deemed herself far too old to go on day trips with her father during the summertime. She hadn't remembered the gold filigree and heavy, wooden embellishments. She hadn't remembered the rich carpets or the flapper-era mystique of the place.

"I know," Nathan whispered. "Isn't it grand?"

"It really is."

"The hotel was originally built in the late 1800s at another location, but they rebuilt here in 1925," Nathan said. "It feels like stepping into a time capsule."

"I sort of wish I was wearing a dress with fringe and a headband," Brydie said.

"Sit down," Nathan said, gesturing to a table in the middle of the lobby.

Brydie sat. There were several tables roped off in the middle of the expansive room, and at one end there was a bar. At the other end there was another staircase that Brydie knew led to a restaurant and bakery. The elevators were to their left, and the front desk, with its smartly dressed employees, was to their right.

"Let's have a drink," Nathan said. "What would you like?"

Brydie squinted at the little menu on the table. She considered for a moment the Peabody Mint Julep, but decided instead on the Lucille, a drink that was named after B. B. King's famous guitar. It also had blackberries and tequila, which sounded like they'd go perfectly together. "I'll have the Lucille."

"I'll be right back," Nathan replied. "They don't seem too busy today, so it probably won't take long. It must be the weather."

Brydie didn't say it out loud, but she was glad that the place was practically deserted. She liked the quiet. She liked the way she could hear the people at the front desk chatting with each other, the occasional bout of laughter echoing off the walls. She liked that the hustle and bustle was on the outside instead of inside.

After a few minutes, Nathan returned with their drinks. "I thought we could have a couple of drinks here first, and then maybe we could go into the restaurant for a late lunch. I'm sorry—I didn't even think to ask if you were hungry."

"No, I'm fine," Brydie replied, taking a sip of her drink.

"There's something happening later here in the lobby that I think you'll love," Nathan said.

"Oh yeah?"

"Yeah."

Brydie had a hunch about what it was, but she didn't say anything. Her drink was so good. She hoped there would be time for another.

"My grandfather used to take my sisters and me on day trips when we visited him during the summertime," Nathan continued. "He thought we needed to learn more about where we came from. He didn't think much of the East Coast and never quite understood why my mother married a Yankee."

"My ex-husband is from Kansas," Brydie said. "Not quite a Yankee, but good enough for everyone down here."

Nathan laughed and took a sip of his Tom Collins. "Yeah, so you can imagine how well being from the East Coast went over. Anyway, my sister hated it down here. She thought people were backwards and she often found it hard to hide her contempt. But she went along with the outings anyway, I suppose because it was better than staying home with our grandmother and baking all day."

"I guess your sister was right in some ways," Brydie said. "It's not as fast-paced as the coast. It's not as forward-thinking in a lot of ways, especially with older generations."

"True," Nathan replied. "My grandfather didn't mind showing us the uglier side of life down here, either, and it was sometimes hard to swallow. My sister stopped coming to visit when she was in high school. My grandparents never said anything, but I think it hurt them deeply."

"Did they ever come up to visit you?"

"They came up for Christmas, until they got too

old to travel much," Nathan said. "But they didn't like it up there any more than the rest of my family liked it down here."

"But you liked it here?"

"Obviously," Nathan replied. "I visited until I moved down here for medical school. My grandfather and I were very close. That's why, I guess, they left their house to me instead of my mother. That was quite the argument. My mother expected to inherit everything. When she didn't, well, she blamed me. She said I'd taken advantage of my grandparents—that as they got older, I somehow convinced them to bypass the rightful heir."

"That hardly seems fair," Brydie said.

"My mother has always been concerned with money," Nathan said, taking another, larger swig of his drink. "We don't get along very well."

"They must've been proud that you became a doctor, your parents," Brydie said. "I know my mother would have been thrilled if I'd done something with my life other than 'baking brownies' for people, as she calls it."

"They like telling people I'm a doctor, if that's the same thing," Nathan said. "I think my mother was always a little jealous of my relationship with her parents. She put on a good show when I got the bulk of their estate, but to tell you the truth, I think she half-expected it."

Brydie hadn't known either set of her grandparents very well. Her father's parents died when she was too young to remember them, and her mother's parents spent most of their time in a nursing home. Visits were rare. It occurred to her that her mother and Nathan's mother might share more than a few similarities. "My mother and I don't get along very well, either," she said quietly. "It's been that way for as long as I can remember, but I think from now on, we're going to try a bit harder."

"I'm glad."

"It's just complicated," she said. "It's been worse since my dad died."

Nathan nodded. "The last time my parents came for a visit was after I'd moved into the house in Germantown. I'd remodeled it, and I was so proud. When my mother came in, she broke down into tears. She said all of her memories were gone. I thought that was ridiculous, because she'd only lived there the last couple years of high school. I'd taken everything I thought she might want and put it in one of the spare rooms. We argued that night about how she thought I'd relegated her old life to one room—the smallest room in the house. We didn't speak again for almost a year."

Brydie wished she had something encouraging to say—words of wisdom about raw emotions after death—but she didn't. She had not yet learned how to navigate the waters of grief or guilt or anything else that came along with having a family member who didn't understand you. She couldn't tell him about how she sort of understood his mother's reaction. She'd had the same visceral response when her mother redecorated after her father died. Everything of Gerald Benson's had been stuffed into his old study, and it was almost as if he hadn't existed. It was one of the worst fights she and her mother had ever had. Now, of course, she knew that her mother had been grieving just like she'd been grieving, but in a different way. She wished she could go back to that moment and take back the words she'd said.

"Do you want another?" Nathan motioned to her empty drink. "I think I'd like one more."

"Yes, please," Brydie answered, smiling over at him.

Nathan walked away and back over toward the lobby bar, and Brydie noticed that a setup of sorts was taking place in the middle of the lobby by the large fountain. A walkway to the lobby elevators had been blocked off, and a middle-aged man in a dapper red jacket and a cane with a golden duck head was rolling out a thick red carpet.

Traffic in the lobby had picked up, and children had begun to sit down by the carpet. People were milling about, shaking rain off their umbrellas and ordering drinks. Brydie shifted in her seat to get a better view of the goings-on in the middle of the room.

"Sorry that took so long," Nathan said when he finally returned with their drinks. "It's starting to liven up in here."

"I've noticed." Brydie took another sip of her Lucille. "This is one of the most delicious drinks I've ever had."

"Can you see okay?" Nathan asked. His eyes were dancing around excitedly. "I want to make sure you can see everything."

"I can see just fine," Brydie replied. She knew what was about to happen, but his enthusiasm was so cute, so genuine, she was glad she hadn't told him about visiting the Peabody before.

In front of them, the man with the red coat began to speak. "Gather round, ladies and gentlemen, and let me tell you the illustrious story of the Peabody Ducks."

"Are you listening?" Nathan whispered.

Brydie nodded, grinning.

"Way back in the 1930s, the general manager of the Peabody, Frank Schutt, and a friend came back to Memphis from a hunting trip to Arkansas. The men had a little too much whiskey, and they thought it would be funny to place some of their live duck decoys in the beautiful Peabody fountain. Three small English call ducks were selected as 'guinea pigs,' and the reaction was nothing short of enthusiastic. Thus began a Peabody tradition, which was to become internationally famous. In 1940, a former circus-animal trainer offered to help with marching the ducks to the fountain each day and taught them the Peabody Duck March. This man became the Peabody Duckmaster, serving for fifty years until 1991. Decades after that very first march, ducks still visit the lobby fountain. What you are about to witness, ladies and gentlemen, is the march of the Peabody Ducks."

Brydie watched as one of the lobby elevators opened and several ducks waddled out, led by the Duckmaster. Using his cane as guidance, the ducks followed him to the fountain, amid cheering children and smiling adults. One by one, the ducks marched around the fountain and jumped in, seemingly oblivious to the people around them.

"What do you think?" Nathan asked her.

"It's wonderful," Brydie whispered, truly meaning it.

The last time she'd seen the march of the ducks, she'd been seven years old. Her father woke her up one morning and told her that she was going to be taking the day off school, as he had some business to attend to in Memphis. At first she'd been wary about going with her father on a "business" outing. She'd been on them before, and they were always impossibly boring and consisted of delivering real estate paperwork for her mother. He usually had a drink or five, and they had to wait long enough for him to be able to drive again. Sometimes that was hours. But this day, her father didn't have any paperwork. He didn't have any drinks. Instead he bundled her up into the car, and they drove along the interstate singing George Michael songs.

When they had pulled up to the Peabody, Brydie knew she was in for a delight. First, Gerald Benson treated her to lunch at the restaurant, where she got to eat her fill of cheese grits, before heading over to the bakery for a duck-shaped cookie. In the lobby, he'd let her order a Fuzzy Duckling drink while he nursed a beer, and they waited.

"Now, you can't tell your mother where we've gone today," he'd said to her with a wink. "She needs to think you've been slaving away at school for the last eight hours."

Brydie had grinned at him. Secrets between her and her father were her favorite things. They shared lots of them, and it felt like they lived in their own, private world that was impenetrable from the outside. He was her best friend, and at seven years old, she couldn't imagine that it would ever change between them.

Of course, things had changed. She'd grown up, and her father had gotten older. When he hurt his back when Brydie was sixteen, life changed even more. Life in the house became unbearable—her father's constant pain and her mother's constant reminders that her father was not as he once was. She supposed that it was one of the reasons she'd been so keen to marry Allan. Marrying him meant getting away from it all, and when she came to visit, everyone seemed to be on their best behavior.

The summer before her father died, he and Brydie had the last conversation they ever would about her having children. He'd been so insistent about a grandchild, and Brydie hadn't been in the mood to talk about it.

"I just need one," he'd said one afternoon over coffee at the bakery. "Just one little girl or boy on whom to dote. It's lonely having no one to take on adventures."

"You can't go on adventures, Dad," she'd said, motioning for him to eat the last cranberry scone. "Not anymore, at least."

At that, her father had grown very quiet and said nothing more. Brydie spent the rest of the afternoon feeling guilty about it, but she'd never apologized.

Now, as Brydie watched the children laughing and clapping for the ducks, their mothers and fathers looking on with smiles on their faces, Brydie felt the absence of her father more than she had in years. She felt the absence, too, of the child she never had—that her father never had the chance to meet.

She sat back in her chair, allowing the two Lucilles she'd drunk and her emotions to wash over her. She'd told herself a million times not to dwell, but the wound was still fresh. She didn't know at that moment if it would ever heal. How could the words she'd never said, the life she'd never created, fester so? Would she always feel this raw?

Brydie didn't even realize that she'd gotten lost inside of her own head until Nathan pulled his chair up close to her and said, "Didn't you like the ducks?"

"What?" Brydie looked around, blinking, as if she'd just woken up. "Oh, yes, I loved them," she said.

"Then what's wrong?"

"Nothing!"

"I can tell there's something bothering you," Nathan replied. "You had this faraway look on your face. And I thought for a moment that you might just burst into tears."

"Did I?" Brydie feigned surprise. "I didn't tell you the truth earlier," she said.

"Oh?"

"I've been here before, to the Peabody." Brydie looked up at him and tried to smile. "My dad used to bring me here when I was a kid. We'd make a day of it. He'd take me out to eat and let me order a fancy drink here in the lobby." She paused, trying to find the right words. "They're tender memories for me, and I haven't thought about this place in a very long time."

"I wish you'd told me," Nathan said. "I wouldn't have brought you here if I'd known you were going to be upset."

"I'm not upset," Brydie said, and she realized it was true. Being there was maybe a bit bittersweet, but she wasn't upset. "I'm glad you brought me here. It's just that it reminds me so much of my father. And until recently, I'd always thought he was the perfect father, the perfect husband. But it wasn't true."

"Nobody is perfect."

"I know," Brydie said. "I just wasn't ready to admit it."

"And you are now?"

Brydie shrugged. "No, not really," she said. "My mother and I had this awful fight before I moved to Memphis. I was living with her after my divorce. I guess I was putting a lot of blame on myself for what happened with Allan. I guess I was putting a lot of blame on my mother, too."

"I see that sometimes at the hospital," Nathan said. "Sometimes when something terrible happens, something tragic, it's much easier to assign blame than it is to come to terms with your own sadness."

Brydie nodded. "Yes, it was a whole lot easier to be angry," she said. "Anyway, my mom told me some things about my dad, about his drinking, that upset me. I'd known, of course, but I didn't want to hear it. Not from her."

"Your dad drank a lot?"

"He did," Brydie replied. "She called him an alcoholic and a terrible husband."

"Ouch."

"She apologized for it. Yesterday, actually," Brydie said. "But I ignored it for so long, pushed it down for so long, that now I can't stop thinking about it."

"You can still love him, you know," Nathan said. His voice was quiet and tender. "You can even love him more for it, knowing what you do."

"Really?"

"Of course." Nathan scooted his chair over to her side and draped his arm around her. "He loved you, and that had nothing at all to do with his faults or a disease he was unable to control. You were his greatest accomplishment, and I'm sure he knew it."

Brydie felt a tear slide down her cheek, and she wiped at it furiously with the back of her hand. "Thank you," she whispered.

"I'm glad this is something I can share with you." Nathan was looking her in the eyes. "I think your father and my grandfather would be pleased to find us here together."

"I think they *are* pleased that we're here."

"Let's go get something to eat," Nathan said, standing up. "I'm starving all of a sudden."

Brydie stood and together they walked across the lobby and up the marble staircase toward the restaurant. As they passed by the bakery, Brydie couldn't help but poke her head inside, smelling the delicious delights of the little shop.

"Do you want to go inside?" Nathan asked.

"If you don't mind," she said. "I'd just like to look around." Brydie wandered around, taking in the pastries and resisting an urge to walk behind the case and hold a few of them in her hands, warm and gooey.

"Hey, come over here," Nathan said, pulling her out of her thoughts and leading her over to a small display case toward the entrance of the bakery. "Look, they've got dog treats."

Brydie bent down to look at the display. They did have dog treats—gorgeous ones, wrapped in crinkly cellophane of all colors. There was a card attached to each one promoting a business in Southaven, Mississippi, just about a twenty-minute drive from Memphis. "These look fancy," she said, admiring them. "I love the packaging. That's half of the sales pitch, right there."

"I wonder if they're any good," Nathan said. "I'm always suspicious of anything in too pretty a package."

Brydie rolled her eyes. "This from a man who drives a Range Rover."

"Okay," Nathan conceded. "The Range Rover and you are my exceptions to the rule."

Brydie tried not to grin at his cheesy line, but she couldn't help herself. "It's very clever, though, to put fancy dog treats in a fancy bakery for people. I bet they sell lots of these."

"I'm sure they do."

Brydie resisted the urge to ask the woman behind the glass case how many of those dog treats they sold in a week. This bakery, all of the Peabody really, catered to a very specific clientele—people who could afford certain luxuries. It was something she hadn't realized as a child, but was all too aware of now. She wondered how a bakery that specialized in treats for both dogs and people would do in Memphis, the kind of place where someone could stop in and grab coffee and a scone *and* a treat for their dog as they went about their morning walk. She was positive that every person she'd baked dog treats for in the last couple of months, Nathan included, would visit a place like that, and the more she thought about this idea, the more she liked it.

"You don't want to buy any of those, do you?" Nathan asked. "Surely what you make is better."

"No," Brydie answered, turning to face him. "Let's go eat."

As they approached the maître d', a tall, balding man in a flashy black tuxedo, Nathan's phone began to ring. "It's Myriah," he said. "Let me just take this real quick."

Brydie nodded and watched a group of people rush into the lobby from the front door, their laughter and the sound of the rain tinkling up to where she stood. They looked like they'd just come from an office, and she followed them with her eyes as they made their way over to the lobby bar. When she felt Nathan tap her on the shoulder she turned around and said, "Is everything all right?"

"Not exactly," Nathan replied. "Myriah says that the basement is starting to flood. I think I'd better get home and check it out."

Brydie's eyes widened. "Okay, of course," she said. "Let's go."

"I'm sorry about lunch."

"Don't be," she said.

"We'll grab something on the way home if you want," Nathan said.

"I'm fine," Brydie insisted. "Let's just go."

Nathan nodded, and Brydie followed him back out of the grand hotel, allowing her one last look before they disappeared into the parking garage and headed back to Germantown to face whatever it was that awaited them.

CHAPTER 31

THE RAIN WAS STILL COMING DOWN IN JAGGED layers when Nathan pulled into his garage. "Just let me check on this, and then I'll take you and Teddy home," he said.

"Of course."

When they got inside, Myriah was pacing worriedly in the living room, with Sasha at her heels. In front of the fireplace, Teddy snored. Brydie couldn't help but smile amusedly at him. She could hear him over the crackle of the logs.

"I brought up a bunch of the boxes and totes on the floor," Myriah said, motioning to one corner of the room. "I don't think the water leaked into the totes, but the boxes, well . . ."

"It's okay," Nathan replied, placing a hand lightly on her shoulder. "There isn't much more you could have done."

"But the furniture down there," Myriah lamented. "Your grandmother's antique couch!"

"It was in terrible shape anyway," Nathan said. "I kept saying I was going to have it reupholstered, but I never did. It's not your fault, Myriah."

Myriah smiled gratefully at him. "A couple of the neighbors have already been over to check on things," she said. "I guess several houses have flooded on the bottom floor."

"We'd better go down and see the damage," Nathan said. "Nothing to do but wait until the morning to make calls."

Above them, the lights flickered once, twice, and then went out for good.

"Great," Nathan muttered. "Just great."

Other houses had flooded? What about her house? She hadn't thought about it until just then, but all of the houses on the block were so similar. It seemed a logical conclusion to draw—her basement might be flooded as well. "I'd better go home," she said, striding over to Teddy. "Now I'm worried that my basement might look like yours."

"You should go home and check," Nathan said in agreement. "I'll take you home."

"I hate for you to do that. You've got enough to deal with here."

"I can take her," Myriah offered. "It's the least I can do."

Nathan nodded. "Okay, thanks."

Brydie wanted a minute alone with him to thank him for the day. She wanted to say something to him about the night before, and the curious side of her, the side of her she was trying to quiet, wanted to make sure that if not for the events unfolding right this minute, he'd ask for her to stay again.

But Myriah was already clipping Teddy's leash to his harness and ushering them out the door and back into the rain.

"It's really comin' down out there," Myriah said once they were in the safety of her car. "It's a wonder we aren't all floating down the Mississippi River by now."

"At least it's not ice," Brydie said. "That's one nice thing about living this far south. We won't get too many ice storms."

Myriah nodded into the dark. "True enough."

"It looks like the power is off on the whole street," Brydie said. "I hope I can remember where I saw that flashlight."

Myriah pulled into the driveway and put her car in park. "Here we are," she said.

"Thanks for taking me home," Brydie said, truly grateful. "Nathan is lucky to have you. And so are Sasha and Teddy."

"Teddy is a doll," Myriah said. "And Sasha adores him."

"I think the feeling is mutual."

"And what about Nathan?" Myriah asked. "You like him a lot, huh?"

Brydie was taken aback, but she answered truthfully, "I do."

"I can tell," Myriah said.

"He's been good for me," Brydie said. "The last year has been . . . difficult."

Myriah turned to face her. "Dr. Reid is one of the greatest men I know," she said. "He's been there for me when my own father couldn't be."

Brydie smiled, not knowing what to say.

"You know he's the reason I decided to become a

doctor?" Myriah continued. "I'm getting a degree in biology, and my dad thinks it's because of him. But it's not. It's because of Nathan."

Brydie wasn't sure why Myriah had picked now to have a heart-to-heart with her, now when all Brydie wanted to do was to get inside her house and check on the basement. "I'm sure he'd be very flattered to hear that," she said. "He says you're a great student."

"I love him," Myriah said, her voice barely above a whisper. "I know I'm too young for him, but I guess I'd been holding out hope. After seeing him with you, though, I know that it's never going to happen."

Brydie felt her chest tighten, and an unexpected sympathy for the young woman came over her. She knew what it was like, better than anyone, to be in love with someone when there was no hope of the love being returned. She'd seen it in Allan's face the night he'd told her he wanted a divorce. It wasn't exactly the same, she knew, but it was painful nonetheless.

"I'm sorry," Myriah said before Brydie could think of something to say. "I shouldn't have said anything. Please don't tell Nathan."

"It's okay," Brydie said. "I won't say anything."

"I hope I haven't made things weird between us." Brydie shook her head. "You haven't."

"It's just I don't want to lose . . . my place, I guess," Myriah said. Her hands were gripping the steering wheel.

Now Brydie understood. Myriah was afraid that if Nathan and Brydie became too serious, she would no longer be a part of his life. "Look," Brydie said, "I can't speak for Nathan, but I can tell you that he depends on you. And I can promise you that I'd never do anything to keep him from depending on you."

A look of relief washed over Myriah's face that was evident even in the dim light of the car. "Thank you, Brydie."

"I really need to get inside," Brydie said. "I should check on the basement."

"Of course," Myriah replied. "Do you need some help getting inside?"

Brydie was already out of the car and in the backseat, removing Teddy. "I think I'm all right," she said. "Thank you, though."

"I'll just wait until you get inside," Myriah said, craning her neck to face Brydie in the backseat.

Brydie didn't even bother to set Teddy down on the ground and instead carried him up the front steps, putting him down only when she needed to fish the key out of her purse. The dog shook himself as rain pelted onto him and snorted his disapproval to her until they were safely inside the house. Despite the lack of power and the possible flooding of the basement, Brydie was happy to be home. An overwhelming sense of exhaustion washed over her, and she wished more than anything she could crawl into bed.

She felt her way toward the cabinet by Teddy's food bowls, cursing when she accidentally stepped in his water, sloshing it all over the floor. She grabbed the flashlight she'd used the first night she went to the basement. She was relieved that the batteries were still charged enough for the flashlight to work.

It occurred to Brydie that the house was more than a little bit creepy at night, especially with the flashlight beam bouncing off the pictureless walls. She went into the bedroom to retrieve the key and Teddy followed, jumping up onto the bed.

"Teddy, no!" Brydie hissed, helplessly watching

him burrow down onto the comforter, pieces of the blanket sticking to his wet fur. He looked over at her and cocked his head to the side before rolling over onto his back.

Brydie sighed and shone the beam away from Teddy and traced her steps back out into the hallway and to the basement door. She could feel her heart beating in her throat as she turned the lock. What would she find? Would the basement be underwater? Who would she call if it were? Did she call Mrs. Neumann? She realized that she didn't know whom she was supposed to contact in a time of crisis.

When Brydie reached the bottom step, she found there was water up to her ankle. She resisted the urge to turn and run back upstairs, and instead shone the flashlight around the room. There was only one thing she needed to save—one reason for wading through the murky water in the dark—Pauline's trunk at the far corner of the basement. That trunk held all of Pauline's memories, the memories she'd been so afraid of forgetting about the last time they spoke.

Brydie couldn't leave it.

She set the flashlight down on its side on one of the steps that remained dry and waded through the water, ignoring whatever it was that was brushing up against her legs as she moved. The dim light was just enough for her to find the handle at one end of the trunk. She took a hold of it and pulled. It was heavy, and the inches of water that had accumulated over the last few hours weren't helping.

She was out of strength by the time she got to the top of the stairs, and she collapsed into a soggy heap in the hallway next to the trunk. She hoped that she wasn't too late to save whatever was inside. Pushing herself up from the floor, Brydie went to the bathroom and pulled out as many towels as she could carry and brought them into the living room. She spread them out one by one and then pulled the trunk on top.

Satisfied for the moment, Brydie picked up her phone, still ignoring the missed calls from her mother, and called Elliott to tell her about the flooding of the basement. She hadn't answered, of course. But Elliott had said to call if there was an emergency, and Brydie was certain that this qualified.

Exhaling a breath she hadn't known she'd been holding inside, she stared at the newly liberated trunk. Dragging her eyes away from it, Brydie went into the kitchen and searched the cabinets for a wineglass and then poured into it what was left of a cheap ShopCo bottle of Pinot Noir that Rosa had brought for Thanksgiving. She took a sip and scowled; it wasn't her favorite. She resisted the urge to gulp it down, hopeful that the wine would help her make a decision about what to do with the trunk. Surely it would have to be opened to make sure whatever was inside wouldn't be ruined.

She wished Elliott had answered her phone, and thought somewhat jealously about the demanding schedule of her best friend's life. It was evening, and Brydie was sure it was Mia's bath time or bedtime or something or other. When she'd lived there, she'd tried to remember the strict schedule that Elliott followed, but Brydie found that she was constantly forgetting it. She thought, as the childless often do, that if she'd had a child, she wouldn't be so ridiculous about scheduling. Surely a baby didn't *have* to breastfeed every four hours. Surely a toddler didn't *have* to have a bath at 6 P.M. on the dot.

Although their relationship remained close, it had been difficult for Brydie when Elliott announced her second pregnancy. She'd told Brydie before she'd told anyone else. She'd gone down to the basement one night when Mia was staying with her friend Gigi and told her friend that she was expecting a baby. The way Elliott had looked at her—at her face but not in her eyes, told Brydie that her friend expected a negative reaction. Elliott knew how badly Brydie wanted a baby, wanted one still, despite the fact that her marriage had crumbled before her very eyes.

"I'm so happy for you," Brydie had said, a genuine smile on her face.

"Really?" Elliott asked. "You're not upset?"

"Just because I'm sad for myself right now doesn't mean I can't be happy for you," Brydie said. "And you and I both know you've been through something far worse than a divorce."

Elliott rarely mentioned her miscarriage, and Brydie respected that, so of course she didn't come out and say what worse thing her friend had been through. Brydie truly couldn't imagine much worse than a miscarriage, to have wanted a baby as much as Elliott and Leo had wanted that baby and then to have heard the words "We can't find a heartbeat."

Brydie took another swill of the Pinot. She guessed that Leo and Elliott had wanted her to move out for reasons other than the space she was taking up in their basement. She hadn't meant to, but she'd made them uncomfortable. They'd wanted to be happy, to be cautiously optimistic, and there was Brydie, acting like a sad sack on their basement sectional. Ordinarily the thought would have upset her, but this time it didn't. She'd needed to move out. She'd *needed* to live on her own—even if she was basically living some-one else's life.

No, Brydie thought. *I'm living my own life. I'm living my own life for the first time in thirty-four years.*

It was the first time in her life she'd lived alone. It was the first time in her life she'd done anything without waiting for someone else's cue. She stole a look over at the trunk. She had to find a way to get inside of it, if for no other reason than to make sure that whatever was inside was not damaged.

Brydie walked over to the trunk and ran a finger across the lid. There was no way she could open it without the key unless she damaged the lock. She moved around to the back and suddenly had an idea. Maybe she could take the hinges off. With new pur-pose, she set down the empty glass and grabbed her keys. She kept a small tool kit in her glove box, and she figured a screwdriver would do the trick.

Brydie knelt down and located the hinges on the back of the lid. Then she removed the screws with her screwdriver. Once the hinges were detached, she carefully lifted the back of the cedar chest lid and looked inside.

There was a blanket on top—a thick, lavender-colored wool that Brydie thought might just come apart in her hands. Placing the blanket on the floor beside her, Brydie peered farther down into the trunk. What she saw surprised her. Instead of a hodgepodge of items or more blankets, there were two large Tupperware containers, like what Brydie might have used for storing cookies or cupcakes, sitting neatly at the bottom of the trunk.

Brydie reached inside and picked one of them up.

It was heavy, and whatever was inside slid from one side to the other when she pulled it out of the trunk. She sat the box down and got up to pour herself another glass of wine. If she was being honest with herself, she felt guilty for what she was about to do. She didn't have to look in the containers. She could put them away in the closet until the basement dried out enough for the trunk and all of its contents to be returned to the moldy corner.

Brydie pressed the corkscrew down into an unopened bottle of Merlot and sighed. By now Teddy had jumped down from the bed and waddled into the living room. He sniffed the trunk and then lay down next to it.

"You stink," Brydie said to him, sitting down crisscross applesauce beside him, careful not to slosh any Merlot from her overfull glass onto the floor. "You smell like a wet dog."

Teddy looked up at her, indignant for a moment before sneezing onto her bare leg.

Two months ago, any dog sneezing on her would have sent her into fits. She would have been running to take a shower. Now she simply used her free hand to wipe her leg before turning back to the trunk. "Have you ever seen this before?" Brydie asked Teddy, setting down her wineglass and picking up the first plastic tub. She slid two of her fingernails underneath the lid and pulled. With a pop, the lid disconnected with the base and what could only be described as years of dust came flying off and settled on both Teddy and Brydie.

This time, they both sneezed.

When Brydie was able to make her eyes stop watering and the sneezing subsided, she gazed down into the tub. Inside, there were pictures. Old pictures, and as she lifted them out and started to go through them, she realized that they must be the missing pictures from the photo album she'd found during her first trip to the basement. The people were the same, and so were the clothes. There was one of Pauline and her third husband—what was his name? Bill? They were standing next to an older couple, a man and a woman, and Brydie recognized the woman's fur coat in the picture as the same one Pauline mentioned in the story about the Thanksgiving fire. That must mean that the man and woman standing next to Pauline and Bill were Bill's parents. *Did Pauline take the pictures out of the album because she didn't like Bill's mother?* Brydie wondered. *If that was the case, why keep them at all?*

She continued to shuffle through the pictures. About halfway through, she noticed something. The pictures were faded, and the images slightly blurry and yellowed, but it looked like Pauline was gaining weight. Her face had become more rounded. Her dresses had become more flowing. And in one picture, Bill stood beside Pauline, beaming down at her, one hand pressed against her belly.

That's when it hit Brydie—Pauline had been pregnant. She flipped through the pictures faster, as Pauline's belly expanded with each faded scene. It didn't make sense. Hadn't Pauline told Brydie during her first visit that she didn't have children? She'd said four husbands . . . four husbands, but no children.

And then Brydie was at the end of the stack of pictures. She turned them over in her hands and then looked back into the plastic tub. There weren't any more. She held up the last picture, willing it to tell her its secrets. She turned it over, hoping for some sort of notation, anything to explain the mystery baby contained in the trunk—the one Pauline failed to tell her about, the one whose presence had seemingly been erased from the old woman's life.

Maybe, Brydie thought, *they had a falling-out. Maybe they haven't spoken in decades. Maybe one of them did something so awful to the other that they couldn't get past it.*

Brydie set the stack of photos down and reached for the second tub. As she did so, she thought about all the fights she and her own mother had had. She couldn't remember a time when they'd actually gotten along. Her father, with his quiet nature, had always acted as the buffer between the two of them. When he died, Brydie felt alone, but worse, she'd felt exposed—left to weather the storm that was her mother without any protection. Still, she couldn't imagine not ever speaking to her again. She couldn't imagine something so bad that she wouldn't eventually return her calls.

Lost in her own thoughts, Brydie pulled the top off the second tub. This one was lighter, and inside she found a white cotton blanket, yellowed with age. Absently, she plucked it from the tub and held it up. It took her a moment to realize that it was a hospital blanket. It had little blue and pink stripes in one corner and the name of the hospital, Memphis Memorial. Beneath the blanket, Brydie found a tiny pink stocking cap and a pink crochet dress with bows at the neck and at the end of each sleeve.

With the blanket and the cap resting in her lap, she held up the dress. It was slightly dingy and the bows were tattered, but Brydie could see that it had once been beautiful, and probably, she mused, hand-made. Brydie moved to replace the delicate pieces of clothing and noticed that the tub wasn't empty. At the bottom of the tub were two sheets of paper. The first one, the top one, was a birth certificate for Elise Elizabeth Forrester, born December 26, 1963, at 2:30 A.M. to William Forrester and Pauline Radcliff.

The second piece of paper, Brydie realized, was much different. As thoughts of her own life, her own parents, faded from her mind, she held the piece of paper closer to her face, willing what she was read-ing to be different. But no matter how she read it, the death certificate of Elise Elizabeth Forrester read the same way. She'd been born on December 26 at 2:30 A.M., and she'd died less than four hours later, at 6:07 A.M.

Brydie blinked, hard. She hadn't had that much to drink, but for some reason her stomach had soured, and she felt as if she might be sick. Her head was fuzzy, and she threw the contents of her lap back into the tub and pulled herself up, stumbling toward the bathroom with Teddy at her heels.

She knelt down at the base of the toilet, her knees pressing hard into the linoleum, and rested her head against the lid. There hadn't been a falling-out like she'd thought. There hadn't been anything, except for a short few hours of life. Brydie wished more than anything she hadn't snooped into the old wom-an's secrets to find out. How could she face her on Sunday?

Brydie sat up and scooted herself over to the bath-tub. The cool porcelain felt good on her back. She knew that she could never say anything to Pauline, lest she find out that Brydie had violated her privacy in the worst possible way. Clearly, she hadn't wanted anyone to know, let alone the near stranger living in her house. But all Brydie wanted to do was to hug her and tell her that she was sorry, like she'd done with Elliott.

At the other end of the bathroom, Teddy crept closer to her. He paused for a moment to sniff her bare feet before coming up beside her and resting his paw on her lap. When Brydie reached down to pet him, he jumped up onto her lap and began to lick at the tears on her cheeks that she hadn't even realized were falling.

Brydie put her forehead up to his and smiled. "You've done this before," she whispered to him. "I'm sorry I'm not her."

Teddy, for his part, didn't respond, except to settle himself into her lap and fall asleep, quietly snoring.

CHAPTER 32

BRYDIE TOSSED AND TURNED ALL NIGHT. HER dreams were scattered and vivid, waking her up more than once from her fretful sleep, only to be met by darkness and the reminder of what she'd discovered hours before. She dreamt of rainbow babies and lavender-colored blankets only to plummet into a horrible nightmare that she couldn't remember when she finally pulled herself out of bed the next morning.

What she really wanted to do was stay in bed all day. She was exhausted, but she'd promised Pauline that she would go and get her lunch from Gus's, and she couldn't back out, especially now.

By the time she got there, it was 11 A.M. and the place was as crowded as a Beale Street bar during Mardi Gras. She pushed through a line of people and managed to grab one of the last paper menus at the register. She'd thought she could just go up and order fried chicken or maybe even get lucky and go through a drive-thru. Now she was overwhelmed with choices of sides and pieces of chicken as an overworked waitress brushed past her with a tray of glistening chicken held high.

"Can I help you?" came a voice in front of her. "Hey, ma'am?"

Brydie looked up. "Oh, yes, I'm sorry. I've never been here before. I was just looking at the menu."

The woman didn't respond. She simply looked past her at the line and rolled her eyes up toward the ceiling. "Well, everything's good, so . . ."

"Of course," Brydie replied, feeling herself blush under the pressure. "Um, I'll take two of the three-piece all-white-meat dinners, I guess."

"That'll be seventeen fifty-six. For here or to go?"

"To go."

The woman held out her hand to accept Brydie's money. "What's your name?"

"Brydie."

The woman narrowed her eyes. "Brydie Benson?"

"Yes?" Brydie's response came out as more of a question than an answer. "That's me?"

"Oh, honey." The woman handed Brydie's money back to her. "Pauline called this morning and told me to watch out for you. She said you'd probably order the wrong thing."

"She called you?"

The woman nodded. "She used to be a regular up until a few months ago," she said. "I'd been worried about her."

"She had a stroke," Brydie said, suddenly realizing how very little she knew about Pauline's medical history. "She's doing okay. Some days are better than others."

"Well, a bit of fried chicken ain't gonna hurt," the

woman replied. "But she'll want the three pieces of dark, the slaw, and the fried pickles."

"I'll take the same thing then," Brydie replied. "Except I do want white meat."

"Have a seat on one of the benches over there," the woman said, waving off Brydie's money. "It's on the house for Mrs. Pauline."

Brydie sat down on the bench as she was told and marveled at Pauline's foresight. Of course she would have picked the wrong food, and the old woman knew it. However, when the waitress approached her and handed her two plastic bags full of delicious-smelling chicken, Brydie was grateful that Pauline had been a regular customer for so long. Despite the crowd, the service was fast, and she was relieved to step back outside and into the chilly November air.

As she walked toward her car, Brydie marveled at all of the old buildings in downtown Memphis. This was twice in a few days that she'd been downtown in the daytime, but it was the first time she'd actually noticed any of the buildings around her. One of them, a tall, skinny building in the middle of two squat ones, was empty. Brydie crossed the street to look at it, much to the chagrin of a horse-drawn carriage that seemed to come out of nowhere. After she waved her apologies to the harried driver, she jumped up onto the sidewalk and peered inside the window.

The glass was warbled and slightly dusty, but she could see the bare hardwood floors and vaulted ceilings. It probably needed a bit of work, like most untended older buildings, but still, it was beautiful. She wondered if there was an apartment upstairs, as most of the buildings of its generation had once boasted. She remembered as a child visiting her grandparents in the nursing home with her mother. Once, after a particularly boring visit where she was forced to re-count what happened at her Christmas program no fewer than ten times, her mother took her downtown for lunch at a diner with black-and-white–tiled floors and waitresses in poodle skirts.

Afterward, she and Brydie had taken a walk, Ruth Benson pointing out the old building where her par-ents had owned their dry cleaning business, Calla-han Family Cleaners.

"We lived upstairs," her mother told her. "On the second floor."

"You lived *here*?" Brydie asked, bewildered. She'd always pictured the farm outside the city limits that they'd visited before her grandparents moved to the nursing home as the only home her mother ever had before marrying her father.

Her mother nodded. "We lived here until I was nearly fifteen," she said. "Until the fire burned the downstairs, and Nanny and Poppy sold it."

"It doesn't look like anybody lives here now."

"Well, people don't do that much anymore," her mother replied. "But in the old days, when I was a kid, it was normal for shop owners to live above their businesses."

Now, as Brydie stood pressed against the runny glass, she thought about how much fun it might be to live above a bakery . . . her bakery.

There was a "For Sale or Lease" sign on the door with the name of the realty company Elliott worked for, and Brydie made a mental note to ask her about it, even though she knew she was nowhere near ready to have another bakery of her own. She likely wouldn't have the money for a long time, especially given the exorbitant rent prices downtown. Still, she couldn't help but daydream about what it might be like to have her own place again. Right now, however, it was time for her to find her car and get Pauline's Sunday dinner to her before the chicken got cold.

CHAPTER 33

Brydie went home before visiting Pauline to get Teddy, who was sufficiently annoyed at being left at home. He barked his indignation at her until they got to the car and he smelled the chicken. He spent the drive to the nursing home sniffing into the air and gazing longingly into the backseat, where the plastic bags were nestled on the floor.

"Well, you've sure got your hands full," the receptionist said when she saw Brydie lumbering in with her arms full of chicken and dog. "Do you want some help?"

"No," Brydie huffed. "I'm all right." She set Teddy down on the tile. "I don't know why he refuses to walk in the parking lot."

"Because he knows you'll carry him," the receptionist replied with a wink.

Brydie grinned and started toward Pauline's room. As she neared it, she heard a familiar voice wafting down the hallway. When she got to the door, she saw the white coat and curly hair and realized it was Nathan.

He turned around when Brydie released Teddy's leash and he ran to Pauline and put his paws up on the side of her bed. "Brydie," he said, giving her a half smile. "Mrs. Neumann and I were just talking about you."

"You were?"

"I told him I hoped Missy down at Gus's set you straight about what to order," Pauline spoke up, motioning for Nathan to lift Teddy up onto the bed. "I was worried you'd order me something ridiculous like chicken strips."

Brydie held up the plastic bags. "She set me straight, but I hope it hasn't gotten too cold. I had to run home and get Teddy."

"I'm sure it's fine." Pauline waved her off. "I had the gals down in the dining room bring up some proper plates."

Brydie released a breath she didn't realize she'd been holding, relieved that Pauline seemed to be in good spirits. She opened her mouth to speak and then the events of Friday night came rushing back to her—the flood, the trunk, the pictures . . . and everything else.

"You okay?" Nathan asked, taking a step closer to her. "You've got a weird look on your face."

"I'm fine," Brydie replied, turning her attention to the plates on the table by the window. She took a deep breath and turned back around. "But could we talk out in the hallway real quick?"

Nathan shrugged. "Sure."

"We'll be right back," she said to Pauline.

"Take your time," Pauline replied, her attention

fixed on Teddy. "I think you've gained some weight," she said to him. "What's Brydie been feeding you?"

"Is everything okay?" Nathan asked once they were out of earshot of Pauline. "I tried calling yesterday."

"It's fine," Brydie replied. "I'm sorry I didn't call you back. But hey, where's Dr. Sower?"

"She's got the stomach flu," Nathan said. "Seems to be going around to all the patients here. Half the staff has already caught it."

"Yuck. I saw the signs about the possibility of flu and to wash hands when coming and going."

"You're telling me," Nathan said. "I'm not thrilled to be here, to tell you the truth, but Dr. Sower wanted me to come and take a look at Mrs. Neumann anyway."

"Why?"

"She's having more bad days than good days," Nathan said. "I'm sure you've noticed. Her congestive heart failure is getting worse, and there are a myriad of other problems I'm probably not supposed to go into with you."

Brydie swallowed. "But she's feeling okay right now?" She wasn't sure what else to say.

"She feels okay today."

"Did you say anything about your basement being flooded?" Brydie asked. "Mrs. Neumann's basement flooded, too, and I don't know if I should tell her."

"I just got here," Nathan said. "We haven't talked about anything other than you coming to visit."

"Do you think I should tell her?"

Nathan shrugged. "It's up to you."

"I know you said once you can't tell me anything, but Nathan, I found something last night," Brydie said.

"What did you find?"

Brydie shifted from one foot to the other. "You know that trunk I told you about?"

"Yes."

"Well, I had to pull it upstairs to keep it out of the water," she said. "And then I opened it."

"You did what?"

"I had to," she said. "I was afraid what was inside might have gotten wet."

"Or maybe you just wanted to see what was inside," Nathan replied.

"I did want to see what was inside," Brydie admitted. "But now I wish I hadn't."

"Why?"

Brydie took a deep breath, willing herself not to cry in front of him like she'd done that night at the Peabody. "There were pictures," she said. "There were pictures of Mrs. Neumann when she was pregnant. Must've been in the early sixties. But Nathan, her baby, died. There was a death certificate."

Nathan cleared his throat, pulling at the stethoscope around his neck. "I know," he said finally.

"Did you know what was in the trunk?"

"Of course not," Nathan replied. He pulled her farther from the doorway. "But as one of her doctors, I have seen her complete medical history, and I don't think it would be wise for you to say anything to her about it."

"Are you sure?" Brydie asked. "I don't want to upset her. But I also don't want to lie to her."

"I wouldn't upset her if you can help it," Nathan said. "Brydie, she's very . . . delicate right now. I need you to understand that."

"I do," Brydie replied, her voice barely above a whisper.

Nathan took a step closer to her and brushed a piece of flyaway hair behind her ear. "Try not to dwell on it," he said. "Maybe tomorrow night you'd let me take you out to dinner?"

Brydie bit at the bottom of her lip. "I have to work tomorrow night," she said.

"How about breakfast Tuesday morning once you're off work?"

"I'd like that," Brydie replied.

"We'd better get back inside," Nathan said. "Mrs. Neumann was pretty excited about that chicken."

The two headed back into the room, and Brydie busied herself with taking the food out of the bags and warming it in the little microwave above the mini fridge. "Do you want your coleslaw and fried pickles, too?" Brydie asked.

"I do," Pauline replied. "Just put it all on the same plate."

"I'm glad you're feeling up to a big meal this afternoon," Nathan said, still standing in the doorway. "Some of the nurses have told me you haven't been eating much."

Brydie handed Pauline her plate and sat down beside her. "Is that true?"

"I swear, those nurses have nothing better to do than talk about us every chance they get," Pauline replied. "I ate the food you brought me on Thanksgiving."

"But not much since," Nathan replied. "And Mrs. Neumann, you know it's their job to talk about you."

Pauline sighed and then pointed her fork at Brydie. "That pie was delicious. I could eat that every day."

"I'll bake you another," Brydie replied. "Do you have a favorite?"

"Cherry icebox pie is my favorite," Pauline said just

before shoveling a forkful of chicken into her mouth. "My mother used to make it for me as a girl."

"I don't think I've ever made one," Brydie replied. "But I can get a recipe and have it for you next Sunday."

"I'd love that, dear girl."

Brydie felt herself warm from the inside out. "I'll look up a recipe as soon as I get back to your house."

"I've got one," Pauline replied. "In that cookbook in the pantry. *Better Homes and Gardens,* I think."

"Okay, I'll find it. I think I saw that cookbook the other day when I was putting away groceries."

"I'm going to leave you two," Nathan said, tipping an imaginary hat to them. "I haven't been home since midnight, and I desperately need a shower."

"Well, I wasn't going to say anything," Pauline replied, licking her fingers. "But you do need a shower, Doctor."

Brydie burst out laughing, causing Teddy to divert his attention away from the chicken and Pauline. He tilted his head from one side to the other as Brydie laughed.

Nathan grinned good-naturedly over at the two of them and then said, "I'll call you about breakfast, Brydie. See you on Tuesday."

Brydie nodded, wiping an errant tear from her eye from her fit of giggles. "Okay," she finally managed to gasp.

Pauline handed Brydie her empty plate. "I'm going to need another piece of chicken, and honey, I wouldn't say this in mixed company, but it wouldn't matter how many showers Dr. Reid missed, I'd meet him for breakfast any day of the week."

CHAPTER 34

ON MONDAY MORNING, BRYDIE WAS AWOKEN by her cell phone ringing and the doorbell ringing simultaneously. For a moment, she thought it was happening in her dream—one in which she and Pauline were sitting on the couch in the living room and gazing over the photos in the trunk.

"This one is the last one," Dream Pauline said, running her thumb over Bill's faded smile. "The last photo taken when we were happy."

"I'm so sorry," was all Brydie could think of to say, even though she knew it was inadequate. Even though she knew how much it angered her when people said it to her after her father died. Now she understood that sometimes, there was nothing else to say. "Is there anything I can do?"

Pauline looked over at her, her blue eyes glassy with nostalgia. "Don't forget about her, my Elise, when I'm gone."

Brydie sat up, shaking herself out of the dream.

She reached over to the nightstand and grabbed her phone. It was Elliott. "Hello?" Brydie croaked.

"I've been calling you for fifteen minutes!"

Brydie pulled her phone away from her ear and looked at the phone. "It's seven fifteen in the morning."

"And the guys are on their way to look at the basement. I'm on the front porch. Come let me in," Elliott replied, her annoyance evident. "I texted you last night and told you what time I'd be here."

"I guess I was asleep."

"Just open the door."

Brydie pulled herself out of bed, rolling over a sleeping Teddy in the process. He let out a yelp and army-crawled to the other side of the mattress. "Sorry, buddy," she said. "The mean lady at the door made me do it."

"It took you long enough," Elliott huffed, stepping inside the house. "It's cold out there."

"Don't you have a key?" Brydie asked.

"I left it at the office," Elliott said. "I figured you'd be up and waiting for me."

Brydie closed the door behind her friend and followed her into the living room. "I'm sorry. I hadn't meant to fall asleep so early, but I was exhausted. And I do have to work tonight, you know."

"Which is why you probably shouldn't have slept all night."

"I know," Brydie admitted. "It's going to mess me up for days."

Elliott didn't answer. She was too busy staring at the trunk still sitting in the middle of the living room. "What is this?"

"I brought it up from the basement the night of the

flood," Brydie replied, trying to sound nonchalant. "I thought Mrs. Neumann might want it saved."

"Did you tell her about the basement?"

"No," Brydie said. "I was afraid it might upset her, and I didn't want to do that."

"The company is responsible for repairs, so she may not need to know," Elliott said. "At least not now."

"I agree."

Brydie was about to respond when, much to her relief, there was another knock at the door.

"Those must be the guys I had sent over," Elliott said, turning around and heading back to the door, stopping for a moment to hold her belly.

"Are you okay?" Brydie asked. "What's wrong?"

"More Braxton Hicks contractions," Elliott replied, waving her off.

"Well, sit down," Brydie said, alarmed by the pained look on Elliott's face. "I can let the workers in."

"I'm fine," Elliott protested, but sat down anyway.

"Are you sure it's just Braxton Hicks contractions?" Brydie asked, once she'd shown the men the mess downstairs. They'd come back upstairs a few minutes later and told Brydie and Elliott that they were going to need a few different tools and left, one of the men muttering about the "damn Memphis rain," and how he missed the snow up north.

Elliott nodded.

"That sounds awful."

"It's the joy of the third trimester," Elliott replied, giving Brydie a weak smile. "I also have swollen feet and weird varicose veins on my legs and ankles. Oh, and let's not forget the gas so bad that Leo has to sleep in the guest room at night."

Brydie filled a glass with water and handed it to

her. "I'm sorry you had to come all the way out here this morning."

"It's my job," Elliott replied. "Besides, I'll be on maternity leave in a few weeks. I've just got to make it through Christmas."

"I can't believe it's almost December," Brydie said, sitting down next to her.

"What are your plans for Christmas?" Elliott asked. "You know you're always welcome to spend it with us."

Brydie shrugged. "I don't know. I haven't even thought about it yet."

"Have you talked to your mom?"

"No."

Elliott sat back and put her hands on her belly. "Oh, the baby's kicking!" she squealed. "Do you want to feel him?"

Brydie hesitated. She'd never felt a baby move before. Elliott had lived in Memphis when she was pregnant with Mia, and she'd hardly seen her then. "I guess," she said finally.

"Here." Elliott took Brydie's hand and pressed it to the side of her stomach. "Can you feel it?"

Brydie wasn't sure. She pushed down just a bit farther and concentrated. After a few moments, she felt a pulse against her fingertips, a soft *thump, thump, thump*. She looked up at Elliott. "I feel him!"

"Leo will be jealous," Elliott said. "Little man is most active in the morning when I'm at work. He hardly ever moves at night when we're at home."

Brydie was amazed that she could feel the little life inside of Elliott, all the way on the outside of her body. She thought, not for the first time, about what it must be like to carry that life all the way from conception to birth—what it must be like to hold the child you felt inside of you for nine months and know that you'd nurtured it into existence. "I can't wait to meet him," she said, grinning at her best friend. "I can't wait to meet our new baby."

BRYDIE WAS ALREADY exhausted by the time she got to work that night. She'd tried to go back to bed after Elliott left, but the men working downstairs spent what felt like hours clomping up and down the steps, their voices echoing around the house so loudly that she couldn't stay asleep. She'd thought that having an extra day off would be a glorious relief after the rush leading up to Thanksgiving at ShopCo, and it had been. However, in the meantime, she'd gotten off her sleeping schedule, and now she was feeling the effects.

"Well, you look like death warmed over," Joe said when he saw her.

Brydie wrinkled her nose at him. "Gee, thanks."

"You don't look half as bad as the poor assholes that had to work on Black Friday," Joe continued as Brydie tried unsuccessfully to straighten her name tag. "Belinda over in Toys got knocked down in the rush and broke both of her big toes."

"That's awful," Brydie replied. "I've never really understood Black Friday shopping. It hardly seems like it would be worth the risk of injury just to get an Xbox for a few bucks cheaper."

"I went to Target once for Rosa a few years ago when there was something that Lillian wanted. I think it might have been a Furby or something, I can't remember. I stood outside in line for three fuck-ing hours."

"Language!" came the automatic response from somewhere deep in the back room.

Joe rolled his eyes.

Rosa came out carrying a tray of cookies, Christmas trees, and Santa Claus heads with large, rosy cheeks. "Do these Santas look off to you?"

Brydie and Joe peered down at the cookies. They looked fine to Brydie, except for one thing. "Santa's eyes are all white."

"Well good grief," Rosa replied. "I can't believe I missed that." She turned around and hurried off, muttering to herself as she went.

"We need to get twenty dozen cookies packaged and ready to get out on the shelves," Joe said. "The day shift left us half of their work, so we've got twice as much to do tonight."

"Fantastic," Brydie muttered, feeling her head begin to throb. Had she eaten that day? She couldn't remember. Then she felt her phone vibrating in her pocket. Nathan was supposed to call about meeting in the morning for breakfast. "Care if I take this?" she asked Joe.

"You're on the clock," he replied. "Five minutes."

Brydie nodded. "Hello?" she said, scuttling away from the bakery and from Joe.

"Finally," said a voice that was decidedly not Nathan's.

"Mom," Brydie said. She wished she'd taken the time to look at her screen before she answered. "I'm at work."

"Well, I'll just hang up, call back, and leave a message," her mother said. "At least your voicemail doesn't interrupt me."

Brydie sighed.

"Or sigh."

"I've got about three minutes, Mom."

"Roger and I were thinking of having Christmas together this year," Ruth Benson said. "At my house."

"That sounds nice, Mom," Brydie said. "But I really need to get back to work."

"I was hoping maybe you and that doctor might like to come down."

"Oh, I don't know."

"Just think about it, okay?" Ruth said. "I'd really like for us to spend more time together."

"I'd like that, too, Mom," Brydie said. "I really would."

"Then it's settled. We'll see you on Christmas Eve."

"I'll be there," Brydie said. "But only if I can bring Teddy."

There was a pause, and then her mother said, "Okay. But make sure you bring plenty of lint rollers."

AS THE NIGHT transitioned into the wee hours of the morning, Brydie found herself struggling to stay awake in a way that she hadn't since she first started working at ShopCo. She almost burned more than one batch of cookies; she forgot to turn on the oven, allowing a cake to sit inside for nearly half an hour before she remembered; and she accidentally dozed off while putting buttercream on a Santa beard.

Brydie was working to complete a batch of wreaths when Rosa plopped down in front of her a plastic container of Christmas tree cookies with red and gold ornaments. "Do you think these trees look lopsided?"

"Lopsided?" Brydie knit her eyebrows together. "What do you mean?"

"Look how there is more icing on one side than the other," Rosa said, tracing a gloved finger around the outline of one of the trees.

"Maybe a little," Brydie conceded. "Do you think I need to redo them?"

"And give Joe another reason to complain tonight?" Rosa raised an eyebrow. "Absolutely not. Just place them thickest side out."

"Okay," Brydie said, feeling relieved. "I'm already behind about four batches."

"It won't get any better," Rosa said. "Joe and I have a meeting with the morning bakery manager in about ten minutes."

"Why?"

Rosa rolled her eyes clear up to the ceiling. "Apparently one of the other staff heard him complaining in the break room about all the work his crew left us," she said. "And she called Ronnie, and now he's here, demanding to talk to Joe."

Brydie set down her frosting gun. "And you're going, because?"

"I'm the buffer," Rosa said. "I'm always Joe's buffer."

Sometimes Brydie wished she had a buffer. "Okay," she said. "I'll get done what I can before you all get back."

"Lillian is out front," Rosa said. "Keep an eye on her for me. She doesn't usually work without me, but I can't imagine we'll be gone long. Ronnie and Joe fight like an old married couple."

Brydie resisted the urge to tell her that she and Joe also fought like an old married couple. She nodded instead. "I'll go out front just as soon as I'm finished back here."

"Thanks," Rosa said. "Be back in a jiffy."

Brydie went back to icing the cookies. She hadn't looked at her phone since her conversation with her mother, and she couldn't help but think about Roger and her mother in her childhood home together, decorating for Christmas the way her parents used to. She was glad her mother had Roger. Brydie knew her mother deserved to find someone she enjoyed spending time with, just like she enjoyed spending time with Nathan, but she couldn't help but wonder what it would be like to spend Christmas at home with her mother and someone who wasn't her father.

She remembered in junior high when Elliott's parents got divorced around Christmastime and Elliott's mother started dating someone new—their basketball coach, to be exact. At first Elliott had been furious. For nearly two weeks she'd refused to go home, staying instead at Brydie's house in the spare bedroom.

"You don't understand what I'm going through," Elliott had said, flouncing down on Brydie's bed one afternoon after school. "Everything in my house is exactly the same as it used to be, except my mom has replaced my dad with someone else. He even sits in my dad's chair at night watching football."

"Your mom didn't replace your dad," Brydie replied, picking at the friendship bracelet she'd made over the summer at 4-H camp. She'd tried to give it to a boy named Bryce on their last day, but he'd already gotten one from a fourteen-year-old with boobs and hair past her rear end. When Brydie asked her about how she'd managed to get such long, shiny hair, she'd just smiled and said in a quiet voice, "Mane 'n Tail," and showed her a bottle with horses on it.

She'd begged her mother to buy it for weeks after she got home from camp, but her mother said that Herbal Essences, despite the *grotesque commercials*, was the best shampoo that money could buy.

"You're not listening," Elliott said, rolling her eyes at her friend. "You're thinking about that stupid guy from camp again."

"I wasn't," Brydie protested, but even she had to admit it was a weak defense. It was just that talking about Elliott's parents' divorce made Brydie uncomfortable. She didn't know what to say to her friend. Sure, her own parents didn't seem to like each other much, but she knew that it was unlikely they'd have ever gotten divorced. Her mother had depended upon her father too much. "I'm sorry. I really am. My mom talked to your mom today, and she says your mom said you could stay this whole weekend. And you don't even have to call and check in. Not even once!"

"It's just," Elliott began, tucking her feet up under her legs, "Coach Hugh isn't my dad. And now it feels like my dad isn't even my dad anymore. He lives in an apartment *by the college*. Like, right next door to Lauren's sister Elizabeth. He doesn't even have a kitchen. Just a microwave and a pullout bed in the living room."

"I'm sure he won't live there forever."

Elliott shrugged. "Maybe."

"It will get better," Brydie said. "I know it will."

"I don't want things to get better. I just want things to go back to the way they were," Elliott said.

"With your parents fighting all the time?" Brydie asked. "You were here just as much before as you are now. It's just that this time you have a different reason to be here."

Elliott was quiet for a minute before she said, "No, I guess I don't want for things to go back to the way they were. But I don't want Coach Hugh walking around in his underwear and sitting in my dad's chair, either."

"Oh my God," Brydie replied, horrified. "Coach Hugh walks around in his underwear?"

Elliott giggled. "Only once. I screamed so loud when I saw him that he dropped the coffee cup in his hand, and it cut his foot open. He had to go to urgent care and get six stitches."

"No wonder he was limping in gym class the other day," Brydie said. "I'm glad I didn't ask him what happened."

"He told me to tell everyone he dropped a box of Christmas ornaments on it," Elliott replied, giving in to laughter. "I told him that as long as I never have to see him in his tighty-whities ever again, we had a deal."

Brydie smiled recalling the memory. And for the first time, she thought she understood just exactly what Elliott had been trying to say nearly two decades ago. If she was honest, she didn't want to go back to the way things had been before her father died. True, what happened with Elliott's parents hadn't been the same thing, but now Brydie knew what it was like to pine for a reality that probably never even existed to begin with.

Her parents had been unhappy since she'd been old enough to realize that not all parents stayed silent at the dinner table. Not all dads "fell asleep" on the sofa four nights a week. Not all parents existed in a world where the tension was so tight, their only daughter could cut it with a knife. No, what Brydie longed for were the kind of memories like the ones her mother was probably making with Roger right this very second. She was sure her mother was listening to Bing Crosby and decorating the Christmas tree. She was sure she'd had Roger pull out all the boxes labeled "X-Mas Decor" and not used a single ornament, instead going out and buying a whole new set to match the year's theme, which she knew from the years of rotation would be snowmen this time.

Brydie pushed open the doors to the front of the bakery and peered out at Lillian. She was putting the finishing touches on a wedding cake with yellow and red roses. It had three tiers, and as always, Lillian's work was impeccable. Brydie smiled with satisfaction and went back to her own project.

Really, all she wanted was a nap. She couldn't wait to get home and crawl under the covers, with Teddy's warm body snoring beside her. It had become her favorite thing about the day—their routine. When she got home from work, she fed him and herself, usually baked a couple of batches of fresh dog treats, and then the two of them retreated to the bedroom, where she would flip through the newest issues of cooking magazines she bought at ShopCo until she fell asleep.

Brydie sat down on a ten-pound tub of Satin Ice fondant icing and leaned her back against the wall. She closed her eyes. All she had to do was get through another hour or so, and she'd be off work and out to breakfast with Nathan. *I'll just rest my eyes for five minutes,* she thought.

The next time she opened her eyes, it was because she heard yelling coming from the front of the bakery. She jumped up from the tub of icing and hurried to the front. She saw Lillian facing the bakery case, where a tall, thin woman with dozens of bangle bracelets jangling from her wrist was standing.

"I just don't understand how you could have messed this up," the woman was saying. "I put in the order nearly two months ago."

Lillian said nothing, her eyes darting around in all directions like a caged animal at the circus. She shook her head at the woman.

"*No?*" The woman crowed. "No? What do you mean, *no*? I have the receipt right here! It says red and pink carnations! Not red and yellow roses!"

By now Lillian had covered her ears in addition to shaking her head side to side. Her mouth made a little O, but no sound came out. It took Brydie a minute to find her feet but when she did, she scurried to Lillian's side, gently pulling her away from the woman's line of fire.

"I'm so sorry, ma'am. What seems to be the problem?"

The woman sighed deeply. "I've already repeated myself four or five times to *that girl*."

"Maybe I can help you."

"I doubt it," the woman replied. "She brought me the wrong cake." She pointed to the box sitting on the counter. "It's nothing like I ordered, and when I tried to explain that to her, she just stood there like an idiot and refused to speak to me."

Brydie felt her blood begin to boil. "It's not her fault, ma'am," she said.

"No, no, it's certainly not," the woman replied. "It's the manager's fault for hiring an idiot!"

"I'm the manager," came a voice from behind the woman. "What seems to be the problem?"

"I think Lillian accidentally gave her the wrong cake," Brydie replied before the woman had a chance to answer. "If you'll just give me a second, I'm sure the right one is in the back."

"It better be," the woman snipped. "The wedding is tomorrow, and I don't have time to get another one. And we surely aren't going to use this abomination *that girl* tried to give me."

Gritting her teeth, Brydie went to the back and checked the shelf of finished cakes. It wasn't even 7 A.M. How could anyone be so angry that early? She check the receipts taped to the side of each cake box, and after a few minutes of searching, managed to find the cake with the pink and red carnations. "Here we are," Brydie said, carrying the cake around to the woman's cart and placing it inside for her. "I believe this is the correct cake."

The woman looked doubtful, but her face relaxed when she opened the box and looked inside. "Finally," she said. "You know," she continued, turning to Joe, "you really ought to hire more competent people to work up here. Either that, or not leave people who can't read up here by themselves."

The vein on the side of Joe's bald head was beginning to throb, but he managed to plaster a smile on his face. "I do apologize, ma'am. Let me write you a ticket for a discount when you get to the register."

Brydie watched the woman leave, still in a huff, and then she turned her attention to Rosa and Lillian. Lillian was still standing up, her hands no longer covering her ears. Fat tears were rolling down her cheeks, and Rosa was whispering to her, wiping at her cheeks as she spoke.

"Brydie," came Joe's voice, "come over here."

Brydie took a deep breath and tore her eyes away from Lillian and Rosa. She felt awful. She hadn't meant to fall asleep and leave Lillian alone. They hardly ever had customers before the shift change at 7 A.M. Why, this one time, did someone awful have to come in and scream at Lillian that way? "I'm sorry," she blurted.

"What happened?"

"I got busy in the back," Brydie replied. "And then I sat down for a minute, and I guess I dozed off . . ."

"You fell asleep?" Joe's voice sizzled. "You fell asleep and left Lillian all alone at the front?"

"I didn't mean to!"

"The first time you've ever been left in charge up here, and you fall asleep?"

Brydie bit at the corners of her lip. "I'm so sorry, Joe."

"I thought you understood that Lillian can't be left alone up front," Joe continued. "Rosa and I trusted you to take care of any customers while we were in our meeting."

"I know," Brydie replied, her cheeks flaming. "I just meant to sit down for a few minutes."

"Lillian will probably have to stay home tomorrow," Joe said. "You're responsible for this."

"I said I was sorry."

"It was incredibly irresponsible of you to leave her at the front on her own," Joe said. He was scowling at her now, the vein still throbbing.

"Joe, I'm sorry. I don't know what else to say," Brydie said. "It won't happen again."

"You're damn right it won't," Joe replied.

"Brydie?"

Brydie turned around to see Nathan standing

there, a tentative smile on his face. "Nathan?" she asked. "What are you doing here?"

"I couldn't get you to answer your phone," Nathan said, his tone apologetic. "I didn't mean to interrupt anything . . ."

Joe waved him off with a grunt and said, "We're done here," before walking around the glass bakery case and through the double doors to where Rosa and Lillian were still huddled.

"Everything okay?" Nathan asked. "That looked like a pretty intense conversation."

"It's fine," Brydie replied, sounding a bit shorter than she would have liked. "It's just been a long night."

"Do you still want to go to breakfast?"

"Yes," Brydie said. "I'm sorry I didn't answer my phone. I switched it to silent earlier."

"That's all right," Nathan said. "But when I couldn't get you, I figured I'd better come down and make sure everything is all right."

Brydie felt herself soften, and she had to resist the urge to pull him in close for a kiss. "I'm okay. I promise."

"I'm glad to hear it," Nathan said. "Are you off work now, or should I walk around and buy a bunch of things I don't need?"

Brydie grinned. "Don't go anywhere," she said. "I'll be right back. I just have to finish up a couple of things."

Nathan gave her a cheesy salute and said, "I'll just wait right here."

Brydie turned and headed around the bakery counter to the back, where she'd seen Lillian and Rosa slip when Joe finished talking with them. She thought for a moment that maybe she shouldn't bother them, that maybe she should just let it rest until the next night, but she didn't want either of them to think that she didn't care about how terribly Lillian had been treated.

"Rosa?" Brydie said, tapping lightly on the swinging door. "Lillian?"

"We're back here," came Rosa's voice, soft and low.

Brydie pressed through to find Lillian, no longer shaking or covering her ears, but calmly frosting the cookies that Brydie had failed to finish. She looked beyond the two at the clock on the wall. It was almost 7:15. "Aren't you finished for the day?" she asked, feeling guilty that she hadn't completed the cookies. That would be another thing for Joe to be angry about with her tomorrow.

"It calms her down," Rosa replied.

Brydie took a tentative step forward. "I'm really sorry about what happened," she said. "I didn't mean to leave Lillian at the front all by herself."

Rosa didn't look angry, but she also didn't look Brydie in the eye. "I know you didn't."

"It's just that I've had an exhausting few days, and I thought if I could just sit down for a few minutes—"

"It's okay," Rosa said, raising a hand to cut her off. "I'm not upset with anybody but myself. I know better than to leave her with strangers."

Rosa's words stung, and Brydie thought for a terrifying moment that she might just begin to cry right there in front of both of them. She wasn't a stranger, was she? They'd been working together for almost two months. She'd invited them to Thanksgiving. Had Rosa just said that to be mean? She couldn't imagine Rosa saying *anything* just to be mean, and the realization that Rosa actually meant it was more hurtful than the words themselves. She opened up her mouth to speak, but thought better of it, instead turning around and walking back out of the bakery and to breakfast with Nathan.

CHAPTER 35

THE LITTLE DINER CALLED THE HAPPY PAPPY was nestled in between an abandoned garage and a shoe repair shop just outside Germantown. The businesses around the diner had obviously fallen on hard times, but the parking lot at the Happy Pappy was completely full, and Brydie had to park on the side of the street and pay a meter.

"One of the nurses I used to work with at the hospital told me about this place," Nathan said as they stood beneath the diner's faded blue-and-white striped awning. "She used to drive almost an hour from the hospital to here three or four times a week for breakfast."

"That's dedication," Brydie replied, still trying to shake the morning's commotion from her mind.

"Their biscuits and gravy are amazing."

A young woman in a striped uniform matching the awning led them to the only empty booth, near the back of the restaurant. "What can I get y'all to drink?" she drawled, chewing on her pencil and eyeing Nathan. "Ain't I seen you in here before, sugar?"

Nathan nodded. "Every Tuesday for the last three years."

"I'm new," she said. "Just been here for the past couple of months. But I remember you."

Brydie felt an unwelcome sense of jealousy overcome her. The waitress hadn't even so much as looked at Brydie since they sat down. For the second time that morning, she resisted the urge to pull him close to her. It wasn't a feeling she was used to, and she found herself becoming annoyed not only with the waitress, but with Nathan as well.

"What can I get y'all to drink?" the waitress droned on. "Coffee?"

"Chicory, please," Nathan replied.

"And for you?" She turned to Brydie. "The same?"

"Orange juice," Brydie said. "Thanks."

The waitress nodded and scurried off, leaving the two of them alone, and Nathan grinned at her from across the booth. "So you said your basement flooded, too?" he asked. "How bad was it?"

"Not bad," Brydie replied. "Just a little bit of water, and now it actually looks better than it did before."

"I wish I could say the same for mine," Nathan said. "I refinished the basement when I moved in—put in carpet and a pool table and a bar. Everything had to come out, and what wasn't ruined is just sitting in my living room. Getting a pool table upstairs is significantly harder than getting it downstairs."

"That sounds awful."

"Could be worse, I guess," Nathan said, taking his coffee from the waitress. "Thanks."

"Here's your orange juice." The waitress handed a glass to Brydie. "Can I get your orders?"

"Biscuits and gravy," Nathan said without hesitating. "A double order, please."

"Where do you put all of that, sugar?" the waitress asked.

"I'll have the same thing," Brydie spoke up, her arm brushing Nathan's as she handed the menu back to the waitress.

"A double?"

"Sure."

"That's a lot of biscuits," the woman, whose name tag Brydie just now realized read Tina, said.

"I can handle it."

Tina raised an eyebrow. "I'm sure you can."

"I don't think she likes me," Brydie said once Tina had gone. "But she sure seems to like you."

"She says the same thing to me every time I come in here," Nathan said, giving Brydie a lopsided grin. "She's been here at least a year, and she always pretends that she's new and that she doesn't recognize me."

Brydie knitted her eyebrows together. "That's weird."

Nathan shrugged. "That's what makes it fun."

Brydie wasn't so sure about that, but she didn't say anything. The adrenaline from what happened at ShopCo was beginning to wear off, and now she felt like she might fall asleep sitting up.

"Are you sure everything's okay?" Nathan asked, his hand now warm on hers.

"I haven't gotten much sleep in the last few days," Brydie replied. "It's been hard getting back on a routine, and last night I fell asleep when I should have been icing cookies."

"Joe seemed pretty upset with you," Nathan said. "I wanted to talk to him about his shepherd's pie for a charity auction at the hospital, but he didn't look like he was in the mood for a chat."

"He was more than upset with me," Brydie admitted. "He'd been in a meeting, and I was left in charge up front. Lillian—you met her at Thanksgiving, too— she's a brilliant baker, but she has trouble interacting with people. After I fell asleep, she gave the wrong cake to a customer, and the lady got so angry she called Lillian an idiot."

"That's terrible."

"It was, and I should have been there to make sure it never happened," Brydie replied, pressing the palms of her hands into her forehead.

"I'm sure they'll forgive you."

"I just feel so rotten," Brydie replied. "So rotten."

"Well, I can tell you something that might make you feel better," Nathan said, grinning over at her.

"What is it?"

"Mrs. Neumann has been eating very well since you brought her the chicken on Sunday afternoon. Her spirits have been up."

"That does make me feel better," she said. "I just can't stop thinking about that damn trunk and everything that was inside of it."

"I know that was hard."

"I just want to talk to her about it," Brydie said. "I hate the thought of her bearing this alone."

"She clearly doesn't want anyone to know," Nathan said. "I shouldn't be telling you this, but there were notations in her chart not to mention the pregnancy or the child at all, for any reason."

"Elliott had a miscarriage in between Mia and this new baby," Brydie said. "It's not a secret, but she doesn't like to talk about it much."

"Not everybody feels better talking about these things," Nathan said.

"But what if she wants to talk about it?" Brydie asked. "What if she wants to talk about it, and she just doesn't have anyone to talk about it with?"

"She *doesn't*," Nathan said. "She doesn't want to talk about it."

"I think I might want to talk about it," Brydie said. "If it were me."

"But it's not you," Nathan said. "You can't possibly understand what she went through. You've never even been pregnant."

"*I know*," Brydie replied. His words stung her.

"I didn't mean it like that," Nathan said. "Look, from a medical perspective, this just isn't something you can start a conversation about. The trauma lasts for a long time, and clearly Mrs. Neumann isn't comfortable telling anyone about it. You should respect her privacy."

"I think you're wrong."

"I'm not."

"I just want to help."

"Then maybe you should stop meddling in her life and do what you're supposed to be doing—taking care of her house and her dog."

Brydie's eyes flicked up to his. He wasn't looking at her. He was staring off past her at the waitress, who was pouring coffee and laughing with a couple of men in expensive-looking suits.

Nathan ran his hands through his hair and said,

"I know it might *seem* like it would help for you to ask her about it, but it won't. It's only going to make *you* feel better, and it's a selfish thing to do."

"I should go," Brydie said.

"Don't," Nathan said. "I'm sorry. I wasn't trying to hurt your feelings. But I'm her doctor."

"And you know what's best."

"In this case, yes."

"Fine," Brydie said at last. "I won't say anything to her. I won't breathe a word of it, but I really do have to go." Keeping her head down so he wouldn't see the tears that were threatening to overwhelm her, she stood up, grabbed her purse, and hurried out of the diner, nearly knocking over the waitress with their steaming plates of food.

"She all right?" Brydie heard the waitress ask.

"She had to leave," Nathan replied.

"Huh," the waitress said. "I guess she couldn't handle it after all."

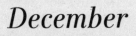

December

CHAPTER 36

I T WAS FINALLY DECEMBER. BRYDIE WASN'T SURE
how she thought the month would begin, but she'd
hoped it would be better than this. She was glad for
the new chill in the air, however, and tried to enjoy it.
She hadn't told anyone about her fight with Nathan,
a fight that she was now beginning to realize was a
stupid one. Of course he was right. She *knew* he was
right, but she couldn't bring herself to call him and
apologize. She was embarrassed about the way she'd
acted. There wasn't anything she could say to Pauline
to change what had happened, and it was wrong and,
yes, selfish of her to think that there was.

She tried to put those thoughts out of her mind by
doing what she did best—baking. Both Lloyd and
MaryAnn had placed orders for Christmas treats,
and this time, instead of looking on Pinterest for
ideas, Brydie came up with a few new recipes of her
own. So far, she'd created a candy cane treat, gingerbread treats with carob icing, and regular paws with
green and red glaze.

Teddy, of course, sat patiently waiting for his reward, which consisted of defective batches, and Brydie wondered what the year ahead would bring for them. She wondered if next year would be the same—if she'd still have his little face full of wrinkles staring up at her expectantly.

Brydie's earliest Christmas memory was from when she was four years old. She hadn't known it at that age, but her parents' Christmas tradition was to put the tree up the day after Thanksgiving. Her mother would take the day off and they'd pile into the car and go to a tree farm in Bono, a little town just outside of Jonesboro, where there was a place called Leo's Tree Farm. They'd eat breakfast out and listen to Christmas music on tape all the way there.

As a child, Brydie believed that the tree farm was magic. It probably came from the stories her father told her about how the trees were planted and tended by Christmas fairies all throughout the year, until it was time for families to come and chop down the perfect tree. But even at four years old, the farm was more than that for Brydie. It was just about the only time of year that her parents were both happy at the same time. They held hands walking through the forest of trees, and even her mother sang the Christmas carols as they drove from their house to the farm and back again.

This particular Christmas, her mother told her she could pick out the tree all by herself, and it was a job Brydie took very seriously. She walked around the farm with the little Polaroid camera her grandparents had given her for her birthday and took pictures of the trees she thought were the prettiest. The tree she ultimately picked was in the middle of the park and just a smidge too tall for their living room. Try as they might, though, her parents couldn't talk her out of it, and they drove home with the tree strapped with bungee cords to the top of their Camry station wagon.

While her mother wrestled with how to get the snowman Christmas topper on a tree that brushed the ceiling, Brydie and her father baked cookies and drank eggnog out of special mugs that her father ordered from the JCPenney catalog. Although she generally attributed her love for baking to the time after her father's accident when she assumed the role of "cook" for the family, if she was honest it was the Christmas thirty years ago that planted in her a love for food, because for Brydie, food meant that perfect, long-ago Christmas. It meant comfort.

That was why, after that morning at the diner with Nathan, Brydie's house—rather, *Pauline's house* looked like the inside of the bakery at ShopCo. One side of the kitchen was reserved for human treats, and the other side was reserved for Teddy treats.

She'd baked for everyone she could think of— human treats for Elliott and her family, Dr. Sower and Mrs. Neumann, and MaryAnn and Fred. Once she'd finished with that, she started on treats for both of Dr. Sower's dogs and every dog she knew in Germantown, which amounted to exactly two— Thor and Arlow.

She'd delivered dozens of snickerdoodles and her newest pet-created treat—peanut butter and carob cupcakes—to everyone. Dr. Sower had been delighted and told her as much, her mouth full of a snickerdoodle. But she hadn't allowed Brydie and Teddy to visit Pauline. She explained that the old woman was back on oxygen and sleeping much of the time. She'd looked at Brydie the same way Nathan had looked at her in the hallway the afternoon she brought food from Gus's to Pauline for lunch.

"The congestive heart failure makes it difficult," Dr. Sower explained. "Some days are better than others."

"It seems like the better days are becoming less and less frequent," Brydie replied, crossing her arms over her chest in an effort to keep herself from shivering in the chilly lobby. "Is there anything I can do?"

"Her visits with you and Teddy are her favorite part of the week," Dr. Sower said, sneaking another cookie from the tin on the receptionist's desk. "If she wakes up today and is feeling better, I'll give you a call and you can come back."

Brydie took Teddy back home and channeled all of her energy into baking. She listened to Christmas music that reminded her of the tree farm and tried her best not to think about Mrs. Neumann or Nathan, or Joe and Rosa and the fact that neither one of them had seemed to forgive her.

That's how, after there was no more room in the kitchen or on the dining room table, Brydie found herself on December 15, her arms full of food, sitting on one of the cold benches in the dog park, surrounded on all sides by baked goods she couldn't bear to throw away. On her last night at work before her days off, she'd bought red and green cellophane and twist ties that looked like candy canes. That morning, Brydie busied herself wrapping up everything in her kitchen—cookies for people in red cellophane, and cookies for dogs in green.

She knew it was a risk, going to the dog park. There was always a chance she might see Nathan.

Even after months of knowing him, she still had no idea what his schedule was at the hospital, and the thought of seeing him, even in the distance, made her stomach roil.

When she'd left the diner that morning, the morning Nathan told her she had too much baggage, she'd sat in her car for a long time, watching him eat his breakfast through the window. Brydie was so confused.

When she got home, she'd gone to bed and slept until it was time for work. The next day she did the same thing, and the cycle continued throughout the first week of December, until, realizing she couldn't sleep another wink, she took to baking. Now she was starting to suspect that she *and* Teddy had put on a few pounds, as she eyed the way his sides were bulging out through the leg and neck holes of his harness.

"Excuse me?"

Brydie was jolted out of her thoughts and looked up from her spot on the bench to see a woman in a fuchsia pea coat standing in front of her. "Oh, hi," Brydie said, smiling up at the woman. "I'm sorry. I guess I didn't see you standing there."

"Are you having a bake sale?" the woman asked, eyeing the box to Brydie's left.

"What?" Brydie suddenly remembered why she'd come to the park in the first place. "No, they aren't for sale."

The woman's face fell.

"They're free," Brydie finished. "I may have gone a little overboard with the baking this year. The box to my left is full of dog treats, and the box to my right is full of human treats. Feel free to take a couple from each box."

"Really?" the woman asked, glancing around the park suspiciously.

"They're not poison or anything." Brydie laughed nervously. "I work at ShopCo in the bakery. Before that, I had my own shop. I just really love to bake."

The woman took a gloved hand and lifted the lid to the box on Brydie's right. "Is that . . . ?"

"Pumpkin bread," Brydie finished for her. "Yes."

The woman unwrapped the red cellophane and held the pumpkin bread to her nose before taking a petite bite. She took another. And another. After a few seconds of slow, thoughtful chewing, she said, "This is wonderful." She leaned in closer to Brydie and continued, "It's even better than my Nana's, God rest her soul."

Brydie beamed. "Take another!"

The woman reached greedily back down into the box and pulled out another cellophane-wrapped piece of pumpkin bread. Then she turned, cupping her free hand around her mouth and hollering, "Melanie! Get over here!"

After a few minutes, a woman in a pea coat in another shade of pink came trotting up to them, two little, black French bulldogs at her side. "You've got to try this pumpkin bread," the first woman said. "It's amazing, and it's free!"

The woman whose name was Melanie screwed up her nose. "You know I don't like pumpkin cake, Alicia."

Alicia rolled her eyes and turned her attention back to Brydie, as the dogs sniffed around Teddy, causing him to roll over on his back and play dead. "Do you have anything else?"

"I do," Brydie replied, standing up. "And in this

other box," Brydie motioned to the box full of green cellophane, "are dog treats if your dogs are allowed to have them."

"They are," Melanie replied. "But they can only have wheat-free treats." She shrugged her shoulders as if to say, *I'm sure you don't have any of those.*

"Well, then they're in luck," Brydie replied. She rummaged through the box to pull out two wrapped treats tied with solid red ties. "I've got a few of those."

"Really?" Alicia asked, raising her eyebrows to her hairline. "Roscoe and Rufus will be so excited to hear this."

Brydie assumed Roscoe and Rufus were the two French bulldogs now tugging on each one of Teddy's ears, but she didn't ask. Instead she said, "I think I've got some more wheat-free treats down at the bottom. Let me check."

By the time Brydie came up for air, a small crowd had amassed in front of her. People were plucking treats from both boxes, and before long, a chorus of chewing began. Many of the visitors to the park asked for her business card, and Brydie gave them her phone number instead, making a mental note to finally order cards that didn't have the old business information on them. To her surprise, a few people even wanted to place orders right then and there for food of both the human and the dog variety.

After half an hour, both boxes were empty, and a feeling of satisfaction warmed Brydie. Teddy, however, exhausted from babysitting the two cantankerous French bulldogs, was hiding behind her legs, peeking around them occasionally to make sure it was safe.

Brydie was about to pack up and head home when

she saw a familiar flourish of fur sprinting toward her. It was Sasha, her leash dangling behind her, her tongue out, licking the air furiously as she ran. Brydie paid no attention to her, and instead glanced hotly around the park for Nathan. She let out a sigh of relief when she saw Myriah coming toward them, waving her stocking cap like a white flag of surrender.

"I'm . . . so . . . sorry," Myriah huffed when she finally reached them. "She got away from me . . . She must've heard your voice or something . . . because the next thing I know . . . she's dashing off across the park."

Brydie couldn't help but smile at her. Myriah was bent over now, gulping at the air and giving Sasha the most withering look anyone wearing tie-dyed yoga pants and a Hello Kitty sweatshirt could possibly have it in them to give.

"It's okay," Brydie said. "She's fine." She bent down to give Sasha's head a pat.

"Oh," Myriah replied, erecting herself upright. "I didn't think . . . I mean, I didn't know . . . I wasn't sure if you'd want to see us."

So she knew.

Brydie turned away from Myriah, stacking one box on top of the other. "I don't mind," she said with her back still turned. It was true. She didn't mind seeing them. Not exactly.

"So, you're not upset?"

Brydie wasn't sure how to answer that. Of course she was upset. She'd just given away a metric ton of baked goods as proof. But she couldn't just tell that to Myriah. She might go back and tell Nathan. "I'm okay," was all she could think of to say. And then, because she couldn't help herself, "How is Nathan?"

There was a pause, giving Brydie enough time to turn around, and then Myriah said, "I haven't seen him much lately. He's been working a lot. Pulling lots of doubles. Sometimes he even sleeps at the hospital and showers there."

"I guess that means you've been hanging out with Sasha all the time," Brydie replied, trying to smile.

"Constantly," Myriah said. "Nathan said he was coming home tonight. I'm cooking him dinner. And then we're going to put up the Christmas tree. It's beginning to look a lot like Christmas, you know."

Brydie knew she wasn't mistaking the tinge of hopefulness in Myriah's voice. She thought back to the night of the flood, when Myriah confessed that she was in love with Nathan. She'd forgotten about it until now, glowing and secure in her budding relationship with Nathan—and now it was *all* she could think about.

"Well," Brydie finally managed to say, "I'd better get going." She leaned down to hook Teddy's leash to his harness and was given a swift lick to the side of the face by Sasha, and for some reason, it made her want to cry.

"Byeeeeee," Myriah called after them.

Brydie fought the urge to put one of the boxes she was carrying over her head until New Year's, and kept walking. If she hurried, she could run by ShopCo and use her employee discount to buy roughly four dozen eggs and twenty-eight pounds of sugar to once again fill her kitchen in a gallant effort to clear her mind before it even got dark.

CHAPTER 37

B RYDIE STOOD IN FRONT OF THE CHRISTMAS
tree and shut one eye and then the other. After
that, she squinted, tilting her head from side to side.
"I don't know," she said at last, turning around to
face Elliott. "It *does* look sort of lopsided to me."

"That's what I told Leo!" Elliott said, throwing her
hands up in the air from her position on the couch.
She was lying back against one of the arms, her feet
propped up by several pillows. "He told me I must
have vertigo."

Brydie grinned. "That sounds exactly like something he'd say."

"Doesn't it?" Elliott shifted her weight, groaning
as she moved from her back to her side. "Anyway, I
really appreciate you coming to help decorate. I can't
believe we let it go so long. We always have our tree
up on the first day of December!"

"Well, you are pregnant," Brydie reminded her
friend. "And you and Leo both work."

"He works too much," Elliott grumbled. "He

promised he'd stay home today and help me decorate. And instead, he went off to chase some ambulance!"

"He'd kill you if he heard you say that," Brydie replied. "You know he hates it when people call him an ambulance chaser." Brydie cleared her throat and adopted her deep, self-important lawyer voice and said, "I'm a *personal injury lawyer,* ladies."

"Speaking of ambulances," Elliott began, "are you ever going to tell me what happened with Nathan?"

Brydie sighed. "There's nothing to tell. It just didn't work out, that's all."

"Oh, come on," Elliott said. "You brought me five pounds of peanut brittle today. And peanut butter bone-shaped cookies for a dog that I don't even have. You're clearly upset about it."

"It doesn't matter," Brydie said.

"It matters to me."

Brydie turned from the Christmas tree to look at Elliott. "Do you think I have too much baggage?"

Elliott's eyes widened. "Is that what he said to you?"

"He met me at the store for breakfast a couple of weeks ago," Brydie said, walking over to the couch and sitting down beside Elliott's elevated feet. "I was in a terrible mood. And then I fell asleep at work when I was supposed to be in charge up front. Some lady came in and yelled at Lillian, and I was too busy sleeping to be there."

"Oh, Brydie."

Brydie closed her eyes, willing herself not to cry. That's when she felt Elliott's hand on her shoulder.

"Brydie? Brydie?"

Brydie opened her eyes.

"Brydie, oh my God, Brydie, my water just broke!"

"What?" Brydie blinked. "Your water broke? But it's not time!"

Elliott held her stomach with one hand and gestured to Brydie with the other. "Go get Mia. I'll go grab my bag."

Brydie hurried up the stairs to the end of the hallway where Mia slept. She grabbed the little girl a change of clothes and stuffed them into a bag hanging on the closet doorknob. Then she picked up a sleeping Mia, shushing her back to sleep as she walked back downstairs to find Elliott.

"I called Leo," Elliott said, handing Brydie the keys. "He'll meet us there."

"Which hospital are we going to?" Brydie asked Elliott, realizing she had no idea where she was supposed to be taking her.

Elliott ushered them outside and locked the door behind them. "What? Oh, Baptist Memorial."

THE WAITING ROOM in the maternity ward of the hospital wasn't exactly where Brydie thought she'd be spending her evening. Mia, for her part, was behaving herself splendidly. They'd been there all of five minutes before Leo came rushing in and was ushered back to labor and delivery. Since Elliott's parents were on their way from Jonesboro and Leo's parents wouldn't be down from Missouri until the morning, Brydie had been recruited to watch over Mia until someone arrived.

Truthfully, she didn't mind, although she was a little worried about Teddy. She knew he'd be pacing in front of the door, expecting his supper. There would be hell to pay when she got home, and she just hoped that he didn't take it out on the trash can.

Brydie glanced around the small, square room. There were two televisions sitting up high and a little play area for kids—currently Mia's favorite spot. The windows that looked out into the whitewashed hallway were covered with spray snow, and someone had drawn snowmen on each of them. There was also a Christmas tree in another corner with blinking lights and a nativity scene set up next to the coffeemaker and packets of powdered creamer.

There was something both comforting and disconcerting about seeing a hospital decorated all festive and cheerful. Brydie was sure that it was mostly, hopefully happy on the maternity ward floor. But in general, people didn't come to hospitals for happy reasons. She wondered how it would feel to receive news that a loved one had died while a cherubic Santa waved at you in the background. She wondered if it made it easier or worse for doctors, for Nathan, to deliver such news.

"Bwydee?" Brydie was pulled out of her daydream by two tiny hands patting her legs. "Bwyyyydee."

"Mia, what's wrong?" Brydie asked, alarmed that she'd not been paying attention to the little girl. "Do you need to go to the bathroom or something?"

Mia shook her head. "I'm hungry."

Brydie looked at the clock above the Christmas tree. They'd been sitting in the waiting room for nearly four hours. "Okay," she said, standing up. "Let's walk down to the cafeteria and see if we can find something."

Mia took Brydie's hand as they walked out of the waiting room. She wanted to inquire about Elliott at the nurses' station, but decided to wait until they came back. Maybe by that time Elliott's parents would be there and could get some information. Since she wasn't family, the nurses had made it pretty clear to Brydie that they wouldn't be able to tell her much, and she knew that childbirth could take a long time. When she'd been married to Allan and trying to get pregnant, she'd read as many books as she could on the subject. Brydie could say, with absolute certainty, that she wasn't jealous of the actual birth part of pregnancy. It seemed exhausting at best and excruciating at worst, and there were some women, like Pauline, who had to go home without a child.

The thought made Brydie wince, and she pushed those thoughts from her mind. Elliott's baby might be coming early, but he was going to be fine—better than fine. He'd be perfect.

"I want cereal," Mia whispered to Brydie as they entered the all-but-deserted cafeteria.

It was the middle of the night, and it surprised Brydie that it was even open. She smiled at Mia and sat her down at one of the tables. "Wait here," she said. "What kind of cereal do you want?"

"Mommy doesn't like me to eat Lucky Charms," Mia replied. She balled her hands into fists and rubbed at her eyes, yawning sleepily. "But it's my favorite."

"Lucky Charms it is," Brydie said, giving her a wink. "Just don't tell your mom, or I'll be in trouble."

Mia nodded and gave Brydie the kind of smile children give when they're conspiring against their parents. "Okay."

Brydie plucked two bowls from a stack at the cereal bar and filled one with Lucky Charms and the other with Frosted Flakes. She turned around to grab two boxes of milk and ran right into Nathan.

"Whoa, careful," Nathan said, taking one of the

bowls from her as she was about to drop it. "Let me help."

Brydie opened her mouth to ask him what he was doing there, but closed it up again. She knew what he was doing here. He *worked* here. She made her way over to Mia and put the bowl down in front of her. "I'll go get you some milk," she said.

"Brydie, I need to talk to you," Nathan said. "I've got some news about . . ."

Brydie's heart leapt into her throat. "Is everything okay? Is it Elliott . . . or the baby . . . ?"

"No, no, it's nothing like that," Nathan replied. "As far as I know, everything is fine with Elliott and the baby."

"Then what is it?" Brydie asked.

"It's Mrs. Neumann," he said. "I guess Dr. Sower's been trying to call you."

"I left my phone at Elliott's," Brydie explained, pouring milk over Mia's cereal. "What's wrong?"

Nathan pulled Brydie away from Mia. "It's not good. Dr. Sower says that if you want to see her . . ." He stopped, removing his glasses from his face and jamming them down into his white coat. "If you want to see her before she goes, you need to get there as soon as you can."

Brydie covered her mouth with her hand. "Are you sure? I mean, is Dr. Sower sure?"

Nathan nodded. "She wouldn't have called if she weren't certain."

"I can't leave Mia," Brydie replied.

"I checked the waiting room first," Nathan said. "When I couldn't get you, either, I called maternity on a hunch. I didn't find you, but I did find Elliott's parents."

"Mia, baby," Brydie said, hurrying back over to where the child was eating. "We have to get back upstairs."

"I'm still eating."

"Nana and Papa are upstairs," Brydie coaxed.

"Okay," Mia said, her eyes lighting up. "Can I take my cereal?"

Brydie looked at Nathan.

"Sure," Nathan said. "I don't see why not."

Nathan followed them out of the cafeteria and into the elevator. He went with them to the waiting room, where Brydie delivered Mia into the waiting arms of her grandparents.

"Have you heard anything?" Brydie asked.

Elliott's mother nodded. "Leo came out for a minute to tell us they were taking her to the OR for a C-section. It may be a while yet before we hear anything else," she said, wiping remnants of Lucky Charms marshmallows off Mia's face.

"I've got to go for a little while," Brydie said. "But I'll be back as soon as I can."

"Okay, sweetheart," Elliott's mother replied, distractedly. She was now on the floor with Mia, trying to keep Mia from spilling her cereal on the carpet. "Don't worry. Everything is fine."

Brydie nodded and took off for the elevator. She didn't realize that Nathan was still following her until he cleared his throat and said, "Brydie?"

She turned around. "Yeah?"

"Let me drive you to the nursing home."

"I'm fine," Brydie replied.

"I insist," Nathan said. "You've been up all night."

"I'm used to it."

"So am I."

They were at a standstill, the two of them staring at each other trying to determine their next move. "I don't have time for this," Brydie said finally, saved by the ding of the elevator.

"Please just let me take you," Nathan replied. "I want to see her, too, you know."

Brydie sighed in an attempt to keep him from noticing that she was touched by his admission. "Okay, fine," she said.

CHAPTER 38

THEY RODE TO THE NURSING HOME IN SILENCE. Brydie would have been uncomfortable under normal circumstances, but she was too busy thinking about Pauline to care. When they pulled into the parking lot, Nathan made no attempt to get out. He simply put the car in park and sat there.

"I've been meaning to call you," he said.

Brydie looked over at him. "What for?"

"I don't like the way we left things."

"I don't, either."

"It's just that I have so much going on right now between this place and the hospital," Nathan continued. "I don't have the time that I thought I would. I don't have the time . . ."

"You don't have time for what?"

"Brydie . . ."

"No, it's okay," Brydie said. "You don't have to explain yourself to me."

"I want to explain myself," Nathan said. He was

rigid, his hands still gripping the steering wheel. "But I'm not sure how."

"I have to go and be with Pauline," Brydie said. "She needs me."

Nathan led her straight back to Pauline's room, not even stopping to tell the front desk that they were there. Inside, the room was much quieter than Brydie thought it would be. There was one nurse monitoring Pauline, who was lying on the bed, covered up to her chin with a blanket. Her breath was coming out in short, ragged spurts.

The nurse smiled at Brydie and Nathan. "Dr. Reid," she said. "I'll just go tell Dr. Sower that you're here."

"I'm off duty tonight," he said.

"Still, she'll want to know," the nurse replied. She turned her attention to Brydie. "She's in and out of it."

While Nathan, the nurse, and Dr. Sower busied themselves with a discussion out in the hallway, Brydie sat down on the chair beside Pauline's bed and wiped her sweaty palms onto her jeans. She didn't know what to say. What could she say? She took the old woman's hand in hers and strained to hear the hushed conversation going on outside.

If not for the way she was breathing, Brydie wouldn't have believed she was sick. She was pale, yes, but she looked peaceful. Her eyes were closed, and her lips were parted in a silent O.

"I'm here, Pauline," Brydie finally managed. "I'm here with you right now. Teddy's at home, but he's here with you in spirit. I'm sorry I didn't bring him. I left him at home tonight, because my friend Elliott is in the hospital having her baby." Brydie thought she felt Pauline's grip on her hand tighten, and so she went on. "I was at her house helping her decorate for Christmas. The baby isn't due for another three weeks, but her water broke."

Pauline's eyelids fluttered, and she began to mumble something.

Brydie stood up and put her head closer to Pauline's. "What? What is it?"

"M . . . m . . . my . . . mine."

"It's me," Brydie said. "It's Brydie."

"My," Pauline said, so softly Brydie almost didn't hear her. "My baby."

Brydie's breath hitched in her throat. "What about your baby?"

"My baby," Pauline whispered. "Elise."

"I know," Brydie said, squeezing her hand. "I know about your baby. I know about Elise."

Pauline's eyes fluttered open. They were glassy, but focused. "She was my baby," she said. "She was our baby. Mine and Bill's."

"Yes."

"She died."

"Yes."

"I'm going to die."

Brydie could no longer keep the sobs at bay. She let it out, allowing the tears to fall down onto her cheeks and onto the old woman's blanket. "You aren't going to die," she managed to reply. "I won't let you die."

"It's time," Pauline said.

"No." Brydie shook her head. "No, it's not time."

"It's time to see Elise."

"I know."

"Will you take care of Teddy for me?"

Brydie nodded, using her free hand to smooth the old woman's white hair. "I will," she said. "I promise."

Pauline smiled, ever so slightly, and closed her eyes. She took a breath in and with a sigh let it all back out again for the last time. And off in the distance, not too many miles away, a brand-new baby took his very first breath and a nurse swaddled him up tight to be placed into the waiting arms of his mother.

CHAPTER 39

BRYDIE HADN'T ORIGINALLY INTENDED TO DEC-orate for Christmas at Pauline's house. She didn't see a reason to, especially if she wasn't going to be going home on Christmas Eve. But the day after Pauline died, Brydie went to work and bought every-thing she could think of to make the house festive. It made her feel better somehow for everything around her to be beautiful.

She put up the tree and the next day brought Mia over to help hang up the lights and garlands around the house. Leo had been thrilled to drop her off with Brydie, as Elliott and the new baby were still at the hospital—she'd had to have a C-section, just like she'd had with Mia.

Three days later, Brydie found herself standing, staring into her closet, looking for something suitable to wear for Pauline's funeral. At her own request, it was only a short graveside service. Brydie planned to invite everyone over for a little something to eat afterward. It was the least she could do, she thought.

After a few minutes of scanning the closet, Brydie gave up and went into the bathroom. She turned on the shower and watched the mirror above the sink fog, her reflection erased with each new billow of steam. The house, for its part, seemed to know its owner was gone, and its reaction was eerie. It creaked in the places where it was usually silent and was silent in the places where it usually creaked. It was as if a great shift had taken place, and it was waiting with bated breath for word from someone, anyone, about its fate.

Teddy seemed to know as well. After Brydie came home from the nursing home that night, he'd been waiting for her at the front door. She'd expected a mess of trash strewn across the kitchen floor and a couple of mysterious wet spots on the carpet, but she found none of that. Instead Teddy followed her straight to bed and lay down, sleeping next to her the entire night. He didn't even bark at her when she overslept, missing his usual afternoon snack, and he'd been following her everywhere ever since.

He was waiting for her after she got out of the shower and returned once again to the closet. She leaned down to pet him, and noticed something sticking out from in between two blankets on the closet floor. It was the photo album from the basement. She'd forgotten all about it since the discovery of the missing photos. She pulled it out from between the blankets, sat down on the bed, and began to flip through it aimlessly. When she got to the blank pages, she had an idea. Tightening the towel closer around her, she got up and went back to the closet. She reached up to the top shelf and pulled down the Tupperware tub containing the pictures from the trunk.

Carefully, painstakingly, she lifted the film on each of the blank pages and began to replace the photos. She didn't know if Pauline would have wanted her to repopulate the album with the pictures, but for a reason she couldn't explain, it felt like the right thing to do. Finally, after all this time, after all these years, the story was complete again, even if she was the only person left who knew about the album, who knew about Elise. She'd told Pauline she'd keep her memories safe. And she would do just that.

Brydie glanced around the room. She couldn't believe it had been just three months since she moved in. She'd come here as a last resort, at the urging of Elliott. She'd come because she felt like she had no other option. If she'd had another option, she surely would have taken it, and now, leaving here was the last thing on earth she wanted to do. Saying goodbye to Pauline was the last thing she wanted to do.

The day was crisp, clear, and sunny. It was a lovely day for December, and it made the little cemetery in Germantown look almost cheerful when Brydie arrived with Teddy in tow. She knew that there would probably be funeral-goers who thought bringing a dog to a graveside was inappropriate, and that's why she was relieved to see Fred and Arlow standing next to MaryAnn and Thor.

"Hello, Brydie," Fred said when he saw her. "And hello there, Mr. Roosevelt."

MaryAnn pulled a tissue from the pocket of her crimson cardigan and wiped at her watery eyes. "I told Fred that having a dog at a funeral doesn't seem altogether respectful."

"But we knew that Pauline would have wanted us

to bring them," Fred said. "She woulda got a kick out of it at least."

Brydie smiled. "I think you're right. I couldn't leave Teddy at home. Not today."

Behind them, people were starting to emerge from their cars and make their way over to the graveside. Some of them Brydie knew, and some of them she didn't. Many of them, like Fred and MaryAnn, had their dogs with them.

"We made sure everyone knew," MaryAnn said. "We wanted to send her off right, me and Fred."

"She was one of us," Fred said with a shrug. "And now you are, too, kiddo."

Brydie bit her lip and looked away in a feeble attempt to hold back tears, and that's when she saw Nathan and Sasha coming toward them.

He didn't say anything as he took his place between her and Fred, but she could feel his eyes on her as she looked straight ahead and at the priest readying himself for the service. They hadn't spoken since the night he took her to the nursing home to say goodbye to Pauline, and little had been said then. She'd been too upset, too tired, to have a conversation with him about anything other than Pauline, and so the air hung thick between them with everything they couldn't say. *Besides,* she told herself. *He's already made himself quite clear.*

"Friends, we are gathered here today to honor the life of Pauline Elizabeth Neumann . . ."

Brydie closed her eyes. She let the priest's words wash over her as he spoke. She wanted nothing more than to sit down on the chilly ground and stretch out her legs. She wanted Teddy to sit on her lap while she cried. She wanted to be back in Pauline's small shoe box of a room and talk about how she burned down her house on Thanksgiving.

She didn't open her eyes until she felt a gloved hand on her arm. She looked over to see Rosa standing beside her, wearing a small, sympathetic smile. Joe was standing stoically beside her. "How did you know?" Brydie mouthed to her.

Rosa inclined her head toward Nathan. "He told us," she replied. "Came by the store the next evening when you were home taking care of details," she whispered back. "Wanted us to know you were having a hard time right now."

Next to Rosa, Joe cleared his throat and nodded toward the priest. "Shhh . . ."

Rosa rolled her eyes, but complied. She kept her hand on Brydie's arm, squeezing every so often.

When they had bowed their heads and prayed for the last time, the priest said, "Now Brydie Benson would like to make an announcement before we all disperse on this beautiful day the Lord has given us."

Brydie took a deep breath and handed Teddy's leash off to Rosa. She walked around to where the priest was standing and smiled at everyone. "Some of you may know that I live in Pauline's house. I've been there for about three months, taking care of her home and of her dog. I'd like to take this time to invite you all over to the house to celebrate Pauline one last time. Pets are welcome, and there will be food."

Rosa handed the leash back to Brydie when she was finished. "Honey, I'm sorry about how tense things have been at work," Rosa said. "What happened wasn't your fault. It's not your job to watch over Lillian."

"It's not my job to fall asleep at work, either," Brydie replied. "I'm sorry, too."

"Well, now that that's all settled," Joe said, interrupting the two, "Brydie, I'm deeply sorry for your loss."

Brydie was touched. It was such an un-Joe like thing to say. "Thank you, Joe."

"And I spoke to the big man up in his ivory tower," he continued. "They'll agree to keep you full-time after Christmas if you're interested."

"Really?"

Joe nodded.

"Thank you," Brydie said, reaching up to give Joe a hug. "I promise not to fall asleep again on a tub of frosting."

"You'd better not," he replied. "But Rosa and I both know you won't stay with us forever. Just hopin' you'll stick with us long enough to train your replacement."

Memories of the shop building in downtown Memphis came to Brydie's mind, and she couldn't help but smile. "Thanks, Joe. But that won't be for a while yet."

"Ms. Benson?"

Brydie turned around to see a balding man wearing a black trench coat staring at her. "Yes?"

"My name is Jacob Dwyer, and I'm an attorney for the estate of Mrs. Pauline Neumann. Do you have a few minutes?"

"Sure." Brydie turned back to Rosa and Joe. "I'd better talk to this guy," she said, taking Teddy's leash from Rosa.

"We'd better get going, anyway," Rosa said. "I left Lillian with a neighbor, and she gets anxious if I'm gone too long."

Brydie waved them off and turned her attention back to the lawyer. "So," she said, "what can I do for you?"

"Mrs. Neumann called me a few weeks ago. She wanted to make some changes to her last will and testament," the man said. "She wanted to include you."

"What?"

"Her most urgent request was that of Teddy," he said. "She wanted to make sure that you had the option of keeping him if you desired."

Brydie looked down at Teddy. He was looking from Brydie to the lawyer, cocking his head from side to side as the lawyer spoke. "She asked me to take care of him just before she passed away," Brydie said.

"Of course, if you don't want to keep him, she also arranged for him to go to a pug rescue in the Memphis area. They're ready for him if that happens to be the case."

Brydie's grip on Teddy's leash tightened. "No," she said. "I don't want him to go to a rescue. I want to keep him."

The man nodded.

"I would never," Brydie said, her voice cracking slightly. "I would never send him away."

"Good," he said. "Now that we have that issue settled." He reached into his coat pocket and handed Brydie a sealed envelope. "She wanted me to give you this."

Brydie took the envelope from his hand.

"Mrs. Neumann asked me to give this to you upon your agreement to take care of the animal," he said. "She gave me express instructions that you not open it until Christmas Eve."

Brydie turned the envelope over in her hands. It smelled vaguely of lavender and vanilla. "I don't understand."

"It's all in the letter," the lawyer said. "We'll talk again after the holidays." He gave her a warm smile and a pat on the shoulder before walking away, his shoes crunching against the dead leaves as he went.

Brydie stood there for a few minutes holding the envelope. She wanted to tear it open right then. She wanted to know what was so important that Pauline had called her lawyer and made him promise to tell Brydie to wait nearly another week, until Christmas Eve. She sighed, and shoved the letter into her pocket. She took a last look at Pauline's casket before she turned away and beckoned for Teddy to follow. "It's just you and me now, buddy," she said.

As she walked toward her car, she noticed a man standing at one of the large oak trees. At first she thought it was the lawyer, Dwyer, but as she got closer she realized that this man was much older. He was wearing dark wool slacks and a matching blazer with circular leather patches on each arm. There was something oddly familiar about him, although Brydie couldn't quite put her finger on it. When he saw Brydie, he turned and walked away, hurrying toward the edge of the cemetery.

"Excuse me," Brydie said, calling out to him. "Excuse me, sir?"

At her beckoning, the man paused for a moment before turning around to face her. "Yes?" he said.

"I'm sorry," Brydie said, out of breath from following him. She'd had to stop and pick up Teddy as she hurried. "Did you come for Pauline Neumann's service?"

"Yes," the man said.

"I'm sorry, you've just missed it," she said. "Did you know her?"

"Yes," the man said again.

Brydie was beginning to think that that was all the man could say. His face was deeply lined with age, but his eyes were bright and dark. She'd seen them before, those eyes. She knew she had. "I'm having a few of her friends back at my house," Brydie said, still trying to figure out where she'd seen him. "You're welcome to come by. I can give you the address."

"No," the man replied. "I just came to . . . I just came to pay my respects to Polly." He turned and continued on toward his car.

There was something about the way he called her "Polly," some kind of familiarity in his voice, that gave Brydie pause. He'd clearly known her for a long time, in another life. Nobody she knew called Pauline "Polly." And that's when it hit her. The man's eyes. His lined face. The way he spoke. She knew who he was. She knew who he was, because she'd seen him before—a much younger version of him in pictures.

"Excuse me," Brydie said, hurrying after him again.

"Yes?"

"I'm sorry to bother you again, but are you . . . would you happen to be . . . well, is your name Bill?"

The man's mouth dropped open just slightly. After a few seconds of weighty pause, he said, "It is."

"You were married to her once?"

"I was," he said. "A long time ago."

Brydie reached out and touched his arm, her fingers

brushing against the smooth leather patch on his elbow. "Please," she said. "Please come back to her house with me. I have something that I think belongs to you."

"I'm sorry?" The man knit his bushy white eyebrows together. "Something of . . . *mine*?"

"It's yours now," Brydie said. "It won't take but just a couple of minutes, and the house isn't far from here."

The man hesitated, clearly hedging his bets with this woman standing in front of him, arms full with a chubby pug. "Okay," he said. "I will stop by."

"Thank you," Brydie said, putting Teddy back down onto the ground. "Thank you so much."

CHAPTER 40

NEARLY EVERYBODY CAME BACK TO PAULINE'S house after the service, and the living room and kitchen were both full of people and their dogs. Brydie was relieved she'd been up half the night baking.

"Brydie," MaryAnn said, approaching her before Brydie had even taken off her coat. "I have someone I want you to meet. This is Marshall Good. He has the most glorious little gift shop near Midtown."

Marshall stuck out his hand to Brydie. "It's a gift shop and bakery," he said. "We're expanding the first of the year, and MaryAnn tells me you make treats for Thor that are out of this world."

"She does," MaryAnn replied. "They're simply amazing, and my Thor can't get enough."

"It's just a hobby," Brydie said, feeling her cheeks redden. "But Thor does seem to like them."

"Well," Marshall said, "if you change your mind . . ." He handed her a business card. "Give me a call. I'd love to stock them in my shop."

"Thank you," Brydie said. From the corner of her

eye, she saw Bill enter the house, and when he saw her, he gave her a small wave. "I'll give you a call. If you'll excuse me, I've got to go and speak with someone. It was nice to meet you."

Brydie set the card down on the dining room table next to her keys and made her way over to Bill. "Bill," she said, "I'm glad you decided to come."

"You've made me quite curious, I must admit," he said.

Brydie motioned for him to follow her. "It's back in the bedroom," she said.

BRYDIE LED HIM to the bedroom, where the photo album was still sitting on the bed. She reached up into the closet and pulled down the Tupperware tote with the hospital blanket and birth certificate. She sat down on the bed.

Bill was standing in the middle of the room looking around. He walked over to the crimson curtains and touched them lightly. "This whole house looks like Polly," he said.

"What I want to show you is right here," Brydie said. She held up the tote and the album. "I think that Pauline would want you to have them."

Bill sat down next to her and placed the tub on his lap and the album on top of the tub. He opened the album to the first page. "I haven't seen these in such a long time," he said. "Such a long time."

"They were in the basement," Brydie replied. "They'd been down there for a long time. I found some of the pictures and that tub there in a trunk a few weeks ago when there was a flash flood and some water got into the basement. The trunk was locked." She looked down at her hands. "I took the hinges off."

"That's just like Polly," Bill mumbled, turning the pages. "Just like her."

"There was a chair by the trunk," Brydie continued. "I think she must've gone down there often . . . when she was still able."

Bill looked up at her. "After we lost our baby," he said. "After we lost our Elise, Polly took down all of the pictures in our house. All of them. She packed them away and told me that if we couldn't have pictures of our child to fill our house, then we wouldn't have any pictures at all."

"I can't imagine."

"No," Bill said, circling a picture of Pauline with his thumb. "If you've never lost a child, then you certainly cannot."

"I used to think never having a baby was the worst thing that could happen," she said.

"She never got over it," Bill said. "She was never the same. I was never the same. I told her we could try again, but she wouldn't hear of it. She left six months after. I always hoped she would go on to have a happy life."

"Did you?"

Now Bill offered her a smile. "In my own way. I married the local florist's daughter and we had three girls."

"That's wonderful."

"It is," Bill said. "They're lovely. They take good care of their old father. But I've always felt like I was betraying Polly and Elise somehow. By never . . . by never telling people that I had four daughters instead of three."

Brydie felt her chest tighten. "I think both of them would have wanted you to be happy."

"I loved her," Bill said. "Polly was the love of my life."

"She told me about you," Brydie said. "I've been living here for the last few months taking care of her house and her dog. She was in a nursing home, but she was feisty right up until the very end. She told about being married to you, and she told me about how she burned your house down one Thanksgiving."

Bill laughed. It was a deep, throaty laugh. "She always used to love to tell that story. Especially because my mother hated it."

"That's what she said."

Bill closed the album. "Thank you for showing these to me."

Brydie nodded. "I'm going to give you some time," she said, standing up. "Can I get you anything?"

"You've given me quite enough," Bill said. "Thank you."

Brydie left the old man staring at a younger version of himself and went back out into the living room to where everyone else had congregated. Someone had taken it upon themselves to go outside with the dogs, and through the sliding glass doors that led to the patio, Brydie could see Teddy and Sasha outside giving chase to Thor.

If Sasha is here, thought Brydie, *then Nathan must be around here somewhere.*

Brydie glanced around the house. She didn't see Nathan. She considered for a moment that maybe it was Myriah who had come over with Sasha, but she shook her head. That didn't make any sense. Nathan had been at the cemetery with Sasha. She'd invited everyone back to Pauline's house. She just hadn't anticipated that *he* would come.

She wandered into the kitchen, picking up used paper plates and cups as she went. It seemed an odd thing to wish for after a funeral, but she hoped that everyone was having a good time. Rather, she hoped that they were all enjoying their time together, talking about Pauline. She pulled out a plate of peanut butter balls from the refrigerator and busied herself putting them on a platter to take into the living room.

"Brydie?"

Brydie turned around, a peanut butter ball between her fingers. "Hi."

Nathan smiled at her, shoving his hands down into the pockets of his dress slacks. "I've been looking for you."

"Oh yeah?"

"Yeah," Nathan said. "I'm sorry to crash like this. I know you probably don't want me here."

"Everybody is welcome," Brydie said, turning back around to the peanut butter balls. "I invited everyone."

"I know," Nathan said. "I wanted to say so much after Pauline died, but for the first time in my life, I wasn't sure what to say to someone who was grieving."

The peanut butter ball between Brydie's fingers was beginning to melt, and the slightest bit of chocolate was sliding down the inside of her thumb. "It's okay," she said. "Maybe there isn't anything left to be said."

Nathan didn't say another word to her, and Brydie watched as he walked outside to collect Sasha, hooked the leash to her collar, and slid out through the back gate. As she watched, she felt a tap on her shoulder. It was Bill, clutching to his chest everything Brydie had given him.

"Thank you for giving these to me," he said. He used his free hand to touch Brydie lightly on the shoulder. "It means more to me than you could ever know."

"I'm glad," Brydie said. "I know she would want you to have it."

"My daughter is waiting for me outside," he said. "I should probably head home."

"She could have come inside," Brydie said. "Here, let me fix you a plate of cookies to go."

"You're very sweet," Bill replied. "Maura knew how much I needed to be here today, how much I needed to do this alone. She's my youngest. A lot like her dad, that one."

Brydie busied herself collecting a cornucopia of cookies on a red paper plate. When she was done, she covered the top with cellophane and handed it to Bill. "I'm so happy I got to meet you today," she said. "Even if it was under these circumstances."

Bill smiled at her, a bright, wide smile that made him look exactly like the man in the photo album he was grasping. "Circumstances like these are about all an old man like me has left."

Brydie walked him to the door and held it open for him as he made his way down the front steps. "Be careful on your trip home," she said.

Bill turned around to face her once he was on the bottom step. His daughter, out of her car by now, was walking up the driveway to meet him. "These memories in here are both beautiful and ugly," he said, pointing to the photo album he was carrying. "They are as beautiful to me today as they were ugly to me sixty years ago. They make up part of who I am, but they don't define me. Not then. Not today," he said, his voice quavering ever so slightly. "Do you understand?"

Brydie nodded. "I think so."

"Ah, Maura, thank you," he said to his daughter, taking her hand.

Brydie watched them go, hand in hand, father and daughter.

CHAPTER 41

December 23

Brydie was at Elliott's house holding Elliott and Leo's brand-new baby, Oliver Joseph. "He's just beautiful," Brydie said, smiling over at her friend.

"I know," Elliott beamed. "He was totally worth that C-section and the thousands of stitches I now have holding my insides together."

Brydie wrinkled her nose. "How are you feeling?"

"Sore," Elliott said. "But happy."

"That seems like the right combination of feelings."

Elliott took a sip of apple juice out of her mug and said, "I'm sorry I didn't get to go to the funeral."

Brydie looked up from Oliver. "It's okay," she said. "I know you would have been there if you could."

In Brydie's arms, Oliver began to cry. "I think he's hungry," she said. She stood up and carried him over to Elliott.

"Oh, sweet baby," Elliott crooned. "It's okay. Hang on. Just a minute." She pulled her left side out of her gown, and the baby greedily began to suck at her breast.

Brydie reached for her sweatshirt and pulled it on over her head. "I should probably get going," she said.

"Okay," Elliott replied absently, still gazing down at her baby.

"I'll come by again sometime after Christmas to visit," Brydie said, making her way toward the door. "Tell Mia I'll bring her present then."

"Brydie?"

"Hmm?"

"Are you . . . okay?"

Brydie stopped at the doorway and turned around. "I'm okay," she said. "I guess I'm just worried about what will happen to the house now that Pauline is gone and what Teddy and I will do after."

"The house will be put up for sale, but you'll be able to stay there for as long as you'd like until it sells. You know that," Elliott replied. "But are *you* okay? I know you and Pauline had become close. I know that things with Nathan didn't end well."

Brydie didn't want to talk about it. All she wanted to do was look at the beautiful baby. "I thought you knew everything already?"

"Fine," Elliott said, and rolled her eyes. "Don't tell me. But you know I'm always here if you need to talk, right?"

"I do know that," Brydie said.

"So you're going home for Christmas?"

"I am," Brydie said. "I was supposed to leave tomorrow, but I'm off work today, too, so I thought I might bundle Teddy up and leave tonight."

"I'm glad things are going better with your mom," Elliott said. "I know that helps."

"It does," Brydie said. "Surprisingly."

"Nathan will come around," Elliott said. "You'll see."

Brydie shrugged. "I don't know if he will. It's going to be okay even if he doesn't. I have Teddy and my job and you and Leo. I'm okay, you know?"

"Yes," Elliott said, looking up at Brydie from her baby. "You are."

Chapter 42

December 24

BRYDIE WATCHED HER MOTHER AS SHE SERVED Roger dinner. They were sitting right next to each other, despite there being more than enough room at the table. Her mother was laughing at something Roger said as he refilled her mother's wineglass.

It was Christmas Eve, and she'd been shocked when she'd arrived the night before to find that none of the decorations had been put up.

"We wanted to wait for you," her mother said.

This morning, they'd gone to the tree farm and picked over what was left of the scraggly trees and took one home. They'd spent the rest of the day decorating and baking and singing Brydie's favorite Christmas carols. She was surprised and impressed that Roger knew most of them.

She looked down at the envelope sitting next to her plate. She'd meant to open it that morning, but she hadn't. She didn't know why—maybe she was saving it for the right time.

When dinner was done and Roger had retired to the living room to start the fire in the fireplace, Brydie and her mother busied themselves clearing the plates.

"Does that pug always sit next to you like that when you're eating?" her mother asked. "Like he's expecting you to drop half your food on the floor?"

"Roger fed him half of his steak," Brydie replied. "It wasn't me he was sitting next to."

"He loves dogs," her mother said. "He has a French bulldog, you know."

"He does?"

Her mother nodded. "His name is Winston."

"That's an adorable name!"

"He's worse than your dog," her mother replied. "He snores and farts and sometimes he gets so excited he throws up right in the middle of Roger's living room!"

"I don't mind Teddy's snoring," Brydie admitted. "I can't say I love the farting or the throwing up."

"But you love him just the same?" her mother asked.

"I do."

"Roger and I have been talking," Ruth Benson said. "And mind you, this is just *talk*, but we've been talking about moving in together."

Brydie stopped drying the plate in her hand. "Really?"

"He sold his house ages ago, and he's renting a little apartment right now. His original plan was to build a new house, but we both think it seems kind of silly to build a house just for him if we're going to be together for the long haul."

"And you think you will be?"

"Brydie, I do." Her mother's face was beaming.

It had been a long time since she'd seen her mother that happy. In fact, Brydie couldn't remember a time. "I'm so happy for you, Mom," she said.

"Really?"

"Yes." Brydie set the plate down and reached for her mother's hand. "Roger seems really nice. And now I'll have another dog to bake for!"

Her mother laughed and hugged her daughter. "That dog is going to take some getting used to."

"You'll learn to love him," Brydie said. "Trust me."

The front door slammed, letting in a rush of frosty air. Brydie turned around to see Roger standing there with the sack of presents and something else . . . *someone* else.

"I found him outside," Roger said. "He was pacing back and forth in front of the house. I told him he'd better come inside before he catches pneumonia and he has to treat himself."

Nathan stood next to Roger, looking cold and sheepish. "I was going to knock," he said.

"Nathan?" Brydie said, rushing over to him. "What are you doing here?"

Nathan looked from Brydie to Roger to Ruth and then again to Brydie. "Could we talk?"

"Okay," Brydie replied, her brow furrowed with confusion. "Let's go back to my bedroom."

"I'm sorry to just show up like this, but when I got to your house, nobody was there."

"How did you even know where I was?" Brydie asked him.

"I went to ShopCo," he said. "Since you weren't at the house, I thought you'd be at work. But when I got there, Joe told me you'd taken the night off. He didn't seem real happy about it, either."

"He wasn't," Brydie replied with a grin.

"Anyway, he told me you were going home for Christmas, and so I pulled Elliott's info from the hospital system and called her . . ."

"That sounds illegal," Brydie replied.

"Maybe unethical," Nathan admitted. "But I had to find you. I had to see you tonight."

"Why?" Brydie asked. She ushered him into her room and flipped the light switch. "What's so important that it couldn't wait?"

Nathan looked around her childhood bedroom. "This isn't how I pictured it," he said.

"You pictured my bedroom?"

"I mean, *NSYNC? Really?" Nathan asked, pointing to a poster on the wall by her bed. "You were one of *those* girls?"

Brydie crossed her arms over her chest. "What are you doing here, Dr. Reid?"

Nathan tore his eyes from the poster and back to Brydie. "I'm an idiot," he said. "I haven't been able to stop thinking about you. I don't know why I haven't been able to tell you the things I want to tell you. I guess I was just afraid."

"Of what?"

Nathan took a step closer to her. "I'm a doctor," he said. "I fix people. It's what I do. I know that you're not a patient. I know that, but I can't help wanting to fix whatever is wrong in your life. I just care about you so much. And that morning I tried to treat you like someone I didn't know. I spoke to you like I didn't *know you*."

Brydie took a step forward, meeting him in the middle.

"Relationships are messy," he went on. "They're unpredictable. That's why I stuck to medicine for so long. I can clean up those messes, you know?"

"Not all messes have to be cleaned up."

Nathan grabbed Brydie and pulled her close to him. "Can we try this again?"

There wasn't time to answer before Nathan's mouth was on hers, and Brydie felt everything that was tense and lonely and lost begin to unfurl, freeing the knot tied inside of her until at last, at long last, she was free.

From the hallway, there came a thud against the bedroom door, and then a growl, and then someone, her mother, yelling, "*Brydie!*"

Brydie opened her bedroom door. "What is it, Mom?"

"*That dog,*" her mother gasped. "That dog. I can't catch him."

"What's wrong?"

"He grabbed your purse off the couch, pulled something out of it, and now he's running around like he's an escaped convict from Alcatraz!"

Brydie ran out of her bedroom and into the living room. Teddy was sitting at one end by the fireplace, an envelope clenched in his jaws. "Teddy!" Brydie said. "Give me that!"

At her voice, Teddy dropped the envelope at her feet. Brydie picked it up. "It's okay," she said. "It's not torn or anything."

"What is it?" her mother asked.

"I don't know," Brydie said. "It's something from

Pauline. Her lawyer gave it to me at the funeral, and he said not to open it until Christmas Eve."

"It's Christmas Eve now," her mother said. "You haven't opened it yet?"

"Not yet."

"What are you waiting for?"

"I . . . I don't know," Brydie said.

"Well, open it."

Brydie sat down on the couch, and Nathan and her mother sat next to her. Teddy, his energy for the evening spent, lay down at her feet. She tore at the envelope, careful not to rip the contents, and pulled out a piece of stationery with the name of the nursing home at the top. It was a letter from Pauline.

Brydie,

> *I know that you will likely be reading this letter sooner rather than later. I know this, because the doctors have told me as much, and I feel it deep down in my bones. I also know that if you are reading this, then you've agreed to take care of Teddy, and I want you know how grateful I am that you came into our lives when you did. Since the day we met, I haven't worried once about your ability to take care of him.*

> *Enclosed in this letter is a key to a building I own downtown. It belonged to my late husband. It was in his family for years, and I want you to have it. Someday, when you are ready, you can start your own business—a bakery, I hope. If it's not to be, then you can*

sell it. Truly, the building is yours for you to do with what you will. Brydie, I know we haven't known each other for long, merely a matter of months. But I see in you many of the things I would have wanted my own daughter to be—strong, beautiful, and perfectly imperfect. Don't give up on the things you want in life because one part doesn't turn out the way you hoped it would. Be stronger for it, not because of it.

All my love,
Pauline

EPILOGUE

One year later

Brydie stared over the top of the bakery case, at the line of people forming on the sidewalk. There had been a steady stream of people coming in and out since they'd opened an hour ago, and already she was out of four of their signature pastries.

"Rosa!" Brydie called. "We're out of the pupcakes!"

"It'll be ten more minutes!" Rosa hollered, muttering to herself as she worked. "They're going to have to wait!"

Brydie smiled at the man in front her. "It's going to be a few more minutes," she said. "But how about a sugar cookie and a coffee while you wait?" She reached into the case and pulled out a Christmas tree–shaped cookie. "And a reindeer bone for your buddy."

The man took the treat and handed it to the little

Yorkie in his arms. "Theo just loves your pupcakes," he said. "We'll wait. Thank you."

"This is just the cutest little place," the woman behind the man in line said. "I never would have thought to have a bakery for dogs *and* people. How long have you been open?"

"Four months," replied Brydie. "But it feels like a lifetime."

"And . . . how long until . . . ?" She nodded down to Brydie's stomach, which strained the apron she was wearing so much it looked like a tent.

"February second."

As the woman continued to chat and the line continued to grow, she saw Nathan turn the corner, Teddy in front of him and Joe behind him. They were arguing good-naturedly about something, and Brydie suspected it had something to do with Joe's newest recipe—a cookie for people *and* pets. Nathan, for his part, couldn't imagine such a confection existed.

"Sorry we're late, boss," Joe said, sidling past the crowd. "We got caught in traffic. It is Christmas Eve, you know."

"Oh, I know," Brydie replied as Nathan bent to give her a kiss, one hand flush across her belly. "Rosa is dying back there. You'd better see if she needs some help."

"Shit, I forgot about the pupcakes," Joe said, pulling his apron over his head. "We meant to make a triple batch last night."

"Language!" came the only reply from the back.

"I have to get to the hospital," Nathan said. "Is there anything else I can do before I leave?"

Brydie looked around the bakery at the throng of people drinking their coffee and eating their scones, at the children and dogs playing, at the sign above the entryway that read, "Pauline's: A Place for People and Pets," and let out a contented sigh. "No," she said, with a smile as sweet as powdered sugar. "I think I've got everything I could possibly need."

ACKNOWLEDGMENTS

It is with sincere affection and admiration that I'd like to thank the following:

Priya Doraswamy—for being so much more than an agent. You are my friend, dear one, and I love you.

Lucia Macro—for believing in me, and most of all, for being patient when I was having a rough year.

Luke & Taryn England—for being Emilia's parents.

My husband—for bragging about me to his World of Warcraft buddies.

My son—who teaches me something new every single day.

My mom and dad—for loving me no matter what.

Brittany Carter Farmer—for eighteen years of friendship.

The Liberal Lassies—for being my rock, my sounding board, and most of all, for being my friends when I needed them the most.

Pupcakes Recipes

Thor's Grain-Free Peanut Butter Pumpkin Biscuits

INGREDIENTS:
1½ cups coconut flour
½ cup organic peanut butter
3 eggs
½ cup coconut oil, melted then slightly cooled
1 cup pumpkin puree

DIRECTIONS:
Preheat oven to 350°F.

Combine all ingredients in a large mixing bowl.

Roll dough out gently onto a cutting board dusted lightly with additional coconut flour. Roll out to about ¼–½-inch thick.

Cut out shapes using your preferred cookie cutters.

Transfer gently to a parchment-lined baking sheet.

Bake for 13–15 minutes. Treats should have a slightly golden color around the edges.

Cool on cookie sheets before serving.

May be stored in airtight containers for up to three weeks.

Teddy's Apple Cinnamon Cookies

INGREDIENTS:
4 cups whole-wheat flour
½ cup cornmeal
1 teaspoon cinnamon
2 eggs
2 tablespoons vegetable oil
1 small apple, grated
1⅓ cups water

DIRECTIONS:
In a large bowl, combine flour, cornmeal, cinnamon, eggs, and oil.

Grate the apple into the mixture; add the water.

Mix until it starts coming together into a ball.

Turn dough onto a lightly floured surface.

Knead well.

Roll out to a thickness of ¼–½ inch.

Take a straight edge and score the dough horizontally then vertically to make a grid of ¾-inch squares.

Be careful not to score the dough so that it cuts completely through the dough.

Lightly grease a baking sheet.

Place cookie on baking sheet.

Bake for 1 hour at 325°F.

Cool.

Place in a storage container or Ziploc bag and refrigerate.

Sasha's Frozen Yogurt Treats

INGREDIENTS:
4 cups yogurt (flavored or plain, non-fat if needed)
½ cup creamy peanut butter
2 tablespoons honey
1 ripe banana, mashed

DIRECTIONS:
Melt peanut butter in microwave for about
30 seconds.
 Place all of the ingredients into a blender, mixer,
or food processor and mix until smooth.
 Pour into ice cube trays or popsicle trays.
 Freeze until firm.

Arlow's Valentine's Carob Cookies

INGREDIENTS:
1 cup water
1½ teaspoons dry yeast
½ cup carob powder
¼ cup vegetable oil or olive oil
1½ cups whole wheat flour
½ cup cornmeal
1 cup unbleached all purpose flour

DIRECTIONS:
Combine the water and yeast.

Blend the yeast mixture with carob powder and the vegetable oil. Slowly mix in the whole wheat flour, the cornmeal, and the all purpose flour.

To prevent the dough from sticking, sprinkle flour onto your rolling pin.

Roll the dough out to ¼-inch thick and cut into heart shapes.

Place the cookies on a greased cookie sheet or non-greased silicone baking mat. Bake for 55 minutes at 275°F.

Pupcakes

INGREDIENTS:

Muffins:
2 cups shredded carrots
3 eggs
½ cup applesauce, unsweetened
2 teaspoons cinnamon
½ cup rolled oats
3 cups whole wheat flour

FROSTING:
8 oz. low fat cream cheese, softened
¼ cup applesauce, unsweetened

DIRECTIONS:

Muffins:
Preheat oven to 350°F.

Lightly spray cups of muffin tin.

In a large bowl stir together the carrots, eggs, and applesauce. Set aside.

In another medium bowl whisk together the cinnamon, oats, and flour.

Slowly mix in the dry ingredients. Stir until well blended.

Spoon mixture into muffin tin. The dough will be thick, so you may wet your fingers to press the dough into place.

The dog cupcake will not rise very much, so do not worry about over-filling the muffin tin.

Bake for 25 minutes.

Cool completely on a wire rack before frosting or serving.

Frosting:
Blend both ingredients with a hand mixer until well blended.

Spoon into a pastry bag for easy decorating.

Read On

sit! stay! speak!

Who says nothing happens in small towns . . . ?

Tragedy sent Addie Andrews fleeing from Chicago to the shelter of an unexpected inheritance—her beloved aunt's somewhat dilapidated home in Eunice, Arkansas, population very tiny. There she reconnects with some of her most cherished childhood memories. If only they didn't make her feel so much!

People say nothing happens in small towns, but Addie quickly learns better. She's got an elderly next-door neighbor who perplexingly dances outside in his underwear, a house needing more work than she has money, a best friend whose son uncannily predicts the weather, and a local drug dealer holding a massive grudge against her.

Most surprising of all, she's got a dog. Not just any dog, but a bedraggled puppy she discovered abandoned, lost, and in desperate need of love. Kind of like Addie herself. She'd come to Eunice hoping to hide from the world, but soon she discovers that perhaps she's finding her way back—to living, laughing, and loving once more.

just fine with caroline

Whenever someone tells you they're "just fine" . . . they're probably lying!

Caroline O'Connor tells herself everything is "just fine." Never mind that her faithful companion dog is mostly deaf, her best cousin's marriage is on the rocks, her mother has Alzheimer's, her father retreats to his study every night, and she's stuck back in Cold River, Missouri, a place she once thought she'd left for good.

There's all that, and Noah Cranwell, too. A far-flung relative of a local family mostly known for running moonshine, the ex-veteran has come home to Cold River with troubles of his own and he has his eye on Caroline and her dog. He also seems to be the key to something that happened to Caroline's mother in the past, something that's been a secret for decades.

Caroline has always believed she knows everything about Cold River and the people who live in its hills and hollers . . . but occasionally life's greatest surprises happen closest to home.

*G*ive in to your Impulses!

These unforgettable stories only take a second to buy and give you hours of reading pleasure!

Go to *www.AvonImpulse.com* and see what we have to offer.

Available wherever e-books are sold.

AVONIMPULSE